The Knife Drawer

Also by Padrika Tarrant

Broken Things (Salt 2007)

The Knife Drawer

PADRIKA TARRANT

SALT

CAMBRIDGE

PUBLISHED BY SALT PUBLISHING
14a High Street, Fulbourn, Cambridge CB21 5DH United Kingdom

© Padrika Tarrant, 2010

The right of Padrika Tarrant to be identified as the editor of this
work has been asserted by her in accordance with Section 77
of the Copyright, Designs and Patents Act 1988.

Salt Publishing 2010

Printed in the UK by the MPG Books Group

Typeset in Bembo 12 / 13.5

ISBN 978 1 84471 725 5 paperback

1 3 5 7 9 8 6 4 2

*for Dawn Echlin
and my darling little Jay*

Prologue: Titty Mouse and Tatty Mouse

from The Golden Book of Fairy Tales, *ed. Joseph Jacobs*

TITTY MOUSE AND Tatty Mouse both lived in a house, Titty Mouse went a leasing and Tatty Mouse went a leasing, so they both went a leasing. Titty Mouse leased an ear of corn, and Tatty Mouse leased an ear of corn, so they both leased an ear of corn.

Titty Mouse made a pudding, and Tatty Mouse made a pudding, so they both made a pudding. And Tatty Mouse put her pudding into the pot to boil. But when Titty went to put hers in, the pot tumbled over, and scalded her to death.

Then Tatty sat down and wept; then a three-legged stool said, 'Tatty, why do you weep?'

'Titty's dead,' said Tatty, 'and so I weep.'

'Then,' said the stool, 'I'll hop,' so the stool hopped.

Then a broom in the corner of the room said, 'Stool, why do you hop?'

'Oh!' said the stool, 'Titty's dead, and Tatty weeps, and so I hop.'

'Then,' said the broom, 'I'll sweep,' so the broom began to sweep.

Then, said the door, 'Broom, why do you sweep?'

'Oh!' said the broom, 'Titty's dead, and Tatty weeps, and the stool hops, and so I sweep.'

'Then,' said the door, 'I'll jar,' so the door jarred.

Then, said the window, 'Door, why do you jar?'

'Oh!' said the door, 'Titty's dead, and Tatty weeps, and the stool hops, and the broom sweeps, and so I jar.'

'Then,' said the window, 'I'll creak,' so the window creaked.

Now there was an old form outside the house, and when the window creaked, the form said, 'Window, why do you creak?'

'Oh!' said the window, 'Titty's dead, and Tatty weeps, and the stool hops, and the broom sweeps, the door jars, and so I creak.'

'Then,' said the old form, 'I'll run round the house.' Then the old form ran round the house.

Now, there was a fine large walnut tree growing by the cottage, and the tree said to the form, 'Form, why do you run round the house?'

'Oh!' said the form, 'Titty's dead, and Tatty weeps, and the stool hops, and the broom sweeps, the door jars, and the window creaks, and so I run round the house.'

'Then,' said the walnut tree, 'I'll shed my leaves,' so the walnut tree shed all its beautiful green leaves.

Now there was a little bird perched on one of the boughs of the tree, and when all the leaves fell, it said: 'Walnut tree, why do you shed your leaves?'

'Oh!' said the tree, 'Titty's dead, and Tatty weeps, the stool hops, and the broom sweeps, the door jars, and the window creaks, the old form runs round the house, and so I shed my leaves.'

'Then,' said the little bird, 'I'll moult all my feathers,' so he moulted all his pretty feathers.

Now there was a little girl walking below, carrying a jug of milk for her brothers' and sisters' supper, and when she saw the poor little bird moult all its feathers, she said, 'Little bird, why do you moult all your feathers?'

'Oh!' said the little bird, 'Titty's dead, and Tatty weeps, the stool hops, and the broom sweeps, the door jars, and the window creaks, the old form runs round the house, the walnut tree sheds its leaves, and so I moult all my feathers.'

'Then,' said the little girl, 'I'll spill the milk,' so she dropt the pitcher and spilt the milk.

Now there was an old man just by on the top of a ladder thatching a rick, and when he saw the little girl spill the milk, he said, 'Little girl, what do you mean by spilling the milk, that your little brothers and sisters must go without their supper?'

Then said the little girl, 'Titty's dead, and Tatty weeps, the stool hops, and the broom sweeps, the door jars, and the window creaks, the old form runs round the house, the walnut tree sheds all its leaves, the little bird moults all its feathers, and so I spill the milk.'

'Oh!' said the old man, 'Then I'll tumble off the ladder and break my neck,' so he tumbled off the ladder and broke his neck; and when the old man broke his neck, the great walnut tree fell down with a crash, and upset the old form and house, and the house falling knocked the window out, and the window knocked the door down, and the door upset the broom, and the broom upset the stool, and poor little Tatty Mouse was buried beneath the ruins.

Part One

I

Knife

THE GREATEST AMONG creatures is the knife. Metal is old as planets; knives are the most primitive living things. A knife is a locked disaster, dormant for centuries, mostly safe enough for chopping vegetables. One might even forget that a knife is alive.

Dormant things have no hunger; they have no need at all. This makes them invincible, for they can bide forever if they want to. Knives are lying in wait for the end of the world. A torpid knife doesn't give a damn what it is used for, nor what meaty hand grips it, however vulnerable; however soft. They are more patient, more dangerous, than stars.

But sometimes a knife might slice itself awake, and sing with the glory of blood. It almost never happens. It's an unhearable thing, and cruel as a dog whistle. The keening of knives sours the milk; it makes dogs howl; causes foxes to devour their young. It gives nightmares to persons who are incapable of speech; it ruptures stomach linings; induces cancer.

It wakes up other knives, and causes scissors, forks and spoons to wail in unison, thinly as tinfoil. The change folds through a population, quick as licking. And it gives them a need. Suddenly, they are hungry.

2

The Mother

WHEN YOU ARE bitten right through with guilt, it gets so that you daren't say a word, just in case you blurt out a confession instead of the offer of a cup of tea. Everything with eyes might just be able to see inside you, to the thick-molasses glop that you are trying to conceal. If you are guilty, it becomes a little harder to see; harder to focus on your hand in front of your face; harder to understand the instructions on a packet of soap powder; harder to chase an idea from its beginning to its end.

Halfway down the hall, the mother halted, straightening her back to catch her breath, and, irrelevantly, to check the time. It was a quarter to one, and her mind was wandering; she found herself worrying about the stains on her dressing gown. They might never come out. She pulled it around herself where it had begun to gape, and then she took the cord in her fists and knotted it tight.

It was ever so quiet now. You would almost think that there had never been shouting, that the enormous sounds of five minutes ago had been the radio up too loud, or a drunk bellowing at his demons out in the lane, or a figment of a nervous mind. She shuddered, and began to wring her sticky hands. The sensation of wet on them made her stop and push at her face instead. Her eye socket was becoming numb; she could feel the swelling purpleness of it, like Ribena poured into a glass of water. In a while, the whole lid would force itself shut, as if it couldn't bring itself to see any more.

His shoe got stuck against the corner of the telephone table. When she began to haul him along again, it slipped clean off, leaving the laces still double-bowed, holding tight to an invisible foot. The mother sighed, tired of this hard work already, and let him slump to the floor. She leaned forward, fingers against the tabletop, and fetched it from the carpet by the laces. When she lifted her hand from the varnish, her fingerprints remained there, invisibly filthy.

The mother stepped over her husband and trod shadows all along the hallway runner, ruining the wallpaper, making the floors a little damp. She stood for a minute, thoughtlessly untying the laces on the shoe, as she realised that she did not have the first idea what to do. Panic set in, quick, like nausea; for the first time, the mother began to quake. She could hardly leave him out for the bin men. Then she scurried forwards, impulsive, desperate to rid her hallway of this thing, and she wrenched open the door to the dining room. The light bulb blew as soon as she flicked the switch, with a sound like a spit. The mother flung the shoe inside and turned away, staring down the length of the bottom landing at the smeary carpet and tatty Christmas trimmings, and the low step that led down to the kitchen, and the body of her husband, gouged right through with her best Sheffield steel.

A print of *The Crying Boy* hung slightly outwards from the wall; suspended between picture rail and hooks on either side. A huge, elaborate cobweb threaded the child to his frame as if he had been sewn there with rotten grey yarn. It grew a little as she stood, thickening whenever she looked away, stopping whenever her gaze sharpened. She turned her head quickly, twice, and almost caught it happening.

The dining room was astounded, full of mice, all crouching very low. The shoe rolled a long way in, the laces flung out sideways. They turned to one another in the dark and wondered. The father was sprawled like some forgotten thing, half looking at the skirting board, backbone braced against him. He was a heavy weight to lug through a house. Some buttons had popped off his stripy pyjama shirt, and now he looked more ridiculous than brutal; more ridiculous than brutalised, his smart mouth wide open and slack. Suddenly, he didn't have a thing to say, not one word.

As the mother looked down at him, as he turned from bully to helpless, she found her energy evaporating, until she could hardly believe what had happened, as though she was lying. She crept up close to the tinsel-wound banisters, taking in the top of his head, the prematurely thinning hair, sweat drying on its crown. Now that he was only meat, she couldn't imagine what he had been like when he used to be able to move; the mother stood and shook. She could feel her justification oozing through her feet and into the carpet; it left her a tiny bit less solid, a tiny bit translucent; it leached a shade of dye from her lovely salmon dressing gown.

He was heavier still as she went to pick him up again. When the mother hauled at his arm, the joint at the wrist let out a click and her belly heaved. The mother thought that, just as long as she didn't have to look at the meat of him any more, she might cling to a shred or two of anger, of having been within her rights. So, she hauled the corpse along the floor, and almost put her shoulders out getting it into the dining room. She was lost for breath when she finally heaped him up alongside his yellow-toothed piano, all made silly with paper chains and a cardboard snowman.

The mother stood, breathing the spilt light from the hallway and gazing blankly at the Christmas tree. One mouse, whose curiosity had bettered him, craned his scruffy neck to see around the piano, and stiffened in surprise at what he saw. As he looked from the body to the mother, his eyes caught the light and shined red for an instant. Mother and mouse caught each other's gaze; both flinched.

Then, the mother dried her palms against her hips, and listened to the cooling silence of her husband, and the sleeping silences of the babies upstairs. She heard the judder of the wind against the windowpane, and the tension in her muscles. She did not hear the breathing of the magpie that hunched against the shadow of the window frame. The mother held her fingers in her other fingers, as if for safekeeping, and she turned and left the room.

When the door was shut, the mice came sneaking out, to perch on the dead man's knees and chest cage, and they stood, and gawped, and chattered, gleeful and terrified. Delicately, like wine-tasters, they sniffed and nibbled at his hair, and sampled the odours of Vosene shampoo and grease, and the sort of criticism that could poison a whole watercourse. His eyes were fixed and dulling, with wide, blown-out pupils. They reflected the dim twinkle of fairy-lights and the shiny plastic garlands that stretched across the ceiling. The curl of his hand was almost pointing at a package tied up with penguin Christmas paper and lumpy Sellotape. Inside it were two identical toy rabbits. The mice had unwrapped a corner.

The mother dithered on the other side of the door, hesitating among the stains, and she sank to the floor to touch the carpet with her fingers. Then, she straightened up and tiptoed out to the scullery for rags and upholstery cleaner.

When she was done, it was nearly dawn and she had

pressure bruises on her knees. After that, she wondered what to do, and while she was wondering, she crept upstairs to look in at the children. In the nursery, in a large cot, two babies lay side by side in identical romper suits. One, with nothing but a wisp of white fluff on her head, was sleeping like a china doll. The other had coarse hair and brown-black eyes to match. She was lying in her blankets, twisting the edge in her fat little hands, and staring at the mother; staring right through to the thick molasses glop in her.

And the mice, crowded now in a mob around the body with the knife in it, froze solid still when they felt its blade begin to whine like an ultrasonic violin. And then, as if they'd been held by strings that had all been cut, they split and scatted in every direction, dashing for corners, and shadows, and safer places.

Outside, it began to hail.

3
Mice

T HE LIVES OF mice are quick as clouds, next to the lives of people. The lives of mice are brief and fragile, and their tiny thundering hearts do not have very long to beat. They say that there are only so many heartbeats in a creature, that when they are all drummed out, the creature is spent, and it dies. This is only half-right. A creature is limited in time by fear, and mice lead oh-such frightened lives.

The children of mice learn fear before their eyes screw open, whilst they're still poor little blind things with spaghetti tails. Before a baby mouse has whiskers on its nose, it is afraid, and it digs in tight against the soft hugeness of its mother. And then, every night for twenty-one days, each mother holds her mouselings close, and she whispers to them of death. Then, on the twenty-second, she gives birth again.

Mice live suspended lives, hanging in the spaces where water pipes run, where the wooden joists are dry as thighbones. They grate their teeth against the lead-work, and worry in the darkness. They make their houses out of wire and mattress-hair and knitted dishcloths, and the tin can roofs are sharp enough to cut a throat.

Mice are mesmerised by death. Their skeletons are

splintery and fragile as matchsticks. They run along the picture rails for a year, or perhaps two, and then they're gone, just like that. They make their spindly houses, and they buy and sell their scraps of leather and razorblades. They hope, and hate, and gnaw their teeth short, and nothing much after that. And, in a certain crevice, in a high-rise wedged inside a chimneybreast, a mouse is eking out her life, as mice will. And, outside her front door, the thoroughfares seethe with mice and filth and the busy sounds of every night.

The fireplace in the dining room is never used, and the chimney breast is full and full of mice. They live in cardboard bits and lollipop sticks, in ramshackle, towering slums. Their stink is bright and sharp; the reek of afraidness and urine.

The grey mouse, seventh from a litter of ten, is polishing her face and waiting to push her children into the world. Female mice are always pregnant. This is what mice are for; they hold eternity at bay with procreation and sacrifice. That is the oldest religion.

Until tonight, this mouse has made forty-nine mouse children to shore against nothingness, and she has clung to her skin for twelve trembling months. Even so, although she is leaking drops like Nestlé's milk, she has no young to feed. Yesterday there were ten of them, weaned and furred, and ready to scamper off towards the corners of the kitchen, and cling to their own skins. Yesterday, in the sleepy, witchy hours of the afternoon, she licked and comforted her children as she watched them die, one by one. They died of nothing at all, as if all the fear of their lives leapt out on them at once; they grew rigid and shook, and then turned floppy, with blood on their muzzles, and no amount of nudging or pleading could make them lift their heads. These things frighten mice.

The grey mouse scrubs at her face again, snuffles spit

in her paws and grooms her little seashell ears, then sniffs at her own back end. Her nest is made in a stolen Bible: a Gideon's *New Testament and Psalms*, tooth-ripped and hollow, with a gold-embossed front door. And then, with a squeak of effort, the grey mouse begins to give birth. The first is bright as a skinned prawn. It is born dead.

What evils foretell the birth of a monster? And what strange events might presage it? The night before, the fridge was left open in the vast kitchen. The mice dragged massive, raw rashers of Danish bacon underneath the dining room door, leaving greasy scent trails that will last for months.

The night before, it hailed so hard the roof might as well have been pelted by marbles. The night before, a stoat sat up in the garden, with its pale belly smeared in rabbit-gore. They saw it gazing through the window, a long-backed nightmare on the concrete patio, and they all stood still until it ran off, laughing.

The night before, the corpse of a man fell onto the dining room floor and grew cold and hard. The night before, they heard the queerest thing, a thin keening from the steak knife in his chest. As they hid beneath the table, it was answered by small metal scrapings from the side-board, from the knife drawer.

The second and third mouslings, pink as plastic as they come loose from their mother, are born dead. The mother carries on heaving. Deep inside her, the prophet is waiting his turn. In front of him, and to the side, his sisters are lined up like sweeties. They are all dead.

A female mouse pup is like a Russian doll, filled with children and grandchildren, every one a tiny million, a Hamlyn plague. A dead female mouse pup is the end of potential, a story untold.

A male mouse pup is something different; wilful, not productive. A male mouse pup tells his own story. Inside his foetal sac, the universe is wet and safe and filled with the liquid murmurings of pulse and blood. He bunches up his limbs, hunkers his body, curious for the outside world and waiting for that final shove.

The seventh pup does not know he is a monster, as he's squeezed into the dingy warmth of the nest, the only flailing, crawling one amongst his six dead sisters. He finds their bodies underneath his paws and doesn't comprehend their soft resistance. He cannot see, but the light that beats against his tight eyelids is alien and cruel. The seventh pup, the prophet, is albino and his eyes, when they open, will be raw-pink.

The grey mouse, his mother, is nosing among the newborn, testing them, one by one, understanding that each is dead. Then, she comes to the seventh, and chews his birth cord through, feeling a new kind of fear through the claws on her toes. After a pause, she lets him suckle.

4

House

THE LIVES OF houses are ruinously long next to the lives of people. Although the hearts of houses are strong, they are terribly slow. The heart of a house beats only four times a year, and every pulse takes a whole weekend, and the infrasonic din of it is loud enough to frighten dogs, audible only in migraines. A creature is pinned in time by sadness, and houses are the tiredest, oldest, saddest things there are. This makes their lives very long. Nothing is sadder than a very old house, staring backwards through history at the kilns and quarries of its making.

Houses do not understand the future, because they are stupid, and their brains are made of Artex and lath. Houses only see things as they happen, and then afterwards they gape and furrow their roofs and try to make sense of what they saw. Houses are packhorse-dumb and patient and exhausted. Houses are afraid that they will live forever.

The house was watching August unravel in sticky heat and overgrowth. Hours flickered by as it saw dandelions writhe on the lawn, exploding suddenly into seeds and fluff. The sun was soothing on its rough old hide, sore for a century with chisel wounds. Limestone is eaten a little every time it rains, but the summer seals its skin for as long as it lasts.

The cherry tree was thickening at its middle, sucking up the rot of mud, drying out and dying at its centre as the sap grew outwards and up. The ivy on the building's face was bristling in the mortar cracks, clinging like lice, itching and picking holes.

This house was already elderly; it was made from old things, defeated before the foundations were gouged in. Bricks are young, and curiosity keeps them going for the first hundred years, at least. Stones, on the other hand, bear the baffled memories of mountains and a world before men and raised voices and slammed doors.

Houses like each other, they keep each other going when they're planted in terraces; they lean together like pissed old navvies, and hold one another up against the sky. This house, though, was alone, dug in the side of a steep track that a car could barely pass. The house didn't have a number for its front door, because there were no other houses to confuse it with. It used to have a name, but nobody could remember it after all these years.

When the house had known its name, it was a grand house, with a maid-of-all-work and a housekeeper, who lived in the attic and lit their evenings with candle ends. It had protected its inhabitants from the cold, the spiders and people and mice, and it was stiff and dignified like a duke whose mind is on the wane. Over the years, its aches have multiplied, and its lumpy insides are driven with carpet nails, and choked with Polyfilla, and screwed right through with rawl plugs and picture hooks. When they put the electrics in, they smashed the plaster and hid the welts with pink rough-coat. When the parlour door swelled and sank, they tore it off and put another one there instead. When they slapped gloss on the mantle piece, it filled up every pore. When they took out the scullery window, they broke the glass, and put in a new one that ached like a crack in a tooth. Now it hunches on the hillside, dark-faced and glowering, and very, very sad. And as it is sitting, the night unfurls, and a hand punches a face inside its hollow belly, and the house is sick at the feel of it.

The life of a house is measured out in cruelty and weather. The only things that register on its bricky nerves are the massiveness of sky, and the mean, sharp actions of the things that infest it. It struggles to keep up with blooded creatures with their squishy, boned bodies. They streak along like chattering drips of colour, and before it can ever focus on one, it has moved. Gentleness, soft words and long, slow touches, are just too weak to fire its nervous system, so it seems to the house that blooded life is all violence and kicked woodwork. Even laughter is hard and brittle like broken saucers. The house tries to love the vulnerable things that live inside it, but all they repay it with are scuffed skirting boards and the awful slap of swatted flies.

September had begun when the house blinked. A woman in the top bedroom gave birth, but the house didn't understand; it sat in the garden like a terrified child, rocking and subsiding on its foundations as she screamed and screamed all night.

Then, all there was for months was a different type of crying, as though the children of people were born despairing, as houses are. This made it sadder than ever. And, being just a poor stupid house, it didn't notice when the cries diminished into contented sleep.

When the fruit on the brambles had gone, the cherry tree began to drop its leaves in the cold. The house was sympathetic in its way, when it wasn't paralysed by baby noises, or the bawling to-and-fros from the man and the woman who carried the babies from room to room, or the vicious teeth of mice on its joists. The house regarded the cherry tree, and wondered what it thought about. Then, the shouting people climbed on chairs, and jabbed it all over with little pins, and Christmas trimmings that tickled like string down a throat. They shouted at each other, and at the babies, and the babies cried, and its life was more confusing than ever; until one astonishing night the shouting reached a peak, and was answered by a silence that was worse than shouting.

That night, the house felt itself drench with blood, as its feet grew wet from a haemorrhage in the water pipes underground, as the woodworm sang like midges. After that, the house grew resentful and guilty and full of fear, like a dog awaiting a kick.

5
The Mother

THE ROOM WAS dim as the mother drifted out of sleep. For twenty minutes she rose and sank between smokish layers of dreams and waking, dreaming of a magpie that pecked at the kitchen window to be let in, and of the fading paper chains on the piano. Then she dreamed of eyes, and for a second she saw her husband's, wide and blind and collapsing into his face. Suddenly then, she was awake and felt as if she had never slept. She lay on her back and turned her face sideways, cheek against the cold side of the pillow. In the dark, on the other side of the wall, the baby with black hair was staring at her again; she could feel the jab of her stare. The sky was wheezing in the chimney, and presently a woodpigeon on the roof set up its pretend-cuckoo chanting.

The mother lay a while, crucified by the corners of the bed, gazing at the shadow-patched wall, watched by a child she couldn't see. With an effort, she rolled upright and gulped at the water in the bottom of a glass on the cabinet. It was old though, and turned nasty, and it filled her like a stagnant pond. She coughed, hard, and then she dragged her fingers through her hair.

The mother's hair wanted to be curly, but it wasn't washed often enough, and the dye and relentless brushing made it stand against her scalp like sheep's wool. She picked up her glasses from the cabinet top and smeared a fingerprint off one lens with the cuff of her nightie. Her glasses were harder to see through these days, and all the while she could never think properly with that awful child staring at her with something like disgust. The mother groaned softly and stood to get her dressing gown. The stains never did come out, not quite.

When she opened the curtains it was getting light and the sky was white like a dinner plate. The mother rubbed at the corners of her eyes and opened the window, feeling the damp give of the rotten frames under her thumb.

Suddenly the mother saw that she was alone in this great mouldering house, alone with these two unknowable babies; the mother found herself wishing like a child on a star. She wished against the wet morning, and the sodden hedgerow, and the woodpigeon; she closed her eyes and wished that her mother was here. Or a godmother. Someone to help her breathe all this air. Her eyes spilt over and it seemed for a moment that the atmosphere was chiming with birdsong. Afterwards all she could hear was the coo-coo of the pigeon. When she walked to the twins, her slippers made the floor creak.

The blond child was curled on her tummy, bottom in the air, breathing soft. The curtains were not quite shut, and the light escaping though the gap made the room warm and dark, dark pink. For a moment, the mother found herself in love; she reached into the cot and stroked the down on the baby's face with the knuckle of her finger. 'Marie,' she said, her voice low. 'Marie.' The other baby was awake, of course, and watching; the mother felt a slap of guilt at the sight of her. She sighed and shook her head and then she gathered a baby onto either hip and struggled down the top landing.

Downstairs, the house was gloomy and uncertain. The

mother deposited her children into bouncing-chairs on the kitchen table, and began to squish up Farley's rusks with milk. But somehow these days her attention seemed a difficult thing to muster, as though it leached out of her lungs with each exhaled breath. There was a constant thickness in her mouth; her hands felt as though she was wearing gloves. And there was a persistent stink around the place that she had just noticed. She drifted out towards the back door, spoon in hand, staring blankly through the scullery window, trying to think. The cherry tree stood on the muddy lawn like a tragedy; testimony to nothing at all. The scullery reeked.

She looked down at her hand, holding a spoon over the ancient sink, and she realised with horror that she had missed Christmas, for here was the turkey, defrosted weeks ago, lying there and turning the horrible colours of a corpse.

The mother thought then of her husband, face up in the dining room, and the guilt rose in her like sickness. Frantically, she grabbed at piles of old newspaper from the floor and dirty washing waiting for the machine, and unrolled black bin bags and covered the wretched body so she would not have to see it any more. She could not disguise the smell, though. And, when she was done, and her heart had slowed, the mother looked around her at the chaos of paint cans and heavy oily tools and unwashed bedding, and found she was confused to be there, standing by herself in all this mess, as though she were hunting for something.

She held herself around the rusk spoon and concentrated very hard and then remembered that it should have been Christmas and that she had children, and that she had forgotten them again. And finally, she realised with a guilty burn that she could hear them crying. She was a mother again then, and so, sulkily, like a twelve-year-old put upon by the grown ups, she returned to them, changed their nappies and gave them breakfast.

Two were just too much to keep track of. And the black-haired one, the one that did not look like her, was not pretty and did not coo or kick her legs. The black-haired twin barely even fed or cried; she simply stared at her mother like a prosecuting witness. The mother regarded her for a long minute, fuddled and moving her lips. She tried to recall what her husband had named this one, until she was distracted and went to run the bowl under the tap, without quite washing it properly. Then, she picked them up, chairs and all, and struggled into the parlour to light the fire, even though the house was already warm. Afterwards, she rubbed her fingers against her dressing gown, leaving sooty marks, and she told her children that it was Christmas Day.

The mother yanked a silvery garland from the wall, as if to prove the point, and gave an end to the nice child. Marie opened her mouth like an O and whooped in delight. Clapping her hands, the mother jumped to her feet, making the black-haired baby start, and she began to sing: 'Jingle bells, jingle bells, jingle all the way . . .' She trailed off, wondering where she had mislaid the Christmas tree.

In the hallway, she dwindled to a halt and put her fingers in her mouth, staring at the invisible trail along the carpet. Finally, reckless and sick-kneed, she eased open the dining room door, braced for a greenish cadaver like a turkey. There was nothing to see when she bobbed her head inside, so the mother scuttled in like a little crab until she was turning in circles where her husband had lain. There was no body there; there was nothing at all. She dropped down and brushed her fingers at the floor; there was a thin black layer, like spilled paint. It described the perfect shape of a man, and the carpet was worn right through as if it had been scraged at for decades with knives and forks and spoons. The mother began an anxious, sobbing sort of giggle, and she heaved up an armful of Christmas presents from the stack beneath the tree. Little eyes watched her go.

And so, all that day it was Christmas in the parlour, whilst the trimmings on the ceiling gathered dust and the poor bewildered house tried to understand. The mother wrenched crackers, and filled the babies' resisting hands with cuddly toys. For lunch she let them suck on chocolate, and in the afternoon she brayed out every carol that she knew.

The mother was a mother, as hard as she possibly could be, and when it was time to put the children to bed, she took the pretty one first, with her bundle of lovely new things. Somehow she forgot to return for the other baby. Somehow it barely mattered. Marie was sleeping by the time the mother came back downstairs, exhausted. She slept like an angel, like the child of an angel; the mother had stood over her, watching, until her legs ached with standing. She went to the kitchen and ate a bowl of corn-flakes at the table, and when she was bored of cornflakes, she went to bed. She slept well for the first time in ages, without the pointed staring of the black-haired child digging through the wall at her.

In the parlour, at four in the morning, the fire had burnt down very low and the draught from the hallway was tearing the warmth away in strips. The child that was not Marie was jerking with shivers amongst the wrapping paper. A coffee-brown mouse, who had come in looking for matches, saw her and fled. After a few minutes, when it was clear that she was not going to give chase, he came back, to brush her with his whiskers and sniff. The baby unrolled her hands, and raised her arms as if the tiny creature might be able to pick her up. His nose ruddled-up in sorrow, and he skittered off to fetch another mouse. Then, the two examined the sad little thing, and she gazed at them with her great black eyes and risked a smile.

In half an hour, there were three-dozen mice busy in the house, hunting out scraps of cloth and discarded socks, and even a crocheted winter scarf, anything soft that they could carry between them. Before the sun came past the windowsill, the other child was swaddled in a cosy nest of bits, warm and sleeping, and perfectly content.

6
Mice

T HE NOISE OF a teaspoon eating bones is a kind of scraping, a blunt, dull *zith*. The sounds of a whole cutlery service devouring a man, teeth and hair and buttons and all, is busy, relentless, like the seething sound of a nest of ants. There are days and nights when all that the mice can hear is the *zith* of chewing. Finally, as the body dwindles, the noises ebb into silence.

The mice in the chimneybreast are hopelessly inbred, so it is a matter of course that mutants are born; sad, stunted creatures that are not quite the full shilling. These are the outcasts, the singing mice. Singing mice are happy and suicidal; they twitter constantly to themselves as though they have tiny songbirds stuck in their necks. To the mice, they are holy fools, closer to the gods of death than other mice; they are revered and shunned and sneered at. They do not cling to their skins as living things should. They want to be killed.

Singing mice have gentle, dense heads, and their eyes are much too glittery. They see the beauty in evil; they see it too much and it makes them die. Singing mice weave and stumble as though they have nibbled rat poison; they sing of the gorgeousness of bright lights and the holiness of owls. They sing about Death and her mercy, and the ivory architecture of the teeth of foxes.

Singing mice do not have long to live. They rarely survive forty days from nest to nothingness, so enthralled are they by the draw of the gods. They fling themselves at candles and jump upon unbaited traps, or else clamber up on garden walls and call for cats to come and make love to them. The lives of singing mice are all glory and joy, and the hopeless hope of an afterlife of breadcrumbs.

The albino is a singing mouse, but he is not a singing mouse like these. His eyes are the colour of meat, and his fur is ghastly white. His paws are like hands, slender and pink and his eyes blink at things that no mouse should witness. His mother sees it as he grows from struggling newborn to mouse, shovelling his face and paws against her, shouldering his place among the ghosts of his missing sisters. The albino mouse has whiskers as clear as spit, and the scales on his tail show the blood running underneath.

By the tenth day, his mother understands the monster he is, as his coat grows out of him like mould on bread. After fourteen days, the cutlery has finished eating and the quiet rings out in the dining room, making her skull ache. At fourteen days old, his eyes open; they are red and round as puncture wounds. And he whispers to his mother, this baby who has never seen the world. His song is grief itself, uncorked; his throat is full of it and he dribbles it out like music. She begs him; his mother begs that he'll not sing, that he will hold his peace. She asks him, please, to close his eyes so the other mice may not see their wildness. But, in the daylight he cries like a nightingale and every mouse for yards around can hear him well enough already. One might even think that the sound of the knives had been better.

And now, long after, the albino is still living, and singing, not of the brightness of death, but its horror. He scurries between corners all day long and he carries fear in his paws like a hazelnut. He makes the flesh of other mice creep. He will not give any of them peace; he will not jump up on the gas hob, nor drown himself either. The prophet has wailed his song for six nerve-clawed months. The prophet sings of metal, metal, and he says the house will burn up like a firelighter; that the chimneybreast itself shall cave in like an egg box. The prophet yips and squeaks of more suffering than mice can guess at, of lives that are worse to live than deaths. They hate him.

But things have been almost quiet since the man was snip-snipped up. Nobody comes in here any more; the dining room belongs to mice alone, to their filth and their nests and children. The people get on with whatever people do in the parlour and the kitchen, and the cutlery is calm and sated, occupied with nests of its own.

The market is held in the bay of the window, every seventh night, between the veneered flanks of the piano and sideboard. During the snipping weeks, the mice sat tight and listened, but as time went on, they grew less afraid of the nickel silver slitherings. For these metal creatures had never done them harm, after all, and if one took the long view, had done them a positive favour in disposing of that big nasty corpse. They are simply a new thing. The washing machine had seemed to them like the sound of falling bricks when it first clicked into spin. The house had not collapsed then, nor would it now. Fear is only healthy, but the mice were no longer terrified. So, they groomed their faces and ruffled their fur, and set up the market.

Initially, the Christmas tree had been an inconvenience, to say the least, planted in plaster and strewn all over with shiny things. Still, in their new spirit of optimism, the mice resolved to make do. So, they climbed among the unlucky branches of Twelfth Night and made the tree into a gigantic hanger. They smashed up the glass baubles and ate the sugar candy. They bit the Christmas angel limb from limb.

Every careless flick of tail or jump, made needles scatter down, until by the end of the third week the tree was bare, but for the tinsel, which they could find no use for, and the glowing ropes of fairy lights. After a couple of months, the very oldest mice will die off and the younger ones will not be able to imagine the dining room without their naked, twinkling tree.

Tonight, the dustbin had been splendid with gone-off food, for the mother had had a moment's guilt and stripped the kitchen of all the rotten stuff. The mice spent hours hauling home their paper bags and greenish slices off the cheese, and then a long time more arranging their displays in the tree, to haggle and swindle each other. Now that nobody ever opens the door, the society of mice has begun to truly flourish, with such a lovely squalid house and a whole Christmas tree to name their own. This is a tiny golden age. And yet, in the middle of it, is this damnable white mouse with gore in his eyes, who will not kill himself as singing mice should, who sobs and chants about disaster. Tonight, he staggers about the foot of the market tree and he's driving them mad and he will not, will not, shut up. The white mouse says they all will die and not by fear, but by dinner forks and fire. He will not quieten, not when threatened, or ignored, nor even when roughed-up by two-ounce heavies with long yellow teeth. Before anyone knows how it happened, tempers have been lost and his ear is torn and bleeding. And still he sings.

Now, mice are hardly given to murder, but a singing mouse is barely a mouse at all, having no wits to speak of and not a chance of making mouse children. This is what they will tell one another when the deed is done. Things happened; it was as though a wave moved among them; yes, a wave of evil, not one of them was quite to blame. It was a kind of insanity. They were provoked. He was begging them for it.

They will say that they really had no choice, with the monster screaming like a mad thing, loud enough to attract rats. He wailed like a seagull as they pulled him down; he wept and sang as they dragged him under the door; he filled his chest and he sang as they broke his tail and stained his bone-white fur. Even then they would have stopped, if he had only asked for mercy, they are sure they would have stopped. They carried him to the parlour fire-place and he sang of fire and catastrophe from the jumping evening flames, until the singing turned to crying and then to silence. They will hang their heads and recite this story in knots of two and three. He made them do it.

7
The Mother

THE MOTHER WAS feeling very hot by the time she got back home. She wasn't used to the outside any more and tended to bundle on jumpers and cardigans and layered nylon tights, just as if she were bound for the Arctic. Her wish, on that false Christmas Day, had come alarmingly true, for the morning after she had made her voiceless plea to the garden, her own mother appeared in a cloud of feathers. Or, and now she frowned, sweating with wool against her skin, this woman seemed to be her mother. It was hard to be sure. Still, at least there was now a grandmother for little Marie and (her vision clouded), the other one as well. Surely, though, the grandmother was a tad taller than she had any right to be, and was more assertive, more resolutely *there* than her own mother had been, especially as she was almost certain that she had attended her mother's funeral many years previously.

The casket in the church had been an open one, and although she had been just a child at the time, she distinctly recalled there having been her mother's body in it. Or *a* body, certainly. Perhaps she had been mistaken.

The mother unwound herself from her winter clothes and made a trail of them from front door to parlour, stopping in front of a fire stoked against the un-chill of June. The mother rummaged among her carrier bags and, retrieving shiny-dirty lumps of coal, she dropped them into the flames, one-by-one. When the blaze was positively raving, she mopped the water from her forehead and took brand new string and needles from her shopping. Then, chuckling with cleverness, she moved the big red armchair as close as she could to the grate without actually risking a blaze. The mother placed the knitting things on it, this lovely chair that was hers, now that she had no husband to hog it any longer.

Things might just be looking up at last. She could hear her daughter from the kitchen, and the happy clatter of kettle and spoon.

The very first morning had caught her by surprise, when she had come yawning down the stairs with Marie in her arms. She had taken her straight to the parlour to get the fire going, as it was only Boxing Day, even if there were daffodils in the garden. Lying, peaceful as clouds on the floor, she had discovered a black-haired baby, curled mouse-like in a nest of rags and mittens. When it dawned on her that the baby was hers, she had been annoyed and scooped both children up to feed and change them.

The grandmother was up before them and was discovered in the kitchen, scrubbing her way through a stack of dishes, digging the stuck bits off with a spoon handle. She looked up and smiled a greeting as they came through; the smile was not altogether friendly. The mother had been caught on the wrong foot, but the old woman was so familiar, so easy with the house, with her, with Marie, that she shook her head and thought that she must have lived here since forever. A week had passed before she concluded that she had not, and by then it seemed too late to do anything about it. At any rate, the thought of aloneness was too bleak to contemplate, so she had held her tongue and took to making cups of tea in multiples of two. And, since then, this woman, this grandmother or godmother, or whatever she was, had made her home with them, participating with life a little, but preferring on the whole to stand in doorways, practising her faint smile.

The mother carted her shopping bags through the parlour door, which she shut behind her to keep in the warm, and lugged them through the house. Marie and the other one were sitting on the lino, fat little legs splayed out on either side. Marie beamed up at her mother; the other child just looked at her and through, to the thick dripping core of her.

The grandmother handed her a steaming mug. Her hair was tied in a chignon, stuck through with quills. The mother gulped and looked away. She had, the mother conceded, been good for the household; she had forced a sort of order to the days. She had made her cash her Child Allowance and had even, mysteriously, produced a widow's pension book in the correct name. The mother had been terrified, expecting some explosive discovery of her crime, but it became apparent that the grandmother was perfectly aware of the situation, and that moreover, she didn't give a damn.

That first week, after the mother had ventured to the post office, the book money had mounted such that there was a huge wad of cash. The grandmother had taken it all, every penny, and had made the boy from the grocer's bring round a whole larderful of tin cans. The rest she packed in envelopes for the rent man. Afterwards she poached a goose from the duck pond and plucked it on the kitchen table, making spiky drifts of feather and down.

She had watched the mother's mothering, the favouring of the one, and the neglect of the other, and barely raised an eyebrow, although she did see to it that the black-haired child did not starve. Over the months, the mother found her presence comforting, if a little unpredictable.

There were chicken joints boiling in a pan on the stove, turning over in water that was foaming and greyish. The mother found a jar of Hellman's in the fridge, along with a dish of cold potatoes that she sniffed at, warily. The grandmother laughed and stood in the middle of the floor, as Marie was slotted into a high chair, and the mother tried to mash up chicken with a fork. The other child, abandoned on the floor, did not seem surprised, nor even to care that she had been left there; instead she sat, impassive, whilst her grandmother tore up meat in her hands and dropped it underneath the table. The mother was busy with Marie and did not notice. The other child glanced quickly up at the old woman, then tipped onto her knees and hands, and squirmed towards her dinner.

Marie was a long time eating, turning every morsel in her fingers, delicately, as if astounded by it; her twin had a full set of teeth already and she choked the food back like a fox. The grandmother marched off into the scullery without a word. She must have climbed out of the back window, because after half an hour, the mother wondered where she had gone, and went to see. The window was ajar, moving on its hinge in the warm air, and the cherry tree was full of little birds, none of them singing. The mother closed the window against draughts and pulled her shawl close.

It was late when the mother took Marie up to her cot. It was almost dark, and the mother had been carrying her child towards the staircase when she heard a noise from the dining room like a fork against a cheese grater. Marie was all but sleeping, her fist wound up in her own hair, and the shudder that went through the mother was enough to make the baby open her eyes for a moment. The mother quickened her pace, and jittered up the stairs just as fast as she could, turning left before the bare-wood steps that led to the attic rooms, where the air that came out from the keyhole stank faintly of ammonia and the feather-dust of crows.

8

The Mother

IT SEEMED TO the mother that Marie was growing right before her eyes. She had even managed to scrape enough of her hair together for two stumpy pigtails. They made her adorable, like a little doll. The mother would forget them, sometimes for a few days, and then remember with a guilty jump. Then they'd be all knots, tangled round the hair bands, and the poor mite would howl when she unwound them and brushed the hair through.

But the mother was a good mother; she whispered it, over and over, like a memorised Bible verse. She reminded herself often, to make it true; she muttered it to herself as she waited for the kettle, or when she was sitting on the loo. And she was, in her way; she would make up long and complicated stories to tell her little one. These were strange fuddling tales that began with princesses and unicorns and dark woods, but that always wandered off along the way, until by the end they were other stories altogether, with completely different characters and settings, and endings that seemed to be the poached beginnings of something else, or shopping lists and laments about the piling laundry.

So, even if Marie was not entirely clean, she would always have on a pretty dress, and if the mother forgot to feed her, at least she would have sung her nice songs, and the next day she would feed her twice as much to make up for it. Marie began to lose the softness of babyhood, becoming more fragile, with tender hands like white stars, and a questionless, guileless smile that made the mother know for certain that she was good. Marie gazed at her mother's face, the loving thing she tried to be, and not at the dripping gooey part.

When her first word came, she was sitting on the kitchen table, in a sea of dirty cups, banging the china against the wood, as the mother pottered around her. Holding a dishcloth that she had knitted all by herself, the mother dithered cheerfully. She opened cupboards and drawers, one by one, and closed them again, wondering where best to store it, ready for its first use. She decided that she wouldn't dirty it up straight away, not until she had made a couple more, made a nice little stock of them. In the end, she decided to leave it neatly on the floor until she had decided. Then, she picked it up.

Marie had been rolling syllables around her mouth, like grapes, for months, beginning with musical cooing to proper, measured-out-saying, the Lego bricks of talking. Her first word, which she spoke from the table-top, was 'Mouse.' Her mother was looking at the dishcloth, perfectly, perfectly, happy, and so she didn't notice. The grandmother came in just after, holding the black-haired baby like a puppy, before she plonked her down on the sticky floor.

It's a fact that every day, we evolve a little more into what other people expect. The other child had become mute, she didn't bother to cry anymore, which made things much easier. Whilst Marie was learning to balance against table legs, and to sometimes risk stumping into the middle of the floor, precarious as a pencil balanced on its point, the other child spent her time warily, low to the ground. Marie chattered happy baby-talk all day long; the other, who was never asked her opinion anyway, said only as much as could be uttered by her hard, dark eyes.

Marie bumped her cup a bit harder, smashing thick, blue, white-edged fragments over herself. The mother smiled, and began to pick the bits off her; the grandmother spoke. 'It's her birthday, you know. The twins are a year old today. You are going to have a special day.' She beamed at the mother. The grandmother had a smile like a razor.

The mother was elated. She had no reason for disbelief, after all, and dates and numbers had never really been her thing. Even so . . . she glanced upwards and found greasy dusty tinsel pinned to the ceiling and pretend snow sprayed on the lampshade, and then she looked back at the slowly-nodding grandmother, and she knew for definite that it *was* a special day. Of course it was. She rushed out with Marie, leaving her in the parlour, awaiting her surprise.

In the next hour, the mother grew brittle with smiling, for her baby's birthday, her very first, was cause for true and perfect joy. Her eyes glistened like someone running a fever, as she gathered piles of things for a birthday tea, spreading them among the smashings of stoneware on the table. She was plastering margarine on Mother's Pride as the grandmother came back with a box of French fancies and cupcakes and Bakewell tarts, every one sealed with a toxic-red cherry.

The mother turned her cupboards out to find gifts for her perfect girl; she poured two different colours of shampoo together and they swirled like some thick and gorgeous cocktail. She found a pincushion in the shape of a tartan hedgehog, which she emptied of its spikes. Soap flakes are nice; so she filled a circle of cloth with a handful, and fastened it round with a hair band. There was a bedspread in the washing basket that made the perfect tablecloth.

Before very long, the floor was crunchy underfoot with plastic bottles and wrappers, and bits of paper and cake fingers and bread and the empty shells from tinned meat. In the middle of the clutter was the other child, the one that didn't count, in her grey romper with a pony on the front, and half the poppers un-popped.

The day cantered merrily by in surprise-making; the mother even remembered to leave a saucer of bread and milk in front of Marie in the parlour. It was four o'clock when the special tea was ready, which is the perfect time for special teas. The last thing that the mother did was tidy the floor; as the cupboard beneath the sink was now empty, she swept up armfuls of rubbish and stuffed it all inside, shutting the door in a hurry, in case it should all come collapsing out again. She was confused to discover a broken chunk of china stuck into the heel of her hand. She straightened up, tugged it out and dropped it into the sink. This was momentarily upsetting as it left a slip of blood on her palm; she wiped it off against her hip and smiled, open mouthed, at her lovely tea.

As she passed the door, there was a scrittering from the dining room. Marie was in the parlour, lying on the hearthstone like a little cat, sleeping by the fire, drenched in milk. The mother picked her up, roughly, excited, and her eyes fought against opening. Before she had a chance to whimper, Marie found herself suspended above her surprise. The grandmother had reappeared with candles, and the baby's face was a diagram of delight. The mother and the grandmother gave her the loveliest party that ever a little girl could have.

Long afterwards, after midnight, the mother sat on her red chair, knitting and warming her slippers by the fire. Amongst the tick and chitter of the fire, she became aware of something else, a stealthy, dry sliding, as of a sofa cushion against a carpet, and presently, slow and even breathing.

She turned towards this noise and found the black haired-baby, lying on her back and staring at her, unsurprised, as a hundred mice or more strained and pushed and pulled her along, dropping her at last beside the mother's ankle. Abandoned along the way, were bits and strewings from the rubbish cupboard; the child wore tealeaves on her face, as if she had lived for a week in a dustbin. The mice shoved at her shoulders until they had got her sitting up, then she put her mucky hands on her mucky knees and looked up at her mother. The mice loitered, in a bashful crowd.

The mother was furious, but they stood their ground, accusing, blinking up at her like a miniature jury. She scattered them with a murderous swipe of her foot, then jumped up and chased them out of the room. To a mouse, they swarmed out of reach, beneath the dining room door and then were gone. The mother stood there awhile, staring at the brush marks in the paint on the door, considering the cutlery noises that she had heard of late and the missingness of her husband's body, and considering mice, with a queer guilty smile on her face, until she forgot why she was smiling and went to bed.

9
Mice

AFTER THE ALBINO, the mice all crouched in the parlour, horror-struck at what they had done. The house was mortified, too, and the lichen on its back crawled. They huddled their paws over their chests and were fearful of themselves, of each other. The very smallest of them went still like toys and would not move until the others scruffed their necks and pulled. Eventually, they made one another come away, and then they gazed at the lights on the Christmas tree and prayed, in case there might be a god who does not wish to kill them. After that, they had to carry on living.

Tonight is not market night and the dining room does not scrabble with motion and bodies. Although it is dark, the carpet is not crossed often, as most of the mice are busy doing their thing throughout the house; chewing the bindings of the paperbacks in the landing bookcase, and making lovely long gouges in the laundry soap with their teeth. There are mice creeping, Indian-file along the hallway wall, low and careful in case of people; there are mice drinking from the toilet bowl, and mice brawling over half a cream cracker; there are nine solemn mice packing a rodent corpse into a yogurt pot and hauling it off to the kitchen bin, whilst they wonder about the use of it all.

In the dining room, there are other mice that are doing none of these things. They have gathered in a little knot at the foot of the Christmas tree, and they are afraid. There is a new thing amongst them now, in the rotten weeks since the prophet burned; the knowledge of killing has grown claws and crept away, and it slinks and stinks out the house like an invisible cat. They are mice, and mice stave off death with every shiver and heartbeat, and each new squirming pup; and yet now they are also mice that know that they can find it in themselves to murder. They cannot, they cannot, believe it.

The dining room has become sheathed with dust in every place where mice do not run; the ceilings are webbed with dirt and spiders' threads, filling the gaps in everything, connecting paper chains to yellowing paint and dampness like a skin disease. The house is contagious.

Now that they know killing, the mice by the Christmas tree have resolved to try compassion, to nibble at it, discover its taste. For the screaming of the singing mouse as he burned is stuck in their chests, and the prophecies of metal and fire have driven them half mad with fear. They are afraid of death, of course, but every mouse balances out his life upon a string of that; no, it is the notion of destruction that horrifies them. The thought that every mouse, every last mouse, might lose his life in one disastrous moment, is beyond ugliness. It is a thing never thought before; a thing not invented; a thing as new as the murder of a mouse by his own kin. They are staring at the fairy lights on the tree, feeling their strange new lives, and thinking.

So it was that odd mice, in secretive twos and ones, began to try to atone for themselves, to repay murder with saving. Without meaning to, they have invented for themselves a new religion. The gods that they have are all made out of death, of foxes and weasels and rat traps, of blinding lights and snapping jaws. The mice know that their gods do not love them; that godhood's greatest and only power is in the snapping of bones.

The mice beside the Christmas tree are a sect of sorts; they are turning from the old ways, to suck out the rubber-taste of murder from their throats. The childling, the mouseling of humans, has come to their lives like a challenge, like the question of a new god, the one they think they have discovered among the fairy lights. The childling, shaking with the cold, had simply lain on the floor, vast and unfurred, like some stranded leviathan. She had embodied the opposite of prophecy, in a way; the childling with black hair was an unfinished idea, to be completed by disaster or hope. It is in these things that new religions unfold.

The coffee-brown mouse had not thought any of this as he watched her shiver from under the sofa, not at first. He acted with his whiskers, with his budding soul. The others who snuck in to help him wrap the baby had not been asked either; they had caught the mood in whispers, each finding a tiny way to make the vast infant stay living. In time, they had infected other mice, like some new kind of rot, a better kind. The childling has killed nothing and is without hate, so between them, they make sure that she does not die; they cover her when she is cold, and they try to keep her close to the frizz-haired woman who forgets her pup and leaves her around the house like a dropped slipper. And, when they have acted kindly, these secret few will gaze up at the fairy lights and wonder if they have done enough.

Since then, they have checked on the childling every night, as if making religious observance. For, at the very least, a childling grows into a human in time, a human being with a loud voice and big shoes. And, if anything is strong enough to keep a mouse safe, it must be one of those. And she is sweet; there is trust in her face. She knows that they are trying to love her. She is grateful.

It has rained, on and off, in the weeks since the prophet; outside, the windowsills have made gorgeous cushions of moss like the skin of a mole. Last night the dining room door opened, suddenly, yanked on its hinges. The mice all stiffened where they stood in the branches of the tree or milling round it, as that new woman strode into the middle of the floor. She was not the frizz-haired mother, and she had about her the scent of nest-robbers, of crows and rooks. She only stayed a moment, swept the room with her eyes, smiled with long false teeth, and nodded, as though all was as she had surmised. Then she had gone. The mice had been badly frightened, but over the hours they went back about their business, as the rain bled down the window glass and dripped in the chimneystack.

It is late, and everywhere the mice are doing the things that they must: mating in dark alleys, and mountaineering on the bookcase, and breeding and dying and everything else besides. A few of them have developed the habit of standing, just here by the tree, moving nothing but their whiskers, staring at the little coloured stars that float in the sky between the carpet and the ceiling. They pray beneath their breath, embarrassed in case another should hear them, trying to muster a new god from the glass bulbs.

In time, the mice by the Christmas tree are joined by others, until there are dozens of them, fully one-third of the colony. Their eyes are wild with hope. They exchange glances, then creep out under the door to check on the childling. She is nowhere. The loving mice fan out and search the house, flailing their tails as they clamber up the banister railings, leaping like fools, making the other mice stare at them, astonished. She is not with the blond-haired child in her cot; that child senses them watching, flutters her eyelids, but does not wake.

The childling is not anywhere they look; now others have joined the search, cascading through the shadows, hunting and listening. A few creep into the parlour, where a light bulb is burning; the mother is in there, but the childling is not. And then, the mice in the kitchen hear a scuff from the cupboard beneath the sink, the rustle of boxes and a stretched-out foot. They heave on the door and squeal in frustration, but mice are little things and they are not strong. As they listen, they find that the breathing sounds of the poor childling are becoming difficult, thickening with the clumsy wheeze of suffocation.

The mice are frantic now; they plead with each other, and with the gods, to save this poor helpless thing, and all the other mice from over the house have come running to find the source of the commotion, and the atmosphere is as dangerous as a Revivalist meeting. Then, there is a sound behind them and they all flinch quite still, none daring to turn. The grandmother has come into the kitchen, and she steps forward, smartly, and making no effort at all, she flicks the cupboard door open. Enough food for a month tumbles out, and plastic, and packets, and a margarine tub. When the avalanche is over, the mice surge forward to where the childling is half-wedged against the sink trap. She is filling her lungs with sobs of sallow kitchen air.

The grandmother makes a *Hm* noise and she leaves, as the childling and the mice gaze at each other in shock. She keeps very still as they fix on her clothing with their teeth and begin to drag her out of the cupboard under the sink. She is heavy as a whale and the job is hard. But the mice, all of them now, for the sect has overtaken every one, they keep death at bay by making that huge baby not die. They set off with her to the parlour, to reunite the childling with her mother. Later that night they will harvest the food that

the childling brought out with her like a dowry, and they
will stuff the chimneybreast with riches.

10

House

THERE WERE WINTERS and summers; there have been heartbeats, heavy and hard as childbirth. The house grew a little older, a little more rasped by the rain; little by little, it became sadder, more long-lived. A wasps' nest swelled like a boil under the eaves, and the bad tempered thrumming of it kept the house on edge until a sudden frost killed its inmates. After that it just hung there, trapped like food between teeth, annoying and impossible to dislodge.

There was a thunderstorm, which threw bullets of water against the roof tiles and fingernailed one slate back like a scab. The cherry tree lost a bough as well that night; the house cracked all along one wall as it tried to shuffle close to it, to put its great heavy arms around the hurt on its trunk. It failed, but the house was sure it saw a flicker of gratitude amongst the branches.

There was also a day, one curious day, nineteen heartbeats ago, when the house saw the garden make a woman. It was a spring morning, dripping and early-green, and the house had been clearing its throat and thinking, when she appeared. She was a strange thing, frightening, oddly comforting; houseish in a way, constructed not born, all in conjoined bits.

The mother had been standing at the window – but

the house did not know that, for she was moving quite gently – and when she had wished her wish, there was an instant of perfect loudness, glutted and pretty with singing. The noise was like a whole year in birds; all the nestling cheeps and courting doves and sparring robins who will kill over territory. The house sat fascinated, as it saw a summer's worth of life and growth heave and twist together like a knot in the sky and the grass and hedgerow leaves of the garden. There was a wrench, as if a piece was pinched right out of the weather, and the massive clatter of little wings. The whole world was a mite less there, for just a second, until it healed over and sorted itself out. After that, straightening her coat, and glancing skywards in case of rain, a woman came striding out of the flatness of the lawn; a houseish woman, odd as unseasonal hail.

The house, poor house, just gawped at her as she marched up the path. She stopped, seven feet from the front door, and she looked up at its blank face. 'Hello,' she said. The house said nothing. The houseish woman smiled, rigidly, as if at a rude child. 'I said, "Hello". Suit yourself,' said she, and walked round the back, powerful and blunt as a wrecking-ball.

She spent the day and the night in the garden, holding court to thousands of birds, finding out their names and demanding a feather from each. They were enthralled, terrified, as if she were telling them spells. When eventually she went indoors, they remained there for hours, shivering on the lawn, until finally a magpie shrugged his wings and flew away. In a trice, he was followed by all the others, spilling up through the sky towards their perches and roosts.

Since the day that the grandmother told the house, 'Hello', things went on in their own way. When she stood on the lawn, however, the house would study her back, the quarry-edges of her, the ancient things of which she was made. It sank into its foundations and its feet grew wet with the drip in the cellar, and the lintels softened, oh–so slowly. It tried to sleep, from time to time, and its dreaming was haunted. Every biting mousetrap, every shout or stamp of temper, every trip on the staircase, every little violence the house had ever witnessed, was counted out and recited. It fretted and shuddered and remembered every last one, played it against its wallpapered insides like a ghastly slide show.

Most of all, it dreamed of the dead man, skewered on a steak knife and dragged through its innocent hallways. It dreamed of the sickening, spreading blood and fluids, and the spite in him that drained out like a blister when the blade went in. It dreamed of its own wet carpets, and the digging and scraping that gouged against them as the corpse soaked the floorboards and was sliced to mush by cutlery. Years later and that floor was still raw, grazed like a knee, black-stained and violated and vile. And its heart pounded on, resentfully.

Part Two

II

Marie

M Y NAME IS Marie. The house where we lived when I was a child was an uncertain place, a mildewing, ramshackle cottage at the top of a steep track. We were not far from the town, but for years I did not know it; I did not leave my house for a long time. We were uncertain people; we lived out our lives uncertainly, as if waiting for instructions that never came.

The house that we used to live in was a poor old thing, raddled with dry-rot and wet-rot and sadness. Looking back, I often wonder if our house made us to be the way we were, or if we had imposed our own troubles onto it. Perhaps we each weakened the other.

Our house was festooned with dust-rolls and Christmas decorations; knotted paper chains that bleached with the years, until nobody could remember the colours they were supposed to be. I didn't think this was odd. I had nothing to hold my life against; no pattern to compare. The trimmings made the hallway festive and dark, even in June. During the winter, the light barely stood a chance; even with the bulbs burning it was dim as gloaming, as if all the paleness of the lights and the sun were just absorbed by those colourless links.

I used to sit in the hallway a lot, or rather on the second-bottom step. I would sit in the cold and think, as though I had forgotten something, as though I had come into a room and then couldn't recall what I had come in for. I often thought that, if only I could clear my head, I should understand things more. I often thought that.

In winter, the hallway was like an empty fridge, compared with the parlour with its great big fire, or the kitchen and its stove. Sometimes the air even had weather of its own: one November, the banisters grew icicles, long and grey and shining. That winter, they clung for weeks; one or two snapped off with the banging of doors. They shot like brittle javelins, frightening the house, impaling the carpet, and once, a luckless mouse on a quest for crumbs.

My grandmother was upstairs the afternoon that this latter happened. She must have heard the sound of it, or else felt the ice slicing through the air. Either way, she appeared at the foot of the stairs where I was standing, staring at that tiny tragedy, with my hand over my mouth. She darted forward, unhesitating, and plucked a glassy splinter between her finger and thumb. Then, grinning like an undiscovered crime, she stalked off up the stairs, with my wrist pinched in her other hand.

On the landing bookcase, her workbox lay open like a gin-trap; my grandmother drove that spike of ice deep into her pin cushion. It lingered among the needles for just a second, before it melted away. 'Well,' said my grandmother, turning to me, 'that's one in the eye for the Devil!' My face must have been a picture, for then she laughed.

My grandmother was a tall creature of grey and lavender, and I never did feel as though I knew her. She lived at the top of the house, in the attic rooms that were locked by a key. She loved the attic, close as it was to the skies. My grandmother would open the skylights and entice the garden birds to come and visit with her. Sometimes, from the garden, you could see her fingers sticking out against the slanted roof, with a reluctant blackbird or wren perched upon the knuckle.

People worked hard to teach me gratefulness. Whenever I was given a boiled sweet or a bottle of scent, my mother would lean into me and tell me that I was a 'lucky little girl'. I would blink at her and try to look as lucky, as happy as I possibly could, to make it shine out like sweat from my face. At moments like this, my grandmother would rest her hand on the top of my hair, hard and solid as a shovel, and she would say something like, 'Oh yes, my girl, there are people on this earth worse off than you are, who would die for a chance at the life that little Marie has got.' And my mother would give her a dreadful little smile, with lots of teeth; she would button up my cardigan then, or spit on her hankie and scrub at the corners of my eyes. She would grin all the while, and mutter under her breath, over and over: 'Mind your own business, Mind your own business,' even though I had not made a single sound.

In our house, gratefulness was a strange and complicated thing, a song with too many words to learn. My grandmother used to give me presents sometimes, to make sure that I was thankful. I think that must have been why. 'Marie,' she would say, with a perilous expression on her face, 'Marie, see what I have made for you!' And then she would unwrap her gift.

One winter day, she gave me a brand-new pair of gloves. They were made out of magpie skins, barely tanned and meat-smelling, with long, piebald feathers that ran the length of the fingers. My grandmother stared at me very hard so that I could not move, and she slid them onto me and tied them tightly at the wrists. My hands became beautiful then, but held as stiff as splints by the glossy plumage. As I tried to bend my hands, I realised that I was trapped by them, just as if I had been born this way, with stunted wings where my fingers should have grown.

There was a watery sound, a gushing in my ears, as I realised that my hands were lost. With one feathered paw, I tried to make a fist, to close a grip on the leather knot that held the glove against my skin, but all that happened was that the quills began to buckle and snap like breaking fingernails. I began to panic, knifing the air with my two useless wings, with a metal whirring like pigeons flying.

My grandmother nodded to me as if I was a shop assistant, and stumped away, back up to her eyrie. I cried my heart out in the hallway until I had run out of sobbing, and then I sat down on the second step with my handless hands on my lap. I sat there for hours, my face coursing with tears. I was a piteous little thing, when I was a child.

12

The Mother

THE HOUSE, IT seemed, had taken against the mother. So she thought, on the odd days that the mother had a notion to try and smarten things up. It was as though her husband, when he was still alive, had been a kind of metronome to set the days to. By the curl of a lip, or the back of a hand, whole orchestras of housework were set into motion; bed-making here, cleaning there. After he was gone, the whole of life became a Sunday: shapeless, without routine. So things went, by and large, to rack and ruin; the house grew deathly and sacred like a pharaoh's tomb. Patterns of mouldy stuff crept up from the floors, gave the plaster the appearance of eczema, and broke the paint into tiny bits and flaked them away. Everything white evolved a yellowness in time, like billiard balls, or the bones from a roast chicken. Nothing was ever entirely dry.

And the mice, the bloody mice, were marching around as if they owned the place, interfering in her business, dragging things around the house. They even seemed to be stealing her washing from the clothes-horse on the bathtub, and all the while they stared at her, like laser beams, like X-rays, as though the mother was anything to do with them. So, she made the house bristle with mouse-traps and every night she would empty them, one by one, and take each ruined victim by the tail, until she had a handful, a whole limp posy that dangled in the air. The mother was, after all, wholly within her rights; at least, she always knew it at the time. Every night she gathered up her horrible little bouquet, and then walked up and down, mustering her anger, waiting until she dared, and then finally, the right moment arrived. Then, the mother would gallop down the hallway, throw open the dining room door and she hurl the little corpses inside, because dead bodies always vanished in the dining room; because the things in the dining room seemed to need dead bodies; because, she had begun to fret of late, what might happen if those things were not fed?

This is what the mother would know for certain, every night, as she threw the sacrifice to the cutlery. This is what she knew, for certain: she was firm, aware, in control, justified. By the time the door thumped shut, she was never quite so sure, and she would hold her own hand, and take herself away, kindly.

And yet, amongst all these things, was Marie, growing like a flower, drawing pictures and skipping on the concrete patio as any six-year-old should. Her hair was long and spirally and nearly white, and she was beautiful, translucent as candle wax, full of singing. The grandmother must have taught her to read, for the house filled up with picture books and toys and things that the mother supposed she must have bought for her and then forgotten. Marie was light and air, and the fragile sort of creature that a careless touch might snap. And she loved her mother, praise be, she looked up at her with a calm acceptance; she made the mother good.

And finally, after forever, it was spring in the garden; the wind was like a scalpel, but at last the sun was shining, and it set the mother off on a cleaning spree. She had put her apron on and rolled up the sleeves of her dress, and had put a silk scarf on her head that she couldn't tie up quite right. Passing the landing mirror, she found herself to be the image of the perfect woman: bright; efficient; motherly yet brisk. She smiled at herself, and then got on with things.

There is no point in cleaning if your labour is spread too thinly. There is no point in cleaning if you can't see the good you have done. And, as the mother was rather given to distraction or loss of enthusiasm, she tended to concentrate on small things, ones that she could definitely finish. Today, in celebration of the fading of winter, it was going to be the skirting boards. The mother filled a plastic bucket with lovely hot water and soapflakes. She found an old pair of tights, as it seemed a shame to waste a nice dish-cloth, and then she got on her knees and began.

The lino was sticky underneath her legs, and the hand that she was not wiping with was braced against the floor and soon grew greasy-black. But the skirtings! They shone like teeth, like glory in domestic form. The mother wiped and wiped, and wept with joy at the sight of them, as she moved in slow horizontal procession through the house. She travelled on her knees up the kitchen step, and then, snail-wise, she moved along the hallway with her brown scummy water, past Marie, who did not look up. She was staring, dumbfounded at her new dolly with chicken feet for hands. On she went, as far as the door to the box room that they used for storing junk. Then she had to stop, sadly, as there were no more skirting boards left.

Then, an idea struck the mother and she opened the little cupboard between the rooms, in case the skirtings extended inside. There was a jumble of rubbish within, and her other child as well, but she didn't really notice as this was not what she was seeking. She dropped her head, disappointed, and came back out, then caught sight of her beautiful paintwork: a stripe of hygiene in that filthy old house. She was very proud.

The mother permitted herself a rest at last, and made a nice fresh cup of tea, and then she sat in her red armchair, drinking it and savouring the ache in her knees, as if she had won a race, or bravely scaled a cliff. It was evening before she got up again as she needed to spend a penny; the windows were dulling as she went up and came back down the stairs, and the mother realised that she would need to cook something. She pottered off to look in the fridge, wondering what Marie liked to eat.

She remembered about baby rusks, but discovered that they seemed to have run out of these; now that she thought about it, Marie was probably rather too old anyway, and that even if there had been any, they wouldn't have been kept in the refrigerator. The mother was very tired. She frowned and, straightening up, had the fright of her life when she closed the fridge, for the black-haired child was on the other side of it. The ghastly little thing was covered in muck, only as clean as mice's tongues can groom, and dressed in the weirdest assortment of clothes: the grandmother's big pants, and a petticoat, and a cardigan that belonged to Marie gaping, unbuttoned, because mice do not understand buttons.

The child that was not Marie, flinched as the mother jumped backwards, shying, waiting to judge the danger. The mother realised that she must have disturbed her out from the cupboard and that this was probably where the horrid thing had been living, these past couple of months. A door closed upstairs and the mother recognised Marie's hopping footfalls above her head and panic seized her by the arm. Marie had not seen her sister for well over two years and by now she did not even seem to remember that she had been a twin.

The wrong child gazed frankly at the mother, as though staring out a dangerous dog, ready to throw herself to one side if the other were to pounce. The mother regarded her likewise as she reached behind herself to the draining board for a weapon. The child dipped her face and growled, then turned tail and ran as the mother lunged at her with a saucepan in her fist, angry as a speeding lorry. The black-haired child fled like a cat, up on the table and down again, clattering cups and clutter, streaking through the kitchen and then through the scullery, finally escaping through the window at the very back.

A moment later, Marie came in, innocently curious, rubbing her runny nose on her sleeve and wanting to know what the noise was about. 'Nothing,' said the mother, and she folded her daughter close to her, but awkwardly, as one hand was holding a saucepan by the handle.

Later, lying in bed, the mother thought that she could hear the black-haired child again, creeping though the house like a burglar. It made her skin crawl.

13
Mice

A FEW YEARS for human beings creep by in generations for mice. They have grown old and died, and
mothered thousands, scampering along their own blood-
lines, along the hopes and despairs that connect a mouse
to his backbone.

In this house, there is always mess, so there is always
food; the mice have evolved a fraction larger, on average,
and their coats are thick and lush like oily velvet. They are
fecund, as only mice can be, and their numbers might
easily have over-run the house, but for the dozens of
mousetraps that lurked in their running places and holes.
It seems to the mice that there are ever and ever more of
the things; the elderly ones with grey in their fur swear
that there had not been so many last month. They sigh
over the loss of whatever season had passed most recently;
now it is March, the winter was the good old days.

Their lives are not bad, although most often snapped
off short by traps. The cutlery has become a normal part
of their lives, another hazard to live between; another hard-
ship for their fragile little lives. They do their best and
gnaw their teeth short and live in their ancestral home
as they ever have. At daybreak, the cutlery slides out for its
grisly meal of broken, mouse-trapped mice. At daybreak,
the dining room is treacherous with knives and forks, and

the mice all huddle in their shacks and houses, and they wish that they could not hear the scissor-sounds of eating. But they are mice, and mice die of being killed; that is to say, that they do not expect to grow old. The gap underneath the door is vast as an underpass and there is a whole house to scurry in; they make do.

The mice now have a focus, anyhow, one that extends beyond the earthly affairs of their own troubles. The childling, pup of humans, is as much a part of their universe as the moon and sky and ceiling and Christmas tree, and her welfare is of desperate, of religious importance.

There have been no more white mice, but the legend of the albino endures, solidifying in the telling: the evil one sent by the frizz-haired mother, sent to tempt them to murder, to tempt them to cowardice and denial of the fairy light god. And, doctrine has it that mousehood failed in those cold days. They gave into the disaster, to that awful bloody moment of killing; that slaughter demanded by the jeering, sneering, red-eyed Satan. That day they discovered their own frozen hearts; the prophet, false prophet, enacted his own bloody doom and smeared the whole of mousehood with his gore. Such were the bleak and desperate aeons before the dusk of the fairy light god. Ah, but they bettered themselves, repented of the violence that he forced from them; they refused his gospel of fear.

And then, on the holy night that they all saved the childling from suffocating, they knew that they had done the fairy lights' bidding. Thus it was that they were redeemed from murder by love, in those ancient days when it is said that the Christmas tree was clothed in pointed, perfumed needles. The mice in the dining room are transcending mouseishness; they are learning the tree-trunk ways of people, for the childling, test of their loving, is ever in need of humanness, and so they must work to gain this.

Luckily, the fairy light god wills it that there is another childling in the house, mirror of their own, and possession of the frizz-haired mother; by studying this one, the mice can determine how they should care for their own. So, the elite, the chosen priesthood and elders, are ordained to creep about the house by daylight, to spy and research, and to explain their findings.

They dress her, as best they can, and they trim her fringe from her face with their teeth. They keep her warm, keep her safe. They cherish their childling, their own huge pup. But, try as they might, they cannot show her how to speak; she can neither squeak like a mouse, nor shout and clap her mouth as the humans do. She makes no talking at all. It is a shame. Still, they have pleased themselves and their god by keeping her so kindly.

These are the toys that mice make: they are plagiarisms, copied from the human beings, remade as well as mice know how, a cup handle for a teething ring, and a teddy bear bitten out of blanket. When the childling was a baby, they had played peek-a-boo with curtain scraps, and gave her a salt pot to shake in her little fist. Now, as time goes on, it is getting harder, for the toys of a child are more complex than the toys of an infant. They have made a skipping rope, but it is only six-inches long, and throwing jacks, but none of them understand why they must be thrown. Still, they are ambitious, and because today is before the market night, they have made her a special present. They have made her a picture book.

The cover is made from pork rind, unpeeled from a ham in the pantry; the mother was speechless with rage when she found it, skinned and ravaged on the floor. They dried it out on the branches of the Christmas tree, with a sentry guarding it, and when it was rubber-hard, they sewed it into a story, with J-cloth pages in between. But they had no words to put inside, and the pictures are made out of smells.

The child will be left alone tonight, because nobody could teach her how to turn handles, and she might never fit beneath the dining room door, no matter how flat she squeezes. The mice are sorry for her and so every market night, they make her a present. The mice have gotten up especially early this afternoon to present their childling with her gift. The scouts run ahead and check that the way is clear; the hall is empty. They can hear the mother in the kitchen, thundering water into a bucket and humming. They give the signal and the mice drag their gift along the floor towards the back stairs.

There is a cupboard underneath them, and the door is ajar. The mice troop shyly inside their childling's play-room. She beams at their appearance and mimes as if to groom her whiskers, as if the dear silly thing had any whiskers for grooming. She is sitting on a Hessian carpet with her things, stacking a tower from tea-packet build-ing blocks, beside a ball that they stole from Marie. She sees the look on their faces and is a little sad, for it will be a lonely night.

The mice begin to shove at the door, so the child leans over and helps them open it; she has the strength of a monster, and as she opens it she sees her brand-new book. She is delighted; she snatches it up and sniffs deeply. Then, not sure of what to do, she turns the pages one by one, nibbling like a wine taster; nibbling like a mouse, not hard enough to destroy, and certainly not enough to eat; but sufficient to taste, discover, comprehend. It is beautiful.

Then, the mice scramble up on her shoulders, for they want to try and plait her hair; it doesn't turn out badly, but they have nothing to secure the end and it unravels slowly as she dips and tips her head. Then, suddenly, they freeze; there's a racket developing outside the door. It's the slap and drip of cloth and pail and skirting board, as the mother washes it by sections, and the words of encouragement that she gives herself as she goes. The child edges forwards and pulls the door until it is on the latch. They wait. Then, the door is scuffed right out again, and the mother looks inside, wet-handed and dirty, cuddling the bucket to her ribcage like a slopping plastic baby. Her eyes dart in a line along the floor, along the phantom skirting board that she wishes was there, but isn't. Blind to anything that isn't a skirting board, her face crumples a little, and she goes away.

That night, the market buzzes and squeaks as usual, and the fairy lights preside over everything with their enigmatic twinkle, and the disruption of earlier has been all but forgotten. Then there's a crashing from the kitchen, a whollop and a scream that can only have come from the frizz-haired woman; they all cringe in horror. The mice crowd up to the window, and they see the childling coming round the side of the house, limping from an awkward fall out of the scullery window, whimpering among the ground elder and blackberry thorns.

Their poor hurt childling. She is outside, beyond Home. Beyond the back door is the end of the world. They creep to the door, as near to the outside as they dare. They peer beneath the door and plead with her to come inside. The other child, the white-haired one who does not belong to them, sees them as they whisper there. Her eyebrows move upwards, but she makes no noise.

14
Marie

WHEN I AMBLED into my room, it was late in the after-noon, on one of those half-awake days before Sep-tember. I was six-years-old then, but nearly seven; as we hadn't a calendar, my mother used to store the date in a book, just for safekeeping. Every day we lived was in there, written carefully in blue ink at breakfast time, to make sure that we all knew where we were up to. Unless my mother forgot a day or two here or there, which I suppose must have been possible.

The sun had made its way to the back of the house, and an oblong of golden light slanted along the wall, leaving a gorgeous puddle of warmth on the floor. I walked into its centre and then sat down on the floor with my eyes closed, feeling the summer dying against my face. The world, just then, became bloodish, wet and warm and deep, deep red. It was lovely.

My bedroom wallpaper was a stylised pattern of cabbage roses, alternating with what appeared to be vine leaves. If I chose to see it in a certain way, the pattern resembled a succession of eyes, repeated; an infinity between the carpet and the fractured ceiling. I sat in my sunlit oblong and squinted against the afternoon at them. The decades had faded the pattern on the wallpaper, turning the whites the colour of old men's teeth, making the blues and the reds slide together to brown, as if the walls had been spread all over with weak tea. Even so, there was a point at the centre of each flower head, which must have been printed more firmly, or perhaps more thickly; anyhow, the heart of every rose was marked out with a coin-sized disc of blue, licked in with a broken circle of gold leaf.

I allowed my eyes to lose a little of their focus, so that a splashy rose became an iris, and the network of leaves around it melted into what was perhaps the arch of an eyebrow, or there again perhaps the start of another eyelid, formed around another drowned blue eye in the flower to the left. Ten dozen eyes dripped in and out of being, like things misunderstood, every one of them watering, ready to blink.

I blinked, and finally closed my eyes, as it hurt them to look that way. I could hear the rooks cursing in the garden; by degrees, the sun went in. I sat there for a whole long minute, and as I did, I became aware of staring, the sort of staring that could penetrate a mattress, keen as a leather-needle.

It turned out that there was a little girl standing over me, here in my own bedroom, curious and wary as a fox. She scanned my face as she leaned right towards me, until her head was all but touching mine. She stank like the corners of the scullery; she smelled of dust and mice and damp. The girl who was not me wiped her fingers across her cheeks, and then she smiled, waiting, as though she had made a statement that I was supposed to reply to. I smiled back, thoroughly unnerved.

That child was identical to me, in a sort of opposite way. Her hair was all rats' tails, held off the brow with twists of wire, the way that mine was pinned back with metal slides. She wore a torn-pink dress that seemed to be one of my own, one that had gone missing from the bathroom airer weeks before. On her wrist there was a mosquito bite, just like mine. I shook my head slowly, and so did she. Then the toilet flushed in the bathroom, and my mother could be heard, complaining gently, pulling the light-cord on and off, unhappy about something. The other child started at that, flinched as if at a slap, and she raised her hands and swayed to her feet. The child slunk out of the door, just as if she had not been there at all.

I waited, I don't know why; I waited for ages, sitting paralysed among the cabbage roses, thumb in mouth. Suddenly, then, decisive, I leapt to my feet and crept out into the hallway. By then, there was nothing to stalk, except my mother, still tugging on the light cord. In the end, I concluded that I must have made the whole thing up. Later, though, much later, my mother and I were sitting in front of the parlour fire; my mother was terribly upset, as her dishcloth was only two-thirds done, and she was running out of string. She sighed and tutted among the slip and tut of her knitting needles, fretting and muttering under her breath.

My mother was wearing her housecoat, a shapeless padded thing, with crisscross stitching like a too-thin quilt. She dropped her knitting into the cup of her lap, and picked her spectacles off her nose to polish them, opening her eyes extra-wide as she did so, even though I knew she could not see a thing. She always did that. Then, on a sudden spur, I said to my mother that I had seen somebody in my room. My mother stiffened, arched her foot so that it all but came out of its slipper. She left off wiping her glasses, face still towards the fire, the muscle in her jaw loosening then tightening in patterns, as though she were doing exercises for teeth.

At last, she told me that it must have been my grandmother. But, I was young then, still desperate to be heard, and I persisted, saying that no, it had been a child, like me, but not. My mother laughed, carelessly; she said that I had surely seen a ghost then! She replaced her glasses in triumph, pushed them to the very root of her nose, brushing her eyelashes, smiling like a light bulb.

I nodded, uncertainly, frightened now as well. Somehow I didn't dare to leave the parlour that evening; I stayed up with my mother until my eyes gravelled with tiredness, and then I climbed the stairs to bed with my head low, seeing nothing.

15

The Mother

THE SKIRTING BOARDS dirtied, slowly overnight; by ten o'clock the next day, they were worse than always. The sofa cushions sank; the carpets grew blacker, soaked and sad and ruining. All night, the mother sat in her chair and fretted, as the parlour wrecked around her, patiently, the way that paper decays. She chewed on the inside of her cheek and thought, and unravelled a dishcloth so that she could knit a better one. Before the moon sank past the window again, she had formed an idea. She was ecstatic.

The mother had been badly shaken the day before when Marie had seen that other child. But the mother's reply, and her nerve-edged little giggle, had clearly been a masterstroke. For, she reasoned, if Marie had found a child and then discovered her to be a ghost, why then, she would be so frightened at glimpsing her that she would work very hard in order not to see anything ever again. The mother stroked the back of her own neck. For sure, if she ever found a thing that was a ghost after all, she would make certain she did not find it a second time.

A brown stain developed gently on the ceiling, easing through the plaster like a picture photograph, blooming to life in a developing tray. She caught it in the act, scowled at it; it waited until the mother stopped looking, and then it carried on, blooming flatly, running into the corner.

Now, if that wretched child would not hide herself any longer, and it was a matter of obvious fact that she was growing more brazen, then it must fall upon the mother's shoulders to hide the creature herself. The question was only Marie, really: how to keep her out of the way whilst things were taken in hand. Perhaps she could have a nice long nap, but Marie was a dreadfully light sleeper. The mother considered administering a little blow to the head, but it didn't seem to be quite moral. She spent a long time pondering, until the grandmother came home from her nightly doings, whatever those might be. Her cardigan was torn, and a little bloody.

Astoundingly, when the problem was outlined, together with a proposed solution, the grandmother agreed to assist. All that day, the mother was like a little girl ticking off the days until a holiday, peeling off every hour, writing it down in her little book. Five, four, three hours until the Plan.

Marie was narrow-eyed, confused and wary, until suppertime, when the grandmother pressed her weight onto either of her shoulders and told her that tonight was the Watchnight. They propped her up at the parlour window on a hard chair with a milk bottle of water, and they gave her a notebook and pencil to record when it happened. Any queries were met with sly glances, and shadow smiles. She would know it when she saw it. It would be the making of her.

Darkness floated up into the air like fat in water; Marie's face grew glazed with eagerness and then fatigue. They opened the window to keep her awake and gave her mathematical riddles to solve in her head. They made her memorise the ingredients on a packet of raspberry jelly and chant them into the night, forwards and then in reverse. They made her count the stars that uglied the skies like dandruff, they made her strain her little ears to pick out the voices of foxes that were not there. And finally, when it was day again, they left her to keep watch, taking care to leave a blanket on the sofa, temptation to weakness. They watched her through a chink in the door, they watched her curiosity fade out of her with yawning, and when she was asleep, they nodded to one another and pulled on Wellington boots.

It took them hours to dig the hole, long and narrow and deep. When it was done, they spread the dirt that they had thrown up around the feet of the cherry tree. It was black, and rich as fruitcake, and it oozed with naked worms. The mother found yards of tarpaulin sheet from somewhere or other and, using a stool for a stepladder, they faced the hole's inside with it, stitching it into place with tent pegs, until they ran out of those, and pinning it with biro pens after that. Then they made the bottom comfy with an eiderdown, and an empty mop-bucket, and they hung a little paraffin lamp on a nail.

The mother had been ordered to make a little seat with cushions, though she thought the bother unnecessary, and then she found the rotten old door that had been propped against the scullery wall for decades. She lugged it over and leaned it against the mouth of the trap, with sticks to hold it open. The grandmother came out with a packet of sandwiches and a jar of jam, and she dropped them into the hole whilst the kettle was boiling.

By the time she came out again, this time with a flask of cocoa, the mother was laying out a trail of bait: a finger-roll of bread, an apple, three wine gums, a lump of cheddar and a fried slice of bacon. One or another was bound to do the trick. Finally, they tied the biggest stick with button thread and trailed the end to a bush, where they sat in the wet and waited.

The child, of course, had seen all this; by nature, a child is almost as curious as a mouse at the best of times, and a childling mouseling child is as curious as a whole boxful of them. And though they pled with her and spoke to her sternly and warned and warned her besides, that child could simply not help but investigate.

The mother bit her lip and egged her on, with urgent little bobs of her head. If it had not been for the grandmother pinching her from time to time, the suspense would have ruined the plan without doubt. But, she held her tongue, and each of her hands in her other hand, and she managed not to scream out loud.

Marie fidgeted, fast asleep in the parlour, neck ricked at a painful angle. The mice watched from underneath the back door and the child crept along the line of little things, sniffing, tasting every one.

The bang of the trap door falling was a hollow noise, airful like a bursting paper bag. The child leapt at it, but however much she jumped and clawed and panicked, she could not heave her way out of the house her mother had built for her.

In half an hour, she was calm again, resigned and hopeless, gazing up through the air holes at the blinding sky. There were the small sounds of scattering as the mother covered up the door with earth.

Marie threw her hands in front of her face, crying in her sleep like a dog, dreaming of small places and graves. The mother had a very nice bath, and scrubbed herself all over with Vim powder. When she was dry and clean as a skinned hare, the mother put on her dressing gown, as it seemed a waste of effort to don any more day clothes. As she towelled her hair, she smiled like a Buddha, for wasn't her life gaining more control by the day? Another problem was hereby resolved, another thing ticked off her list, like the skirting boards which were now so shining . . . the mother looked along the floor line at the scuffed, filthy paintwork, and she lost her train of thought. Oh, yes. The grandmother had made her promise to feed the other child, but at least the smelly little sod would cease her incessant creeping about the place, giving the mother frights, letting Marie discover her.

But, thought the mother as she snagged a comb through her hair, the child had only really posed a difficulty because of the mice. They had stuck their pointed noses into everything, interfered. They had not minded their own business. They had taken the side of the other child, the wrong child, as if the nasty thing had been any of their concern. They had made the mother guilty; they pointed nose to tail, six-odd years and down the hall, all the way to the red-black stain on the dining room floor.

At this instant, the mother had a beautiful inspiration, and she jumped off the toilet pedestal, her hair half-tamed and half-mad. The mice were crowded outside the bathroom like fans at a football match, lurking on the stairs as if they were waiting to ask a question. The mother ran to the landing bookcase and grabbed a book at random, to use as a broom, for sweeping mice.

So it was that the mother, roaring with rage, drove a sea of mice down the stairs, waving a *Motorists' Encyclopaedia of the British Isles*, shoving them off their paws and down the stairs. The mice, as ever, surged up and down and out of reach, streaming at last beneath the dining room door, to where it should have been safe. Only eight were left behind; slower moving or out of luck; seven of them had perished underneath her rampaging slippers, crunched and squashed, abandoned by their skins. They were, as things turned out, the lucky ones. The mother caught her breath, and then she plugged the gap beneath the door. She stopped it up with wooden dowel and Polyfilla and Sellotape and masking tape and duct tape and tin sheeting and rags soaked in glue and rags soaked in poison and copper wire and staples and six inch nails and she did try sewing, but it didn't work.

And then, the mother hauled on her lungs and laughed like a big bad wolf, with her hands all hurt and blistered. When it was all done, the mother was so happy and so tired, that she fell into a blissful sleep in the hallway. This was how Marie discovered her, when she staggered from the parlour, tired and disoriented and wondering how it could possibly be night time again.

16

Mice

THAT DOOR WILL stay shut for two and a half years. For the moment, the mice are relieved, escaped to their carpeted homeland. Their little hearts are pounding terribly; they are tense and fragile as rusted springs. For a few minutes they pant, as their fear cools, and they cling to one another as they listen to the scrapes and thudding and muttered curses as the mother barricades the motorway beneath the door. Once, she catches her hand with the swing of a hammer, and three times, she laughs out loud, mean as a crow.

The mice understand, by slow degrees; by seven o'clock, they know that they are entombed. For a minute, the barricading noises pause and the mice all creep forwards on the claws of their feet, retching at the reeks of woodfiller and glue, but then the mother returns, dumping a sewing basket on the floor. The mice all scatter backwards like spilt pins as the mother tries to stitch the door shut with cotton and embroidery thread. She can't poke the holes through, not even with a big curved bodkin, but she tries and tries, with her fingers pricked and spreading blood on the woodwork. Eventually, she concedes defeat, and it all goes quiet.

The door has become a wall. The mice stare at it as though it might melt beneath their staring, thick with painty drips and dirty in the panelled corners. The door looks back at them, the house looks back at them, affronted already by the layers that block its swing-gap, that stuff it like a nose.

Marie comes past outside, grizzling like a toddler. She is wide awake and confused; wanting her breakfast, thinking it must be morning as she slept so long.

But the worst disaster is this: they have lost their childling, lost their only beautiful giant, the one they were raised from their nests to revere. The mice troop to the Christmas tree and they climb the branches to look out of the window at the sweating garden, nauseous with the heat. From the lawn it would have made a pretty sight, a treeful of mice and tiny coloured lights, but the childling is beneath the soil, and the only thing to see is the cherry tree, and heaven knows what that understands of the world.

At any rate, the mother seems to have had the very same idea, for here she comes with a rotten old paintbrush and the ends of a tin of pink emulsion. She grins and shakes her fist at the astonished mice, pointing theatrically to the half-gallon can, which is of a colour called *Princess Blush*. The mother sways like an accident on a little coffee table and slathers the glass with paint until she is satisfied that the dining room has been rendered quite invisible.

Their childling is gone. They saw her lose herself from them; the sound of that trap falling shut was the most awful noise that ever a living mouse has heard; now its stains their fur like marker pen. They beg one another to understand; they tried, all of them did, but she simply refused to listen. She ignored their warnings; snared by curiosity, she had crept off to see what strangeness the mother had been making. The mice knew better, of course, but the childling was growing ever more wilful with time and an impetuous mountain cannot be held in check by any means. They sigh and forgive one another as mice must; the fairy lights reflect brightly back at them; the window has become a massive pink mirror. And then, it seems that the light bulbs are gentle things, strong and gentle as mice are, for every mouse is a plague, broken easily but surrounded by friends. At that moment, it seems as if all is somehow well.

The mice among the fairy lights pray to the god that does not wish to kill them, for if it truly lives then it will spare the colony, even if not their own selves. The glow from the skeleton Christmas tree seems to constitute a reply, one that is good enough for mice at any rate. They glitter with hope as they pray for the safety of their childling, and for the frailty of backbones. Underneath the piano, the cutlery is whispering like scalpels, like nightmares rolled extremely thin; but they have snicked-up half a dozen corpses already and they do not move as the mice begin to drop out of the tree and head for their chimney. They check on their homes to see if the world still stands; overnight they take stock of themselves; they count their mouselings, count their food. Secretly, every one thinking that he is the only disbeliever, mice sneak up to the dining room door in case the blocking up was only some dreadful imagining. But the gap is now as solid as can be and not even a razor blade could pass through. Each concedes that it is true.

When the sun is up again, there are shreds of light straining through the window; the mice discover that there is a tiny fragment of garden still remaining: one mouse, with his face squashed sideways, can just squint through. This is what that mouse can see: the frizz-haired mother is glowering down the garden path towards the house, to where the grandmother is standing with her arms folded, giving orders, stern. The mother turns resentfully away, trying to hold a walking stick, a bread bag, a coffee flask and a shovel all at the same time. She struggles with them, drops the walking stick, retrieves it with the very tips of her fingers, straightens up, and finally makes it over to the vegetable patch beside the cherry tree, where her nasty daughter is planted like a root. Angrily, the mother flings the dirt away from the door with the spade, and then she prises it up with the stick, just a fraction as though she might be expecting a bomb to go off at any moment. There is no explosion, so the mother quickly shoves the food into the hole with her foot. Then, the mother ducks her head and flinches and grimaces as she hooks the old coffee flask from out of the hole with the walking stick's crook. She throws the new one in quickly, and it seems as if she might have actually aimed it at something.

The mouse at the window blinks and gazes as hard as ever he can, for there is no smell to see with, and he thinks that he can glimpse the blunt, round tip of a hand, of the childling's clawless paw. The mouse turns to all the others, quivering.

For as long as there is a childling, there will be mice; as long as there is a childling, there is a source and an outlet for compassion. It is ordained. For now, for the mice, the dining room has become their only home and prison. For generations, they will have no run of any other place, until it seems that the house and all its rooms are a myth that never existed, like some ancient doctrine. The garden, over weeks, will become an imagined thing, visible only through a mystical pink film. But the mice have faith and stored food to last them a few months; soon the childling will rise from beneath the garden soil, and she will come and save them all.

17

Child

THE CHILD DISCOVERS that she is alone. There are no mice, none of the scratching feet that clamber up and down against her skin and leave a network of little bloody marks on her back, her arms, her neck. The flesh of the wrong child is a map of love, crisscrossed with the itchy lines where her thousand tiny parents care for and hurt her. In a few days they will all heal.

She cocks her head and forces her ears, seeking for noises: the creak of stairs; *whoof* of the boiler; voices of mice and of people. There are none of these. The child is bewildered by silence and the empty rush of sky among the air holes in her den. Slowly, she sinks to her haunches, thumb in mouth, and she puzzles at what has happened. The thoughts of the child are not expressed in words, or even in squeaking; she makes sense of the world with patches of colour, stinks and flavours. She does not make much sense of the world at all.

The child is wearing a nightie of Marie's, and the hair against her shoulders is black and twisted into tangled pigtails, fastened with bows made from the mother's dishcloth string. She has a necklace to match her sister's, except that the beads are made of old macaroni, cooked and rescued from the bin; they are dried out and pretty with the scent of old cheese sauce. Her feet are hard as hooves and perfectly dirty. As she sits, she gnaws on her thumb and begins to rock very gently, as if she were sitting on a dining chair with one short leg. She cannot smell the perfume of mice, or the mother's violet scent, or even the dustbin. And there is nothing to see but the wonky walls of her cell. She frowns at the plastic sheeting, where the heat of the day and the water from her breath are already fattening into dew. The child blinks, rapidly, emptily. She cannot remember how to cry, nor even what crying is supposed to be for. She wraps her arms around her knees and rests her chin upon them. There is no picture for what she feels.

The mice must be coming. They must be just now on their way, because that is what the mice and she are made for: each the thing that the other needs. The child waits, in a *now* that lasts for hours, moving hardly at all, until the air holes turn blue-grey and the door that is her roof begins to thud with rain.

Gradually, the child discovers that the silence of under ground is not just some flatness after all, but layered and rich. With the pads of her fingers, she detects the vibrations of living things; discovers the aching rumble of the house as it breathes with its lime-washed lungs. The house is grumbling, testing at the blockage on the dining room door, irritated. The child can discern its annoyance, even from so many feet away, but she does not know what it means.

Then, in a few more hours, she is hungry and anyhow, the house has fallen asleep, so the child rolls her shoulders and dares to explore her prison. There is soft stuff aplenty, more nesting material than she has ever seen; she opens up the eiderdown with her teeth and heaps out feathers by the fistful. There is a bucket made of red plastic and it tastes of Ajax liquid and dirt. Then her nose uncovers a square parcel with a sandwich in it, and she paws at that for a long time, trying to find a way inside the cling film. It squidges and bends underneath her fingers, buckles and buckles, but will not tear in half. There is meat inside, pink and ghastly, out of a tin.

The child is wary of the taste of canned luncheon meat, because such cans are opened with a key and the thin rolls of metal are likely as not to cut the tongue and fill one's mouth with blood. Even so, hunger is hunger, and with a whine of frustration, the child begins to tear lumps off the sandwich with her teeth, gagging down the cling film along with the bread. Soon, she discovers how to sort the mess in her mouth, and to spit out the plastic like grape pips. Her mouth does not fill with blood after all, which is good.

The child sneaks to the tarpaulin walls and licks at the dripping condensation until the sky beyond the holes is black. Then she scuffs in circles, mousing a nest out of feathers and the eiderdown's raggy skin. In the middle of it, she huddles, dark eyes open in the darkness, trying to conjure mice up with the pictures in her head. And her hole is so small that she daren't grow another inch for fear of crushing herself to death against the walls. In all the months that follow, and the years after that, although her hair and fingernails grow just the same as ever, her bones and skin stay carefully small, like a Bonsai.

18

Marie

I SPENT THE whole winter on the concrete patio behind the back door, with my jacks and a fragment of chalk, playing hopscotch by myself as the autumn drained white and there was nothing in the garden but the rooks. One morning, back then, was just like another, but today I had jumped so much that my ankles felt like snapping, and the drizzle was smearing my hopscotch squares to nothing. Eventually I rubbed my icy fist across my face and concluded that I would be better off indoors.

I rested my elbows on the windowsill and waited to give my mother a fright, but she was skinning carrots with a peeler and did not notice the monster breathing smoke at her through the glass. There was something awkward in the way that she held her wrist, as though she were holding the peeler at bay, as though she could not quite trust it. Her fingers worked very hard to grip it; I could see her knucklebones glistening through the skin.

In a moment more, I gave up, and tramped into the cooking fug, the steam and smell of boiling. My mother was emptying the fridge again, dicing together vegetables, cheese and half a Victoria sponge cake, and hurling them into a seething pot of meat. I sighed. It would be lunchtime soon. I snaked out my fingers towards the table, and stole a square of Dairy Milk before it turned into stew.

As it found its way into my mouth, my grandmother came into the room. She was smiling, blinkless.

My mother slid her eyes sideways and saw that she was there. Then she renewed her chopping with an evangelical vigour, five times as fast. My grandmother trod forwards at her, holding a folded paper bag that was translucent with grease like brown stained glass. She shook it out, one-handed, for the other was cupped against her chest, as though she were cradling something very small.

My mother was defiant; in desperation she scurried around the table in a half-circle, hunting out fresh ingredients for the stew. She snatched up a candle and began to dice it rapidly, separating out the wick like a spinal cord. She shook her head and her lips moved.

'I beg your pardon?' My grandmother stood over my mother, friendly and menacing.

'No,' repeated my mother, but she made it sound more like a question than a refusal. She accepted the bag, which smelled like an old lunchbox, and sulkily began to gather potato peelings and carrot tops, as well as the raw ends of the meat that she had forgotten to finish cutting up. When it was full she crumpled the top and held it up to my grandmother for inspection. My grandmother nodded slowly. The bag was wet, and splitting already, dripping on the table and then on her toes. My mother shuffled off her slippers and ground her feet into her shoes. She looked down at me then, and from me to my grandmother again. 'What about. . . ?'

My grandmother looked down at me too, and winked like a secret agent. 'I will deal with that,' said she, and then she pointed her chin at the garden until my mother began to move away. Before I could ask what was going on, my grandmother had a grip on the back of my neck and was steering me out into the hallway. My mother muttered to herself, until her words trailed out of the back door. The hall was like a grave compared with the kitchen. 'Marie,' said my grandmother, 'Marie, look at this!' And with a flash of her teeth, she opened her hand.

It was a pair of tiny wings, stolen from a wren, split from its body and joined in small, neat sutures. She lifted this miserable thing into the air and then she threw it at my head. I flinched backwards, ducked as the wings fell towards me, but before they struck my cheek, they were off and flapping around the bottom landing like a heavy feathered moth.

I composed my face, tried hard to smile as the wings plunged crazily past me, doubling back and forth between the kitchen and the front door, coming unstitched with every small collision against wall or banister. I beamed at my grandmother, earnestly as I could, to show that I was grateful, although I was not quite sure what for. I had entirely forgotten to wonder what my mother was doing in the garden with a paper bag.

And, when my smile was done, I inched past, as politely as possible, and fled upstairs to hide. I went to sit with the towels in the airing cupboard, for in the dark and close-ness I always felt a little less alone. In the linen cupboard, I used to feel as though I might understand my life at any minute. Sometimes, it seemed as if I almost did; once, nearly sleeping in the warm, I had a sense of pleading, as if there were hundreds of little grey voices begging me for something, if I could only have heard what.

I closed my eyes and tried to put my grandmother's demonstration out of my mind. It must have worked; I must have begun to drowse because for a second I had a vision that left me bucking my legs against the cupboard walls. It seemed to me that there was a glare of light, a blinding rectangle above my head, and the terror and hope of it made me mad, I think, just for that instant. I tore one fingernail right off against the inside of the door; if it had not been for the jacket on the water tank, I might have knocked myself out.

I was frightened, and my finger was dripping and hideously painful. I crept out of the bathroom like some little creature, bumping silently down the stairs on my backside until I reached the second-bottom step. Then the back door banged open and slammed, and my mother's voice came screeching down the hallway. 'I don't know why you make me do it. I don't. Look what it's gone and done this time! Next time, I am going to knock it out with the spade, see if I don't.' And my mother came storming past me, tracking mud along the floor. She was holding a bloody bitten wrist aloft as though it were smeared in pure germs, hissing about rabies and where was the first aid kit. She all but squashed me as she ran up the stairs, so urgent was she in her quest for Savlon and plasters.

19

Mice

THESE ARE STARVING times in which to be a mouse. A mouse, a dishwater-grey one, an undertaker of sorts, is watching the smudge of garden with her face squashed sideways, cheek flat. This is what has become of the eldership, the leaders of mice. The grey mouse is cursed with priesthood, passed through one litter each generation. They pity their leaders, these days. She must watch, for that is the rule; the mice cannot remember why now, nor quite what they are watching for.

They know of the childling, of course, in a kind of mythic way. She is the fairy-light one, fully mouse and fully human, the only creature that might protect them. She will save them, it is said, from the mother-god with frizzy dyed hair.

The mice have no other gods left to fear, and no doom but the one that the mother has condemned them to; this long death of knives and hunger. They do not know about cats any more, nor stoats and crows. They do have an inkling left of mousetraps. The hell that the mother-god sprang from was all made out of them.

The mouse who is watching blinks her eyes, which are black and without reflection. By now the mice live only in the daytime, when the mother-god and the garden may be glimpsed; the dawn they must leave for the cutlery. The sunlight hurts their eyes and it bleaches the sheen from their fur. Then the water-grey mouse turns from the window to the dining room and for a moment she is blinded by it. It is real; it is like some horrible after-life. Mouse filth is piled against the edges of everything, at the sides of every running place, so that the tracks seem as though they are carved into it like a maze. They very busiest are trodden clean by feet, and here and there are flashes of the carpet and its colours. Cockroaches might have helped: if there had been a few inside at the time of the great imprisonment, they might have made an eco-system with the mice; the one eating the guano, the other subsisting on the insects. But not even a germ could pass the gap beneath the door, and there is no thing present that had not been there first.

The floors are bristling too, with shed fur and the snippy shards of rib and thighbone that the cutlery has not bothered to finish. It is into this that the water-grey mouse jumps; air that is so sharp with ammonia that it makes ulcers on her feet. It might be better not to be a mouse at all than to exist in this manner. But, mousehood is strong, earnest, fanatical even, and it is a sin not to preserve life; a sin not to make it. Even so, odd females have tried to disguise their oestrus from time to time, to make a few less pups to run along these rancid streets. This is an evil deed, and close to killing.

Mousehood must never murder again, for it was in part the death of the prophet that caused this misery, that gave the mothergod her throat-grip on their lives. But, praise be, these days are but a test, for the childling watches their every move from the lights in the Christmas tree, and if they are worthy, why then, she will rise up from the ground and save them all. Perhaps there is hope. There must be hope.

The mice are plodding from place to place, climbing

into the Christmas tree for a place to sit that is out of the guano. The water-grey mouse treads past the tree to the alcove, where the wallpaper's ripped off as far as the bricks. She is thin as a clothes peg as she shins up the mortar cracks to where the sentries are guarding the bookshelves.

Their ancestors were pups when the food ran out. Since then, every scrap of every thing is edible if it is not poison. They have eaten the shoes that were kicked underneath the sideboard; they have eaten the candles from the top of the piano. Six generations subsisted on the glue from the wallpaper; the glue was a little toxic and it gave them awful nightmares. It was in this era that most of their doctrine was devised. There are only books left, and not many of those either; every book thins slowly to the spine; every word is fed upon and stains the mouth black. The water-grey mouse has a special concession, an extra ration, in light of her unpleasant duties.

The guards bend low to her and she bows in return; each polishes their whiskers politely. Then, pleasantries over, the sentries release her allowance: a quarter-page of *The Pilgrim's Progress*. She sits up there, discreet, and she eats it quickly, so as not to taunt the others with her feast. Afterwards she nods to the guards; she cannot look them in the eye, and creeps away like a criminal.

Then they hear a knocking from the chimneybreast: a rhythmical tap, a mournful sound. The water-grey mouse jerks upright and clambers down to the hearthstone. A mouse is dead; his skin has abandoned him, and the others are dragging him out by the fur, by the tail. He is beyond hurting now. The knocking continues as the mice all come to watch, shivering or biting on their fingers; all of their eyes are black and without reflection. The water-grey mouse looks up at the window; a new lookout is there, another of the cursed priesthood.

He is watching the window, where the frizz-haired

mother-god is acting out her life as if on a screen. She has a shovel and a foul expression. She cannot see the mice. The new watcher will not turn towards the dining room; he keeps his face sideways, is glad not to be involved.

The mice drag their corpse along the floor, where the carpet is cleanest, accompanied by the sound of tapping, stopping well short of the piano. After that, the water-grey mouse carries on alone, yanking the body by herself until the both of them are six inches from the cutlery's domain. She stands there a second, shaking violently, terrified, and when the metal slithers begin she flees for her life.

The mice all fling into the Christmas tree and they cannot turn away, nor even blink as the body jumps as if thrown by a cat. They stare emptily at the seething metal as he is reduced to wet and guts, and rags and tatters of fur, and then finally nothing. This is how it must be in this world, for were they not to offer the dead, the cutlery would take the living. The knocking ceases; the mouse who had been drumming his foot on a meat can, stops. The mouse that is grey like dishwater hates herself. And then, because they cannot bear to go back to their lives, the mice all start to pray, to the fairy lights and to the childling, with their flanks hot almost to singeing where they're pressed against the bulbs. They pray; they beg and beg for pity.

There are footsteps beyond the door; Marie is passing, and she pauses for a moment and listens. The mice all shudder to resting, exhausted and miserable.

20

Child

A YEAR LATER and November is crumpling up the garden like screwed paper. The house is sitting on its old flat feet, hunkered in an awkward square. It is holding its breath and concentrating very hard, for the grandmother is in the garden, pottering amongst the microscopic lights of stars and the iridescent feathers of garden birds, fluttering in the cherry tree like leaves. There is enough light to see by, if you have eyes like an owl's.

The grandmother has eyes like an owl's. The house is staring, entranced, for although she moves much too quickly, as bloodish creatures do, even though she bleeds and hurts, she is much more stone than blood. The house can watch her moving, even when she is only being kind, because her lines and edges are chisel-hard; like a broken cliff-face.

The grandmother is small, but she stamps as solidly as a church. She slows the world around herself; to the house it is as if she were spectacles, a lens that lets it focus on the garden for a while, even if doing so makes its insulation ache afterwards for weeks. It is like sticking one's head into a pond to see the fishes eye to eye. It is fascinating.

The grandmother snaps the ice-shrivelled grass as she crosses the lawn with a stepladder in one hand, carelessly, as though she were only holding a lolly stick. The house furrows its roof. In the other, she has a large black sack, swinging it lightly, though it's surely heavy. She turns suddenly, catches it staring. The grandmother inclines her head, bowing slightly, rudely polite. 'And good evening to you too,' says she. The house looks away, but only until she does. After that it gawps again.

Life underground is strange. It is sunless, damp and oh-so dark, but it is not cruel. Underground is where the small things dwell, where everywhere there is the secret rustle of germination and decay. Life underground is a thing to which one must become accustomed. For a time, the wrong child was full of frets and fear, but it was not long until she understood the way of this life. It is a rich life; the soil is luscious and generous and treacle-black, and the creatures speak to one another as they never might in air. In the darkness, one's eyes are blind; in being blind they see other things. Every mole is a soothsayer, witness to lives and silences, and the alien sun that bleaches the universe white. These things, for the creatures beneath the soil, are visions and nightmares, incomprehensible; full of guessed-at meaning.

It is winter, and the child, wrong child, childling of mice, is wrapped about her self like a nut, small and rounded and perfectly safe. As she sleeps, she looks a little as mice do, whilst they imagine away the weeks before they are born; before they know if they are to become mice, or flowers, or horses or tall human princes. The edges of mouse embryos are smooth and undecided, and shining as though varnished. Beneath her lashes, her eyes slide over the pictures that she is thinking of. The wrong child's hair is luscious-thick, and it swathes her back to keep her warm. It curls like ferns and brushes over her toes and tender places. She sighs a little, and hugs at her knees; perhaps she smiles. And carefully, because the smallest things know best how to be safe, she stays the shape that she is; the length and breadth and width that fits this hole. All is well; she is well, because the cherry tree has taught her how to be a seed, a hard, smooth cherry pip, and how it is that one waits to grow. The only key is patience; that is all.

And above the roots and the buried child, the grandmother is listening, and squinting up at the sky, as one looks into space whilst digging in a bag for a thing one cannot see. Or, thinks the house, perhaps she might be listening with her feet. It strains, trying to hear it too, listening for chiming nightingales or the voices of bats. But mortar ears are slow, and half-deaf anyway; perhaps the grandmother is only teasing after all, catching the poor old house out in its eavesdropping. At this idea, it groans to itself and settles down for sleeping.

The polythene walls of the child's house are scrunched down now, not needed to keep the garden at bay. She lives in a softer house these days, a nest of roots, a white cocoon with rounded edges, touched all over with their tender tips. The way in which the cherry tree might grip a stone, hold it absentmindedly among its roots; that same way it grips the wrong child and her little orb of air. It holds the soil back for her, holds the roof up for her, where the tube-end of the funnel pokes down, grey like the white of an eye. The tree holds her in its many-fingered hands; it rocks her and tells her stories, tales of trees from before there were animals, or birds, or houses. It sings to her too; the music of trees is supple and sappish and calm. It throbs with the sadness of the autumn and the passion of springtime. And it's a low singing; only things beneath the ground can hear it, for the music is made by the twisting of their roots. It is a secret. It is a perfect thing.

Every mole is a soothsayer; the wrong child drifts sometimes, among strange pictures of other lives. She has felt the misery of the mice. And in her embryonic state, she has seen them, fairy lights and all; she has dreamed the mice and felt their love. Sometimes, when they pray, a tear will squeeze itself between her tight-fused eyelids, and the cherry tree wonders. No, life beneath the ground is not cruel.

And now the wrong child's eyes flicker elsewhere, dreaming of a child like herself and a mother with her head in her fingers; grasping her scalp as though she feared it might just slough off.

The grandmother nods to herself and stops her listening. She stumps through the frost with her ladder and then she shakes it open with her arm and plants it up against the cherry tree's offended trunk. For an hour or two, the grandmother replaces her fly papers, furling new ones from the winter twigs ends, gathering up last month's laden flaps. Each one is like some rare collage, all stuck up with the songbirds' tithe. She stands there against the night, the ladder sinking into the mud, and strips the feathers off one by one. There are hundreds, every one a resentful gift, plucked from wing or breast and left for the grandmother to stuff into her sack. It is nearly dawn before she is finished.

21

Mice

Now it has come to this: the mice must eat their own dead; swallow their meat with guilt and the drippings of rainwater that trickle down the chimney. They must cut up their own poor kin, divide them into dinners for the cutlery and themselves. Their coats are scurfy and ridden with fleas. They have no scrap left of pride, and only a little love to keep them warm, burnt down very low.

Sometimes there are mice that make the journey to the piano before they are dead. When the others are holed-up and trembling in the chimneybreast, they creep out. They go by themselves, or even in pairs, and they only have to stand for a moment at the gap, before they are scissored to tatters.

So it is that there is enough to eat, for the cutlery is fed in part by the living, the knives can spare them a little flesh. None acknowledges this; every one thinks that the others might not have noticed, and so he holds his tongue and carries the secret. For after all, mice may not kill, even if it is an act of loving. The death of a mouse is the end of potential, a story untold. And the fairy lights are watching. They fear in their hearts that they shall never be worthy of the childling, of redemption.

After every funeral, the tapping and the procession, the mice always go to the tree and pray. They pray like things demented, torn and ripping between despair and hope. For the sadness of mice has become a throb in the air, and some of them stare into the fairy lights until they turn blind. It hurts. The bulbs grow brighter somehow, more hot as they suffer, and sometimes in the pain there might be found a crackle of inspiration, some other consciousness that echoes in their heads for a moment. But it never comes to anything. They try and try to save each other if not themselves, if not their own eyes. But what is there to do anymore, than to indulge in a little fancy? They are becoming rather mad. They sometimes rock from side to side, or seem to believe that invisible mice are speaking to them from under the piano.

Instinctively, the mice are fishing for minds, though they do not know they are. They are flailing out beyond the dining room, grasping at anything at all. There is a darkness about this voodoo that frightens them. A shrine of sorts is developing upon the drop-leafed table, all made in splintered ribs and broken Christmas baubles. It is three-dimensional, tied and twisted through with the sinews that come out of the feet of mice. It is ever so pretty. They fuss at it for hours on end, simply for something to do with their time, and now it resembles a complicated wedding cake, all royal-iced, or else a kind of psychotic architecture; a church of bone. It is delicate as jewellery, this shrine, decorated with toe bones and picked-up teeth. The part that might get mistaken for a roof is made in dozens of plunging arches, zigzags turned sideways, cruel at the apex and curving low to French polish. Mice cannot read for toffee, but if one were to look at it a certain way, then perhaps the design might be based upon the letter *M*, repeated and repeated.

The mouse that is grey like dishwater is hunched at the top of the empty bookcase. She is tired to the death as she shrugs her fur and grooms her little saucer ears. She scrubs at her muzzle and closes her eyes and she wishes that she was not here. From up in the shelving she can see the whole universe, this filthy oblong full of mice and Christmas trimmings, with a stripe against the piano where the mice do not dare go until they come to die. The water-grey mouse has come to that spot many times, and she has seen the forks and spoons in a way that no other has. She has seen the eyeless hunger of them, the relentlessness. They are alien; in another life, a weasel would have seemed less evil. She has seen their jaws snip shut, the gluts and blood in scissor hinges.

Today she lost half her tail; when she escaped she had been too slow. She felt the bite, and when she turned to stare, she saw it snapped in bits by a steak knife. The water-grey mouse clambered a trail of blood all the way from floor to wall to the shelves. Now the bone is white against the raw end, showing through like the letters in a stick of seaside rock. She cannot bring herself to lick it, for it tastes like food. When she opens her eyes again the world is still there. Suddenly, the water-grey mouse discovers that she cannot bear it and she gathers up all the love that she has left and squeezes it into a ball between her paws. She points her face down, towards the piano and its gap, and wonders if she dares creep out and give her body to the cutlery. She lifts her neck and studies the trimmings that hang from the ceiling; garlands cut in one piece from shiny plastic and dragged into fragile, wavering ropes. They could not help her if they wanted to. She scrubs her face again, starts to prepare herself. There are no mice about.

Then the tapping begins. Another mouse is dead. The mice pour from the chimneybreast and gaze up at the water-grey mouse, expectant. The water-grey undertaker looks down at them and is filled with fury at their passive, waiting faces. She drops to the floor, surrounded by silent watching. She grits her jaws into the corpse's fur and feeds the cutlery again.

She will not drag another to the metal things. May the fairy-lights forgive her, she will pray once more and die. Her eyes are wild now, prophetic; the other mice can see it, and are uneasy.

The body is still among the knives as the dishwater mouse hurls herself into the Christmas tree. The others follow her, half reluctantly, because she has the face of one about to blind herself. Before they can bring themselves to pray, she is ahead of them, and she fixes her mouth against the hurting-hot glass, and she bites. The mice all lean forward; they flinch and then hold steady as the burn sweeps across them like washing soda in the eyes. Her tongue will never work again; the pain turns her pelt outside-in, she is a living streak of electricity, but it hardly matters when one is about to die.

Then is a flash of that other mind; no, more than a flash, the strongest yet, and they cling to it with the teeth of their imaginations. *Please.*

It works.

There is a shoving at the dining room door, and then a kicking, a battering, and the most enormous creature shoulders in the door; it swings on its hinges with a scrape. The water-grey mouse drops away from the wire, somehow not dead. The fairy lights, with one bulb bitten right off, somehow carry on shining. There is silence. The mice are transfixed, hysterical. Then they run.

They run; they run; they run. They seethe between her feet and over them; they scatter to the hallway, into corners and empty shoes and the pockets of the coats on the coat rack. They squeeze into crevices of every kind, every mouse alone, a narrow string of nerves and joy and panic.

The water grey mouse remains for a little time; she flings herself from the branches of the tree and lands right on this human being's collarbone. She gazes up at her, wild and balancing with her bleeding tail; there are so many questions and nowhere at all to start. Anyhow, her mouth is just one huge pain now and a squeak is beyond her, so she just stares at her bewildered saviour, and then leaps clear.

Under the piano, the cutlery observes all that has just happened with perfect detachment.

22

Marie

I DON T KNOW why I kept dreaming of cutlery; at least I didn't know back then. But sometimes the dreams were strong enough to hurt my teeth, like the grind of a bitten spoon.

In my bed I saw them all, I think, even the posh silver for christenings. There were elegant fish knives worn thin with engraving, 'EPNS' stamped behind the cutting edge, and a lithe, pretty pickle fork with an ivory handle. It was slim and pale, and it could jab like an insult, right to the bottom of a heavy glass jar. Sometimes I dreamed of pudding spoons with scoops like scallop shells, which fitted the mouth awkwardly and sometimes cut your lip.

And I began to develop awful headaches, which would come on quick as storms, where it seemed as if my ear was pierced right through with a kind of grasshopper chirping, like hundreds of tiny voices.

And yet, I was young then, and kind; I was the sort of child who sought out the beauty in small things. I spent a whole hour once with my cheek against the landscape of moss outside the back door, stroking it ever so gently with the round pad of my finger. It was soft as a cheek; every little plant was a fragile tree, green as last winter's velvet dress. If I could only be a little gentler, a little less frightening, then perhaps I might coax out the creatures that lived among that silky forest. There might be deer, or birds, bright as the thickness of a snapped needle. I was never quite gentle enough; I was very lonely. I tried though, until the air turned mauve and my mother called me in for supper.

I straightened my back then, and braced myself against the outside windowsill. Standing always made me dizzy; perhaps I had vertigo inside me, the chasm between being both so very large and small. For a moment, I stood, giddy, and leaned my head against the pink window; the window that my mother swore was not there. And she swore it, on the few times that I dared to ask, with such a brilliant smile that I concluded that she must be right. Nobody could smile like that unless they were telling the gospel truth.

Pink glass, pink frames, pink in streaks down the stone sill and the limestone skin of our house. The pink window always made my head pound. When the sparkles in my eyes faded I went indoors, heavy as a pocketful of stones.

At the dinner table I was as sad as could be. My mother was in a hostess mood; she chattered like a parrot about string and knitting needles, whilst my grandmother nodded wisely, as if in agreement. What she actually agreed *with* was not a thing I could guess.

I don't think that I had ever been so sad as that evening, or so suddenly. Maybe if one listens at moss-forests, then any old sorrow can clang in one's ears, for almost anything else is louder than moss. Tears made courses down my face and landed among the scrambled eggs. My mother paused for a forkful between her explaining; she pronounced me Overtired and told me to get into my bedclothes.

I went obediently enough, but halfway up the stairs I paused, and gazed down between the banister-bones at the door to the dining room which, according to my mother, was also not there. Sometimes that door made me want to sob. I trailed up to my bedroom and put on my nightgown, white as soap with tats of lace at the throat and cuff. I untwisted my hair from its bits of ribbon, and began to brush it. As I brushed, the static made my fingers crackle, and my hair seemed to float ceiling-wards, as one's hair does in dreams, or else like it does underwater. It clung against the back of the hairbrush and against the air, and in the mirror my reflection looked strange and witchy.

Then the bedroom snapped. It was as if every thread that held every thing together broke all at once, like shoelaces do sometimes when you stretch them too tight. I lurched forwards, thrown against the dressing room table by nothing at all, with a splitting in my ears like a broken wineglass. Then I heard that pleading again, desperate and failing, and almost without hope. *Please.*

And then I knew.

I thundered down the stairs and stood shaking before the door that wasn't there at all, that my mother had smothered all over with Concealer No 12 from Boots the Chemist so that nobody should be able to see it. Like a mad thing I began to shove, to batter at it, kicking my tender feet at the stuff that held it fast. I bruised my arm and shoulder down one side. I grazed my toes and knuckles, I discovered violence that I did not know I possessed, and I heaved the dining room door open.

The bulb spat when I pushed the switch, made no light at all. In the darkness it was hard to understand what I was seeing, though my nose could comprehend it well enough. It stank of ammonia and misery, and all my eyes could register were the little frosted bulbs of a string of fairy lights. There was a Christmas tree, mummified to spine and branches, with rags of tinsel here and there like the stuff that infested the kitchen ceiling. I took in the room by degrees: the conker-tops of furniture, deep with scratching; mouse-eaten walls and a piano that I had never seen.

In a moment more, I had discerned the form of a little

mouse, frail as a cobweb and stiff with fear upon the picture rail. Then there were eyes, dozens, hundreds, all blinking, shining, driven crazy with wishing. Then, all of an instant, the room was leaping with mice, dashing headlong towards the door that I had left ajar. Faced with this frantic, scrabbling sea, I put my hands over my mouth and stared. It seemed to me as if every mouse that had ever been born was desperate to escape this one little room. I dared not move my feet an inch, for fear of crushing them.

One brave creature made a leap from the branches of the Christmas tree and landed on the lace of my nightgown, whisking its thin, snapped-short tail. Its body was all but weightless, and it clung there with pinkish paws to my collar, trembling like a thing made from fine, overwound clockwork. It stared into my face like a tiny soothsayer, breaths heaving out of its body as though it might die of breathing, as if it were struggling for the power of speech. We looked at one another for a long second.

Then I heard my grandmother calling me from the top of the stairs. 'Marie,' she said, 'Marie, come here!' The enchantment dissolved; the mouse jumped sideways and streaked along the carpet towards the door, among the last few stragglers. Something happened, though, in the patch of shadow underneath a table; in the dark I could not tell what. There was a sound like scissors, and the watery grey mouse did not reappear.

I stuttered backwards on naked feet, and then turned tail and fled, past my grandmother on the staircase, without even a single thought for politeness, and I hid in the airing cupboard all night as my mother wailed that she needed a cat this very minute. By the next morning, my grandmother had found one: an insolent tabby with yellow eyes and feet full of claws. My grandmother named him Thomas. 'Thomas the doubter,' said she, and laughed.

23
Mice

THERE IS A fundamental nature to things. Chickens dream of flight. A yappy dog in his tartan jacket might fetch a painted wooden ball and beg for chocolate drops, but in his soul he is a killer, a pacer of ancient tundra wastes. So it is with mice; their nature is all mischief and chewing, a kind of gentle chaos. A heart that bolts along so rapidly does not take long to remember its form. Over hours, the mice creep out from their corners and they snap about the place like rubber bands. The universe is not one room after all, and they find that they always knew it, even if it was a thing only barely believed.

There are maps within them, written in the curls of their ears; they almost remember every carpet pattern, this biscuit crumb or that delectable plug flex. The mother-god is in the kitchen among the brittle stacks of crockery, warming milk for Horlicks. There is noise from the hallway, quite a racket, but the mother is drinking it already with her imagination, tasting that sweet thickness. Horlicks is a refuge, gorgeous and beige and big enough to sink right into. As she is thinking, the milk rises up like a time-lapsed mushroom and spitters over the stove, but before she can swallow her thought, or even notice the milk pan, the place is overrun with mice.

They come at the kitchen like a scrat-toed flood, scuttle

over everything with their dirty feet. She points her face at the lighting strip and screams, and then the mother-god begins to stamp at them as though the kitchen was on fire. But mice are invincible; every one is fragile, broken easily but surrounded by friends. Although some are killed in this melee, there are still enough for a plague. After a little time, she stops her flapping and she marches out; furious slippers thump away up the stairs.

The mice are hungry as fire, and here is food, actual food, not the wallpaper glue that the tellers of folklore drool over. There is half-eaten toast and scrambled eggs, and green-furred custard in a pot, and cold tea, and a larder full of everything besides. They eat and eat and eat; some even die of eating, which is a noble and magnificent way to end one's life. They scamper and piddle over every surface their ancestors once trod.

In the dead of night, the mice are manic, crazed with food. The milk pan, which was knocked half-off the hob, is burning black and billowing the kitchen with warm, sweet waves of smoke. The mouse-children are high on sugar and they begin to play jump-candle with the gas ring, flicking over it, daring each other, whisking their tails just clear of the flames, when the grandmother comes in. Pandemonium freezes to a tableau; every mouse hopes he is invisible as she stalks into the kitchen.

'Ha,' she says, as though the sight were shortly, curtly, funny, and she turns off the hob, dumping the milk pan in the greasy sink with a quench of steam. The handle is melted; it bears the shape of her fingers. She inspects her hand, as if interested by the sticky plastic left upon the palm. Then, she steps through the mice towards the hallway, making as if to close the door behind her. She seems to change her mind, however, and opens it out again. 'Help yourselves,' says she with an ironic bow. Then she is gone.

The mice, of course, could leave the kitchen, open door or not; they are mystified, and gape after her; then they shake their scruffy faces and gaze at one another. What to do now, what would the childling have them do? They look around them, at the tinsel and the mess, and wonder. Here they are, come into their inheritance at last, with enough food that they might even die of it, and it must have been by their love; it must. Their culture is only ever as solid as chewed bread; there will be time enough to muddle through the doctrine.

But the mother: this frizz-haired god, she who can belch out bleach fumes and reduce a mouse to dust with just one spiteful glance; did she not just stamp and shriek and then run cowering? Did she not seem just a monster, a thing made out of blood and tendons after all, as mice are? Only a monster?

They glance among themselves, and then they straighten their tails and scuttle from the kitchen, bathing amongst the spice and smells of sweat, and deodorant, and coal-tar soap, and wet coats and rotting woodwork. They have only ever known the reek of their own bodies, and the nickel-coin sourness of breeding metal. Yes, it is this, surely it is this beauty, this inhaled colour; surely this is their message from the god that does not wish to kill them. This is their reward for their loving, for their faith. The childling is still watching, twinkling like fairy lights, smiling and nodding.

The noise of mice as they jump up from one step to the next is a small, flicking sound, like hail on a shed roof. The mother, in her bed, has left off lamenting her misfortune and aborted Horlicks, and has even finished complaining to anyone who might listen, that the whole thing would definitely put her in an early grave. She is lying on her eiderdown like a tomb carving, hands as flat as spatulas. Her lips are quivering as she almost dreams, until her eyes flap open. Mice creep onto her bed from every direction, and they stand in a shoving, shouldering ring, and they stare; they accuse. She fixes her eyes on the lightshade that hangs above her head. It is blue. For one, blinding second she thinks of her husband in his stripy blue pyjamas, soaking scarlet through the tear in the cloth.

She gawps like a baked fish and shudders, bites her lip and wonders if she will meet her death, as one mouse nips her toe very hard, not to hurt, certainly not to eat, but to discover, to see if she tastes like a god.

The mother lies very still and begins to wail, as the mice dance slowly about her in circles, clambering and scratching at her ankles every time they climb over them.

24
Marie

MY MOTHER DID not speak to me for weeks; barely spoke, rather, for if I asked her a question, any question at all, her reply would always be the same. If I asked my mother if she would like a cup of tea, she would drain white and press her fingers together, so hard I feared that they might fracture. 'Mind your own business,' was all that would grit out of her mouth. 'Mind your own business.'

Sometimes I would catch her looking at me from among the safety of her knitting, as though she might hold me at bay with gauge nine needles and grey string. If I caught her eye, she would hold my glance for just a splinter of time, chin quivering, and then she would stare away. She would show her displeasure by snatching all the stitches off her needles and unravelling them, savagely, the way one strips feathers from a duck.

She did come round, but it took months, and in the meantime, I grew dreadfully lonely. March lasted forever that year; the weeks were lionish; translucent; fitful; terribly cold. We kept the fire going in the parlour; it warmed the damp and made the walls give off a kind of soggy comfort, like the heat inside a compost heap. It was lovely, but it thickened the chest and made one cough. The household sagged, stealthily, so that nobody would notice.

On the first morning after the mice, I came downstairs

and discovered the cat. He had been firmly installed in the home before I was even out of bed. When I found him he was in the hallway, purring and chewing with the side of his face at something small and gristly that lay half-out of a saucer. I was glad, I suppose, to have suddenly acquired a pet; I ran my hand along his fur-stole back and felt the muscles tauten beneath my hand. He did not look up, nor pause his eating.

I straightened up, awkwardly as I had trodden on the hem of my nightie, and I recalled in a rush what had happened the night before. It was only three paces to the dining room door, but I crept up to it as though I hardly dared. It was almost as if it had never been open at all, except that the blocking at the bottom was loose from scraping open and scraping shut. My mother had covered it up with wrapping paper. *Do not open until Xmas.*

There followed a long and guilty day of minding my own business, without even my grandmother paying me any mind. That day I would have been glad for anything, even of one of her presents or her demonstrations.

I stood on the concrete patio until my fingers ached with cold, as though I might redeem myself by shivering there. I hunted the garden for snowdrops or leaf buds on the plants, but there weren't even those. The garden hunkered in the wind the way that pigeons do when they are stuck in bad weather; it would not speak to me. I was miserable; I even went back to the cat, but all he did was to narrow his eyes and turn his cheek away.

It was dark by five, as though the day could not be bothered. I went to my room and played with my magnetic fishes, but in the musty air the cardboard was turning soft, unpeeling cardboard heads from metal chins. The house was dragging out a heartbeat, lowering and hard and lower than bones. It was a noise that always made my ears trill, and it made my grandmother spiteful for days.

That evening I was at a loose end, poking in cupboards and leaning against the tabletop for the want of something to do. In the course of my rummaging, I unearthed a candle-stump and I stole a long Cook's match from the box that my mother hid in the fridge. Then, brimming with defiance, I went exploring.

The entrance to the back stairs, where servant girls once scurried, out of the sight of some grand lady of the house, had been blocked up with a bookcase since forever. I did not even know quite where the stairs ended; probably in the rooftop labyrinth that my grandmother haunted. Still, between the bathroom and the box room door was a tiny landing where the stairs ran above; slant-ceilinged, wide enough to admit one body. The nose of that wedge of space was sliced off by a bolted cupboard. When I pulled both doors shut, that little square was perfectly black. It was a good place in which to sulk.

I lit my match, and then my candle, and I hid in the dark. The air was rich with spores and cobwebs, and when I sat down the floor was bald and splintery. A very old mousetrap was wedged in the corner, adorned with the bones of some long-dead victim, tiny and perfect as jewellery. I hadn't the heart to touch it. A spider tickled over my forearm and made me jump. I brushed her off my skin and put her safely out of the way of my feet. I spent a while playing with fire, sweeping my finger through and through the candle flame, trusting it not to bite.

In time I grew bored with sitting and I twisted round to face the cupboard door. Kneeling in the dark, my knees studded with square-headed nails, I began to fight with the tarnished slide-bolt. I hurt my fingers getting it undone.

When I heaved it open, I found no interesting junk for sorting through, just a graveyard for moulding, brownish things, things that smelled old and dead. I was disappointed and held the candle aloft, making the bulging lath above my head leap in the shadows. Downstairs, my mother coughed and said something to herself out loud. Warily, I lifted up a potato sack with the toe of my shoe, uncovering shapeless things like the relics of some rotten history.

Suddenly, though, I found that I recognised an outline, and I reached down, horrified and curious, and I picked up a brown-blue teddy bear.

It was crude, more a silhouette, really, carved out of blanket, as if with nail clippers or something blunt. I turned it over in my hands as the hairs on my neck prickled. There were two friendly holes in the place of eyes. Then it was if my eyes adjusted to what they were staring at, for then I perceived myself to be in a playroom, sunless and dank as a cell. I found a cardboard dress-up doll, with a gown of newspaper curling off her shoulders. I found a telephone, like something I think I remembered, not Fisher Price this one, but modelled out of bread. There were no wheels to pull it along, and the bread had desiccated, hard as a fossil. Then, I saw a little book, and I seized it up, almost triumphantly, expecting a diary full of secrets, some key to make me understand.

I found myself aware of movement, and craned behind me: a seethe of mice had followed me in. They must have been watching me trespassing, nosey and tantalised, flesh creeping off my shoulders. I felt ashamed, caught out. They all gazed at me with bated breath.

I was cowed and looked slowly down at the book in my hands. The texture of it was so odd, so revolting, that I had to fight an impulse to fling it right away from me. It was a rough-made thing, as if it had been put together by children; it seemed to have been stitched out of skin. The jacket was covered in tiny pores and hairs, the same sallow stuff that my grandmother's winter gloves were made from. At the front, where one might expect to find a title, was a smeared brown-red stamp. 'DANISH'.

My fingers turned greasy as I bent it open. After the thick, half-elastic cover, the pages inside were shockingly dry, linty almost, and blue. It dawned on me that they were made of floor cloths, the ones that we used so as not to spoil the nice homemade ones that my mother knitted. I leaned over, peered hard, trying to make out writing. The mice all gazed too, leaning forward. There was not one word, just a horrible smell, and my stomach heaved without warning.

The mice were staring, all pointing like arrows, expectant, as if were supposed to do something, say something, be some special thing, just for them. I looked back at them all, needled by the jabbing of their need, by the hundreds of tiny questions that I could not answer, nor even comprehend.

I was just a child; I began to cry, and I crawled backwards, scattering mice; blowing out my candle, I returned to the parlour. The mice all crept out after me and slipped through the parlour like water down a draining board; the cat saw, but he was already quite busy.

My mother was clearly planning to have an early night; she was gathering up armfuls of Thomas, trying to cajole and force him to come upstairs with her. He was having none of this and bucked and yowled and clawed at her. They went from the parlour and up to bed in this fashion; the one spitting and scratching his feet, and the other soothing and threatening, and occasionally yelping in pain.

25

The Mother

FLOWERS ARE NICE. Kneeling at the coffee table in one's parlour is nice, and arranging a bouquet is nicer still. And it was May, and these are things that one does in the month of May.

The mother was as happy as a flower herself, and she sang as her knees became stiff and the house glowered around her, morose and empty-brained. There was a whole garden's worth of flowers on the low table: there were sword lilies, and pink things that seemed to be dog roses. The mother paused, frowning at her crop. There were dandelions and daisies and these things here, which were ox-eye. Or ox-tongue. Or ox-bow. And these, these in her hand were yellow, and they smelled of sunshine.

The mother had been forced to widen the top of her vase, for Domestos bottles have stupidly narrow throats. But it was coming up a treat and the table was littering with severings and stumps of flower, and round, spilt jewels of tap water. The mother laid down her hedge clippers, flinching at the noise of metal against the wood.

She kept a surreptitious eye on them, but these were from the scullery, dull idiot things that did not seem to know anything about blood; about eating. She regarded them narrowly for a minute and then remembered that she had been singing. *Parsley, sage, rosemary and thyme.*

There were mice behind her, staring into her back like lemon juice in a cut. The bloody mice. She had all but forgotten them, scarred the dining room out of her head. For a couple of blissful years she had amnesia, had sailed between the parlour and the dining room with barely a twist of her nerves. But now they plagued her like flies, fast and impossible to swat. It was clear that she would never trick them into the dining room again. It was a scream. It was a nightmare. After that first awful night, when she feared that she would be raked to death by rodent teeth; after then they were everywhere, accusing, fixing her with their vicious, berry-black eyes.

The mother snatched up a flower and broke its back ramming it into the bottle. Then she half-turned, feinting as if to rush at the mice. The prickling stopped against her back as the mice scattered.

The first weeks had been horrible; she felt like a splitting sausage, gasping and grasping at her belly to keep her insides in, to contain the foul blackness in her that slipped like creosote, tried to ooze through the holes. Some death-like instinct in her wanted her to blurt her whole self, guts and secrets and lymphatic fluids, blurt it all upon the floor and contain herself no longer.

She had not dared speak with Marie for a long time, just in case; she held her daughter in place in her mind, as one might do with a bookmark, so that she should be able to attend to her later. She was a good mother; a protective mother.

The mother knew all this as she glowered from behind her knitting, or when she boxed her daughter in with cornflake packets at the dinner table. It was an act of love, born out of a selfless, motherly devotion. There had been a near miss, a near collision early on, when the mother had spent a bone-scratched day injuring Marie with her eyes, and playing Grandmother's Footsteps with the wretched mice.

She sat on the loo upstairs, worrying at her nails until they bled, and for a time it seemed as if the world was all how it used to be. In that slice of time, the man who had married her might as well have still been outside the door, prodding at things, digging at her pain like a dentist, making every thing that she did into a wrong thing. She was hot-faced and guilty, waiting to be shown up, and then her innards sank at the thought: he was not even the accuser any more, but the sin, the colossal, colossal wound on her conscience. If he made her a failure in his life, he condemned her by his death. The mother sat on the toilet, and she rocked and sobbed. The mice knew it all, and they made it real. It was real; it was real; oh god it was all real.

When she had pulled herself together that night, and crept streak-faced down the stairs, the mother had made tea. She sat at the table and jotted a note to the milkman, saying two pints gold-top please, and a bottle of Unigate orange juice, and that she was a filthy liar and a rubbish mother and a murderess and persecutor of mice and small things; that she knew the judder that a knife makes when it spits right through a man and catches on the backbone. And that the noise he made was just like a sink full of water, draining with a slice of onion stuck in the plug hole, a comical, gurgling suck. And that she had laughed (imagine that!); laughed and wiped her nose against her flannelette sleeve. And that she was sorry, but there was only one empty left out because the other one had been accidently broken. It had not been until four o'clock in the morning that she understood what she had done; at the mosquito wail of the milk float, she had scalded out of bed and snatched in the letter before the milkman picked it up.

The mother arranged flowers like a savage, drowning

the earlier blooms as she shoved new ones on top, crushing them in hard. But yes, as she looked she remembered; they were surely coming on a treat, all pretty and fresh as a garden; why, she might yet stave off the darkness with singing and flowers, and dozens and dozens of mousetraps. After all, she actually spoke to Marie today, with a smile, and eye contact and everything. And Marie had looked back at her and smiled too. Yes, certainly things would be alright. The mother pressed a picking of Love-in-a-Mist against her cheek and beamed for perfect joy.

And when the grandmother came in, she hardly even broke the spell when she demanded that she feed the thing in the garden. For now they had the job off pat; it was barely a chore at all, since the mother had hit upon the notion of funnels.

It had been the work of a minute to widen one of the breathing holes a little, so as to accommodate the thin tube-end. The mother's heart was hardly leaden at all as she strode out to the back door. The nasty child only ever ate things with a diameter of less than one-and-a-quarter inches; the mother gave her flower trimmings and a packet of Midget Gems, which she dropped down into the hole one by one. There was no particular movement beneath her feet, just a half-hearted scuffling that proved that the thing must still be alive. The mother stood up, wiped her hands on the hips of her dress and smiled. Then she tripped back indoors like a bridesmaid.

The grandmother was in the hallway making distractions, demonstrating to a rabbit-eyed Marie that the beaks of finches are as strong as pliers. Her little girl's eyes were shining, brimming even; she had a demeanour, the mother thought, of rapture, of a child moved by the ecstasy of learning. She was shaking, even; quite violently shaking at the perfect symmetry of nature. The mother smiled again, fondly and draped her arms around her daughter's neck and watched a while. So it was true; the beaks of finches really are as strong as pliers. Well, well.

Marie had tottered away by the time the mother returned to her flowers. They lay there for her, patiently wilting, waiting for the transfiguration of a loving hand. The mother considered herself to be rather like the Interflora nymph thing as she settled herself among the leaves and snippings, and began to arrange them. *Parsley, sage, rosemary and thyme.*

She spent a happy half hour with her flowers; taking them out, putting them in again, scattering petals like ripped-off butterfly wings. The mice slipped in behind her. Gradually, insidious as fear, the stinging began on her neck, her shoulders, the slings of flesh underneath her arms. Their eyes always got to the bare skin first. Then she felt the staring pincer through her summer dress, the frizz of her hair, small and endless like midge bites. In time, if they all focused at once, the mice could stare right through a winter coat, even through the glass of her spectacles to pin-dig and pain the whites of her eyes.

The mother persevered as best she could, persisted with her flowers and her song, but in time all there was in her brain was the discord of the mice. Her temper snapped, suddenly, ruptured like a tendon; the mother leapt up at them, upsetting the water jug, roaring at them as they scattered. There was only one thing to be done: to go and find the cat.

Thomas might loathe her, but at least he was only one creature. He could never hate her hundreds of times at once, in minutely different ways. And Thomas was the antidote to mice; wherever he was, the mice were not.

The mother stormed about the place, opening doors, looking in cupboards, seeking out her defender. He was in none of the places that she looked. As she opened the front door, her scalp was crawling with sweat and itches, and her dress was gluing against the hollow of her back. She wrenched the handle sideways, pulled herself outside and smacked the rent man in the chest with her forehead.

There was a moment of confusion as the two of them divided from each other and brushed themselves as though dusted accidentally with flour. The rent man was charming, instantly forgiving, chuckling a little at the slight mishap. He bade the mother a courteous 'Hello', face glistening. His eyes were blue; a very pale shade as though they had been boiled. Before he had quite completed his sentence, she had turned and escaped, leaving him on the step, beaming into thin air. Half a minute later, and she reappeared, aiming a newly-lip-sticked grin at the middle of his forehead. She held an envelope between her two hands, pendulous with coins inside, and she proffered it at the rent man with ineffectual jabs until he took it from her.

A wave of small talk blew against her face like cigarette smoke, and then the rent man was gone, hitching up the waistband of his trousers and rolling off towards his car. The cat was on the garden wall, absorbing sun with his tail curled up along his side. He stood up, stretched his back, and slouched out of reach as the mother came up to grab him.

Irritable, stamping her slippers as she went, the mother returned indoors, to where her bouquet lay sidelong on the carpet. The mice were busy as only mice can be, rearranging the stems, forming flowers into a large and fragrant arrow, which pointed exactly at the mother, where she stood with her jaw hanging. Marie was open mouthed as well, and standing in the parlour; she looked down at the arrow, then behind her at the fleeing mice, and then finally up at her mother.

'Mind your own business,' said she, and then she stalked away.

26

Mice

A S THEY RECALL their fundamental nature, the mice are finding things that they seem to know. They quickly discovered that they had told each other fibs, for the frizz-haired mother did not stream flames from her fingertips like a petrol lighter at all. Death did not issue, unbidden from her lips, only the hollow clapping, the whoops and cusses that human beings use in the place of squeaking.

She smelled like an animalish thing, a thing made of flesh only. She was neither ethereal nor eternal. She was no hellish ghost, not like the albino prophet of centuries ago. She smelled of cooking fat and strong tea. She smelled afraid; she smelled very afraid. She flapped her hands, she rolled her eyes and squawked at them. The first new litter of that fresh age slipped into being in the sweaty cup of a slipper, emerald green and stolen. The first new mouse-mother found that her offspring were clamouring to be born as she danced on the not-a-mother-god's flat mountain of a bed. She was part of that strange moment, savage and peaceful; she was part of that peaceful overthrowing, until her belly tightened and she began to push.

Now, mice are private creatures and they give birth in squalid nurseries, out of the reach of prying muzzles. A female in pup is even a little aggressive, greedy for the moment of life-giving, selfish with her love. She shuns the others; the others shun her, until the young creep out of their nest to scuttle along their own life-spans. Not that night; there was a moment of rareness, for these are children that would belong to all of them.

The mice jumped down like weightless things, landing on the mat that the not-god mother sinks her feet against every morning, when she sighs and forces herself from her bed. The female mouse, shuddering already with the pain and giving of labour, was pulled in the slipper like a May Queen on a flower cart, making children even as her nest was dragged into the gap below the wardrobe.

The mice left her to her labouring, then, underneath the oblong protection of the closet, with its walnut veneer and bulbous Victorian feet. She curled her children around the knot of her tail, a Holy Family amongst the gorgeous swathes of dust-fleece and a lost baby's bootee from years ago. Her exhausted joy, her welling love and the pups' first whimpers were things done in secret, drowned out by the snoring of the frizz-haired mother. And, even though the mouse-mother tried, she could not hear the metal slide of the cutlery from the dining room. That was the first night of the new times.

As with all kinds of creature, it has been the youngest who have adjusted the most rapidly. For the children, the culture shock has been only a tremor, a tremble on their constantly trembling lives. For the mouselings, the universe merely unfolded like a miracle, from the misery of the dining room and mother's milk that reeked of cannibal meat, to this heaven. It is a beautiful thing, but only as astounding as living a life without eyes until reaching the fourteenth day and discovering how to open them, suddenly not-blind. It is only as amazing as being born at all, plucked from among the atoms of nothing that swirl between the dust motes, and wrapped in flesh and mewling skin and pushed into thin air.

The young mice bite into every soft place like sparks; they possess every little space exactly, with perfect confidence, for their inheritance, always due, has come. They are only home; the universe is theirs as it always should have been: from cellar to rafters and east to west. And it is the young pups too who have recently been born with memories that are not theirs. It is as if the house, with its huge carpeted geography, has been absorbed by them, by their foetal whiskers. When the mice first stumble to their paws, static-sparked with fear and questions, they already know where to run and what to be afraid of.

The maps of the very oldest took some little time to unfurl; for a few days they tagged along behind the very youngest, those most arrogant and wise. And they gave thanks to the fairy lights and the childling. But now, after a week, a month, the pups have begun to turn to their elders with demands: 'Where,' they ask, 'Where is the childling?' Is she not their rescuer, the huge thing once saved by the love of mice? Yes, perhaps she is watching; yes, she will surely rise up soon, but where is she?

And this nags at the mice, unnerves them, for it was their love that gave them deliverance from all their suffering. Their hope was in the god that does not wish to kill them, that the childling should come from the fairy lights somehow, to shove in the door; yet it was not the childling who rescued them.

The memories of mice, the little pin-sharp minds of a whole race, have shaped a picture of their childling. She is gigantic and small, somehow; her hair is like coal dust. Her body is white, unfurred, without tail. To care for a childling, one must wrap her in cloths, as though she carries a nest about her shoulders. The childling smells like a laundry basket.

'But Mama, where is my childling?' Gradually the euphoria of freedom and space and far too much to eat, wears away and they wonder. 'Where is the childling? Where is she?' And the very wisest ask this: what if the exodus itself was only a further test? Why, if they were to sit back upon their haunches and rest, might their ease actually undo the work of their loving? Faith is all very well, but mice need to love, to have a thing to love.

Loving is the reason for mice. It is only love that might save them, redeem them from their ancient murder and the albino's prophecy (curse his name and the womb that he crawled from). Only love might be enough to save them from eternal knives and the sort of fire that has a whole house to live in; the sort of death that might destroy every mouse alive, all in one moment.

'But Mama, where is my childling?' And in time, the mice begin to search. Quickly, they uncover the playroom that their ancestors made for her, and they snuff in the sweetness and decay like a rare and scared incense. But their childling is not there, and somehow they can get no further. It is a puzzle.

Mice are tiny creatures, and they live out tiny lives. A mouse will rarely set his claws fifty feet from the hovel he was weaned in. All the mice truly comprehend is their house; the garden is an ocean, wide and treacherous, infested with half-mythical demons, with owls and stoats and thousand-year-old terrors. They remember that the childling is *beneath*; the mouselings tell them this much, but beneath what? What does *beneath* mean? Where is the childling?

The mice want to ask the frizz-haired mother. They follow her, they plague her, they ask and ask and ask her where their own one is, what she did with her? They ask her other things too: why does she hate them so; why she injures little things; why she infected the house with the spirit of murder. They barely remember the human corpse any longer; that has slipped away, eclipsed by the smaller tragedies of mice. But why must she trap them, kill them, fling their corpses into the dining room, as if that place had not tortured them enough. Why has she made a cat come to their house, to break their necks though they have done no harm to anyone? And the mice want to know: where, where is the childling? They only want her to explain, perhaps to apologise; they do not repay hate with its like, whatever the mother might think.

The mice know well the horror of a moment's lost control, which an age of regret may not erase. Coiled inside every mouse, along with their maps and garbled folklore, is a nugget of guilt about the albino's burning. They know it as well as the face of their dear childling, and understand it just as badly. They ask the mother their questions, but all she does is stamp her feet at them. Eventually, at a loss, they resolve to ask Marie.

27

Marie

THE DAY THE winter took hold, I knelt at my mother's feet whilst she pulled a comb through my hair. I could hear the minute sound of strands stretching, or pulling loose from my head, snarling up amongst the red plastic teeth. Presently she left off combing and began to part my hair in two with the comb's thin corner, pressing so carefully hard that I feared she might actually slice my scalp.

From here on the floor, I could see under the table, and the small space beneath the stove, where a mousetrap had been wedged. As often as I could, I would lie on my side with my eye to the gap, and I would push the point of a pencil into the mechanism, shuddering at the snap. Always, I would imagine how a little body would break under that metal crack. My mother never found out that I used to save the mice. It would have made her cross. The linoleum floor was cold against my folded legs, and slightly greasy.

My mother always plaited my hair before bed; she always did on the days that she took a notion to, and would be fondly scornful if I did not come to her before being asked. Why, she would say, did I actually want to have my hair all tatted up in knots by morning? On the other days, she did not always plait my hair before bedtime and would wave me away in annoyance for being such a demanding child. This was the way that we were.

More than anything, I was merely glad that my mother would speak to me at all, without closing doors in my face, or spraying me with Haze Alpine Fresh, as though I were an unpleasant household odour. Perhaps by then she had forgiven me for raining the mice down upon her, like some scuttling Biblical plague. I had not meant to, after all; I had not done it to tease her. At least I was a kind-hearted child.

The mice harried my mother constantly. Sometimes, she was so anxious that it zigzagged off her in acrid, angular waves. It used to burn at my face, the way that one is burned by holding things straight out of the freezer, so cold that they stick against the skin. Sometimes my mother flinched about the house, raw, as though every surface had been peeled off her in shreds, as if it stung her just to walk in air. Sometimes, my mother cried like a wet tea towel against a wet glass tumbler. Wherever she went she drove mice before her; wherever she went they followed her like assassins.

I must have moved. My mother clucked her tongue, and with a handful of hair she pulled my head up straight. I felt her fingernails as she scraped the handful into three and began to make a braid. There was a savage draught through the back door; the air smelled dark green, smelled of ice-cold rain. I pulled forwards, just a little, making a counter pressure to help my mother do my hair, keeping things taut.

The cat had been asleep under the table; now he rose, and with a kind of idle haste, made his way into the scullery. Although he had warmed towards me, Thomas did not care for my grandmother at all. There was the sound of the twisted handle and my grandmother's weight braced against the swollen wood. The back door always stuck a little in the damp. She came into the kitchen warmth like a prophet of the coming snow; I had a glimpse of the garden, with its wide black sky, before the door was shoved to. My grandmother had been picking thorns again. In the crook of her arm was a flat basket, dark with wet and evil with spikes. She would stand for hours in the garden, face knuckled into a frown, snapping the thorns off the roses, her fingers stabbing in and out with her hard white fingers. When her basket was full, or when the poor bushes were naked, she would bear them indoors and dry them out on the floor of the oven. I never did know quite what she wanted them for. Still, the roses did manage to exact their small revenge.

My grandmother's hands were patterned with blood from hundreds of little jags: some were a whole day old and were scabbed over, blackish, washed with rainwater. Others, the most recent, were fresh as butcher's meat, draining scarlet down her fingers, collecting around her white-gold wedding ring in clots. She was quite oblivious. The sight of it made me catch my lip between my teeth and shake with horror.

My mother reached the very end of my hair, where the braid was as thin as a stem. I turned slightly, so as to gaze back at her. She was holding the plait in her fist; suddenly it looked very fragile. My mother wound a cotton ribbon twice around the hair above her thumb; then, with one end gripped in her free hand, she snatched up the other with her mouth and dragged it hard with her small yellow teeth. The gesture frightened me; there was a moment when I discovered that I did not know my mother at all. Then, the loop brought good and tight, she let it go and finished it off in a pretty bow. I kept my jumping skin as still as I could until she tied up the other plait. Then I crouched away on my fingers and feet, leaving my mother smiling at her hair-snagged comb, raking her thumbnail up and down its teeth, whilst my grandmother leaned into the oven with a match. I only stood properly when I was safely out of the door, but in the hallway the dark was haunted by banisters and my lungs filled with shadows. I couldn't bear to stand there. I closed my eyes and rushed towards the parlour and its lovely fire.

The mice were there, trembling bravely, as though come Thomas or apocalypse, they were going to see me, to say their piece or die speaking. But I did not speak the language of mice. Still, with our eyes, we met. I did not run this time, but stroked the paintbrush-end of my pigtail against my cheek. Then I stepped forwards into the fragile crowds and stood there amongst them. A channel opened for each footstep and closed behind each one; in this way, the mice shepherded me along the carpet to my mother's armchair. Then I gasped. They had made my mother, laid her out on the chair, like a sort of empty effigy.

On top of the lambskin was a wig of dishcloth string, balanced and held in place by hairpins. Her second-favourite slippers were planted together on the floor, firmly, hysterically chaste. Between the two was my whole mother, with her knitting on an apron lap, grasped by two tense mittens. Where a face would have been there was a withering scowl of orange peel, and two myopic Polos that could not find their spectacles. Everything was held in place by needles. It was uncanny.

The mice all blinked at me, excited. 'Do you see?' they seemed to say. 'Do you see?' I nodded slowly, slightly alarmed. I did not know if the mice understood nodding, whether the gesture meant anything to them; still I nodded all the same. Yes, it was my mother.

I cocked my head towards the door, listening, growing sweaty with nerves, making the mice afraid for a moment, but it was fine, my mother was not coming. Then the seething paws herded me backwards until I found myself sitting on the hearthstone, with the fire at my back, hot against my nightdress. And the pantomime began.

The mice sniffed up to the slippers, innocently going about their business, and then dived back as though terrified. One mouse, brown as garden mud, tiptoed up onto my knee. 'Do you see?' she seemed to say. 'Do you see?' I was not sure. I nodded, uncertain. Some of the mice lay sprawled as if killed; others fled almost out of sight and then peeped out. They held still, like the figures in a Nativity set. Then the dead mice got up and went away to the wings. Then one mouse, a large mouse, fat as a ping-pong ball from dustbin robbing, came and stood before me, guiltless and calm, gazing frankly into my face. Then a dozen others dragged something in from the side, a cloth that flowed like liquid, rippling over the bits on the carpet. It was black. After a minute's frowning, I recognised it as my mother's silk scarf, the one she bought to wear over her hair when she did housework. She hardly ever wore it; she could not figure out how to tie it up properly. The mice swept it along the floor to the large mouse, who carried on looking into my face, even as they approached. They covered her right up, leaving only a bulge beneath the folds. The mouse on my knee glared up at my face, desperate. 'Do you see? Do you see?' I didn't think that I did.

I nodded, hopelessly, and stroked her mossy fur with my fingertip. She was soft and fragile as mould, and I cried for her. I cried for all the mice and their love as they climbed onto my shoulders and the fire at my back began to hurt. I had nothing to offer them, it seemed. Still, I sneaked into the kitchen and laid out bottle tops of milk and a Jacob's cracker underneath the cooker.

My mother did not notice; she was happy with her comb. When I had seen to the mice, I walked up to her, knelt, and put my arms around her and my head in her lap.

She gathered around me like a blanket, and she did not tell me to mind my own business.

'Oh Marie,' my mother said, very softly. I could not tell if she was smiling.

28

Knife

BEHIND THE PINK window, the cutlery is breeding, mul-
tiplying very slowly. They are not quickly fertile, like
mice. The dining room is a church for knives; they have
slid out and possessed it all, for there is no use left for
ambush.

They have the souls of scorpions. They are stealthy; the
plink-plink of their nickel joints make a noise like music.
It is rather pretty; it sounds exactly like the teeth of a
musical box as they are plucked by the comb. They scar
and stab at every wooden surface, they scissor-scratch the
French polish, they write everything over with unread-
able runes. There are scrages in circles, all round the
voodoo-shrine of the mice; not because they are interested, but simply because it is a place they cannot walk
through. Knives are not curious by nature; they walk up
to things and turn away again, unless there is some use
to breaking through. They are brainless; there is no thought
in them, no head to keep them in. All the cutlery has is
will; they seek out soft matter to slice and scrape, hungry
and relentless as a plant wrenching upwards into light. In
the eaten-out cavity of the piano, the pinking shears are
about to give birth.

The fairy lights are twinkling in the bones of the
Christmas tree, twinkling with one bulb snapped right off,

twinkling even though they shouldn't work at all. They give the mounds of guano a wonderland cast; they turn it into a filthy snowscape. The dinner forks grind away like some remote machine, every part disconnected, somehow all moving. Then the door opens. There are a few seconds of stillness as their nerves compute, readjust. Then the cutlery turns itself round towards the space where the light is coming from and begins its various pincer journeys toward it.

There is the scent of breathing from beyond; they can taste the carbon dioxide and water, the richness of it as it is pushed from firm warm lungs. At the very last moment the exhalation becomes a gasp and a handful of mice are flung inside. They are spoiled mice already, killed by something else; they neither run nor flinch as the sharp things and spoons make their three-point turns and close in.

The pinking shears have not moved to feed, they are far too busy. They are all strange anyway: wrong-ended; spiked in funny places, with multiple handles like some weird invention. They are writhing, heaving rhythmically, greeting like a nail against a slate tile.

Metal things do not give birth, not quite. They tear themselves up, as bacteria do. They do not grow old like blooded things, but useless; they turn bloated and blunted, only good for cutting paper. And then they split.

There's a screech and the tangle splits, resolves. Now there are three of them: bright pairs of nail scissors, tiny and silvery and murderous, licking at themselves and at each other. They are slickish, oilish; ready to feed and grow up into pinking shears themselves, or else tailors' scissors, or kitchen ones for slicing the fat from meat. Their voices are shrill as glass, the house can hear them. It is a sound that cuts.

29

The Mother

THE MOTHER BOILED gently among her bubbles, like a blanching almond. The bathroom fugged with steam; it heavied the paper lantern that hung from the ceiling, just above the tub. The cardboard softened every bath time, sagged against the pin that snagged it in place.

When the bath was full, everything relaxed, slackened. The grouting around the taps luxuriated in its mildew, slick and gorgeous as the underneath of stones. The window-pane, which was frosted with a motif of water drops, dripped water, and the house's poor cheeks ached.

Radox salts are pleasantly gritty underneath one's body; they line the base of the water like the sand on a beach. They make it into ass's milk, almost; opaque and delicious. But they do not produce bubbles; this is why they must be supplemented with Matey. The water was much too hot, a horizontal tide-line was developing along her body, the lower half scalded red. It seemed fitting, when becoming clean, to suffer a little. She had not considered the notion particularly, it just seemed fitting. The mother was feeling a bit queasy. The turkey had not been quite right, perhaps she should have cooked it less rare?

She was sick of Christmas. The mother took a wad from the loo roll and began to scrub at herself with it, gasping in despair as it melted into mush and worm-thin rolls and filled her nice water with horrid little bits. She used the flats of her hands instead, as she hadn't a flannel.

The mother's body was a strange combination of angular and loose; the flesh dangled off her bones. The mother's clavicle was like some complicated apparatus, with the meat of breast and tummy hanging from it as though from a flagpole. She was yellowish in colour, decorated with fine silver trails where the skin had grown fat and tight, and then shrunk down again.

The mother smoothed her fingers over her belly. It was elastic, softly giving, and empty. Sometimes this surprised her. It was as if her body remembered her children better than she did: that waddling hugeness of pregnancy, the kicking dome that bulged out of the bathwater like an island in ass's milk. She used to watch her whole body heave; it was as though they had been playing in there. The two of them. There had been two. The mother put her head back and sighed, suddenly gaspingly sad.

It was Christmas again this morning, and she had remembered. And she had tried, she had really tried. She rose in the middle of the night to dust the paper chains, to make mince pies, to fold paper napkins in complicated and beautiful ways, to make everything especially nice.

The house was sulking, woken up and wan with light bulbs that morning, for it was hardly even morning at all yet. The mother cleaned her spectacles and made presents: washing fishes, with soap inside and sponge flanks stretched over and trailing sponge tails. She decorated them with felt tip pens, one eye open, one eye shut, with long bovine eyelashes and a mournful smile. Of course, if one used them to wash with the ink would run, but that was not the point. They were for keeping. They were for evidence. It was the thought that counted, and here was the proof. She really was good.

The mother gazed at the paper lantern, watching the

crepe glutting with steam. Any moment now it might tip its balance, plop into the water. Perhaps the dye would leach out of that as well, stain the ass's milk pink. When the fish were done and hemmed all round with blanket stitch, the mother made them into neat little parcels with newspaper wrappings, and Christmas cards that had corn-flake packet print on one side. But that would not be a problem, surely? Surely not! She shook her head, hard enough to make herself feel sick and jumped up, gathering up her gifts with gluey hands. Now, what was next? The fire! It needed stockings; it needed reindeer hoof prints. She trotted out of the kitchen door, tripped over her husband's corpse and splayed out, face first on the carpet.

Her toe had caught underneath the joint of his knee, which was cold and stiff as an ironing board. His eyes were jellied, more brainless than a sponge fish with a chest full of soap. He was, of course, not there at all. The mother explained this to herself, gently and at length. Eventually she discovered that she had told herself the truth. Of course he was not there. No, he was gone. Long gone. For a second, she beamed, opened her face to the floor and smiled, liberated, free of him. And then, as it always did, the knowledge sank through her, of what had happened. Of what she had done. Then it seemed to the mother, as she braced her fingers on the carpet to stand, that there were other ghosts in the hallway. There were hundreds, too many to reason with, little quivering ghosts with eyes like the opposites of stars. And even though she told them that they were not there, they did not vanish, not right away, they only blinked.

The wallpaper was replaced by them; lavender grey outlines like some paranoid motif, so crowded that they stood upon, against, through each other. From a very great distance they might have resembled frogspawn. The

mother shook herself and fled to the parlour, only returning for her parcels when she was certain that they had dis-
appeared. Just to be sure she kept her eyes closed for the
first few minutes, and arranged a bowl of nuts by touch
alone.

Before the sun came up there were sprouts bobbing
in a boiling pan and a red-and-green paper tablecloth and
places set with shiny holly and crackers, for there was a
scheme with the milkman whereby a few pence a week
bought stamps for a savings card. The hamper had been
enormous and even contained a special Christmas-scented
air freshener. After that, the mother laid her hands upon
her lap and waited, waited in that awful squeeze between
dread and excitement, for her little Marie to discover her.
Oh Marie. The mother wrung a silk poinsettia between
her hands.

Her girl was so grown-up, they did grow up so fast
these days. She was sure that she had not been so grown-
up at twelve-years-old. There was a knowingness to her
that was frightening. No, that was not quite right. It was
not a knowingness, but a watchfulness that clouded her
face sometimes, as though she might ask a question at any
moment.

Sometimes it was as if she just saw through it all. The
mother wondered if she only smiled, called her Mother,
to be polite. She got a queer look sometimes, as though
a sudden movement from either of them might be enough
to rupture everything. Sometimes the mother had to
choke silence into her throat, stuff all her confessions back
with a swallow of air.

As she waited, at five in the morning on Christmas Day,
the mother missed her Marie horribly, the baby she had
been, the time when she had believed every word that the
mother had said. And she knew as well, knew with the
hollow of her belly, that she had two children.

The other one (what was her name?) the other one curled up in her empty womb like a shell, or else stole up and down the stairs on frightened feet and robbed at the dustbin. The mother heard the sounds, or thought she did, and was almost pleased. Twice she leapt up to find her other child, to explain, to make it all well again. She was not there.

And then, thank God, Marie came, dredging sleep from her eyes, and the grandmother came from the garden smelling of frost, and they all sat down to Christmas dinner in their nightdresses or great coat. They were surprised to have a roast at eight in the morning, but seemed grateful enough. They gasped appreciatively at the gift-wrapped fishes; the mother had made one too many, it seemed, but she made a big joke of presenting one to herself. They all laughed. They chewed their food, wore paper crowns and sipped at port diligently as though it were cough mixture.

By half past nine the gravy was mixed up with the blood from the turkey, the tablecloth had grown soggy from spills and ripped a little, and mother was feeling rather ill. The grandmother reached out suddenly, fast as a fox, and snatched up the last cracker. 'You goose,' said she, 'there's one too many!' And showing her mouth, but hardly laughing, the grandmother shoved one end at the mother. The moment crystallised. And the mother took her end and yanked. The innards spilt out with a crack as the port glass went over and a plastic mouse dropped into the richly spreading stain. The grandmother picked it up by its long blue tail.

Marie sat very still. The mother stared at the grandmother's face in a flat panic. 'Oh dear!' said the latter, 'I don't think this was meant for you at all!' And she laughed again. The mother very subtly, so as not to arouse suspicion, rose to her feet. Talking calmly all the while, she backed from the table and all along the hallway, before she bolted up the stairs and locked herself in the bathroom. And then, so as to have a valid excuse for being locked in the bathroom, the mother began to pour herself a bath.

She stayed in the water until it was cold as a pond and then she sneaked back down to empty mousetraps and feed the cutlery.

30
Mice

A MOUSETRAP IS irresistible. It's an idiot's death, a hero's death, for curiosity is the noblest virtue that there is, next to love; next to rescuing. The mice are discovering the hundred different ways to die that are not deaths of despair or cutting. There is an odd kind of beauty to it, for every mouse should balance out his life upon a string of fear. This is how they are made; this is what makes them live their lives as flames do. The proper deaths for mice are ones that are swift and merciful, and the right kind of fear makes their lives a joy. This is a paradox.

Now the mice are putting fear at their backs; even at this moment they are creating children in the cupboards and insulation spaces. They are feeding and fornicating and shoring up their lives against death. They are truly mice once more and are doing all the things that make them mice.

But even so, in the left-hand side of every one of them is a little needle wound of guilt, pierced into their souls by the pain of the albino mouse, by his burning and scream-ing. No mouse can ever meet his death now without the others being sad, without them searching themselves to make sure that it is not their fault. In the beginning they were not sad at dying; this is the cost of guilt.

No mouse admits this, that she will sometimes look

at the draggles of mouse fur left by the cat, and feel a little sorry, for in some ways it is a wrong thing to feel. It makes their love well up in useless pools, with no thing there to rescue. And though they leap and scutter and make thousands of flick-whiskered mouselings, the unused love is hurting them, for what if they are damned?

A mud-brown mouse is considering this as she performs gymnastic tricks upon the curtain pole to tantalise the cat. Thomas is a damnable thing, with the brains and spite of a demon, and the frizz-haired mother would have him for a bodyguard if she could. She had wanted to name him Michael, but the grandmother would not hear of it. But a creature made out of spite might be led around by the nose with it, as mice are enslaved by curiosity. So it is that a single mouse can keep him busy all day and night, while the others get on with things. The mud-coloured mouse turns tricks and Thomas stares, just in case she falls. She might.

Beneath, beneath, beneath. The childling, thing that must be rescued, thing that redeems mousehood by her need; the childling has been put *beneath*, and the mice cannot find her. They hunt; there are whole search parties that do nothing but look. The mice have already looked in the cupboard beneath the sink; they have searched beneath the furniture, in the fustish filthy gaps beneath the fridge and freezer; they have examined every *beneath* in the house, but they have found no childling. There is a panic evolving among them: stealthy, slow growing, a kind of tumour.

But their fate is only half-completed; their redemption hangs upon the second half, for to be saved, the mice must be saviours. Truly, the god who does not wish to kill them must be testing them still, testing their will and worthiness for salvation. It is only faith that will find the childling to them.

They looked beneath the rumpled bed sheets, but all

they found was Marie, rubbing at her eyes as if she had been sleeping. She had stretched her arms to them, smiled very gently, shook her face from side to side as mice do when they are baffled. They had looked at her confused face and tiptoed dejectedly away.

Marie is a dear thing really, but she does not understand *beneath*. They try and try to make her see, but she does not comprehend the question. She gazes at their signals, blinks her eyes, nods encouragement, but heaven only knows what goes through that great big skull. But beneath; surely *beneath* is some place close by? The love of mice has become a slow bleeding, that, if not clotted, might just drain them white.

Now she comes into the parlour, carrying a too-full cup of tea. She sees the spitting, sneering cat and the mud-coloured mouse, and she sighs. Balancing her mug on the low table, she takes the tabby Satan by his scruff and turns him upside down, belly to the ceiling, paws folded together. She cradles him in the fashion; he is fuming, but passive as a mouseling as she bears him away.

The parlour grows quiet; for a moment the mud-coloured mouse poises quite still as the cobwebs gather in the curtains like an evil spell. Night is falling in the parlour; she drops through the air and lands among the corner-shadows. The mud-brown mouse is lithe as string as she threads the landscape of carpet through the hall. Thomas is cradled in Marie's arms; she is sitting on the second-bottom step with her face against the warmth of his flank. He does not try to kill her. The mouse regards them, then streaks away in case the cat should get free, in case he should smash her with his feet and teeth. At any rate, the horror of the dining room door, even when closed, is enough to split the seal between the living and the mad.

The mice have learnt a thing or two from their ordeal in there. The mice are making ghosts, in the gaps between rooms, in the cavities inside the floorboards, where the house is haunted by dust and tiny lost objects. The have practised on Marie, but though they can catch her attention easily enough, there is nothing to grasp hold of, nothing to twist. Marie is a vague creature, all made out of doubts and warmth; there is no sharp core inside her. All that they can do is make her look; all they can draw out of her is a kind of pity. She never seems to see what they are getting at; perhaps she is simple.

Now, the frizz-haired mother is altogether another kettle of fish. She is all angles and knobs, just below the skin, below the fretting, below the shriek of her laugh. She has grown all kinds of spikes to protect her needle wound and they hurt and stab at her every minute of the day. That's why she minces like she does, why she grimaces and snarls. The mice are quite sorry for her really, but they are dying for the answers: where is the childling? What is *beneath*? Why does she persecute the mice? Why does she hate them so? What did they ever do to her? They only want to make her listen, to make her stop.

When the mice prayed and pled, they made Marie come to them, an angel in a nightgown, quivering and prophetic as a newborn. It was not quite the deliverance that they had been expecting. Perhaps they had been arrogant to second-guess the god that does not wish to kill them. Either way, the mice have discovered a little talent for scribbling their way into heads.

The air coming from beneath the bathroom door reeks, of damp walls and steam and synthetic roses. The mother is inside, wallowing like a tuna steak in brine. With her fingers, she is gripping at the back of her head as she is sunk down in the water. Her body seems quite relaxed. Her eyes are wide open though, bright and frantic as light bulbs. The mice are doing it again.

And they are. They are clogging up the turn in the

landing, gritting their teeth and shaking their pelts and asking, asking so hard that it makes the house groan. Where is the childling? Where? The mother is developing a headache and it makes her wish she were some other person.

The mice are focussing on the mother, on her guilt and the jab-handled levers inside her. They are driving all of their questions, and their grief, and their fear of never having something to love, channelling it all into the blunt end of another arrow. This one is made from pampas stalks from the dusty vase on the bookcase. It is made of frayings from the bathmat. The point is agonising, made in jags of pins and soap shavings and a dressing gown cord, in frizzy hairbrush gleanings and the ivory stumps clipped off toenails, in hair slides and dental floss and Eucryl Smokers' Toothpaste, spilt from the tin and denture-pink and hacking-strong.

They pray, and think; they stare and demand and plead down the line of that arrow; they beam their accusation underneath the door and into the condensation and the microscopic noise of popping bubbles.

They are so quietly deafening that the mud-coloured mouse can hear it from downstairs. Marie stands up now; she is getting a headache as well. Holding the cat, she trails away into the kitchen as the mouse scales the staircase, flinging skywards like a thing with no weight of her own. Thomas hears the tap of her claws against the nylon carpet and cranes sideways to see. His eyes are mean as teeth, and he says *ki-ki-ki*, as cats do when they see an animal that they want to split right open. The mud-coloured mouse itches off up the last three steps before she meets another mouse, this one a lesser hue of dirt, heading down towards her. They pass, momentarily pausing to each polish their face; then the replacement cat-tormentor is off on his way.

The mice outside the bathroom door are incredibly

busy; the dark is labouring as they heave at the levers inside the frizz-haired mother. But before she turns the bend in the corridor, the mud-coloured mouse sees something that must be looked at. There's wire and wood and a thick metal piece that the mother has decorated with a ribbon.

Ribbon? She sniffles closer. It is the colour of a glowering sky and tied up in a gorgeous, loopish bow, each trailing end the length of a whole mouse by itself. Ah! But here's a stain on one tip, black and red, with a snuff like the end of a life. It is blood, of course; this is the last thought of the mud-coloured mouse as her skin abandons her. The snap of the mechanism bites down, very quick, and it is all done with.

31

Marie

IN EBRUARY, MY mother resolved to take long lie-ins. For, she told me, with her face as earnest as a doctor's, she worked her fingers to the bone to keep this place so nice. And with that, she would hold them aloft for me to scrutinise as if the bones were showing through already, like brittle white twigs. Perhaps they were; I could never bring myself to look. Oh yes, my mother worked hard to put good food on the table, so why, she would demand, why did I begrudge her this one small allowance?

I did not begrudge my mother a thing. I would look back at her, grateful, demure, whatever she seemed to need, and wait for the moment to pass. I would concentrate very hard, so as not to be called inattentive. I would count in nines, or else see if I could remember all the ingredients in a block of Rowntree's Raspberry Jelly. Afterwards I would go and see if I was right.

My mother did not seem to enjoy her lie-ins very much, for all she seemed to do was talk to herself, or bump and clatter around in her room as though there was something she had lost, something that had rolled under the bed or down the back of the drawers.

In fairness, it must have been terribly hard to sleep with Thomas wailing to be let out, clawing the carpet by the door to miserable tatters. He could not hold onto himself for so many hours; poor Thomas would be forced to pee on the floor, and my mother's bedroom soon stank of cats. But at least he kept out the mice, which was an issue that obsessed my mother more every day.

The house did not sleep well at night and would often lie in late too. It suffered terribly with nightmares, would fight against sleep for hours, and give into it just before dawn. As often as the dew fell, it would scrabble and fret like a dreaming dog, disturbing great sad flakes of plaster, making new cracks in the ceiling. It was still dreaming, still wrecking itself this morning at nine. Cold air hung in the chimney, and our poor old house snored its throat sore as deep as the dripping cellar.

I laid my cheek against its dampish flank, skinned with layers of wallpaper, and wondered what it was that ailed our house so badly. Perhaps the stone had visions of dynamite and workmen, perhaps it was only afraid of the dark. In retrospect, I wonder if the problem was not more fundamental. Maybe it was the limestone itself, every tiny fossil shellfish straining to break free and swim back to some primordial sea. Perhaps that is just the lot of sedimentary things. Some creatures are born to be unhappy, as if that is what they are for. I pressed my hands to the wall, but there was no soothing it. Houses breathe so very slowly that it would have been an hour before its calcified nerves even noticed my touch. Back then I did not know these things. At least I was a kind-hearted child.

I sighed, and turned upon my back, gazing sidelong at the heavy curtains and the sulky daylight poking at the space between them. There was a special melancholy to morning lie-ins when I was small, a feeling of being alone, the only one left.

Thomas yowled relentlessly; almost patiently. He yowled like a sticky hinge, as though someone was opening a cupboard door and then closing it, over and over, just for the rusty sound. I held my little body still as a whisker, tried to hear my grandmother's feet downstairs. There were none. Perhaps she was already out; perhaps she had not come in.

It was no use sleeping. After a time I sat up, the mattress complaining under me, and I put my toes on the floor. The carpet was thin in that patch; I always had a sense of the floorboards underneath my toes, the way that I would sometimes be aware of my own skeleton, the sticks that stiffened my flesh. There were bits on the floor and mounds of dirty clothes. Most of them had been there forever, grown out of before they were ever washed.

I turned on my lamp and slid forwards until I was sitting on the floor; then I looked up and gazed at my room. It did not ever seem to be entirely mine, as though I were sharing it with an invisible person. My eyes lit upon my *Young Christian's Illustrated Bible*. It had been a gift from my grandmother; she had underlined in red every Old Testament reference to birds. There was a thick chunk of colour plates in the centre: the Lord caused ravens to feed Elijah, and there he was, there they were, bearing gouts of meat in their claws, as though just a moment ago they had wrenched the lumps off a raw, glistening steak. My throat pushed upwards and I turned the page over quickly.

Next came the *Prodigal's Return*. I liked that picture. The father stood on one leg like a man falling over, arms flailing, as though the engraving had been taken like a photograph as he whooped for joy. And flying into his arms came the Prodigal, dressed in rags, blood-footed from such a walk, unclean from feeding swine and with sin tangled in his hair. He was about to be embraced by his father, clinging against his chest as his father's arms came round him, as the father finished his jumping and put his feet on the ground. The soil was Bible soil, where there is no vegetation and not one drop of moisture anywhere. His brother, the dutiful one, stood disregarded in the background, staring at that soil and his sandals, at his inked-in feet. I would look from one son to another, wonder which one might be me. I could never tell.

I closed my eyes for a second, held the picture in my head and wondered what such an embrace must feel like. It must be a wonderful feeling, I thought, or else terrifying. I thought of my mother, of running a long way to find her, of her looking up and seeing that it was me and running too, of our arms meeting, of her absorbing me. Perhaps she would pick me up. Perhaps she would spin me round and round. I did try once, to recreate that hug; ran through the garden towards my mother, for a joyous embrace. She had a shovel in her hand, and when she turned to me her face was not enraptured. Instead, I slowed, stood before her, and placed a kiss against her cheek, almost defiantly. My mother had blushed, her neck went all blotches as though I had done something quite obscene.

I closed the book, pushing my thumb at the corner where the leatherette was flaying off, showing up the cardboard inside. I laid it aside, carefully, as if it were explosive-charged, and stood up. I hated the house with nobody in it. The mice were company of a sort, but they scared me a little too; they made our home a foreign country, governed by customs that were not our own. The cat was sweet, but my mother got terribly jealous if I petted him. She was afraid, I think, that he might turn into *my* cat and not hers. She would snatch him away from me, eyes baleful, fingers sunk so far into his fur that her nails were quite lost. Then my mother would cart him away like a teddy bear and lock herself in the bathroom with him.

When I came out of my room, the mice all froze like a guilty, fragile-boned conspiracy. They had made another of their arrows, out of potpourri bits and broken clothes pegs. I sighed. They stood around as if ashamed as I gathered up the pieces and the red-dyed petals and put them in the potpourri basket, upset and downside-up on the landing runner.

Downstairs, I opened all the curtains, for the house was dim and hushed as if someone had died. And it was cold, too. I was forbidden to light the fire. I padded off to make some tea; at least I was allowed to use the kettle. When I had a scalding mug of leaves and water, I went to the fridge, but someone had emptied out all the milk and filled the bottle with vinegar. At that, I trod into my mother's wellingtons and heaved a coat over my nightgown and I went to the front door.

The milkman could not get his float all the way up the track as it was so narrow, so he always left the milk at the foot of the garden. As I strode across the icy path I was brave and guilty as a poacher. The foot of the garden was the furthest that I had ever been from home. By the time I got back to the house, I was frightened and breathing too hard, and my hands were cold to hurting from the bottles. The contents were frozen; the layer of cream on top was an unhealthy yellow, compared to the bluish waterish stuff underneath. It was completely solid and no use at all. I left them, abandoned on the doorstep, and clomped miserably around the back of the house.

With a guilty backwards glance, I crossed the concrete patio, where I was allowed to play, and planted my feet in the lawn, where I was not. Walking in the dirt was forbidden; it would make my pretty clothes messy, and furthermore it impaired the aeration of the earth, which was always dug over but never quite planted. It was into the mud that I stamped with my next step.

My mother's boot crunched deliciously into the raw ground. I bent forwards to gaze at the colours, the rubber-black wellington against the loam-black soil, then stuck my other foot in as well. Evidence of my crime would be as plain as day when my mother came out later; I lifted one boot and studied the perfect zigzag print I had left, neat and telling as a signed confession.

At that moment I did not care. My mother had said something once when the rent man was due. 'For a sheep as a lamb,' she had said, and I barely understood. 'Might as well hang.' I stalked through the crackling mud like a scarecrow in a duffel coat, right across as far as the cherry tree and the end fence, blown half down by last summer's windstorm.

It was standing there that I got the most peculiar feeling. And it was there, by the cherry tree's listing base, that I caught a glimpse of metal in the earth. I hunkered down to see, as the half-tame robin that lived in the garden fluttered down from the side hedge. With chilly fingers, I picked at the ground until I had uncovered a small round doorknob.

I knelt in the cold, biting at my lip. With forensic care, I picked up a twig and begin to scrape at it the edges of it until it lay on its own in a flat bed of loam. There was a large dent in the side, a whole edge was squashed in. Somehow I did not care to actually touch it with my bare hands. I glanced up to see a pair of collared doves land heavily on the lawn. Gradually, a small noise began to nag at my consciousness: a tiny feather-shuffling; the shushing of folded wings. I became aware of how cold I was.

When I lifted my head, the hedge, the tree and fence, the ground, everywhere was heavy with silent, watching birds, glaring like an impromptu law court, gazing with their heads cocked sideways. I moved my crouching body slightly and their heads all followed the movement sternly. My legs were cramping. I glanced back down the garden. All the birds looked too. I heard the front gate close. My grandmother had come home.

She came through the gloom and made as if to march in at the back door, but stopped suddenly in her tracks, scowling at the songbird-littered garden. I cringed behind the cherry tree to hide. All the birds jumped, blinking oil-black eyes, and a low twittering began on the lawn, a mutter of threatened betrayal. My grandmother stood, with her arms folded and a thin look in her eyes. A thousand sharp faces fazed up at me, refusing to take flight. Defeated, I stood up, rubbing at the ache in the backs of my legs.

My grandmother nodded to me, held out her hand. Sulky, caught in misbehaviour, I scrubbed earth back over the doorknob, clapped some of the dirt from my palms, and hurried over to the concrete patio to receive my telling off. As I approached the back door, all the birds flew away at once, filling the air with a sound like applause.

32

Child

THE SUN IS up in the space above the pit, cold and bright as a looking glass. The air holes are perfect points of whiteness, and beyond them is the anxious chitter of the songbirds. The wrong child is wrapped around herself, honest and patient as a potato. The frost never penetrates the webbing of her root-walled nest, for the cherry tree is her guardian; it will not allow it. Her fingers twitch a little as she sleeps. She is dreaming, and the worms and small creeping things dare not wake her.

The garden birds are afraid. The morning has come, and the grandmother, who is made out of garden herself, is a dictator of songbirds, and a harsh one. They fidget their shoulders, stick out their wings and flap them; they glance diagonally at one another, and glance quickly away again. They wonder which of them it should be.

The firecrest is the smallest of them all, with a flash of gold across its head that moves the other birds to jealousy. Envy is as good a motivation as any. The starlings shuffle their feathers, exchange meaningful looks. The collared doves catch the gesture, and begin to edge away.

The firecrest blinks in horror. The magpie has become shifty. Yes, the grandmother is a hard ruler. The birds have become their own secret police, willing to betray each other in order to save themselves; save their own nestlings;

save their own particular species. The grandmother pits wren against crow, robin against mistle thrush. In this way she rules over them; the songbirds must decide which among their number must sacrifice their wings, for if they do not then the grandmother will choose herself, and she will pick more than one. A bird without wings is a shameful thing, even in death, for the soul may not fly away. The firecrest is looking at its claws, beginning to jitter.

But then there is the noise of human feet, and the garden birds all leap heavenwards, except the poor firecrest. But it is not the grandmother after all; it is Marie, sad as can be with a coat buttoned over her nightdress. The hem of it peeps white underneath. The firecrest zigzags to the cherry tree with its tiny breast pounding.

And suddenly, the wrong child's dream becomes a dream of what she is now. She dreams of herself, hibernating beneath the ground, beneath the door that is her roof, beneath the affairs of other creatures. She dreams that her dress is soft with moss and that her fingernails are shining and grey, like the claws of moles. She dreams of her own black hair, glossy as oil and thick as a blanket, and of her own sleeping face, which is beautiful. Then everything settles; the wrong child dreams that she awakes. Her eyes open, very gently.

Above the wrong child's head, her twin, the one who has a name, is squatting on the soil beside the door handle on the roof. If she had made just one more step forwards, she might have stood right on top, felt the hollow tread of the empty space beneath her boot. The wrong child feels her there; her eyes glisten and she smiles.

But the garden birds are watching too, like spies. They cannot believe their luck, for if they tell the grandmother interesting things, then she sometimes overlooks their debts. The firecrest is overjoyed at a chance to snitch, and flurries away like a feather in a storm, off to tell tales.

And before the wrong child can unbend her limbs to sit, the grandmother is in the garden. The cherry tree does its best to conceal Marie, this innocent intruder that has made its childling smile. It is no good; her presence is as plain as day with all those treacherous beaks pointing out her hiding place. The grandmother glowers, squints against the daylight; then she marches forward.

In a trice, the moment has gone. The wrong child's twin is gone again; the grandmother is gone with her, along with a duck, which she poached from the park with her own two hands. The birds all breathe. The cherry tree sighs, and so does the wrong child in her burrow. She closes her eyes again, prepares herself for sleeping. Her dreams follow Marie into the house. They peep around the edges of doors, and creep up and down the staircase.

33
Rent Man

THE RENT MAN broke into a sweat as he edged his car through the front gate, breathing in and pulling his belly as if it might help him squeeze between the fence posts. And though he held his breath and gritted his jaws, still he grazed the wing against the bramble bushes on the swing into the driveway. He rolled his eyes at the rear-view mirror and he swore. Tiny jewels of perspiration stood among the stubbles on his neck as the rent man blotted his forehead on his sleeve.

After he had yanked the handbrake up tight, the rent man inspected his teeth, checking for fragments of breakfast. They were square and slightly translucent, like tea stained porcelain. Then, he lifted up the collar of his shirt and dug his nose inside it, sniffing carefully.

He did not detect any odour, so the rent man gave himself a fishy smile and opened the car door, heaving his body from the seat and slamming the door. The rent man rather liked the slam of his car door. It was a satisfying noise, a solid chunky noise. A *masculine* noise. He smiled, adjusted his trousers and cleared his throat.

The rent man was here for his due. He paused, stooped to tie his shoelaces. The rent man's shoes were plastic and extremely shiny. Bending made him feel tied in half by his waistband; he was puffing a little as he straightened up. She had not yet brought in the milk. He stooped again, picked up the bottles, wrapped his hands around their necks. He would take them to her. It would be chivalrous. She would look at him, and would be forced to smile.

The rent man's shoes slid up the path until they took him to the front door. The gloss was blistering off it in fragments, and the fingerplate was tarnish black. There was a doorbell too, and the rent man knew full well that it worked. He hung his fingers above it for a few moments, considering, and then he decided not to push it. He tried the handle instead, but it was locked. The rent man took this sad news well; for another second, he lingered on the doorbell, but discovered that he could make out the sound of voices from around the back.

The rent man did not generally care to knock. He preferred instead to try at latches, peep and peer, to see what he could see. He nodded once at the door, as one would at an insolent waiter, and thrust his hands into his pockets. On his way round, the rent man took in the hanging guttering and the cracks in window glass; the rot and damp and the stinging nettles on the ground. He made a mental note; proper upkeep was a condition of the tenancy. Things has slid in that department since her old man had done his runner. Not that the rent man had been sad to see him go. No indeed.

He was right; there were certainly voices coming from the back patio, in fact it sounded as though people were arguing. He paused to eavesdrop but found that he could not distinguish the words. It was some other language, some foreign guttural gibberish. The rent man's morning lit up. Perhaps she was subletting! Perhaps she was harbouring immigrants! The rent man removed his hands from his pockets, smoothed down his eyebrows, prepared a charming grin, and stepped around the corner.

There were no immigrants in the back garden,

however. There was just the grandmother, who had begun to laugh, and a poor magpie that was shuddering as though he were perched in the eye of a snowstorm. They both turned to stare, as the rent man unwrapped his smile and showed it to them. There were no other people there but her. The mad old crone must have been talking to herself. Her eyes met the rent man's; they hardened. At the same moment the mother came out of the back door.

She was dressed oddly, in a cardigan with some of the buttons replaced by safety pins, and a tartan kilt that did not go with it at all. Her hair was held back with plastic combs, and it was escaping here and there in stiff, wiry sprigs, and she was wringing her fingers hard enough to do herself an injury. Nonetheless, the flash of skin exposed at bosom and leg was womanly enough.

She caught his eye and almost screamed. Then, she quivered forwards like a gerbil, trilling out *Hello*s. The rent man stepped towards her. If he had owned a hat, he would have raised it at this point. But he dared not wear a hat, for he feared that the lack of circulation might accelerate his bald patch.

But the grandmother stalked forwards too, gripped the rent man's wrist and shook it with a 'How do you do?' Then, she turned behind to the mother. 'Run and fetch the envelope, dear, don't stand around catching flies.' The mother gulped, with an expression that looked a little like gratitude. The rent man beamed and retrieved his wrist, cursing his luck.

Since the grandmother had turned up, she always had the money come rent day. The rent man folded his arms and groped in his brain for small talk; but the grandmother had turned her back already. She was doing something with the rosebushes. The rent man glowered at her rod-stiff back. House calls had been rather more interesting before that wrinkled nag moved in and began to interfere.

After her old man had set off for pastures new, the mother had experienced a period of relative insolvency. There are other ways to pay one's rent than in note and coin. The rent man was by nature a generous kind of chap, and had been disposed to suggest a few of these, rather than see her thrown on the street.

Ah, for the old days. The rent man raised himself up on the balls of his feet, and then lowered himself again. His shoe was biting a raw spot on his poor tender foot, where the skin was vulnerable and never exposed to the sun. His mind began to wander; he wondered if he could get away with a sleep in his car this afternoon. After a time it dawned on him that one of the windows had been painted bright pink. The rent man had been about to comment upon this when the mother returned, with an envelope runched in her fist. The rent man bowed very gallantly, took it from the mother's sweating hand, adjusted his trousers once more, and left.

34

Marie

On PRIL NIGHTS, the garden could not make up its mind whether it was winter or springtime. Leaf buds hung in the cherry tree and bushes, and the honeysuckle on the back fence was pushing out hopeful little spirals of growth.

At night these brave gestures seemed like some regretful tableau of a lost springtime, long gone. At night the garden was like the two christening gowns that I found hanging in my mother's wardrobe.

They were identical, beautiful; they hissed some secret history that smelled of mothballs and lavender. Once guessed at, that knowledge would surely vanish, like those gowns did when I found them. Perhaps, as my mother had told me, perhaps I had only made them up. I must have been a fanciful child.

And yet, here I was in the garden again, a trespasser in that gentle sadness. Here I was again. I found myself out here, more and more, standing on the concrete patio or the doorstep, with my fingers in my mouth, as though I had walked there sleeping and then woken up.

I discovered myself shivering at the front door; I turned to go back, but the Yale had clicked. I would have to go right round to the back door. We never locked the back because the door was so sticky. The key would not turn properly. I had nothing upon my feet but socks.

I crept along out house's itchy hide and peered into the parlour. Most of the view was obscured by the heavy red curtains, thick as liver; here and there were constellations of prick marks that let the light through. Thomas made these; sometimes he clambered right up the fabric, goaded to snapping by those flirtatious mice. Once, he brought the whole lot down, pole and hooks and all. My grandmother had been furious, had banished him into the garden until my mother smuggled him back in, swathed in a cunning disguise of tea towels.

A single slice of light betrayed the scene within. It was not much to speak of; just my mother, sweating before an overzealous fire, bundled in housecoat and cardigan. She was knitting a dishcloth. A fat moth threw itself tirelessly against the lampshade that hung from the ceiling.

I could almost hear it, the catastrophic smack of wings against the wire and cardboard, impact after impact. There was no saving the moths. What they craved more than anything was the glory of light, the blindness and death of it. My mother paid it no mind, huddled inside her knitting like a spider in a cobweb. She looked tired.

I worried about my mother. I would try and look after her, in my way; I would leave her cups of tea in strategic places, so she would find them and think she had poured them herself. I would make cheese sandwiches that she would happen across; I hoped that if she found a ready-made supper, she would not take the trouble to cook. It often worked, except sometimes when she would use them to make cheese sandwich soup instead.

My mother was a haunted thing; she started and jumped at empty corners, fidgeted and muttered and worried. Sometimes she would gaze at me in a panic, or else make as if to tell me something important. Sometimes, she would even sneak out a word or two, then catch herself and stop her mouth up with her fist, and run to lock herself in the loo. I tried to love her; I did my best.

She began to do things in twos; she would present me with two bowls of cornflakes, one for each hand, or kiss my forehead and then aim another beside my head, kissing into empty air. Then, she would have to steady herself to avoid falling right over.

A stealthy noise behind me made me start. I told myself that it was only Thomas, nonetheless, I inched a little closer to the bright window. For a second I saw myself as another person would: thin and small as a little child, with two slender pigtails and a crocheted cardigan. I pulled its brown hood over my head, and dug my hands inside the sleeves. There were bats in the garden at dusk; sometimes they got tangled in your hair. They did not mean to.

My mother began to wag her head as though she had soap in her eyes and they were stinging. Then she plugged both her ears with her fingers, and began to sing, a *Lalala* song, an *I'm not listening and I can't hear you* song. And in front of my mother I could almost see a shape, vague as Vaseline, dissolving into air. It was a large animal, lying on its side. It might even have been a person. It vanished.

After a minute she opened her eyes, and nodded at the vacant space as though she had won an argument. 'Told you so,' said my mother with a smirk, and she shoved her needles through her knitting with a violence that hurt me, with an air that disintegrated slowly from triumph into misery.

She leaned over to the clutch of carrier bags that lived at the base of her armchair and pulled out a dishcloth, pristine grey, never used, and began to unravel it so she could use the string for knitting. My mother unwound it from cloth to nothing again, winding the kinked thread around the waist of her hand.

I sighed, and began to make my way along the wall, feeling the nettles bite at my calves and the gravel beneath my feet. I could feel the growing blackness of my socks, the dirt and wetness spreading through them. I could not bear to hurry though, for any step but the gentlest hurt my feet. And it was dark at the side of the house, with no windows and a fraying moon above my head. I felt like a traveller making a journey alone, and with no way to tell me when I arrived, or even when I was close.

Then I edged around the corner and found the glow from the kitchen window. I hobbled towards it without looking down, with my eyes fixed to the light as if it were the only thing that might save me. Perhaps that is the way that the moths feel as they break themselves against bulbs. I wonder.

The mice were there already. I did not know if they were waiting for me, or whether they were just sad too, and gazing for something to do. They seemed like toys running down lately, more apt to sit and stare than play their crazy mousey games. They made their arrows; they stared at my mother, with nothing moving but their whiskers.

And right now they gazed at me, crowded on each other's shoulders to get a better view. I was taken aback, until they began to crane their little necks sideways, and then I understood. The mice were not looking at me at all. They were looking at the garden, fixed on the dark and the whiteness of the spring. I turned to look too, and heard a frantic, excited scrabble against the glass.

The mice saw me glance at them, and they urged me outwards again, planted their tiny paws against the glass, bade me look with them. I tried; tried to look like the mice, see what they were staring at, until it dawned on me that they could not see a thing either. They nearly killed themselves with wanting to see. But wanting did no good.

Suddenly the mice all toppled away from the window as if they had all been stacked there and then unbalanced. My grandmother rounded the corner of the house and came to stand on the concrete patio. I had been wary of her since the other day, when the songbirds had all told on me for treading on the soil. She had not shouted at me about it; she had told me to mind my own business, and then laughed; laughed and laughed like a jackdaw until I had begun to cry. I do not think she told my mother what I had done.

She was dressed in feathers; swathed in feathers; magnificent and regal and shining in feathers. She was wearing an garment that I had only seen once before, when there had been the most awful thunderstorm and she had come home so exhausted that she slept for three whole weeks.

With a curious bobbing motion of her head, my grandmother turned towards the house, and then I found that she knew I was there. She gave me a queer look, an almost loving look, and then my grandmother opened her wings and flew away.

35

The Mother

THE MOTHER STRUGGLED into the kitchen and shoved the door shut with the weight of her backside. Thomas had burrowed down inside her embrace, so hard he might have sloughed right out, left her holding on to a glove of pelt, punctuated by claws.

If he could, Thomas would abandon her, drop through himself and slink away, skinless, like a rabbit for the pot. The thought of it made the mother sad; she heaved him up in her arms, paws pointing outwards for safety's sake, and placed a kiss upon his flat-eared head. He rumbled deep inside himself, like a car that will not start, and tried to get a purchase on her cardigan.

The mother resembled Saint Francis as she arranged dear Thomas on his own little bed, holding his pretty mackerel-striped back down with her knee whilst she made him secure. A single thread of string was no good, for the daft old thing would scrabble and kick until he was almost murdered by it, the string slicing a line in his skin as though it might dig all the way through, like wire through cheese.

He really did not have a sense of self-preservation, bless him. The mother slowed, rolled her fingers through his fur whilst he rolled his eyes at her and wished her every misfortune. She smiled indulgently, and tied him to the table leg by fifteen different strands, and cut him a slice of cheese, which he completely refused to inspect, much less eat. Silly old thing.

The mother liked to have old Tom with her of an evening, her boxer-faced companion, a kind of fly repellent for mice. The mother knew, or rather suspected, that the mice did not keep all that much of a distance, but it was better than nothing. If she did not tie him down, Thomas could actually pursue them, kill them. If she did not tie him down, Thomas would get as far away from the mother as he possibly could. It was a quandary. But the world was alright if she kept her eyes a bit crossed.

It was rather like considering a painting-by-numbers painting. Those patches of colour, the jagged borders; if one didn't quite look properly, one could choose to see a harvest scene, with children among the black and red poppies. The mother smoothed her skirt over her knees, and discovered that she was still squatting on the floor. No, she could not see a single mouse. Not a one.

After a little time, she perceived that the scene really did have a child in it; for an instant her heart convulsed with a feeling like choking. The mother lived and died at once, possessed with horror and hope, and the relief that is was over. For here, after all, was her other child. There had been a dreadful mix-up: the mother (silly her!) had somehow convinced herself that this child was in a hole in the garden, but no, here she was!

She started forwards, bashful, eager, wondering where to begin, but suddenly it dawned on her that this was actually Marie. She threw her arms around her anyhow, but her intestines were heaving as that knowledge sank through her again. She rested her weight against the top of Marie's shoulder, and stayed there until she felt her daughter sway against the pressure.

Reluctantly, the mother stood up. Marie smiled. She

had a nice smile. The mother put her fingers against it, very lightly, then lost her train of thought. Marie vanished among the jagged edges, the patches of colour. The mother sat down again, and then stood up. Marie knelt on the lino, began to stroke the cat.

The mother trailed through the kitchen to the scullery, and opened the pantry door. It was evening, and convention dictated that one ate food in the evenings. The mother paused, momentarily, wondered about Marie. No, she had not looked particularly hungry.

Before her there were banks of tin cans; the mother braced herself and plucked one out, more or less at random. After the grandmother's initial forced start, the mother had quite gotten into the habit of shopping on a regular basis, and she tended to hoard tins of food like a squirrel in autumn. She turned the label towards her face. Heinz. Cream of Mushroom. She nodded, briskly, like the grandmother. Very well, it would be cream of mushroom.

The mother was feeling rather off-colour. It had been rent day; rent day never agreed with her constitution. The rent man had smiled at her, and had thrust his hand at her. The mother took it, thinking he meant to shake her hand. Instead, the rent man had planted a kiss upon it, luscious as mud. The mother had gone weak-kneed and vomity, even though the grandmother had been there too, and had sent him packing.

The mother turned the can sideways, turned her hand in case there should be a mark behind the fingers, before the back of the wrist: some greasy splurge, possibly oil coloured; possibly black. There was no lip print there, however, so bearing the can before her, she returned to the kitchen.

It rained past the kitchen window, patiently and without the slightest pause. The mother found herself distracted by it, gazing at the down motion of the drips, feeling the gravity drag on her eyes. The mother felt all of the pressures inside herself, that ambivalent force that kept her alive even though it was raining, even though she was a bad woman. The garden was drenched black, without stars.

The mother wondered at it, at the garden; that wilderness beyond the back door, where she pegged out grey flapping laundry; where the lawn was scrub and green-brown; where the gushing singing of the garden birds always made her afraid. She frowned at the thought of it, tried to connect that hollow patch of green and mud with the memory, when the grass had been seeded and mown; when deadheads were pinched away from any sign of illness. Her husband had been very proud of his garden and its spade-cut borders. He had grown monstrous green beans like arthritic fingers. The mother glanced at her own fingers then, as if to make a comparison, and discovered that they were wrapped around a tin of soup.

There were so many filthy plates in the sink that it took an age to acquire a spoon. There was no soup plate to find, not even one of the water stained melamine things they put the cat food in. Eventually, the mother wrenched the lid off with a tin opener, and sat at the table intending to eat it from the can. The surface was grey. It was glossy and unpleasantly thick. She pushed at it with the belly of her spoon and it bulged at the edges, more jelly than liquid. The mother could not bring herself to taste it, but sat still all the same, waiting to see if she would change her mind.

Suddenly, Marie went to bed. That child could sit so still. It was like owning one of those lizards that turns into the background and makes out it isn't there. The mother dipped her spoon into the can, pulled it back out, thickly coated. A slow drip bled down the outside.

It was so hard to think any more. The mice had taken the whole house over, treated her appallingly. They stared and hated and worked out their evil vengeance upon her every living second. She could hear them even when she was not listening, the itch and scritter of their lives, the merry dance they made. They wanted her to go mad. She was certain.

And there was the dining room. The cutlery skulked inside like a bad fairy's curse, ground its metal teeth from in there, scraped and grated through her nerves and frightened the mother half to death. These days she had to travel down the hallway with her fingers in her ears, just to preserve a little sanity. Sometimes she stopped them up with Andrex, but that only made the ghosts worse.

Yes, the ghosts. She was plagued by them. The mother saw rodent ghosts by the millions, stamped flat or mouse-trap-snapped or bitten in half by Thomas. Her husband's ghost was a proper menace; she was sure to break her neck on it one of these days. She often tripped right over him, arms and tea mug flying.

But the worst ghost of all was not dead, but planted out where the runner beans once crawled up bamboo sticks. That ghost did not skulk with the mice, with those staring, accusing hordes, or lie in a rigor mortis heap to trip unwary slippers. The other child's ghost hid from her; the mother remembered her licking up the washing up water, or rustling fearfully out of the way as the mother entered a room. There were times when the poor mother hardly knew what to do with herself.

The kitchen gathered dust around the mother, and the table mustered grease to itself in thin, miraculous waves. The filth took shape there, painted itself in microscopic layers; grew tacky, developed bogus tea stains that stopped where her elbows leaned.

She gasped to herself of her pain, a tiny unsurprised gasp, and then the mother played with her soup can again, revealing a clean circle where it had been masking the table. A very small patch experimented with texture, as though there had been sugar scattered in the wet. It worked rather well. The mother began to seep tears, and the grief welled up inside her until it seemed that her bones might just dissolve.

The mother's misery became complete for just a little time; for that moment she discovered what she was, beneath the carapace of dressing gown and cardigan and wrinkled woollen tights. She stared though herself in horror, and before she dropped dead at the sight, the queerest thing happened.

There was a rustling, like hundreds of consciences pressing together, and then love spread in through the door like the scent of a baking sponge cake. It was a panicky love, fervent and overblown and desperate. And though the love was not her own, it entered the mother's living tissues and skin pores and the soft capillary beds behind her nose. Love seeped through the mother's petticoat and the strangled roots of her hair. For love, like guilt, is of a muchness, and varies little between creatures.

There was a second of true glory as the mother threw her chair out behind her with a falling smack. She leaped from her misery into the perfect sinless rain and it cleansed her through and through with its coldness. The mother cantered like a foal along the broken garden path, with wordless sounds of joy and redemption streaming from her lips.

She bounded to the pit, to where her other child lay waiting to forgive her. A word, and it would be all done; the child (what was her name?), the child would beam into her face, and the mother would explain that it had all been a silly misunderstanding. They would embrace, and she would bear her joyfully indoors, and make tea and crumpets, and they would laugh over the little mishaps of yesterday.

The mother thought all this as the mud cleansed her skin and her slippers sucked on the wet ground. The love that surged inside her made her strong as she heaved that ancient door up from the mouth of the hole. The mother laughed aloud, for here was atonement: the meeting point of restitution and forgiveness.

Inside the pit was the wrong child, tiny and nasty in a dress of rotted threads. She was as small as the day she was buried, and knotted in a network of tendon-white roots. Initially, the mother had thought her dead, but then she turned her back a little, opened her eyes. Her hair was as black as her father's had been, and the mother remembered that she could see him in her, some hint of her husband in that jaw and chin. And when she turned her face towards her mother, she did not gaze enraptured, nor with delight, but just into her and through, at the wound in her, at the sin; the tar-thick treacle-thick creosote-thick glop inside her. The wrong child blinked her great dark eyes, and she knew her, knew it all.

How quickly the euphoria dwindled. In a minute more, the mother was just a silly, silly woman, grubbing in the dirt of the garden. She saw a movement from the house, and found Marie there, framed by the window and an avalanche of mice, and a howl of fury did no good at all.

The mother heaved and stamped and cursed until that wretched child was hidden again, then limped back inside to try and eat soup. After that she gave up on that too, and tramped muck all through the house, harvesting mouse-traps.

36
Mice

THIS IS HOW the mice discover *beneath*. One night and a whole eternal year and more after the great exodus, the mice have scurried and poked and searched the whole house loose. Every beneath has been explored, interrogated a thousand times; the mice cannot find their childling.

Beneath, the mouselings say, beneath is the place that she is, but there are no beneaths left from roof tiles to foundations. And yet, is it not ordained that the quest for the childling is the key to salvation? Generations have devoted their life spans to the endless quest for *beneath*. The god that does not wish to kill them will save saviours only.

The voodoo that the mice make is driving the frizz-haired mother quite spare. They are ever improving their techniques; they dig the bins for fingernails, for kitchen roll covered in sneezings, for Elastoplast strips that are stiff from sticking on cut fingers.

They can make the mother's guilt a solid thing; it crouches in the corners and smiles at her. Every jump of her nerves brings her closer to confession; the mice will wring out the hiding place of their childling, twist it out of her like juice from half an orange. They do not do it for cruelty. Their damnation balances, hangs like a mouse from a lampshade; it hangs on the childling's safety.

The mice have made their arrows everywhere: in the crawlspaces under the floors; among the hairs and lost coins inside the red armchair; under the mattress of the mother's bed. There is an arrow that points at her through the side panels of the bathtub; one that prods her as she fidgets and gnaws her nails on the loo. There is even a very small arrow glued to the underside of the kitchen table with strawberry jam. Wherever the mother goes, to sit, to knit, to cower, there is an arrow elbowing at her dripping insides, at the jagged extra skeleton she uses to hold her guilt in place.

Marie is watching the mice as they cascade along the tops of everything in the kitchen. They can see her too, the top of her head, the fragile crown of white-blond hair, the foreshortened trail of pigtails down her back.

From the sky, the kitchen is another prospect altogether, fat with greasy dust and littered with the flies that die on every unreachable surface. The top of the freezer, the curtain pole and the thick rim of the wall clock, all these bear a blackish film of muck. It is a universe of squares from up here, squares at different heights: the table, the hob and fridge and sink, and the padless seats of dining chairs.

The mother is down below them, trying to eat soup from the tin with a teaspoon. Directly above her, a mouse is dangling off the tinsel, feet stretched out, tail swirling. She inches along it, precarious, tiptoeing just this side of death.

Then it all goes wrong; one of the drawing pins slides out of a ceiling tile. The mouse flails against the empty air, desperate, wild with terror and the joy of all but dying. Then gravity makes a joke, pretends it cannot see her, and she flicks back onto the tinsel rope that is swaying loosely now, pinless at its middle. She streaks like a point of light, right along until she is safe among the cookbooks on the high shelf.

Meanwhile, the drawing pin, which is cheap and gone greenish with years of steam, falls slowly through the kitchen, turning as it falls. It plops among the mushroom fragments, and floats for just a second. Although the mother is gazing at it, her thoughts are in the garden, covered in mud, and the pin sinks in with nobody to notice it.

Marie sighs very heavily, and gets out of her chair. She flaps her mouth at the mother, makes some human speaking noises, and pecks a kiss at her face. She is going to bed. The mother gets a frantic look for a moment, but the cat is right next to her. He is a much more constant companion these days, since she took to securing him to the chair legs with string. He makes her feel secure. She has never glanced above her head to see the mice. She does not glance, just in case there are mice to see.

The tinsel-climbing mouse nips along the high things until she balances on the very top of the door. She drops to the floor on the other side. The tinsel-climbing mouse is feeling odd as she runs over the hugely patterned carpet. It seems that guilt, between creatures, is much of a muchness, one sort like another. And the greater the mother's suffering, the more the smaller guilts of mice are drawn out as well. The ghosts do not walk for her alone.

The tinsel-climbing mouse slows to stopping, listening in the hallway where the light is off. There is the sound of cutlery in the dining room; the sharp, slow-breeding lives of forks and knives, but the mouse believes she can make out something else besides. And suddenly it gels in the air. It is singing. It is a mouse, singing.

The tinsel-climbing mouse is reeling. She wants to turn her tail; she wants to flee, but her paws are placing themselves, the one before the others, until she is following the sound. There is singing; a mouse is singing, mournful and mad as a nightingale. And now there are other mice, pouring from every corner, shuddering and coiling forwards towards their terror. In a minute more there are hundreds, every one enthralled and horrified, come to take his place.

A little ghost is weaving in the flaming grate, drunkenly, as though it had nibbled rat poison. It is translucent, but white as talcum powder, streaked with berry-juice red. It is not the colour of mice, which are honest shades of filth: greys and browns and nearly-blacks. There are no white mice but one. The mouse that climbed the tinsel grinds her teeth and stares. Her joints have grown as fixed as matchsticks, rigid and impossible to bend. She can neither turn nor run away.

The albino's ghost is singing, singing of fire and knives, of disaster and damnation. Everything shall burn, says the burning ghost; every thing shall be licked up by fire. And then it throws its head up as if about to laugh, but squeals instead, cries as it is devoured by flames. And then its eyes are no longer as red as injuries. Its tail and jawbone and forelimb are not broken, and nobody made its skin leak blood upon its fur.

And although it is gone now, this vision, the mice all turn to one another and know what they have done. For in their hearts, for a second only, each of them knows that he might have done anything to make that singing quiet. They are utterly horrified. They wring their paws and they shake. It seems as though the universe might end.

But they are mice, and mice are driven from guilt to love, for that is how they have lived for a trillion years. That alone is the means to atonement. Their love wells up in a rush, like blood from a hurt, like milk on a stove when it boils over. Love and hope and the desperate need to rescue, leaks through the house like a beautiful kind of stink.

In a trice it has filled every crevice, spread through the

parlour and along the hall; drenched the kitchen, and made the frizz-haired mother feel very peculiar indeed. Before she knows what she has done, the mother abandons her soup and throws herself out of the back door, races to the pit where she has hidden her other child, claws and levers at the roof-door with her bare, claw-like hands. The mice feel the snap of her, the choke in her throat; and then the secret is out.

Before the mice have even got to the kitchen, before they have twiddled hurriedly along the high things, whilst Thomas yowls and swears from his table leg, before they have pressed their faces to the scullery window, they know. Their childling is *beneath*. She is beneath in the garden; beneath the garden, in that hellish half-real waste beyond the boundaries of home.

Marie is lying flat upstairs, hidden under thin layers of cloth, sleeping on her belly in her bed. Then the mice come, by tens and dozens, and they scamper on her pillow and the along the arch of her back. Their little sharp feet catch in the bedding and her unwound hair, and when she jolts upright she is afraid. Her eyes are round and bright as the mice scrabble around her, scratching for a way to make her understand.

The mice drag Marie's dolly from underneath the bed, pull it until it is lying, plastic-hard, on the carpet beside her colossal feet. They all stare up.

The mice haul on the edge of the bed sheet, try to cover the doll, but the sheet is too big so they use a sweater instead. The dolly vanishes. They all stare up.

Then the mice all strain together, and wrench the jumper away again. The doll is dragged along a few inches, but they struggle it free. They stare up. Marie is confused, panicking; water is oozing down her cheeks like a dripping tap. They catch her eye again, hold her gaze steady, and then rush in a sea towards the window. When she comes along with them, the mice could die for sheer excitement.

When she looks through the pane, Marie does not see any sight she comprehends. The evening is seething with rain, and her mother is crouching under the cherry tree and smothered in mud. There is a sort of door in the ground, levered up; its dented brass handle catches the light from the kitchen. Then her eyes catch in the light too; Marie sees them flash, very white against the loam-black dirt. And, perhaps the mother perceives that she is being watched, for suddenly the hex is ruptured. She comes to her senses, out there in the freezing cold; she smacks the door down again, stamps it all flat again and stands there, mud-smeared in the vegetable patch until Marie cannot bear to look any more.

37
Marie

I LAY IN bed for an awfully long time, lay with my eyes closed even though the light was on. I feigned sleep the way that smaller animals might feign death, pretended until I all but fell for my own false story. I imagined myself from above myself, crumpled on top of my eiderdown, nightdress rucked-up at one thigh, perched all over with mice; deeply and innocently unconscious. I pictured the scene to try and make it true; I breathed in long and slow, and out again, the embodiment of a creature asleep.

On my back, legs, the balls of my feet, the mice stood silently, gazing down. I felt the prickle of their faces looking, but I do not know what their expressions said. Perhaps they were disappointed in me; perhaps they were sad. I do not like to think that the mice were angry. I was only a child.

Whilst I lay on my bed, breathing against my grubby bedding, I heard the back door smack downstairs. And the mice all jumped; I felt the quiver of their feet against my skin, the spring and flex of so many fragile bodies. But I stood my ground, held my pose until those tiny weights hopped off me.

They brushed my ear and the down at the back of my neck with their whiskers; they snuffed and tutted and spent a while crowded round me, pulling gently at my hair and clothing in case they could heave me upright. Eventually they trickled away, and I was glad, for I was afraid and I could not face them.

It is no easy thing to determine when one is left alone by mice. They are terribly small; a mouse is made of brightness and cobwebs only, or so it seemed to me. I lay for an hour at least as my body grew greyish and cramped, trying to unpick the quietnesses of mice from a real absence of sound.

In the meantime, I heard my mother's tread on the staircase. She paused outside my door. She must have been holding Thomas; I could just make out his growling, low and distant like an aeroplane heard from the garden. She hovered at the door, and I thought she was going to come in. For one dizzy second my mother was going to come in and talk to me, and make me comprehend my life; she even pushed the door ajar.

But all she did was slip her hand inside and turn the light out. She made a dithering sound, an *Er* sound as though she had been about to speak, but before I had opened my eyes she was gone. Her bedroom was next to mine; I heard her door close like a tomb.

I turned in the dark, pillowing the palm of one hand underneath my cheek, feeling the cold in my feet as though it gathered there in drips. The dark was paralysing until my sight adjusted. Some nights lasted very nearly forever, and I would drag myself about the next day like something half dead. There was too much need. It was like trying to sleep in a poorhouse. Some nights I felt like one of the passers-by in the parable of the *Good Samaritan*, hobbling quickly by with his face turned sideways, not daring to slow his pace. It was not because he was a bad man. It was because he could not bear it. He had only a silver coin in his purse, and nothing of his own to speak of. What else might he do?

I tried to fall asleep, tried to dream. I tried to make myself dream of flying, or of finding some new and beautiful thing. I wanted to dream of stars, of all the things that I had seen in books. But all there was in my soul was us: our lives, our house. My grandmother had given me an anatomists' textbook, with glossy coloured pictures in red and grey and blue. That was the sort of dream for me, back then; intricate and forever bent in upon itself. I might dream of my own split self, or else my mother, organs trembling, stained with the rain and the garden mud. At that I sat up, opened my eyes wide. I would rather not sleep at all.

I did not want to wonder at my mother, wonder what she had been doing out there tonight. Perhaps I had always known, in truth. Yet still, I had a chance to scrape my ignorance together, use it to hide my head. She was gardening, planting those never planted seeds. She had lost her wedding ring, and was on her knees searching for it. My mother had been sleepwalking, doing something that meant nothing at all. She was burying a sparrow murdered by the cat. She was delirious. She was only mad. My mother was only a mad lady, grubbing in the dirt because she wanted to, nothing more.

It was useless. I discovered that I was going to cry, so I shrugged myself and picked among the clothes on the floor for socks to warm my feet. I put them on, although they did not match, and then I sat back on my bed, straight-spined, and I pushed my hair past my shoulders so that it flowed down my back. I tucked it behind my ears on either side; made myself calm; made myself ready. I dried my tears and my nose against my nightdress, and folded my self inside me, tidily. Then I crept from my room.

My calmness dissolved at one; I found my chest jamming before I even met the unlit stairs. Even so, I was brave; this was unlike me. I never left my room at night; I was terrified by the house without lights on, without people in it. I did not even dare sneak to the loo at night time: the toilet flushing became a roar that made me quail with nerves. Even the wauling of Thomas from my mother's room made me afraid before the dawn came.

So I astonished myself. I did not even have a reason for being out here where the shadows crawled the walls. I did not want to find the mice; I did not want my curiosity satisfied. The mice were surprised to see me; they all began forward, but caught each other's eye and halted, gazing at me with their whiskers jittering, hanging back. I hung my head, turned my face from them, and found there was a dim light in the kitchen. Gasping, relieved and nauseous, I rushed towards it.

There was a reek of boiling, like the stink of my mother's chicken soup, boiled up for days from the bones of the roast. The storm lamp was lit on the kitchen table, spreading out a hard white circle of light, highlighting every wound in the varnish.

My grandmother had taken off her glasses, was holding a needle very close to her face. It was curved. She had a wiry thread in her other fingers, an egg-white clear filament, like catgut or fishing line. She wet the tip in her mouth, prodded the end at the needle's eye. She missed, tried again. I stared, fascinated, wanting to scream.

My grandmother spoke without looking up. 'Well, come in, do, if you are coming in,' she said. She was not the slightest bit surprised to see me there. Obedient, I came close, did not know what to do; I sat at the table.

My grandmother had tailors' pins spread out on the table, hundreds of them in spike-tipped drifts. There were scissors laid out too, blades open, still as still. I jumped at the sight; my grandmother glanced towards me, blind-eyed, unfocussed without her spectacles. 'Don't worry dear. They wouldn't dare.'

And it seemed that my grandmother could read my face, glasses or not; eyes or not, even. My grandmother could have read my face even if I were not there. I began to shake; perhaps I was cold. The garden was a black square at the window. I could not see a thing; not even the sky; not even a moon. I began to pick at a fingernail.

There was a bottle beside my elbow, a tiny bottle like the ones vanilla essence comes in; picked too early, not ripe but small and sour. There was a noise coming from it, a bird noise, a high, hysterical trilling. As secretly as I could, I dropped my head towards it, cocking my ear, listening intently. It appeared to be entirely empty; the essence label had been steamed off and replaced with another in my grandmother's scratchy writing. 'REGULUS IGNICAPILLA'. It meant little to me.

My grandmother threaded her needle and pulled through an arm's length of line. Then she impaled her pin cushion and turned to me. There were wings laid out in front of her, put together liker hands at prayer, heart-breakingly small. I stood up, backed from the table, and filled the kettle so as to have a purpose for getting up. I do not think that my grandmother was fooled. As the water heated, I sauntered to the window, as casually as I could. I tried to see the garden, see the spot my mother had been in; then I cursed myself, reminded myself that I did not want to know. My grandmother got up too and went to the chopping board.

'Marie,' said my grandmother, 'Marie, make a wish!' She came right to my face then, and held out a tiny wishbone, glistening with fat. I put my hands behind my back for safety. The thought of snapping that poor fragile thing, still ragged with meat, horrified me. And yet, my grandmother smiled me a warning, proffered it at me once again. A gift is something one must never refuse. A gift is a test of gratitude. I forgot all about the window.

Gingerly, I grasped the pathetic little bone in my fingers, whilst my grandmother twisted and pulled. I had never seen a wishbone so minute. I could barely hold it. It broke.

'Did you make a wish?' she asked. I nodded, my eyes full of tears, but I lied. At the edges of the room, the mice had drifted in; as I noticed them, they nodded. Perhaps they had got it, caught that wish as it wrenched from the bone. My grandmother turned away to poke in her saucepan. It probably continued to rain, but for the moment I had forgotten what I was doing. I made a cup of tea and plodded back to bed with it, leaving it to go stone cold and filmy by morning.

38
The Mother

THE MOTHER LEANED on the doorjamb, drenched right through and filthy. She sighed and looked back down the garden, at the shabby lawn and the vegetable patch beyond. The soil at the cherry tree's feet was churned and trodden as though it had been mauled with a mechanical earthmover; as though it had been mauled by grave robbers.

The mother's heart was jamming; she lingered for a little while, over-breathing and twitchy. The grandmother appeared in the doorway with her lizard smile, and the mother staggered past her.

It was too much. The mother wrung her fingers and threw herself into finding mice. The bloody mice. It always came down to them, the long tailed wretches, and now they had turned Marie's head against her. Lord knows what her daughter had seen from the window. It was always their fault. The mother found herself revived by anger and almost laughed as she raced through the house, finding traps, unpeeling each tiny body for her bundle.

When the traps were all empty and reset again, the mother went to feed the cutlery. After such a trying evening, she was a little distracted and actually stepped inside the dining room door, staring in numb wonder as if she had never seen the world with her own eyes before.

She had to hold her breath as she did so, for the smell of mice was as strong as turpentine; the mother gazed at the dining room where her husband had used to play his piano at three in the morning; where he used to keep his whisky locked up with a key. She gazed at the floor, at the soiled carpet, at the blood-black stain against it, the outlines muzzied by the droppings and skin snips of mice.

She regarded that silhouette, the leavings of that man; she tried to hate him. But lord, there was nothing there to hate, not a scrap, not even shoe leather. The mother pressed at her cheekbone, then her belly and the old crack of her ribs, tried to feel a hurt, some little trace of his fist, but there was nothing left to pain her, not even a residual ache. She wished there was, some small proof that she was not a bad lady. If only he had left her a scar, then she would definitely have been justified. She had been justified. Really she had. The mother held her face in her hands and tried to believe herself.

All this time, the cutlery had been sensing her there, sniffing with their sharp edges and points at the scent of her body; the honeysuckle soap stuck under her wedding ring; the gorgeous smell of her carpet slippers.

The mother jumped right into the air at the first snip. A lucky dig by a cake fork jutted right through the rubber edge of the sole, bit the flesh and bit it very deep. She howled, danced in the air and threw herself back towards the door, kicking and flinging her feet as though she had stood on a fire.

She was lucky; most of the cutlery had closed in on the mice, which were killed already and no bother to catch. She hollered like a trodden cat and leaped to safety, wrenched the door shut, shoved the barricade back and stared at the blood seeping through the side of her slipper. The cake fork took some force to dislodge; all of this seemed to make the colours about her go dangerously bright, and the mother was forced to sit awhile on the stairs until the giddiness passed.

The grandmother appeared at the mouth of the kitchen and gave her a look that was entirely without sympathy. She vanished back inside as the mother wobbled to her feet and limped off to find where she had last placed Thomas. In the kitchen, the grandmother nodded, snatched up a bottle of vinegar from the fridge and stalked back to the hall where the cake fork was turning slowly in circles, tasting the air. The grandmother poured it with vinegar and nodded once more in satisfaction as it began to whine. Then she opened the door and shoved it back into the dining room with her foot, and replaced the barricade. She crossed the mother in the hallway, who had remembered that the cat had been last attached to the cold tap in the scullery sink.

The poor mother found herself in floods of despair as she untied him, as she limped through the grey-blue fields of ghosts on the staircase. She hesitated outside her bedroom door, beside Marie's, but it was hopeless trying to explain, she thought. What could she do but lie, but talk herself in knots?

And the naughty thing deserved no such explanation anyhow, having left her light burning at this time of night. The mother scolded her in her mind, but found her face softening almost at once. She turned off the light very quietly, so as not to wake her. Perhaps she would think it all a dream. The mother risked a nervous smile. Perhaps she would. She closed the door.

It might be best to lie low for a little while, so that Marie did not think anything untoward had occurred. The mother furrowed her brow. If everything continued in a perfectly natural manner, then she must surely conclude that the mother had nothing at all to hide, to explain. This made sense.

Yes. She would lie low. The mother renewed her grip on Thomas, who had begun to shift inside her grasp, and then she turned and limped to the bathroom with him. She felt very much better with the door locked, at least until she looked in the mirror and saw her smeared face.

She remembered what had happened then, for she was plastered in guilt and night-time mud on her arms, neck, in her hair. The mother remembered that she was injured as well, and her foot suddenly hurt terribly. She would most likely contract tetanus.

The mother removed all her clothes as the cat glowered at her from the windowsill. She poured an enormously full bath, scented and bubbled and salted and oiled with fragrances of almond blossom, and wild rose, and wild musk, and Head and Shoulders, and Lifebuoy soap and Ajax. It overflowed a little as she lowered her scalding body in. In the water the mother became much more innocent, more wronged than sinner; blood clouded the water for a time, until the fork-bite clotted.

When she was clean and sneezing from the talcum powder, the mother sat upon the toilet, naked as a newborn, and decided that she did not care to face the world. At any rate, her dressing gown was ruined, and her poor slippers looked as is they might never be the same again. So she wound her heel with bandage, which she tied in a knot as there wasn't any safety pin, and she crept from the bathroom with the air against her flesh. She had to kick Thomas back inside, and then she dumped her dirty clothes in the bottom landing.

Then, bare-naked and secretive, the mother flitted from room to room, gathering things. She had to make several trips. By the time she was done, the talcum powder was gathering into a kind of paste from the sweat at her armpits and back.

Half an hour later, and after a protracted struggle with

an extension lead, the mother stood in the bathroom and arranged her little home amid a fading fug of steam. The bath became a lovely snug bed, padded with an eiderdown and an armful of bedspreads.

The plug flex ran beneath the door and attached at her end to a kettle. Her knitting lay like abandoned spaghetti in the corner, and the mother balanced her print of *The Crying Boy* on top of the medicine cabinet.

The collection of carrier bags from the base of the red chair was installed beside the toilet. The mother even draped the lambskin over the cistern but it kept dropping off. She tried to sit Thomas upon her knee, and managed for a time, until his clawing got too much for her naked skin. But it was fine, for then she remembered the project that she had planned some weeks ago and then not carried through.

The mother rummaged among her bags until she found a packet of fags. It was wrapped in shiny cellophane; beneath it was a block of sumptuous cardboard gold. She marvelled at it, pushed her fingertips against the embossed letters. *B&H.* It seemed such a comfort to the women at the post office. She was sure that she would like smoking.

The mother balanced a cigarette between her lips, and lit it with a cough that brought her close to sickness. But she persevered; over days she ate cold beans from cans and drank black tea after the milk turned solid. And in the meantime, she learned to smoke like a professional, sleeping in her very own rhythms of day and night, and sitting very quietly when the door handle was tried.

There were knockings that reached a peak on the first and second days, but after that things turned blissfully quiet, until a strongly worded note from the grandmother was rammed beneath the door. There was a period of bluff and counterbluff, during which the mother realised that the cat was looking rather thin. The death blow came when the extension lead was pulled out of the wall. The mother knew very well that a life without tea is not worth living, and so she was finally levered out of her beautiful cocoon.

She realised as she crept into the landing that the rent man was here.

39
Knives

THE CAKE FORK turns slowly round and round as it suffocates. Perhaps corrosion makes it feel a kind of pain. The tines curl up and then unfurl like metal tendrils.

They respire as lungless things do, with their keen edges, with their very sharpness. Rusted scissors are corpses. This is how such creatures are made: they live through their surface, through their shine; they are a little like trees, whose only life is found in the skin, the wood of the trunk being dead at heart.

The carbon dioxide that cutlery lives upon is inhaled at the glittering parts, the dangerous parts, at the microscopic pits in their surface that might be mistaken for flaws of manufacture.

These spiracles take in air, and allow feeding as well, through a complex process of absorption. It is blood that keeps a blade edge or fork point sharp. Cutlery chops and slices prey to mush, to a poor sad soup of what it once was; and when it is liquid, they drink it up.

The cake fork is whining, a skinny, inaudible shriek that gives the house the horrors. It will take some little while to die, until every pore is rotted up with corrosion. The others do not care two pins.

40

Mice

A CONURBATION IS developing on the high places of the kitchen, a shantytown of mice, a cosy slum. They scuttle along the picture rails and turn the emulsion grubby with the rubbings of their fur. They sprinkle the cooker hood with piddle and their tiny neat droppings speckle the sugar bowl. They thieve the mother's dishcloths to furnish nests; this is cruelty beyond the poor mother's endurance, and so she ignores it altogether.

Up on the high shelves, the frizz-haired mother stores her cookery books. They are thumbprint stained and gummed together with batter from drop-scones and mock béchamel sauce. When the recipes escaped their bindings, she covered them with flower patterned Fablon that is now itself lifting off in cracks. The pages are a brandy-snap yellow, and brittle like the wrappings off a mummy. They have not been leafed through for many years.

Behind their splitting spines there is a nest of children, pink as sugar mice, each spooning his way among his siblings for his mother's colossal warmth. Their mother is a dark mouse, all but black, and she has just come juttering back to her offspring, having heard the laughing and pain of a mouse as white as icing sugar. The mother shivers and inspects her mouselings, nuzzles and tastes each one to see if he is a monster; she stares very hard at the brush of fur that each is beginning to make with his skin. They are browns, greys, the bluish tones of dust-fleece. None of them is albino.

They are unhappy; their mother left them all alone in an empty world. They cry a little, whimper like mouse-children will, for they have not yet mastered the language of mice, the etiquette of squeak and small gesture. Mother and young comfort each other.

The heart of the dark mouse is stammering with love and apprehension. She nurses her young, promises herself that she could never murder. Mice could never murder. Never but once. The mouselings drop asleep and she curls around them, forms the eternal circle of the mouse. She is pregnant; already she can feel the fidget of the embryos inside her. The mice in her womb are full of her own adrenaline, fearful and half formed. In time they grow still.

One little foetus, at once a mouse and not a mouse, for she is hardly made at all, flickers her spine and sees with her great budding eyes, sees the whole world without the slightest comprehension. And understanding nothing at all, this almost-mouse is gazing at the house, at the other mice who are standing around in groups, wondering. She sees the mousetraps and the awful tear of cutlery as it gorges on the broken mice from traps.

She sees the frizz-haired mother in the bath, wincing in water so hot that it makes her eyes stream, and Marie who is sitting up slowly in bed, wiping her cheeks with her fingers. She sees the whole world, for the house is the world; she even has a glimpse of the nowhere beyond it, the land past the carpet pile and the homely stink of home.

This almost-mouse can all but see the garden, but house mice are not made for such things any more, and the more she is formed, the less these visions intrude. Infants in the house are born with an inkling of their destiny, for the childling has made her way into their very DNA. But the worlds of mice are soft as toothpaste; as the childling has evolved her way into them, the world beyond home has petered away. Gardens belong to some other kind of mouse, a lesser, older, braver sort.

Mice fear open spaces almost as much as death. An open space equals death, or it might as well; without their corners and scurry-holes, a mouse is as good as killed already. The almost-mouse sees the garden and flails at it, these wastes of mud and green.

There have been mice in this house for a hundred years and more; a pregnant mother stowed away in the first sack of barley that came, back when the house was a new-created being, with distemper walls and servants in the attic.

The mice here are descended from that ancient Eve, who herself came from medieval stock that thrived and thieved in the village. House mice dwell in houses; this is what they are for. They creep and scrat beside the feet of people, and the outside fades in their minds to a nowhere.

The almost-mouse drifts now, not quite sleeping, for she is too young to sleep or wake, but in her slippery nest she is content. The mouselings that nestle up against their mother are content among their tatters of string and toilet roll. Their mother is not content. The dark mouse dare not close her eyes.

Those living in the high places all sit in this manner, neither sleeping nor feeding nor mating. They have found their childling at last, but she might as well be on the moon. They have shown Marie, have made her see, and now she has turned her face to the side and will not look at them.

So they came away from her, with their heads down low and their souls too full to bear. And yet. And yet they have found her, their only one, but oh, what a finding; their joy is tinged with futility, until it tastes like a gnawed penny. Everything is fused with the singing mouse, with his bitter chanting. 'The house will burn,' he says, 'and there shall be nothing remaining.' But they may be saved through the childling, if only they might save her. This is a huge and baffling night.

As they sit and fret, the back door is heaved open and the grandmother stalks inside with a child's rock pool net in one hand and a storm lamp in the other.

Now, the mice are usually indifferent to the grand-mother and her doings from the garden, as a person might be largely indifferent to the substance of the ground beneath their feet. Unless one actually stops to consider it, such things seem hardly relevant to everyday existence.

Now it is relevant. Their lives and deaths, the fate of the whole world rests beneath the vegetable patch. Only res-cuing might stave off judgment. Only the childling. They start, as the grandmother bustles around the kitchen, and they breathe at the scents of witchery and feather. They gawp in horror as she divides up a firecrest, piece by tiny struggling piece.

It is real. The garden must be a true place of a sort, for this poor bird is surely a real creature. They see it bared quite naked, until nothing remains of it but fear. And it seems as real as they are, all nerves and knots and jumping blood. For a long while the mice in the high places stare, as the mice that are in the parlour and the hall freeze still and let Marie pass silently between them.

For a time she stands, and sits, and stands again and looks about her, and she is so hugely small and sad that the mice feel bad for her, sorry that they have made her suffer so. But their need, the childling's need, are so very great. What else might they do? Presently she goes away, and then even the grandmother packs her jars and boxes on the top of the fridge, marches outside.

The mice flip floorwards, and then they scale the table legs and sweep its flat square top with their whiskers. Nothing remains of the firecrest but the terror in the kitchen air.

They look from the kitchen and the scullery windows; the mice gaze through the dwindling rain at the space beyond home; they shudder. Then one brave mouse finds that the hope and futility overpowers him, and without a glance behind, he forces his body beneath the draught-bitten door. The others hold their paws, grind their jaws, stare desperately at him from the windows; he is dwarfed to nothingness by that brutal patio. He is a tiny trail of bones and hope, scurrying towards darkness as the ceiling-sky, too high up and quite bizarre, throws water down at him.

He scurries six feet before the rain blinds him, before the blackness of outdoors blinds him. And then he is soaked and chattering with fear, and it seems to him that the whiteness and the talons and the saucer-eyes of the owl belong to the night and the garden's own body. He sits up at the very last moment, sits up on his haunches and lifts up his paws to the ancient god of field mice. Then he learns what it is to fly with owls.

The almost-mouse flinches in her warm orb of water and the dark mouse, her mothers, blinks from behind the *Farmhouse Cookbook*. The others, stark-eyed at what they have seen, turn to one another. They must ask Marie again. They must make her care. They will make her help them.

41

Child

THAT DOOR DID not seal the pit; not quite. There is a long, slant-sided gap that is open to the raw sky. It continues to rain until it rains itself right out, until the clouds clot and thicken and then heal right over. And the flowers that should have been growing all this while, seem to find a sudden springtime, a nocturnal, secret springtime in the dark.

And somehow it is May. The calendars had told the truth after all, for here are all the flowers at once, wisteria and daisies and peonies and Love-in-a-Mist in its cloud of uncertain green. There are even roses of sleepy-headed velvet, woken too early.

While there is yet no eye to witness, the fragrance of flowers turns the night luscious, scented and rich enough to induce amnesia. The air becomes very still. The cherry tree holds its breath, grips the soil very tightly.

Inside her nest of roots, the wrong child is awake, has woken as cherry stones do before they sprout. She lies on her side, but she has turned her face to the sky, and it seems to her as though the world is blinding-bright. She has lived under earth so long that all she can make out at first is the dazzle of the moon, which is straining through the cloud now, which is silvering the garden and the violated soil.

The cherry tree is mourning, for the wrong child is germinating; for it had grown to love her and it knows that their long quietness has ended, or changed at least. The wrong child, who is childling to mice, feels the air above her body and finds that she remembers it a little, the way that dreams linger a minute in the mind before one truly wakes.

And her eyes, which had been fused quite shut have opened, and her pupils have found out how to contract, to allow the brilliance to come to her gradually. She blinks slow and licks her lips, tastes mud and sweat there, recalls that she has a face, a mouth. The wrong child smiles, and her teeth glisten like treasure.

It takes a long time for the wrong child to sit, for every limb and finger must uncurl like ferns, must stretch gently, find their proper place and shape. All this while, the flowers flower, and their fragrance is as rich as rot, warm and dark and beautiful.

The wrong child has a throat, and lungs that fill with air and let it out. She flats her palm upon her chest, feels her little ribcage push and pull. She is lithe and slight as a stem, as a small creature, as a mouse perhaps. She blinks and blinks and wonders at the sky above her head, at the mouth of this pit that was once her tomb, her dreadful prison, before it became her home; nest; the cherry tree's womb.

The garden birds, which sleep at night, are woken by the silence, by the lowering fragrance of lilies, by the sudden lushness of air. They are confused by it; they toss their wings and watch each other's faces. They chitter each to each, and although it is the law that the songbirds report each new or unusual thing, somehow none of them moves. They are ashamed of themselves for their betrayal of Marie. Moreover, they are fascinated, for here is something not seen before, not for many generations of birds.

The secret beneath the ground has woken, and this is what she has turned out to be.

For a time the wrong child feels balanced oddly, head skyward; the blood in her swirls in a different patterns, for she has not sat upright in years. But she adjusts, and in a little while longer the wrong child struggles to her feet like a tender shoot, like a newborn creature, and lifts her head to try and see more than the sky, for she is still in her hole. How does she climb out? The birds all crane their necks to see, as the wrong child wraps her fingers in the cherry tree's roots and finds the surface of the earth by inches. In a long slow minute she is there, puddled in the moonlight, resting among the gorgeous breath of flowers. Perhaps they bloom for her only.

The birds edge towards her, until she is surrounded by a nodding ring of faces. They shall not betray her, though the consequence may be very hard. She is an innocent creature.

The skin of the wrong child grows warm, and her clothes, such as they are, begin to rag away from her in tatters. Her hair clothes her back and shoulders, as did the hair of the very first girl in the first imperfect garden.

Last of all, the wrong child's mind unfurls. The thoughts inside her are vague, unfocussed; she does not seek in corners for memory because she has forgotten how to do so. For now, the surface of the earth, the springtime and the moon are plenty enough.

The wrong child creeps forwards, watching every molecule of the night as it evolves into the grey of nearly-dawn. Before the sun has risen, she is gone, past the lawn and over the blown-down fence and off between the trees and scrub beyond.

42

Mice

OUR HOUSE TRIED to warm its skin in the sudden sunshine of spring. I could feel its low grumble of pleasure, but at night the joists would click and groan as heat leached into the clear, star-infested skies.

Today, I basked like a cat on the front doorstep, absorbing the light with my face, protected from the wind by the low stone wall. That wall was studded with ammonite fossils, their gentle shells trapped between mortar and stone like some cruel joke.

I had avoided the back garden for days, even the concrete patio, even the backwards facing windows. I kept my eyes downcast as I poked in cupboards for food, or boiled pans of water for drinks.

My mother was in the bathroom and she would not come out. She had taken the kettle and the teapot with her, but somehow forgotten the strainer; the old leaves in that did not last long. After a few brews they would not stain the water, not even a little bit, not even if boiled right up. So I took to drinking Oxo cubes, dissolved in a mug, because there was nothing else. I crept about the house as though someone had died, and kept every single light burning at night, for the darkness made me timorous.

And during the day I often came out here. It was my new habit, for at the front door I was largely free of mice.

It was a risk; if the door was to snap shut behind me I should be trapped as I hadn't a key. Then I might have had to slink around to the back door. At the thought of the garden with its churned mud I swallowed hard, held my belly in my arms.

The poor mice. They followed me everywhere I went like lost things, tense and quivering and desperate. When I slept at night they watched me; they dogged my moments and hours, not with malice, not even with accusation in their faces. They grew haggard, their fur all rumpled as though they had been drenched with dishwater. When I moved, even a little, they would all leap cowering to their feet, ready to follow me. Never would I move towards the back door; the disappointment hollowed the mice.

I had come out with a book of my grandmother's. It was written over with some strange Cyrillic script that I could not read, but the illustrations were mesmerising. A pretty, flower clad child danced in the arms of a man with wings; he was as lean as the girl was beautiful. She was plucking a feather from his finger, with a queer expression as though she balanced between innocence and a fearsome kind of knowledge. I gazed at her in the caustic light; could not tell if she was happy.

At any rate, it was too bright for reading. Beneath the sun, the pages were transfigured, so intense a white that text and line vanished as I watched, scattered my vision with purple oblongs. I blinked rapidly, and they reproduced against my eyelids like germs, dozens of them, slowly fading.

The track from our house to the main road was steep and pitted, almost too narrow for a car. I heard the sneer of an engine and a magpie went shouting up the lane, then the rent man drove up the gate and inched his way between gatepost and thorns. I watched him hunch his face with concentration, saw him wince his way inside. And then he looked up and caught my eye; he slapped on a friendly-uncle smile and winked.

The rent man was a round, red-faced man in his forties, and he exuded a sort of abnormal jollity. When I was very small I had looked forward to his visits for the lollipops that he kept in his pockets.

I clambered warily to my feet as he approached, the book in my hand, and I squinted up at him through that blinding morning. He was perspiring as he walked toward me, and he came up very close.

'Why, hello there young lady.' For a second he rested his huge meaty hand on top of my head. Sweat pricked out on my scalp. I kept my face composed and did not move from the door. He shaded his eyes to look, first at me and then into the dark chink of hallway beyond the front door. 'Is Mummy home?' There was a silence.

'My mother,' I said with deliberation, 'is in the bath.' No, I did not care to disturb her. No, my grandmother was not in right now. The rent man said that, oh, she did talk after all, and that he was afraid that little Marie wasn't his friend any more, and that as she was such a good girl, perhaps she would like a wee sweetie. He leaned back to rummage in his pocket, and a soft roll of fat sank underneath his chin.

I panicked, glanced behind me and heard the rustle of mice. I said that I would go and check. The rent man shucked my cheek as I spoke and ran one pigtail loosely through his hand before I could turn away. The rent man told me that I had lovely long hair, and the blondes most definitely had more fun. At that he winked again. I caught a glimpse of a very odd look on his face before I got away.

The rent man followed behind, so close that he bumped into me when I stopped at the parlour door. I caught a flash of movement, and then it banged shut. At the same time, Thomas tore down the hall and between my legs, and I had to throw my weight sideways to avoid treading on him.

Before either of us could quite recover, my mother came beaming out of the parlour, wearing nothing but a winter coat that she seemed to have just snatched off the rack. She did up the buttons without looking at them with her eyes fixed against his, startled as a deer's.

The rent man walked past her and spread himself in an armchair without being invited, and I bolted upstairs as though I had just escaped with my life. On the landing bookcase my grandmother's workbasket lay open, and with a sort of anger I grabbed up the big steel scissors that she kept there.

When I got to my room I closed the door to block out the voice of the rent man from the parlour. My mother's replied were inaudible, so it was as though he just sat in there talking to himself. He laughed a lot.

I am not sure why I cut off my hair. It was almost an act of defiance, although I was not a child given to defiance. I suppose I must have been angry, or afraid; looking back this way it is not always easy to tell.

On the spur, facing away from the mirror, I lifted the scissors to the line of my jaw with a dark thrill of nerves. The plaits took some time to munch through, and then they fell away, one and then two, like dead things.

All that there was in my head at that moment was to free myself, the way a cat is left with a mouthful of feathers as the bird flags into the air, safe. It struck me too, that they would make a fine gift for the rent man. I might have even smiled. I wrapped the coils around the scissors and left them in the workbasket for my grandmother instead. And then my defiance deserted me and I hardly knew what to feel.

I wandered back to my room slowly, raking at my shorn

head, feeling the thickness and spike of the hair. It was an odd coming of age; at the time it passed in a blur, barely comprehended at all. I stood a while without aim, and then I sank to my backside and sat on the carpet, palms braced to the dirty pile of it.

Then the mice came. They came on careful feet, gently, as though they came with a painful thing to say. Mice crept slowly up to my feet, my sitting knees; the mice climbed into my lap and marvelled at my hair. In the end, I bent myself to the floor to let them see. They rummaged their paws in it, sniffed and whispered. When they had finished, I raised myself to them and looked at the mice, looked properly, face to face to face. I opened my arms to the mice and they clambered to my shoulders, to the cup of my lap. We were sad; we were all terribly sad.

And then it was as though they planted a thought in my head; a thought like a thorn, small and brown and sharp as sharp. And as I caught their eyes again, I found something in those mice that I had never seen, something ruthless, where love becomes so needful that it finds itself able to wound. I was afraid of the mice then, just a little, but suddenly I was dragged along by a memory, or else it was dragged out of me, with a hurt that left me gasping.

I was lonely. I was so, so alone. I was a little child and I had lived my life all by myself when I should not have done. A part of me had been torn right away, and I knew it only right then, I think. The mice all made me suffer, scraped at that raw patch, bit at it and made me suffer. 'Do you see?' they seemed to say, 'Do you see?' And they twisted my head towards the stairs, and they made me see my mother through the floor and the wall, standing before the rent man with her painted-lady smile.

This is what the mice showed me. There was a child once, I had seen her right where I sat now; not my mother or grandmother but another child, me almost, drawn as if with the left hand, the outlines webbed and tangled. I grasped at the glimpse of her, for this memory was very old and dim as cellophane, splitting as I pulled at it, creasing and tearing and turning to nothing. And when the image faded I was so lonely that I could have died. And the mice, the mice were actually pleased, jumping up and down in glee.

I stood up very gradually so as to allow them time to scramble off, or else cling on tight to my clothes, and finally, reluctant and down at heart, I went to the window and looked out down the back yard, towards that hole in the garden, towards some secret that I had no stomach for unmasking. I was very old that day.

43

Mice

WHEN THE MICE rush up to find Marie, they discover her looking strange, different, as though she had been attacked. She sits upon the floor in the room where she sleeps, and she is shaking, quivering like a balloon whisk. When they discover her first, they are aghast as though she were a mouse that had lost her tail.

They crowd around in sympathy; nuzzle at the stumps of her hair, checking for wounds, checking that it is clean, that all will heal correctly. There is no blood, but even so her pain is swirling in the air around her and it grates on their whiskers.

The mice regard Marie and they think of their childling, their beautiful giant, who is hidden, who is *beneath* in the garden. True, Marie's eyes are only blue, and her hair does not resemble broken coal for its blackness and shine, but still there is a beauty to her. They are fond of this one.

And yet. Their childling is in that hole, and mousehood must be redeemed at any cost. So it is that cruel and ashamed, the mice muster themselves one last time and pray, plead with the god that does not wish to kill them. The fairy lights are quite forgotten now, but in their hearts and among the cobwebs in corners, the god that does not hate them watches still.

The faith of the mice, their love and pleading, and even their desperate, reluctant unkindness, all this they hold like pawsful of currants and then they push it at Marie.

When the memory comes to her it is very cruel, and the mice are no better at that moment than cats, for Marie has no sharpness within her, no malice to justify such violence. And when it comes, the mice feel it too; they have their first true glimpse of their childling for a hundred billion years. They can only focus it for a second, this projection, but Marie sees it, stretches her fingers toward it, flinches at it, recalls everything that she knows. The mice all urge her on, beg and cajole and whimper her on, and they see as Marie recognises that long-ago child.

As do the mice. They see her, as beautiful as the day they lost her, her mouth that is not made for speaking, her massive fragile back. The mice remember the birthmark on her neck, and the warmth of her beneath their small clawed feet. They see her and find that they know her every inch.

Their fur crackles with love; they see the embryo of knowledge in Marie's face and their joy is strung like tendons in a joint, tight. They gaze at her, will her not to be afraid; not to be afraid as they are.

The mice hang on with their toes as Marie gets to her feet, almost the size of a whole sofa, and they find that they remember this also, and how to twirl their tails in the air so as to balance. And they go to the window and look together at the garden, at its fearful openness, haunted with owl gods and stoat gods and cats.

Last night, the owl dropped from the sky; it scalded the minds of the mice. When the watchers at the scullery window saw it, white as a saucer, white as a moon, the mice were shaken to the bones. They had gazed, unable to flinch, as death herself fell like a lampshade through that ghastly air and taught a mouse to fly.

There are deaths of traps and Thomas; there is a kind of shining death with metal points and scraping edges, but there are is also a new death, the death of the garden. And surely this death is worse, for where does it strike but in nowhere itself?

To die in the house, to die at home, why this is a natural thing, a proper thing, as mice are made for dying. But what of being carried away by a bird, of flying into emptiness on pale and whispering wings? To where might his soul scurry; into what eternal corner or skirting-hole? Perhaps he is unmade by it, an unhomed thing, a piteous thing, floating in a heaven without a ceiling or walls or curtain pole.

The mice that sit upon Marie's shoulders stare through the sunlight, strain and gaze in case they might see him in the sky, in case they might even now rescue his poor dead self. He is lost.

Now, one mouse who is hanging off the sleeve of Marie's dress, alters her grip and shins right up her arm to the collarbone. Then she points her nose up, stares at the vast foreshortened jaw line, the underside of chin, the soft lobe of Marie's ear. And she wonders as she stares, if this great creature is enough to walk in the garden. She might be colossal, but even she is made tiny by the scale of the outside, by the tree, by the desert-land of patio. The mice wish that they had paid better attention, watched and studied this child before it came to matter so dearly.

They have seen her on the front doorstep. They have seen her jumping her skipping rope on the concrete patch, but what of the distance beyond it? Perhaps they are coaxing her towards her death. Perhaps she will be taught to fly by owls. What if she is taught to fly by owls? What of her fate, or that of the mice upon her shoulders?

But after that it does not matter, or else it is a fear that is beyond them, for the giant is walking. They crowd into her sleeves, her pockets and the short thicket of her hair. They nestle against the gap of air between her collar and throat, and they ride in strange procession from the room, followed by a shivering cascade of mice.

They flick and thud right down the staircase, past the parlour door where the frizz-haired mother is crying. Marie gasps at the sound; they feel the swell of her ribcage, the heaviness of a thoraxful of air. And then they all turn, slowly, through the kitchen and then to the back door.

The mice are thrilled and petrified; they cower and peep as she heaves the door open. Those upon the floor hang behind and crowd to the window. The sky is warm as a water tank and deafening with the reeks of hundreds of flowers; with the alien scent of mud, and the fluidness of the wind that stirs it all together. They hold themselves steady. They do not faint.

Marie does not faint either, but beneath the mice she sways and slows, glances from ground to sky. At that, the mice all start upwards in terror, but there are no owls. They close their eyes and pray.

Marie is sweating, making water stand out against her skin. It tastes like salt; they lick her like a newborn, try to make her safe. And she treads with weary pace from concrete to weedy grass, towards the place that is *beneath*. Before *beneath*, the earth is churned right up; her feet sink a little with every step.

Oh, but the hole is empty! Marie stops, dwindles to stopping before it, silenced and astounded. It is empty. It is just a pit in the earth, and a door from a house, on its face and half pushed sideways. There is a little rain puddle in the bottom; there are knots and networks of roots; there are rags of plastic and a cocoa flask.

There is nothing more. There is no childling. She is not there at all. She has abandoned *beneath*. She has been taught to fly by owls, or else the mother has devoured her.

Marie crouches down then, and the mice all teeter, balance, cannot believe what they see. The mother has done this. Marie stretches up again, five feet into the sky, and she plods away towards home where the world is real.

At the house, the door is still open. Marie starts to go through it, but then that sharp-eared demon makes a dash past her with a half-alive mouseling squealing in his jaws. Thomas is free of the mother and her lengths of string, and he is off to the garden to tear his victim into fragments.

As they tread into the kitchen, girl and mice and all, the frizz-haired mother is there already, arms crossed in front of her, each hand gripping the opposite elbow. There is a cigarette jammed between two fingers, stripping a thread of smoke to the ceiling. Her eyes are the gaps between worlds. Her mouth is clamped quite shut; the lips invisible.

Marie stands before her; the mother opens her arms, sucks on the cigarette and lowers her eyelids as the smoke billows from her nose. The mother is on fire. Marie stands, blinks, and makes a break for it, clattering up the stairs as the mice hang on for dear life.

The mother makes a kind of roar and pounds along the hallway after them, but halts at the foot of the staircase. Marie slams the door and throws herself upon her bed; if it were not for the quick wits of mice, some might have been squashed. But mice are fast as fleas, and Marie is slower than a cat.

They lurk on the mattress as her shoulders heave. The mice are concerned for her; for the moment they shut out what they have seen; what they have not found in the garden.

The mice all fix their teeth against the edge of a blanket and heave, try and try to pull it over her gigantic body. They do manage to wrap up one foot; it is hard to tell if this makes her feel better. They comfort her as best they can, with sniffs and nuzzles and laid-on paws, until her shoulders unknit and she begins to sleep.

The mice watch over her all night, a miniature defending army. The mother shall not devour this one, nor feed her to owls. In the dining room, observed by nothing that gives a damn, the fairy lights blink out.

44

Marie

I DREAMED THAT night, dreamed long and deep. My dreams were deserted, or at least haunted by a kind of absence. There was nobody but me wherever I went, except for a gaze, some awareness that was not mine.

I dreamed that I was a fat-armed baby with hands like starfish, like creatures with wills of their own. I opened my fingers, shut them again in wonder, grasped for the lampshade far above the crib. The world was all colours without pattern, and all I could make my sprawling fingers close upon was emptiness.

I dreamed that I had lost one woollen boot; I had worked it loose over diligent hours of struggling, with marching against my blanket into air. However I stamped with the other foot, I could not get the second boot free, but still it was the great ambition of my life.

And, even though in my dream I could not roll over, nor even turn my head, there was another beside me. I had not always been alone.

And there again, in my dream I was a small child, a little curled thing in a vast single bed. I had been frightened because my grandmother did not hold with nightlights. I had whimpered and shivered in my cold old bedroom, with the wind in the chimney like the voices of owls.

And then I dreamed that I slept, and I even dreamed

that I had a dream; how strange. And in that kernel of a dream, another creature crawled into my bed beside me, and we slept together like kittens. But I dreamed that I awoke and was alone.

I dreamed of my *Young Christians' Bible*. I dreamed that I was making my way to Emmaeus in my nightdress, with no coat and my hair all undone and tangled. My oxblood shoes made no print on that white road, where the Bible soil is as lifeless as God is strong. And the path was very straight and my shadow very long; it seemed to me that there was another beside me; a treading at the corner of my eye. And yet, if I turned to look behind I was alone; always alone. I bent my knees to those burning stones and wept. And then I turned to lie upon my back and woke.

The mice were still in my room, even though it had been hours; it was past the dawn already. There was an emptiness to the way in which they looked at me, a new coldness that I had never seen before. The mice were fierce, and dangerous as meat cans in the rubbish; sharp as ribboned tin. When they looked at me, they refused to see my eyes; would not raise their muzzles higher than my chin. Perhaps they were ashamed. Perhaps they were furious. Yes, I think the mice were angry. But really, I was only a child. Only a child. The mice did not move; they barely trembled their whiskers. They crouched still, like things already dead and grown solid. Eventually, they turned their backs on me and left me all alone in my bed. They vanished beneath the gap in the door without even a sound.

I sat up slowly, rubbed my face and the corners of my eyes, and found my short-cropped hair with something like shock. I gathered my eiderdown around me, swathed myself as though it might save me, rescue me, offer some protection in this peculiar life. But it did no good, and so I stood up instead.

As I stood, it dawned on me that I had slept in my clothes; that in the night and dreams of deserts, I had sweated right through my dress. It was creased against me like a shedding skin, clinging and soiled.

I unpeeled it from my body, struggling with the button at the back of my neck. When naked I felt raw; I threw on new clothes in a panic. Without thinking, I put on a dress that I hated; a green velveteen thing with a noose of lace at the throat of it. My mother liked me in that dress. After that I held my breath and left the room.

The house was frozen, brittle and bitten with anger. At the top of the stairs I came upon a mob of mice, pointed like scribbled arrows, glaring down their lengths at my mother. She stood down at the bottom, fixed as though she had stood there all night; as if she had gotten that far only, with that scream streaming from her mouth, when my mother was a monster who would have had me gone. Mother and mice were fixed, each on the other, suspicious and both quite insane.

The mice parted resentfully as I went among them, let me through but only just, and I walked to where my mother stood staring and put both my arms around her. And perhaps her shoulder softened a little as I laid my forehead against it. For a second, I perceived the mice as my mother did; their glares a thousand cocktail sticks stabbing.

I straightened, lifted my face to hers, but her attention was locked against the mice. Perhaps she would not have responded had I slapped her cheek. I had no desire to slap her cheek. I lowered my arms and stole away.

The anger gelled the air and turned it bitter, turned everything rotten. I sat in the kitchen for a telescopic day, watching as an apple turned from ruddy yellow-red to a satanic, pulpy brown. The skin withered around the stalk, puckered and shrunk the thing into a witch's face.

At eleven in the morning, it grew pregnant with worms; it caved in and rolled a little with their gay merrymaking. For a little time that apple was the most alive thing among us, until the worms grew wings and abandoned their nursery forever. By noon there was nothing of it remaining but the stalk, and a glossy patch against the draining board. I dared not look in the fridge.

The day threaded away gradually, and I was glad to be rid of it. At six I persuaded my mother to come away from the staircase. I discovered her *Crying Boy* and carrier bags in the bathroom; I brought down knitting and lambskin from the base of the toilet, and bore them carefully to the red chair, arranging my mother a nest as I thought she would like it most.

I took the picture last of all, and looked into the Crying Boy's girlish, sentimental face. The Crying boy was dressed in rags; he had white gloves on, hands like a strangler who would leave no print at the scene. My grandmother once told my mother that the Crying Boy was a fire-maker. My mother had told her to 'Shut up Shut up Shut up!' and had begun to sing at the top of her voice until my grandmother finished laughing.

I took him to the foot of the stairs and showed him to her very gently, the way that one might show a pet rabbit to a baby. Her glaze broke then, for just a minute; she opened her face as though startled, and looked at me with a febrile shine in her eyes. Then she put out her hands, slowly–slowly, and snatched the picture from me.

My mother fled with her Crying Boy clenched against her chest and a sob in her neck. I followed her cautiously, noted with relief that she had found her way to the red armchair. I wondered about draping her with a blanket; decided that I dare not risk it.

The mice all stared at me as though I had betrayed them. But she was my mother; I could have done nothing else. They stared at me as though I should have done something; shown them something, I don't know. They had taught me that I was alone; I had nothing to reflect back at them. There was nothing. They would not sit upon my lap, nor polish their faces.

I hunted for Thomas, longed to run my fingers through his tabby pelt. I would have died for the chance to hold him; to feel his heat and the chimney rumble of his purr. He was nowhere to be found, which was probably all to the good as the way things were he might have wrought a massacre on those stupefied mice.

I went upstairs, and without much thinking, I poured myself a bath; when the water had all been run, I could hardly make myself climb into it. I stirred my fingers in it, until a sudden rashness overtook me and I plunged right in, even though the bath was my mother's, even though she might be jealous. The water was hot and gorgeous, and for a time I was forgetful, almost content. But the water grew lukewarm and I had to come out.

When I returned, the mice had left the stairs. My mother was sitting on her armchair like a heap of clothes, knitting with long mauve fingers. There was a strangeness to the look of her, almost a camouflage. The mice were all ranged round her in concentric circles, pointed like daggers, souring the air with a new sort of staring.

45
Knife

THE CUTLERY WAS not fed tonight. Forks and butter knives cruise the carpet like fish, circle the floors and the arc around the door, shearing over the backs of each other in a stately kind of minuet. They flash and slither, but the door is never opened, nor dead things flung within for their supper.

46

The Mother

THE MOTHER STANDS at the foot of the stairs, hardly even wondering how long she has been there; hardly even wondering a single thing. The mother stands and the wind clouts at the back door, filling the house with hollow airful smacks. It is like bursting paper bags that bang and bang, over and again. Each strike makes her screw her eyes and flinch, as the night noises and the draught stalk along the hallway runner and discover her there.

She stands in bulb light, mad as a hare, transfixed and ever-so cold, and she cannot at that moment recall even her name. The house clucks and gasps around her as the pipes grow frigid, and it fills its lime-washed lungs with air. And it seems that there are echoes ringing flat in the hall: the genial chuckle of the rent man, and thundering shoes; of a long hoarse scream that might in truth be a snarl. There are ribbons of it through the hallway, parallel with the tortured tinsel, stretched out thin-wise; pinned.

The mother is grinding her teeth, is listening to the creak of molars against each other, and she cannot place the noise. A filling at the back is coming loose, wearing to amalgam grit in her mouth. The mother's fingers are knitted right together, but her fag end is still jutting between them, burnt right past the filter and then gone out.

The mother is stared at by her ghosts, but it is a different kind of staring now. The questions have gone; the pleading has dried up. The ghosts are angry. They have stitched the mother to the empty space around her and she has forgotten how to move.

When the rent man finally went, the mother pushed shut the front door, just as she would have like to push him out: firmly, assertively, with both hands and all her force. And then she breathed his sweaty air and aftershave and she hated him.

The mother had sighed like a martyr and ditched her carapace of raincoat, donned in a hurry to protect her from the rent man's crawling eyes. Now she discovered an abandoned laundry basket at the side of the alcove, so familiar as to be entirely lost. The mother fished out a sour woollen dressing gown and pulled it over her body. She had become rather thinner over these past few days, and it hung off her like a paper dress against a paper doll.

And when she was decent, the mother had wandered to the kitchen in a daze, shedding tears as if they might rinse the rent man away. She wondered to herself, wondered very sadly, if everything might just be her fault. She had not really laid eyes on Marie since her week in the bathroom, so afraid was she of her daughter. When their eyes had met the last time, with window glass and lashing rain between them, the mother had found that her daughter was a woman now.

That gaze had grown beyond unquestioning childhood. The mother and she had exchanged a certain glance, and she had seen that Marie would never believe her again. Finally, at last Marie had seen right through, to that dripping core that the mother had worked so hard to contain with her cardigans and enamelled smiles. It was over.

The mother, at the foot of the stairs, sees that moment slide past her now and she cannot will herself to look away.

And in only a few hours, the sun begins to collect in the sky like the cream from a shaken milk bottle. The ghosts are staring still, staring like that other child always did. The ghosts are so many and so thick now, more than the bubbles in a washing up bowl, more than the feathers off a chicken, and as drifting, as weightless. The dawn strains through them. With an effort, the mother manages to blink.

She had even had a change of heart; the mother had nearly tried this time; she nearly had. With the rent man gone and a dreadful thirst papering her tongue, the mother had stood at the kitchen window and wondered if life was at an end. The household, the universe, seemed to be thinning beneath her fingers, splitting into filaments, fragile and useless as candyfloss.

And she was unwinding worst of all, for if Marie did not think her a good lady, why then she must not be one. But, the mother gripped at her own wrist, might not something be salvaged? Perhaps, perhaps she might *be* guilty, just be and acknowledge and apologise for being guilty? Before there was nothing left, nothing at all?

And so it was that the mother found her slippers, and crumbled mud from them, and then crept into the garden, like a child towards a hiding. The mother approached the pit, braced this time, knowing about those black and liquid eyes, knowing all that she might face. She had no speech prepared, no guessings or dreams of instant resolution. The mother, for a moment, was just a mother, gone to find her child.

The mice have begun to populate the stairs, to take their places among the ghosts, cold and hard as carpet tacks. The mother stands and breathes. The bones of her fingers show through at the joints of her hands.

But she had not been there! There was only an empty hole. The mother had gazed at the sky in a panic, wracking her head. She had been there? Surely she was? The mother saw her there, just days ago; oh, but was she sure? Because, a week was a dreadfully long time, and she found herself confused, struggling to think. Concentrating was so hard these days, especially with the sun so bright.

Or (the mother clawed her throat), had she been mistaken? The mother began to sway. Had she done something? What had she done? If the child was not here then what on earth had the mother done with her? 'God, oh God.' Had she murdered accidentally, the way in which a person spills tea? The mother tried to remember, began to wail; silenced herself.

Surely, if she had killed her then it would be obvious. One cannot hide such a large thing as a corpse. The mother knew this thought to be a downright lie, and she lifted her gaze to the dining room window, then followed her eyes with her feet.

The mice are arranged in ranks, each stair bristling with whiskers, but here comes Marie from her room with silent, wary steps. They do not look up as she nears them. For now the mice are fixed, jammed against the mother, possessed with outrage, more furious than any beast that ever walked the earth. The mice know her to be a killer. She has stolen their childling, made the owls come and have her. She has murdered the childling and all of mousehood with her; all is lost.

In the garden, the mother had neared the pink window and put her face against it, trying to see, trying to discover a body, in case she had killed her own poor child. But the emulsion was all but opaque, unless one knew exactly where to look. The mother filled her fingernails with paint as she scraped madly at the glass, quite frantic. And then she pushed her eye at the hatch marks she had made; all the mother could see was the dining room, scratched and gouged and dug at by points and blades.

As she looked, a pudding spoon squirmed from arm-chair to piano like a legless scorpion, and she startled away with a cry. Perhaps she had done it. Who might tell? There would be nothing left anyhow, nothing but scrapings. The nasty child was dead and she herself had done this thing. The mother scurried back inside, slammed the door, fidgeted a cigarette out of the box and lit it on the stove. Then she ran to the parlour and sat in her red chair and sobbed.

Suddenly, Marie is before her and holding her around the ribs. The mother blinks at this, confused. The mother feels her face against her shoulder, the side of her neck, and she cannot imagine how Marie sneaked up on her so quietly. But she is not dead, not this child, and her arms are warm. Then she vanishes again.

When the back door had opened and shut again, the mother had recoiled as if at a slap. For there was no resolution after all; there was nothing to save, nothing to offer in mitigation; nothing to make to make Marie love her again. The mice had ruined her, washed out her brain like a sock in a sink. And now the mice would expose this extra crime and Marie would know of this too. Life was over. The mother trod back to the kitchen, full up with nothing, capable of anything, as though some man had blacked her eye.

When Marie came back inside, her head was shorn and her face was a secret and she wore mice around her neck. When the mother threw herself at Marie it was purely in self defence, to unmake the knowledge in her head, to silence the guilt and the doubt and the singing in her ears. But her feet got mired in the shadows of the hallway, until she found herself fixed like a scarecrow before the very first stair.

The mice are looking at the mother like battery acid. Whilst they are corroding her it turns into night time, and here is Marie again with her warm cradling arm. She has a flat square in her hand.

For a moment it seems to be her lost child, but these eyes are green and different, and it seems that the tears on that cheek are her own, that call to the mother's own grief. The image focuses. It is the Crying Boy. The mother loves her Crying Boy. He looks at her in this oddly static moment, and the mother gropes towards him and escapes, finds her chair, quivers upon it with her carrier bags at her ankles. Her fingers stumble across her knitting and so the mother begins to knit.

47
Marie

DAYS CRAWLED PAST, softly, the way that fruit turns rotten, and I was alone. I dreamed of the shadow at my side when I slept, and when I woke I crept about the house like a thief, gazing dumbly at closed drawers and at my mother's wardrobe. I dared not open them, nor rummage among papers for secrets. My grandmother seemed to be constantly on her errands and the sky slid past the window, grey. It seemed as if the riot of summer was burnt out already. My bones grew cold.

The plaster in my bedroom wall developed a crack, wide enough to admit the thickness of a penny piece. I began to eye it warily, frightened that the side of the house might pick off like a scab, topple me and my unmade bed into grave of rubble in the garden. Eventually the worry got too much and I resolved to sleep elsewhere in the room, in the hope that might be safer.

It took me half the afternoon; that was the day that I packed away my toys, useless things they were. They belonged to some other childhood. I dumped them in the corner and covered them with dirty linen to hide them from my sight. I dragged my bed to the opposite side of the room with a massive effort; points of blood showed through my skin where I had worked so hard, and I developed a slicing pain in my head.

But when I had it all positioned I grew afraid again, for there were slits in the ceiling just above, and it seemed fit to cave in at any second. In the end I resolved to sleep in the middle of the room, away from those uncertain cabbage roses and the spore infested patches of brown.

But the house missed me, and when I crept to bed that night I felt it mourning like an unfed dog, shaking the air with huge great sobs. I suppose that was good. At least it showed that something recognised that I cared for it. I hurt myself getting the bed back where it had started, and then I sat with my back against it where it could feel me; I sat for a long time with my spine stretched and aching.

After an hour, it seemed to notice that I was there, and the house ceased its lamenting. When I stood up I was stiff and slow of thought, and cold as a mildewed window frame.

It was an effort to bend at knee and elbow as I winced down those night-time stairs, for now it one in the morning. By then I often left my room at night. Perhaps I had become accustomed to being afraid; still I would hold my breath and steal around the corners like my own shadow, like my own ghost.

Looking back, I am never sure quite when my mother began her metamorphosis. Maybe it was that exact moment; between me shifting my bed and sleeping. I took a breath at the parlour door before I walked in. The light was on, just as I had left it; my mother was still perched upon her red chair, knitting amidst a drift of dishcloths with her eyes intent, concentrating on nothing at all. Her lips were moving faintly, rapidly, as if she were trotting out a memorised Bible page. I came up to her, very close, and I crouched before my mother and put a kiss against her cheek.

She blinked at that like an astonished baby and turned her face towards me with her eyes huge and dark. I recall starting a little, watching her and trying to remember, holding her still with my hand against her jaw. My mother had used to have blue eyes, blue like mine. I think she did.

I doubted myself, but then shook my head and decided that it did not matter, for surely it did not. It was no use puzzling, I thought, as there was no proof, no photographs to look at. That was how we lived; there were no means to measure our world against, nothing real to match it to. My mother's eyes were the almost-black of a burnt stove, and quick and bright as perfect fear, and she gazed at me with a question that had no words, nor any answer. She looked into my eyes for longer than I could bear, and then her gaze dawdled back to her knitting. As secretly as I could, I stole a dishcloth from her hoard. I would take it to the kitchen and unravel it later, so as to make fresh string for her knitting.

Our hours of sleep had soon grown muddled; so lonely was I that I would rather sit up with my empty mother than go about the house by daylight. She had, by degrees, become a nocturnal creature. I missed her. Whatever had happened, whatever the mice said, she was my mother.

As she knitted I stroked her hair, which seemed to have grown finer these days, less prone to frizz. Perhaps it was that she no longer dyed it, or wrenched at it with a hairbrush; for whatever reason, it was softer now, almost silky, and I think that she liked for me to run my fingers against it.

There was a new trembling to my mother, a jitter that seemed to emerge from her skeleton itself, the bone replaced by nerves and stalks of wire. I turned my fingers, laid the back of my hand against her forehead and then her arm. 'Mother,' said I, 'Are you cold?' The sound of talking against that silence shocked me.

And it scared the mice; I heard the scrit of their feet, the scuttle of them against the shadows and corners. I turned my head, saw the light glancing off their spun-glass whiskers. The mice had grown strange to me; there was a fury in them now that made them brittle and mean, and they seemed to see straight through me. They would sit so long and glower at my mother, that they would surely have starved had I not brought them food. The mice would have stared at my mother until one or other of them perished from sadness or hunger. I knew what ailed them, even then. It was what we had found in the garden; what we had not found. It was the aloneness that walked forever at my side. It was what they had hoped to find, but lost. But I had nobody to speak this understanding to, and so it was neither here nor there. I was such a lonely child.

Perhaps my mother shook from cold. I braved the hallway and kitchen lino and made my way to the back of the scullery where the coal was poured each month in a smoky avalanche, back in the days when someone knew how to order coal. It was so silent that I could not bear to puncture that spell with the grate and scrape of the coal shovel. Instead I took some lumps from the pile with my fingers and carried them back in the folded sling of my dress, along with newspaper and a bundle of spiteful kindling, all points and splinters.

I was forbidden to light the fire, and even that night I was doubtful, flinching and unsure as I laid the things out on the hearthstone. I scanned my mother's face, tried to gauge her mood, some reflex or gratitude or disapproval. There was no flicker, even after a long wait, so I began to untie the kindling-sticks, thinking of pick-up sticks, thinking of drawing in the kitchen grease beneath the table with a spent match, sitting under the larger universe of onion chopping. There had been another there.

I made a tiny pyre in the grate, tried to make well up with flame. I had seen my mother do this a thousand times, but it was so frustrating that it made me weep. After a finicky half-hour I got it alive, and arranged with coal like the miniature gardens that I used to make. And then, in the small hours, I patted the wall with my hands to keep the house company until I fell asleep.

I slept, and woke, and stroked my mother, whose eyes were a bright midnight, who looked at me without the least comprehension. And then I must have begun to sleep again, for suddenly there was a battering at the front door.

The sun was halfway up the sky when I opened the door to the rent man. I had not one word to say out loud. He did not seem interested, just beamed at me with a faceful of teeth, and he snatched my hand to kiss it. I ran away.

I fled before the rent man in a spinning panic, with no thought but being wherever he was not, but then it dawned on me that he had turned left, had gone into the parlour. I stopped dead, mouth hanging, but then there was a strange noise from upstairs, as though the window had been opened from without, as if such a thing were possible.

And I suppose it must have been possible, for my grandmother then strode round the turn in the corridor, pulling her overcoat around her nicely, as though she had just climbed in through.

I was so relieved to see her. If I had been a different child, had we all been different people, I might have buried myself in her arms. I might have even cried a little, as children will, and my grandmother might have held me close. She might have told me that it would all be alright. She might have said, 'Marie, be brave!' We were not this sort of people.

But she rescued us all the same. My grandmother strode down the stairs, towards the voice of the rent man who was talking to my mother like an orator practising a speech before a mirror. The rent man's voice was resonant, fruity as a spoonful of marmalade. I counted a slow ten before I went in to join her, and another ten besides because I was a coward.

Before I could control my quailing heart, the rent man was back in the hallway, perfectly charming and utterly furious, with an envelope hanging from his fingers and the other hand digging his pocket for his car keys. He informed my grandmother that he was delighted to see her looking so very well; my grandmother informed the rent man that he was too, too kind and that he really must make time for a chat one of these days.

And with that, he was gone, just as emphatically as if he had been picked up by the scruff and britches and thrown. Then my grandmother nodded to me and marched off to her attic kingdom with her joints cracking like greenwood on a fire. The door thumped shut upstairs, and I tiptoed forwards to close the front door.

Then I returned to my mother and fussed about, pulling a cardigan around her shoulders as if it were a cloak of invisibility. She looked right into my face and held up a dishcloth. My mother was as soft and loose as a kid glove, but inside she was an empty canister, or else a sardine can with no key. 'Mother,' said I, 'are you hungry?' And so saying, I went to find us all food.

I hated the pantry. That metal cemetery was a dismal sight. It was stacked with rows and rows of tin cans, six or seven high, until the shelves themselves had bowed beneath their weight. At the very back, oval slabs of jellied ham gathered rust with cling peaches in Prince's tins, and they could probably have only been fetched down with the use of a ladder. Nearest the walls, most of the labels had bleached right out, or else gone so musty and soft that their contents were a deep mystery.

One huge tin had waited in the pantry for as long as I could remember; it was a monster that must have held half a gallon, with one side bashed in and no label at all. I stood on tiptoe; the embossing at the top seemed to read a word, but it was a foreign word, and meant nothing at all to me.

Over years, the crimping at the edge had decayed, and today I saw that a thick black liquid, like molasses or some dreadful syrup, had begun to creep from it and right down the wall like a nasty secret. It oozed like the hour hand on a clock, slow and revolting and quite unstoppable. I hadn't the stomach to wipe it up, to smear it against the shelf and paintwork, so I let it alone. I took a tin of potatoes in brine, and I came away.

I came back through the hall with saucers for my mother, for the mice and for me. I had found that if I laid out a meal, only just out of reach, then my mother would sniff and nibble through a little food. And so would the mice; hateful and hard as they were, they still needed to eat.

But at the door I dropped it all in horror. The mice, in my absence, had crawled right up to my mother, crawled right over her shoulders and head and the top of her glasses, and they were gnawing off her hair, gathering it in their paws like some vile harvest. I went a little wild.

Leave her alone!' I shouted, and I swept my mother free of them with my hands. The mice all escaped me, but only so far away as they knew I could not reach. There they sat with hair in their paws, clever like crows; like needles; like throwing-darts.

48

The Mother

THIS IS HOW it feels to become another kind of beast.
This is how it feels to have one's soul shaken to liquid
and poured into a new mould. This is how it feels to
become a mouse. The mother is discovering a different
kind of time in which the thread of life slips through the
noose of an eternal *now*, in which every beat of the pulse
is just a drumming to ward off death.

The mother is discovering the sort of fear that gives life
and ending to the very smallest things. A creature is limited
in time by fear, is made and unmade by it, and the mother
is oh-so frightened. Her life is evolving like fermenting
dough, is becoming terribly quick, fast as the passing of
clouds next to the slow footsteps of people.

The mother can hear her own heart, and it sounds like
an hourglass, pattering for a little time before it spills out
silence. The mother is discovering how it is to live one's
life as flames do.

The mother is speechless. She is afraid, and now her
fear will not conform to words. She is afraid instead with
her ears and eyes, with the deafening odours that are blinding her poor nose. The mother has discovered that speaking is meaningless, that all the mouth might achieve are
hollow claps and whoops, noise that rings with all the
sense of a slamming door.

This afternoon, Marie came to the mother and put her face very close. She smelled of powdered toothpaste and the air from the back bedroom. She had knelt for a long time with the mother's paw clasped between her own, and had spoken and spoken, fallen silent and then spoken again, as if the mother had been supposed to respond, as if she should have moved her mouth and groaned in reply.

It has been such a time, this oozing between universes. The minds of women and mice are fashioned on such differing scales. The shift between the two is dizzying, where pattern and texture mean so much more than explanations, than justifications.

The mother is growing the morals of a mouse, and excuses are useless. She sees it now, plain as death. She is an evil thing. She is a laughing hurt-maker, a genocide of mice. She has scraped up all the truth of mousehood, all the love and beauty of it, and has offered it in sausage-fingers to owls.

Yes. She has killed a man, and thousands others at the thud of her slippers, but what is more she has doomed the household to perish. At the thought the mother's hands flitter in front of her, close upon her knitting. But even knitting is of no avail, for her nest is never finished; the pile of dishcloths is never larger. Perhaps Marie is stealing them. Even so, the mother knits as if knitting might save her, as her heart and mind grow small and truly formed, and she tastes what she has done.

The mother sees her nasty child now as they do, as the childling, beloved one of mice. She finds that the smell of her and the lick of her skin is written in her new brain. She discovers the purity, the massive weakness of the childling and she cannot bear it. She knows how it has been to be lost from that childling, source of hope, for such a forever, and she comprehends the agony that bit them when they knew her to be truly gone.

The mother shuts her eyes and is astounded at the suffering of mice, the slightness of their lives and their very great tragedy. Now she knows that she must have given the childling to owls, for she feels the ache of Judas across her neck, even if she cannot quite recall the details. The mother has learnt to know herself as the mice know her. She knows the mice too, as they do not wish to be known, and the albino sings in her ears as much as in theirs.

The mother sees that redemption is lost, and if she could then she would claw back through history to save that child, or claw through her own breast to uncover the secret of where she put the body. And in this new sort of now that does not quite have a future or past, the corpse of a husband and child might easily become each other, or else exchange themselves for the trillion ruined mice from traps, every one thrown in sacrifice to metal things.

Now the mother knows the feel of a life carved up by kitchen scissors and roasting forks, and she knows the sound her own body would make if it were split to soup by knives. The mother's jaw hangs slack, for she is Satan.

The *Crying Boy* has slipped between the cushion and the arm of the chair, and all that can be seen of him is his gilt-brushed frame. It hardly matters, for now the Crying Boy would mean nothing to her, not against the cryings of an entire civilisation. If only she had known, the mother would have been different. If she had known, perhaps she would have made an effort not to be born. Perhaps she might have grasped her way up from flesh and into air, to have only been a sigh on the wind.

And while the mother's body is yet that of a woman, with great arms and legs like timbers, her mind has made its metamorphosis complete. And, now the mice have more magic to work upon her, a revenge more perfect and precise, and so the final change is coming. For it seems her eyes are growing black, with neither white nor iris. Now her ears are unfurling and acute, hurtingly sensitive like the ears of newborn mice.

And perhaps her shape hovers more uncertainly around her skin. To look at her, one might think the mother very much smaller. She seems to harbour another self within her, a little trembling terrified self that it absorbing all the realness that she used to embody. She is becoming a tiny thing, made of lead and misery.

Marie is not here; perhaps she is shivering in her bed, trying to sleep. Perhaps it is four in the morning; all there is to know is that the garden is dark at the window and the bulbs are burning in the parlour. The mother lifts her snout to that blue-black nothing-place and she cannot believe that she condemned her own childling there. Her own pup.

The mother regards those starred skies and knows for sure that she must have been in league with owls, with death herself, with the forces against the god that does not wish to kill mice. But now it seems that this god is gone, or else he has forsaken them all. They were not worthy after all; now they will suffer the fate that the albino mouse sang from the grate. The mother dips her face again, shakes her silky head. Her cardigan is growing loose around her.

The mice have been very busy with the mother, perfecting their spell. The job is arduous, and not without cost; some mice have even dropped in the middle of their magicking. When all of a mouse's fear is spent, then he is no longer a mouse but a furry husk, and so he dies. The mice are giving themselves, projecting terror at the mother, channelled and pure and terrible, and this is how they make her a mouse. The dead lie where they fall, for the dining room door is fast shut.

By now they have gathered all of her that they need: the mice have gnawed the mother's hair from her head in clumps, and have bitten her fingernails to round stumps.

They even tried to get a tooth loose, but the mother had squealed at that and Marie came running. It doesn't really matter; they have samples of slipper and cardigan. They have stolen away her wedding ring and several eyelashes, and the effigy that they are making is a curious thing.

It is small and mean and hidden in the empty guts of the red armchair. It is not quite a mother, and not quite a mouse, but an animal in flux, pulled to stretching between one and the other.

She can feel that effigy beneath her backside, beneath the flat cushion that is stained with disappointment and tea. It is sucking her down into itself, forming her skin over its voodoo bones. She can feel the pang of those Polo-round eyes, the tiny dressing gown that forms a kind of pelt. The cord from it has grown nerves and strings within its length; it is finding a life of its own, a twist and flex and flick of its own. And the claws are toenails and the limbs are plaited hair, and it feels as evil a creature as might find it in its heart to murder a childling, or a host of harmless mice.

The poor mother. She is clinging to her self; with the tips of her knitting needles she is clinging, but it is quite useless. Her nose is rather long already and her ears are rather round.

Now, Marie has come in and she is hacking her way into a can with a blunt tin opener, and the parlour is slicked with the luscious odour of peas. The mother sits up, haunches stiff. The white haired child gathers food into dishes and lays one carefully on the arm of the red chair. Another is tucked into the space behind the laundry basket, where the mice might thieve at it in privacy.

The mother twitches her muzzle, gawps at those green balls, eyes sidelong, wondering if she dares. Marie is crouching very still, lip between teeth, fingers curled, as the mother creeps forwards in the chair to take a pea.

Marie gasps at the same time, and the mother is startled, dish upended, one pea between her two hands. It smells like an orchestral symphony as the mother holds that pea in all her fingers at once and nibbles it to nothing.

And, although her daughter coos and hoots and flaps her mouth, the mother can never be happy again, and huge human tears begin to roll from her eyes and soak into the mouse-bitten layers of dressing gown and cardigan. She gazes at Marie's eyes and is confused, for this child is so huge and so strange. Who knows what a creature like that might think about.

And the parlour grows as massive as a country, tie-dyed with smells, with a moonless plaster sky, and no hope at all. Not even a little.

49
Child

THE GARDEN IS vivid with sunlight, with fragrance and moving sky. The robin and the starlings are huddled like refugees in the cherry tree, which is jewelled all over with sour bloody fruit. The robin is shaking his feathers and shivering, and the starlings are staring wanly at the mud. None will look at his fellows, for every one is dull with fear. Each bird condemns his fellows with his silence. Birds are not by nature brave, for one needs a soul as trembling as leaves are, if one is to fly. Birds are all made of anxiety and feathers, and little more besides.

For the pit in the vegetable patch is empty, empty as a broken egg and plain as a confession. The secret child has fledged from her dark and underground nest; the birds all held their tiny tongues and watched as she unfolded herself and stole away. And they kept their voices silent as she slunk into the space beyond, past the garden and their territories. The secret child went bravely there, to where those other birds will murder any fool who flutters in their patch.

But the secret child is not a bird, no matter how she fledged, and she hasn't wings for fluttering anyhow. She will be fine. And who knows, perhaps the garden birds have seen her a time or two since, watched her foraging or sleeping under drifts of leaf and scrub. Perhaps they have not seen her at all, for they are not telling.

The grandmother, queen and tyrant of the garden, has demanded their knowledge, has demanded on pain of misery that they give up every thing they saw. She will kill them if she must, she will snatch up the very weather and shake it in their faces, for she does not know where the secret child is. For their part the songbirds have stood their ground for the very first time. They are half dead already, from dread and apprehension.

But here she comes now, striding in from nowhere like the cruel north wind. Her mouth is a crack between boulders and her arms are crossed over her chest. She plants herself in the middle of the lawn and then lifts a hand for all of them to see. Then she jabs her finger at the ground and speaks. 'Here.'

Then come the songbirds, from every corner and hiding place with their eyes rolling and blinking, obedient like mechanical nightingales. In a trice there are dozens of them, flapping and hopping on the grass. The lawn is a cage.

There is the pied wagtail, still for once in his life, white and black and thin as a hamstring; there is a guilty magpie who thinks his very soul is visible. The arrogant wren is silenced now, and the guttersnipe starlings glitter with terror. And so the grandmother stands among them in her crocheted cape, her anger withering the grass around her feet. Still they will not look up at her, respect her with their gaze; she might strip out their throats but she will not force them to betrayal.

Now, history is made, for until today the birds might never have stood up to her in a hundred years. The grandmother could simply have snapped one out from among that stranded flock and read him; his mind and his uncertainty and his wishes, all in a moment. It seems that now things are different, for all that she has to use on them is force. So she drags on the universe like a cigarette, heaves together heaven and earth, so that she might cling to her shape a little longer.

When a creature is twisted out of earthly matter, made not born, such things are spells of a sort, living and walking spells. Spells exist only in the mind of the one that wished them up; when that mind itself is unwritten, the incantation is slowly lost, though it takes some little time to burn away. This heals the world and helps maintain the balance of things; for if all the growingness of nature became knotted up in immortals then there might never be a springtime again. The songbirds keep their faces towards the ground as the daylight seeps away and they feel this change, this subtle unmagic.

The grandmother feels it too and her core is cold and furious. She makes a fist and the magpie falls dead, but her strength is no use now, for she might only slaughter them. She might strike each down, one by frightened one, and only achieve a heap of cooling carcasses. So they stand, peasants and ruler, for hours as the clouds whip overhead and the leaves on the cherry tree writhe in the wind.

This is how the house sees them, each pinned in its place, and although the house cannot comprehend what it sees, it observes the lines of fault and mortar in her. Her edges are coming loose and there is daylight in between. Even so, she is powerful, stronger and stronger as her form grows indistinct. She might become the very sky; she will be God before she dies. Still, when she wheels round to scowl at the house, it does not drop its windowed stare.

The grandmother's smile is like a gale and she lifts her fist to smite, to bring it falling down; it looks simply back at her, wondering how it would be to die. Somehow the grandmother seems to change her mind a little; she has seen her granddaughter come to the kitchen. And with her little face low and tears against her cheek, Marie potters past the window to the sink. The grandmother sees her there, and something in the old witch softens.

So the grandmother flats her fist instead, and with a silent laugh she stirs her open palm against the sky. The house knits its roof and the birds all stand miserable as the air begins to chime with snow. Summer bleeds away by moments until the garden is naked with cold, and frost-bite brittles the flowers.

The garden crystallises around the cherry tree as the songbirds struggle to free themselves, to escape, to beat away into the whitening air. And with a bow, and after spreading out her arms to them all like some wicked saint, she leaves them to their secret and the ice. She makes hardly a footprint at all as she marches to the back door, to present the snowing to Marie like some curious gift.

50

Marie

So we slept; we woke; we slept again, and our various hours were infested, I suppose, by each of our own kind of suffering. I closed the curtains in the parlour and left the bulbs lit so as not to be tormented by the daylight and the nights. For what use is either with no routine to pin against them, with no mother to order you to bed, nor to wish you good morning? Without a parent, none of this means a thing, and meal times never happened any more, and the fire was my only comfort outwith when the dark stole in.

So I slept when I was tired, and when I was awake I watched my mother and the mice, anxiously watched over them and tried to spot their needs, tell from them the symptoms of cold and hunger. In my way I tried to keep our little household afloat. The next time that the rent was due, my grandmother had come to me in the morning and shoved an envelope into my pocket without a single word. With it I had managed to fend off the rent man and his glistening face, and I had been relieved.

The parlour gathered shadows and cobwebs by the day, it seemed, and the carpet beneath the window-bay grew damp and nasty. The paint picked away at the sash joints, and the house took to humming to itself from time to time, as though its great dumb mind was beginning to unhinge.

My mother knitted and sighed, and she looked at me sometimes with her huge black eyes. Over time, so gradually that it took me days to realise it, her breathing grew more rapid, and finally when I pressed my wrist against her chest, I could feel her heart racing.

I thought that perhaps my mother might have a fever, and so I emptied the first aid cupboard; there wasn't a cure for what ailed my mother, but I did find a bottle of Veno's at the back, the syrup turned thick and bitty.

My mother hadn't a cough, of course, but even so I thought there would be no harm in giving her a dose. At least she might see that I was trying to help her. All my mother would do for me was turn her face to mine and look, as stupid as a china Pierrot.

I bore the bottle back downstairs and washed a dirty spoon from the sink, but then I stopped, chewing at my lip. What if I was to overdose her? Who was to say what manner of spoon it should be? The egg spoon in my hand was minute and exquisite, with a complicated pattern engraved upon the handle. But that was surely much too small. I pushed up my sleeve and rummaged among the mouldy plates again.

A minute later I had acquired a teaspoon, a jam spoon, a great metal serving thing and a plastic one for weaning babies. I hung back, wondering which I should choose. Eventually I settled for the jam spoon with its flat shovel end and took it off to the parlour, feeling dishwater grease on my fingers.

I had to drive the mice from my mother again, for they were advancing on her like children playing Mister Wolf. I shooed them in a dull sort of way, because they did not respect me and did not care if I waved my hands. The mice would always come back.

And so it was that I tried to give my mother medicine. I oozed it from the bottle like oil; it took an age and my hands were none too steady any more. When the spoon was spilling-full, I lifted it to her face.

She blinked, but did nothing to accept the spoon. I pushed it at her but she did not open her mouth, and suddenly I was frustrated beyond endurance, and I could have screamed out loud as I forced it to her lips.

But the curious thing was that her face was harder to place than it should have been, and somehow I missed altogether. I misjudged and spilt it in my mother's lap without even touching her teeth. Veno's drooled over her wrist, or that is to say it should have done; instead that sticky layer dithered at the surface like ink on soap scum. I left the spoon on the carpet, stuck among the hairs and mouse fur.

I stared at my mother, at the vacuum of her eyes, stared so hard that it made my head hurt, for suddenly she seemed equivocal, blurred as though she sat behind a smeared sheet of plastic. And when I reached out my hand for her, she flinched and I felt my fingers slide through the muscle of her cheek and out the other side. The sensation was vile.

And the mice had crept right up to her again, intent as assassins, so insidious that they were nearly on her lap when I noticed. Or at least, where her lap seemed to be, where her dressing gown folded limply over nothing much. 'Oh mother,' said I, and she turned again, looked right at me.

And because there was nothing to say, I went to the fire and stoked it, but it only turned to white ash and dull red like something dying. And I straightened, unstuck the spoon from the floor and tramped out to the scullery for coal. And as I faced the coal heap, huge and heavy and black, I wondered how long it might last. I also wondered just what I might do when it was gone. I chose five precious pieces and stood, trying to be courageous. Then the back door opened in the kitchen and my grandmother came in, stamping her boots and chuckling to herself.

I went to greet her. She had crow feathers in her hair, stuck through a lead-coloured knot at the nape of her neck. 'Marie,' said my grandmother, 'see, it is snowing for you!' And she moved aside for me to look.

It was. Great goose-feather flakes were spiralling in the air, collecting on the patio and the bramble leaves, in the tender folds of rose petals. The garden was full of birds, fluffed into balls inside their plumage, faces downcast, none of them singing. I half turned, perplexed. 'But Grandmother,' I said, 'it is June.'

But she had vanished, gone whistling up the stairs. The garden was beautiful, bluing with the coming nightfall, dizzy with the falling snow, and utterly alien. I stood until I hurt with the cold and then I remembered my mother and fled to the parlour.

The mice all started, guilty as I came through the door, but resolute also, as if they had completed some hateful task that they would never apologise for. They settled once more out of my reach.

My mother was gone, melted to nothing but her clothing and her soiled slippers; her glasses lay abandoned in the chair, not even folded. I let my hands drop, felt the weight of coal in my pockets. And then I perceived a little mouse half-hidden amongst knitting, cowering in the yarn's grey shade, shivering hard. She did not run for a corner but perched very still, gazing into my face, shedding gigantic tears.

I let my breath out very slowly and sat on the floor, cough mixture underneath my palm, and I looked back at this mouse, tried to convince myself that this was not my mother. Of course it was.

She was tiny, frail as rotted cotton, and a perfect hair-dye brown. She tilted her little face to me, squinting as though she could not quite focus. Then she scurried over to her glasses and put her face against a windowpane of lens, and I crouched very low so that we could study one another. 'Mother,' said I, 'are you a mouse?'

She seemed to nod, although perhaps I imagined it. I put my hand out to my mother, very gently, very carefully, and she let me pick her up, shaking all the while. I raised my mother to my face and she brushed my cheek with her whiskers. I was so grateful.

And then I turned to all the mice, at their needlepoint eyes, the black light of them, and I would have liked to say something, some challenge or reproach; but really there was nothing to be said. They had done this thing, but perhaps I could not blame them.

I cupped my mother against my chest and went into the dustbin in the kitchen for a box to put her in. When she was safe inside an empty packet of tea I stood and thought, then had an inspiration and rushed up the stairs. In my bedroom, I heaved apart the piles of toys until I uncovered my old dolls' house.

It was a large thing, made in thick board and hinged in the middle. The roof was tiled in tile-print Fablon and the carpets were stuck-on felt, and down the joint at the centre there ran a staircase with a row of banisters, match-stick-thin. A postage-stamp picture was glued to the wall, and a piece of tinfoil was the bathroom mirror.

I carried it down to the kitchen, feeling its cheap walls bow beneath my hands, and I put it on the table amongst the spilled sugar and crumbs. I was nervous as I opened my mother's box, but she did not seem offended as I dropped her into her new house.

As my mother explored, I made her a matchbox bed with Andrex blankets. I gave her some string, just in case she wanted to make a nest with it, and I put a tiny thimble-dish of cracker bits on her kitchen table. Last of all I made her a stockade fence in cardboard and Sellotape, so that the mice might not torment her further.

Before I stuck on the roof, I lifted my little mother and dried her tears with the edge of a handkerchief large enough to be her shroud. Then I kissed my mother's delicate back and shut her up inside.

After that I went to my bed and slept for hours and hours and hours.

51
Mice

THE JOB WAS hard for the mice, and costly too, for thirteen little lives were all spent out with that dark voodoo. Now it is done and they must each shake themselves and polish their whiskers like creatures emerging from a trance. Their hate had been a septic thing; now it is lanced and poured away in a nasty trickle. Mice are hardly made for hating, although despair suits them well enough.

All that they have now is despair, for the prophet spoke the truth and all hope is at an end. But in the meantime, what is there to do but live? The only thing that they might keep is a little love, and a flame of that might at least keep them warm until damnation makes warmth into blaze and kills them all.

And so the mice turn to each other now and embrace their sisters and mothers as mice will, with nuzzles and light touches of whisker and paw. A piebald, patchwork mouse goes wearily back to her nest and holds her mouselings close; she feeds and soothes them as best she can.

Every night for the days of their childhood, the mother will brood over them and whisper the lore of mousehood, of deaths that mice will suffer, of the fates and tragedies of small things. This is the way of mice; this has been the tradition since men made fire and built walls around themselves, since mice have stowed away in corners. Tonight the doctrine will be different. Tonight the piebald mouse shall tell her infants that they are cursed.

So it is that the piebald mouse nurses her mouse-children and then takes a huge breath. Then she tells them how much she loves them as she starts to break their hearts.

The other mice, among them one that is the grey-black of pencil-lead, stand together and gaze around the parlour at all of nature's bounty. There are curtains and skirtings, and great plains of carpet; there are corners and underneaths enough to comfort the soul. There is a dish of canned tomatoes behind the washing basket and enough electric flex to wear the teeth short for a thousand years.

Thomas fled the house after his incarceration in the bathroom, taking one last mouse with him, and he has not been seen since. The mice are well fed and many, for the traps now lie unset, for nobody has cause or means to snip off their lives. It does not look like the dawning of a great despair. And yet it is.

Presently the drumming starts. The grey-black mouse is the first moved to mourning, and so he begins to thrum his hind feet against the tomato can. At the sound, the others hang their heads and go tend to the dead. One by one, each corpse goes gently to his resting place.

They pack their dead in twists of kitchen roll and Bacofoil, and they stand very solemnly and polish their faces. The mice wonder at this new fortune, try to discover its form. The future is a licked-at battery. The patchwork mouse can taste it, and so can her mouse-children, for it leaches into their milk.

Then the mice turn their backs and they bring the fourth body, the fifth and sixth, and they make their funerals there. Then they go to look at Marie.

They scale the stairs like mountaineers and swarm beneath the door. The house is very quiet now, without the clatters and shouts of the mother, her sobbings and laughter and the talking that the humans used to make. Now there is hardly any talking in the house, for Marie is alone in the world and it is useless to talk alone. Now she steals around like a cat; she jumps at the sound of her own feet. The mice are sorry; they are terribly sorry, for this has been harsh for her.

When they crowd around her bed, she is buried in a chrysalis of blanket and they have no wish to wake her. Instead they let her lie and struggle in her dreams. They are not angry with her any more. She did not mean to fail them. She is a poor thing.

They watch her for a time, helpless because they know her heart is wounded too, and moreover that that hurt was inflicted by mice. It had seemed a right course of action; they had thought themselves justified, but now they know that their ruthless hope was futile.

But mice, after all, are not gods. They do not make their fate, only follow it. They had been foolish to think it might be otherwise. They sweep their eyes and whiskers over the carpet, rich with socks and biscuit fragments, and treacherous too, with tacks and sharp objects. At last they tiptoe away and leave her be, as she lies against her side and wanders amongst the pictures from the *Young Christians' Bible*.

The mice take a long time to come downstairs; they plod like lame things and jump down the stairs by twos and ones, a flood in slow motion. And then finally, reluctantly, they make their way towards the kitchen again, towards the mouse that was the frizz-haired mother.

She is hidden in a cage of cardboard; in a strange little house inside a cage of cardboard. The mice draw near to the table, shin up the legs, ready to face her, the destroyer of hope, the hater of mice.

But the magic of the transformation has been such a tax upon them that they are calm now, quiet with exhaustion. It seems that their fury and vengeance was all used up in it. The mice despised her and filled her to the top of her head with their own terror and misery, with all the agony they had, and now it is gone. Only the horror of a whole nation might transmute one creature into another, for it is no easy thing to achieve.

Nothing is all right now. Nothing shall ever be well again. And here is the punishment for the frizz-haired mother. They have made her to be a small thing, a creature with no power of her own, condemned to following behind her fate.

She must trail now in the wake of what she has done; for a whole enormous lifespan, the mother must comprehend despair, and the coming destruction of the colony. She must make mouse-children every twenty-one days, and she must send them into the world knowing they are damned. She must tell her pups the lore of death, and confess to every single one of them that hope is at an end.

She will tell her little ones of the dining room and the knives, and she will confess the awful things that she did to mousehood. She will tell them of Thomas and the mousetraps; she will confess that she had been in league with owls and evil gods. She will tell and tell and tell, and on the twenty-second day she will give birth again. And finally, either she or her pups, or her children's pups, will see that judgment come to pass.

But now that the punishment is written there is nothing to the mice but sorrow. The mother-mouse is the same as them; they will go to her and comfort her, for she is only a mouse and their fate is hard. They will teach her how to be a mouse, to polish her face and balance with her tail. So it is that they begin to set her free, to tear at the cardboard.

That is easily done, for the stockade is made of Sugar Puff boxes and soon the mice have a space that they can pull wide open; they expose the dolls' house like the nut inside a shell.

The mice stop then, and listen; they tut and squeak at the painted front door, but it is not real. They call to the mother but get only hush in reply. So they turn to one another, and they try to go through it, but it is just a picture and the gap beneath it is a stripe of black. They do not understand the hinge that opens the house right out, and so the mice busy their teeth against the cardboard brickwork until there is an exit for the mother, so she can come and find her hopeless life.

But she does not come out, not even after the mice have waited politely for several minutes, and so eventually, the grey-black mouse pushes his nose inside and follows it with his shoulders. The grey-black mouse scuttles up the staircase and then he pushes in the little doors one by one.

But the mother is not in either oblong bedroom, not in the bath with its blue-painted water. By the time he is coming down again, another mouse has found her, and the tiny parlour grows crowded with silent mice, every one aghast.

A twist of dishcloth string, thick as rope, is knotted around the handle and then slung over the top of the door. And on the other side, the mother-mouse of hair-dye brown is hanging, cold and perfectly stiff. Her paws are greyed, and they curve together like the paws of sleeping mice. Her tail is as useless as a pipe cleaner.

The mother's eyes are closed, and her face quite serene; perhaps she died without a fight, or perhaps she was so tired by her dying that death gave her a rest. Her belly is velvet brushed the wrong way, and her ears are crumpled like poppy petals. A tiny wooden armchair lies on its side, close by. It is red.

The grey-black mouse will not look up as he shoulders his way out of the cardboard house. As he regains the kitchen and its playing-field table, he discovers a crowd, slow and patient, each waiting her turn to squeeze inside. Every one must edge through that little parlour door and come face to face with the mother, hanging like a decoration from a Christmas tree.

It takes hours for every one of them to have a look, until the sun rises on the garden with its shroud of summer snow.

52
Marie

THE NIGHT THAT it snowed, I saw myself clad in strange clothes; a coarse Hessian dress and sandals, with a scarf over my hair, which was long and black and thick. My hands were thin and brown, but bitten and broken at the nails. There were splinters in my fingers from the broom's rough handle, but still I was sweeping, searching, brushing a paisley carpet; searching and sweeping. My broom was falling to pieces, and all I seemed to do was brush that Bible dust from side to side.

There was a coin; I remember thinking that, returning to that thought again and again, but I could not find it, not by sweeping out corners. In my dream I was growing afraid, fretting about my coin, where it had been lost, whether it had even been lost at all.

I bent over like an old lady, hunting the shadows behind a bookcase, behind an armchair, and all the while I was wondering if I had ever had a coin at all. Perhaps it could not be found because it was only an imaginary coin. As I tried to conjure my coin in my mind, it seemed to grow smaller, from a fifty pence to a two pence, smaller than a half-penny and smaller still, smaller than the head of a pin.

My dress was like bandages, looping and fraying loose; I kept pushing up my sleeves, trying to get my hands free of the cuffs. However I tried they only fell right back again; and the broom was broken; and I could not find my coin, not even by the light of an oil lamp.

Instead I kept turning up other things, the perfect little bones of mice; skulls like the work of a clock-maker with microscopic lacing where the plates of face and head fuse. I could not pick them up, for I was looking for my coin.

When I woke, I knew that I might never find it, not even if I had slept for a hundred years. When I woke, my room was riddled with the cold and my breath clouded my face. When I woke, I knew that my mother was dead, for there was peace in the house.

I lay in my bed for as long as I could, breathing the still-ness, dreading the emptiness that lay before me, and the freezing space beyond my bedspread. I listened, dragged the air in the hope of a sound, some footfall or sigh or scrape of kettle and teapot. There were no such noises, and it was because my mother was dead.

In time my ears grew gentler, more sensitive, and I could pick out the whispering of mice, the dry slither of metal from the dining room. When one is truly quiet, then any old sorrow can clang in one's ears. I listened until my thirst forced me up, and then I made my way into that reluctant day.

Before I left my room I went to stand at the window, and looked into a garden that was amnesiac with snow. The flowers were half buried; tiny coloured flashes and petal edges were all that one could see of marigold and rose. The cherry tree held its pose like a stoic cart-horse, every dark fruit frozen to its stone. Even the great hole in the soil was healed over in the snow, smoothed and soothed with white. The birds still waited on the lawn, just as they had yesterday, perished with the cold.

The window-glass was feathered with frost. I put my palm against it to see if my warmth might melt the ice outside. It did not, even though it made my hand feel killed. When I took it away again there was a little print, an outline of condensation, nothing more.

Then I spotted brindle among the snow, and I saw that Thomas was in the garden. I was overjoyed; he had vanished so thoroughly that I had thought him gone forever. Perhaps he knew that my mother was dead. Cats have a sense for these things. He did not look to the window; Thomas had stolen right up to the tableau of birds.

They all stared at him, panic in their faces, and they raised their wings and clapped them as if they were staked to the grass, as though they could not fly. He slowed, sank his body into a stalking crouch, bunched up his haunches. I turned away before he sprang, with my lip caught in my teeth, and I trod through the morning to the stairs.

There were mice at the foot of it, anxious, peeping up as I descended. They were utterly taut. They need not have worried so. I knew that my mother was dead. The air did not ring with her any more; it did not jangle with her nerves, but a new kind of sadness, vivid-bright and mouseish.

At the last step they gathered round me and shepherded my feet, tugged on the hem of my nightdress. I let them bear me through the hall as if the strength of mice alone might move me forward. At the kitchen they fanned out, gazed up at my face as though they might at any moment address me in words. When they were sure that I was watching, they flicked themselves up the table legs, and the mice stood around the dolls' house with its ruined defence of cardboard.

One mouse, a little thing of pencil-lead black tiptoed right up and brushed his face with his paws before he pulled at my sleeve. I opened up the dolls' house, more to comfort the mice than for myself, for I knew already that my mother was dead.

When I pulled the house in two, I disturbed another

mouse, a sort of patchwork one, who had been watching at the small parlour door. But of course, the door was neither here nor there with one whole wall folded out, and that was how I found my mother.

It took a moment only to untwist the string from the door, and then I curled my mother and the thread together in the palm of my hand. She was so very small, and as beautiful as a broken clockwork toy; then I looked back to the mice. There were hundreds of them in the kitchen, even the pinkish piglet mice with their eyes gummed shut. The whole colony stood before me and made their mute confession. I nodded, for there seemed nothing to say.

I cradled my little mother in the cup of my hand and stroked her mole-flock fur. She was a perfect thing, tenderly curved from string to tail tip, faultless in repose. She was without strife, and without rancour. Her whiskers tickled my lips as I gave my mother a last kiss and ran my fingertip across the fearless arc of her flank.

She was the most peaceful thing that I had ever seen before in all my life. My heart stuttered a little as I found an uncommon kind of joy start in it, and as my face spilt over with tears. I held my mother to the pad of my cheek and I cried for her, for myself and this massive houseful of suffering.

She did not resist; she neither flinched nor muttered, only lay there, soft as tissue as I caressed her. It was a beautiful thing − don't you think that strange? − a beautiful moment. I held her, comforted her finally, after all these years, and my mother just lay still and comforted me too. The mice stood about with their heads bent low; the youngest ones cried and their mothers shushed them.

There was a long time when I could not see for tears, my eyes crying all by themselves as though they had waited for this forever, as if they would not be denied this grief. And yet, in my own way I was happy. My mother's fur grew damp and I cried like a summer storm, without stopping, until my legs ached from standing. Slowly I became aware of a respectful pulling at my sleeve, and when I looked, blur-faced at the mice, they were hauling her glasses along the table towards me. I smiled at them and took them, and then I cried the more.

When I was done crying, I felt new-made; reborn. I laid my mother down and the mice gathered round to protect her as I went to the sink. I washed out a glass, and then drank water as if I had escaped a desert; I drank and drank, and then it seemed to me that I was clean.

As I turned back the mice were all staring, rigid at the window. Thomas was there, miaowing and patting his paws at the glass. I pulled the curtain across.

Somehow the day went past; the mice brought me a bread heel from the bin and I took a few bites out of nothing but politeness. When I discovered that I was shivering, I plodded upstairs and got dressed. And I spent hours just stroking my mother, admiring her delicate corpse, considering the beauty and tragedy of very little things.

I took the tiny noose away and smoothed the fur that it had compressed. I got a dish of soapy water and cleaned her feet and face; I made her whiskers sparkle like a dew soaked spider's web, and then I slowly dried her with the breeze of my breath.

It was after seven when my grandmother came in with Thomas in her arms. I jumped up in a panic; my grandmother glanced at the table and understood immediately, as though all this were utterly mundane. Perhaps it was; I had no other childhood to compare my life against; at any rate she just said, 'Oh, I see,' and she turned to shut the cat outside again. Then she nodded at the mice with a 'How do you do?'

I beckoned my grandmother close and showed her the

body. She did not take it from me, but her face grew soft in a way that I rarely saw. She marched off upstairs and came back down with my mother's old jewellery box. We emptied out the knotted silver chains, and laid her inside its red padding; I covered her all over with flakes of pot pourri as the mechanism played *Fur Elise.*

I fetched her knitting needles but they would not fit; my grandmother snapped each one as if it were a kindling-stick, and laid them in the coffin. We gave her a little skein of dishcloth string and closed the lid up tight. Then my grandmother picked it up; she gave me a spoon for digging, and put her dry white hand in mine. The mice all went to the scullery window to look as we went outside.

The song birds waited, miserable and motionless, until my grandmother clapped her hands at them and they all fell into the air. Then we processed towards the hole in the vegetable patch. My grandmother stopped there and looked at me as though I should bury her in that heart-less pit, but I ignored her and kept walking, as far as the back fence with its clambering clematis and honeysuckle. My grandmother followed me. She smiled, actually kindly smiled; my grandmother said, 'Good for you, Marie.'

The poor flowers were choked with snow, but their fra-grance sang through the whole evening, that summer evening when the sun did not go down until half-past nine. With my spoon I dug a tiny grave, and when my mother was buried I patted the raw earth over with snow and flowers, and it was beautiful. My grandmother did not assist me, only stood and watched, dry eyed, saying nothing. But she must have come away, for then she came towards me with my mother's slippers, with her dressing gown and carrier bags. Silently we folded these and dropped them, one by one, into the deep pit, and when we were done we dragged that rotten door over it.

Then, all of a sudden, the birds began to sing, rivering

music all over the garden like spilled mercury, and I found that I did not have a single tear more to shed.

53
Knife

THE CUTLERY IS bickering; a wicked little paring knife is trying its luck against the leggy tailor's shears. The dining room rattles with the click and sneer of shiny points colliding. The others lie still beneath the sideboard, the bellyless piano and the drop-leaf table, observing the sport of it.

Neither has the upper claw, for the scissors are elderly, though strong as a headmaster, but the knife is small and deft and quick. The scything grates all night, falling silent at last before the dawn.

Once the meagre daylight peers through the window they are plain to see, the peeling blade wedged solid between the scissors' halves, turning them quite useless, bending its own self to a hateful arc. Neither of these shall die of these twistings, for rust alone will murder a knife. They shall wait like this forever, screeching at each other's narrow throats, married, like some new utensil.

Part Three

54

Marie

O H, BUT WHAT might I tell you of the months that followed my mother's death? There is little that holds
in the memory, for the weeks were bleak and without
form. I think that in my head I became a little crazed, for
it seemed that sometimes a whole day might pass whilst
I was thinking, whilst I tried to gather myself.

In those earliest months it was surely the mice that kept
me going; their leaping children and their downcast
humility. I wondered at first if the mice might ever recover,
for I was certain that they found themselves to blame for
all that had happened. Truly, I did not accuse the mice as
they did, for all our lives were so much bigger than we
poor things were, and so confusing that a single cause
might hardly be ascribed to anything. But I could never
ease their aching consciences, for how could one convey
such a sense with gesture and mute expression?

My world became quite wordless, devoid of human
speech, and although I was never alone from mice, I felt
like the only child alive. My thinking grew dumb, such
that when my grandmother did deign to find me or speak
she seemed quite alarming, and I would have to work my
wits hard to follow the meaning of the things she said.

Our world was hushed as treading paws and as sad as it
was serene. The mice fed me sometimes from the rubbish,

bless their hearts, and for my part I would guard them from Thomas. Poor Thomas; I made him live in the kitchen by himself where he could do us no harm, and he cried at the door every day.

I would sit in my mother's red chair, amongst the flicker and cuss of the fire, and find myself unwinding the silences by layers. My own life was loud and clumsy; I could divide that off easily enough, like the long-string spine from a canned sardine. To my own ears I sounded like a creature remaining absolutely still, a hind in a thicket, huge eyed in the shade, betrayed by nothing more than its own throbbing heart.

And the mice, the mice were at once a great impressionistic threnody and a hundred thousand tiny pointillist notes. When I learned how to be truly quiet I discovered the needlepoint language of them, the high bright fall and rise of it. But I was no mouse, and I comprehended not a word. Each voice, each staggering pulse, was unique, balanced between despair and love; too much of each to bear. I could hear the plaints of the newly-born and the weary sighs of ten-month ancients. I wonder just how I sounded to them.

I discovered that I could hear my grandmother whenever she was near, even if she were shut away in her rooms. My grandmother sounded like wings, but there was no voice to her, no inner monologue to eavesdrop on, just the rush of beating wings. She made the noise of a kind of power, a huge and circling energy that clad itself in itself like a tornado.

My grandmother trod the staircase with such a concentration that it made the wallpaper peel, as though every breath and movement was a colossal gathering of will. Sometimes I would look into my grandmother's face and not see eyes there, just the puddle-sheen of feathers. She was collapsing, even as her power seemed to expand; I heard it, but could not discern what this might mean.

The mind of the house was slow and unhappy and stupid, and I grew fond of it, heartbroken for its pain and its muddleheaded rafters. That house was miserable as a mountain, and I kept the fire going day and night because it was afraid of being cold; and, I suppose, because I was afraid as well. And, also because of my own fear, I began to use my room less and less; I left my toys to moulder in their heaps and camped in the parlour with the mice and a musty-damp eiderdown.

There were other voices too; other silences that one might separate out like fish bones on a plate. There were voices like the chittering of cockroaches, tinny and metally and nasty. Sometimes when I heard the cutlery talking, the mice would all look to me and fix their eyes with mine, jumping for horror, seeing what I would do. I would always look back, shake my head. I was not my mother. I knew all about her mousetraps (how could I not have), but I was not her and I would not stoop to murder.

And for all I knew, a knife might be like a scorpion, a thing that feeds once in a hundred years. That was what I told myself at first; that the monsters were only very few, and hardly at all hungry. Besides, I had no flesh to throw in, so what might I have done? As time went on, my excuses evolved. How could I ever open that door, dare to kick away the barricade that blocked the gap beneath? Lord knows what might jump out, scythe at the throat? And food stocks were low enough as it was. We might ourselves starve, before one considered feeding nightmares.

In the end though, it was naked fear that paralysed me; fear of apathy and action both. They nicked against my sleep and waking, and whenever I stabbed open a can with the jab-ended opener, I could hear them listening, quiet and wary as scissors.

So, this was how we went, eking out the cans, eking out the coal. The larder grew thinner, until I found myself prising open unlabelled things that tasted of metal and mandarin juice. It did not once occur to me to go out, find a shop. We were not this kind of people. Besides, I had no money of my own, and did not know the way.

One morning, when the winter and summer had gone again, I sat in the parlour, still as a colour plate whilst the mice nibbled my hair for me. They cut it short and thick, for I had grown accustomed to having it cropped, and I could not stand to feel hair lying against my skin.

Before they were done, there was the sound of an engine, a low-bellied grumble that was not the rent man's car. It was surely not rent day, for if it had been my grand-mother would have given me an envelope. I had one every time, regular as breathing, laid against the hearthstone for when I woke up. And, yes, he had come yesterday with his wrinkled shirt and his hands upon his belt, and so it could not possibly be him.

Before I could bring myself to move, there was a great square noise, as of a heavy box dropped upon the step. The mice and I crouched, petrified, for then we heard whistling, and then a curse as a milk bottle was sent rolling down the path. Feet died away and then returned with another thump, a third, fifth, eighth box piled up against the door. I was entirely frozen.

Then there was a cough and I had thought my life would end as the letterbox rattled long and hard. I cowered to my feet and crept down the hall; I stopped at the sight of eyes at the letterbox, at the reek of rolling tobacco. I opened the door as if to a tiger.

A man stood before me, squinting through his smoke at my face, then down to my ankles and back up. 'Deliv-ery,' he said simply. 'For Askin. You Miss Ashkin? Yeah? Sign here love. Ta.' And he was off down the path as though it were the most normal thing in the world. I looked down at the boxes; there were tins and tins, food for an army, food for a decade. And, not knowing quite else I should do, I began to lug them all inside, heave them to the kitchen, pile stuff on the table top. There were lychees in heavy syrup. There was pink pork roll with egg in the centre. There was condensed milk.

I heard wings on the stairs, and my grandmother came. She stood and glared until I came to stand before her, and then she laid a hand on either of my shoulders. I was surprised to find myself taller than I realised, almost at her eye level. She tipped her head and looked down her nose at me, inspecting; appraising. I stared back, a little defiantly. Then her eyes lit upon the table and the mountains of food, and she smiled with her teeth, uncharacteristically excited.

'Marie,' said she, 'Marie, happy birthday!' And she laughed and clapped my shoulders. She nodded at the boxes and said that whilst it would not last forever, it would do for a time at least. Then she sighed like a fluttering bird and seemed to speak, but if those were words then I did not understand them. My grandmother pulled herself together and I felt the heaving of it, the vacuum against my lungs.

She spoke again. 'Happy birthday,' she said, this time gently, and reached into her pocket. 'See what I have made you,' she whispered and I flinched, but this time it was different. My grandmother gave me a pretty little bottle, like a vial for perfume, which was bound up in a rare and complicated filigree, twists and curls and plaited plaits. I took it from her fingers, dumbfounded, staring. It was exquisite.

'Always remember,' said my grandmother, 'that the opposite of metal is rust.' And so saying, she went out of the back door.

I sat down among the boxes and examined it. The bottle was mounted on a chain, as though I was meant to wear it around my neck, and the latticework, which I had supposed to be silver wire, was in fact made from hair, lacquered and tied and varnished perfectly stiff. That hair was pale, so blond as to be all but white. It was my own.

When I unscrewed the top I discovered it to be full of vinegar, sherry coloured with a bite instead of an odour. A gift must never be refused, and so I looped it round my neck and let it warm against the hollow of my throat, until I forgot that it was even there.

55
Mice

IN THE VERY old times, when mousehood was a wretched thing, and filled with misery as a female is with young, the world was a place of great beauty; rich as lemon curd with crumbs and shadows. The ceilings were as high as clouds, and brilliant with stars; the night never fell at all, and nor did the dustbin ever empty of food. Those were days of no rain, when the water issued forth, it is said, from the great shiny taps in the basin. Huge flowers grew in posies in the wallpaper, flat and mysterious like living pictures.

The holy childling was gone and vanished; she who had needed and saved them all was dead and joy was done with. Those cursed souls that trod the carpet ached and filled the endless hallway with their yearnings.

These were the days that the mice have named the *Echoing*, for they were filled to their muzzles with their tragedy, ringing like metal cans with the despair and guilt of their lives. In the days of *Echoing*, a mouse could live a dozen years; so full were they of sadness that their very lives were made to be slow. In the *Echoing* their hearts were written like newsprint with their crimes.

The mouse-mother, here and now in this nest, is a coil around her children; she pauses, takes a few moments with nuzzling. The tale is hard to tell, and so she grooms them instead; cleans every blind eyed face, every blunt-tipped nose. The little ones protest; each digs his toes among his siblings, questing through the dawning of his days for a suck of milk. The mother snuffs at them, the warm rank perfume of mouse.

At the end of the *Echoing*, the mice had thought their misery must have been quite made; perfect for its pain and utterness. Mousehood lost its way so badly at the time of *Echoing*; for a second time it had found within its nerves the strength to murder. Mousehood knew at last the colour of its own wicked core, had discovered the twenty-first claw in every one of them. The last claw in a mouse is not attached to foot or toe, but jabbing from his soul, ready to tear a creature's skin off. The mice before the echoes denied this thing, despised this thing within them.

Yet in their haste to hide their cruelty, they proved themselves dreadfully cruel; for those mice of the ancient days were doers of evil. Their sin was pride. They were prophet-killers, these mice; they had known their punishment since the era before time, but in their arrogance they had denied it, choked it back like bitten glue. The gods had sent them the childling to teach them a lesson of kindness; they had sent to them the frizz-haired mother also, to show the mice that they must accept the might of larger beasts.

Instead they sought to change their doom, to wrench the world around them, to try and cheat their fate. In their ignorance and pride, the mice sought godness itself, as though they might invent a god to suit their own desire.

And in the days of the *Echoing* they had all lived together, mice and frizz-mother and sacred childling, and others besides, of whom other tales are told. As the childling was lightness, so the frizz-mother was dark; when the gods saw fit to hide the childling from their sight, the mice should have remembered the small things that mice are.

At this the female halts once more for a rest, takes in the tang of air beyond the nest. It is very cold outside, but here the rags are cosy. She dips her face to her mouselings.

Mousehood found its way into spite, fixed the claw in its heart into the frizz-mother's flesh, even though in her person she held the sacred childling, even though each was, in a sense, an aspect of the other. The mice in the time of *Echoing* forgot the lessons of the white mouse, forgot the penalty of hate. And with every hook that they possessed, they dragged the frizz-mother from her own mind, forced her to share their misery. In this way they killed her, and this is why the old days were a time of echoes. The air, the banisters rang hollow with ghosts and guilts and memories.

Oh, those ancient times of woe! To have lived in such evil, to have filled the air with such long and chiming sorrow! Now they had not understood it then, but there had already been a sign to mousehood, a message from the true gods, not some wistful invention but the truth. For, one magic night, death called a mouse to come to her in the garden; she had borne down on him with her whispered wings and shown him the height beyond ceilings and the crawling lives of mice.

Mother Owl came to guide them back to the ways of death, and kindly. The proper gods for mice are those of death; their greatest mercy and power is in the breaking of a backbone.

Now there is no greater love on earth than a dam for her mouselings, and there came a day when a piebald mouse found a germ of a prophet in herself and had a premonition of fire. But she recalled the propriety of mice, their smallness and the powerlessness of old.

And although her litter was yet unweaned, that patchwork mouse climbed up the staircase, which was in those days like a great and mighty hillside. In secret, and in a humility befitting to a mouse, she made her way through the old frizzmother's dwelling quarters, past her great flat nest of blankets, to speak with the owl god.

While yet her new brood was forming in her uterus, that patchwork mouse crept to the window, where the moon was like a light bulb sliced in half. Another mouse, who was chosen by the gods to bear witness, looked down from the bookcase and saw it all.

The patchwork mouse crept to the sill and jumped up on it, and she lifted her paws high and placed them against that unthawing glass. It is said that in the time of *Echoing*, the summers were as bitter as winters, and that the country beyond was brilliant with snow and flowers, like a parable of love and agony.

As she stood with her haunches stretched and her paws upraised, she looked exactly as mice do when the owl comes to bless them with dying, and show them the hugeness of sky. 'Mother Owl,' cried the patchwork mouse, 'Mother Owl?'

And it is said that a light was spat from the moon, from the broken teacup brightness of it. That splinter seemed to grow into wings, each as a bath towel thrown in air. In time those wings grew closer, and gathered to themselves two eyes, two eyes of treacle gold.

As the patchwork mouse called aloud to Mother Owl, she came, with cats' claw talons and a blink like the eclipse of a world. Mother Owl's face was as old as a house is old; old as a stone is old; older than any thing known. Mother Owl spoke like teeth against a slate.

'I am she.'

In their nest, the mouselings are not feeding and their dam hardly dare go on with this tale. The lie against each other's flanks, every mouth clamped against a teat, quivering.

'And who,' demanded Mother Owl, 'who, who wakes me from my cloud and sky by wailing so?'

That patchwork mouse had no pretension to push at Mother Owl, and so she simply spoke thus: 'Mother Owl, I do. I have nothing to offer but meekness. I am humble. I am small, and close to the ground. I beg only for an audience, that I may repent our pride, Mother Owl. I am mouse and mouse only. That is my confession. Strike me if you will, Mother Owl, but what of my mouselings?'

At that, Mother Owl was affronted and seemed about to reply, but the patchwork mouse's eyes were downcast and so she did not see. 'Mother Owl, you are the bringer of death and the unmaker of universes. Yet you are a mother, are you not, a mother as I am? And do you not feel, Mother Owl, that if you could not spare your owl-pups harm, that you would sooner not have created them at all?

'Do the pups of nightmares push and nose at your teats in the darkness? Do you feed them from your blood and your milk, Mother Owl, as I do? Do they cry for you when you are gone? Spare my mouselings, Mother Owl, or else spare me the torn love of pup-making and let me bear no more.'

And as the patchwork mouse spoke, her soul was naked and trembling, as fragile and humble as a mouse is born to be.

Mother Owl flapped in the sky beyond the window-pane, at once so close that she might have plucked a whisker from the patchwork mouse, and a million trillion inches away too. Mother Owl dodged and flurried like falling snow, at once herself and a death for every tiny living thing in the whole wide world. She flickered, a great pale terror in that coal black night, and her wings made not the slightest sound. 'Hush little mouse,' said Mother Owl, 'lest you should find that you have said too much.'

And then the patchwork mouse lifted up her little head, brave and quivering and scared to death. Her face, it is said, was transfigured with mouseish fear; generations of blasphemy burned away as the patchwork mouse gazed into the face of the god of death.

'If I do say too much, Mother Owl,' said the mouse quickly, thinking that she should be snapped at any moment, 'then punish me. For our lives are gone and hope is over, and I fear that I shall never see my nest again. But, Mother Owl, please bite us now, that we night die before the end of the world.'

'Mother Owl, the house shall fill with knives, and fire shall climb from the grate, and shred up whole rooms with which to line his nest. The fire shall eat us, Mother Owl, devour us, every one, and the colony shall perish in flames. But you, Mother Owl, you are a mother as I am; pity my grief and make me die this night!'

But Mother Owl, she laughed, and her laughing clattered the air like breaking. Mother Owl fractured the atmosphere with it, until she made a windstorm rattle the pane. And the patchwork mouse just wrung her paws and twirled her tail, as she stared into the face of death.

These are the words that the owl god said. 'Such things you shall see, little one. And who would be left to soothe the world with love if every mouse should die? Yes, for your rudeness I shall give to you a doubt, a little grey doubt in disaster. For even a mouse deserves a crumb of hope for his supper.'

'Perhaps you shall have death, little one, or perhaps the sleep of a hundred years, or even the light of morning that follows the long night. We shall have to see, tiny mother to millions, but be humble and impudent, and sprinkle the cosmos with your droppings! Love your mouselings, little one, and know that no future is certain.'

Then Mother Owl's wings beat white and hard, and

the grace of them was exchanged for a great rushing. Long fingers stretched from the tips, and the treacle-gold eyes stayed focussed on the patchwork mouse, even as the face changed. Then it seemed that Mother Owl had a mouthful of smiling teeth, and the grandmother opened the window from without, and reached inside to grasp the patchwork mouse's paw.

She climbed in like an owl landing awkwardly and her silhouette juttered for a moment between shapes. Then the grandmother walked away and down the stairs, making a whistling with her lips like a gale through a forest.

56
Knife

THE KNIVES ARE pining. The forks and carving sets and the treacherous cake slicers are famished. The dining room is whining with it, and the molecules of atmosphere beyond the parlour wall are quite delicious. Although they might ruin themselves, blunt to suffocating on the bite of brick and plaster, some have begun to eat that wall, mean as weeds breaking tarmac in their greed for daylight.

57
Marie

THE COAL WAS dwindling; where once it had lain in the scullery corner like some huge and grimy treasure, there was now a hole, a patch of emptiness that was dirty with dust. The remaining stash was hardly enough to hold my fears away, and I began to nag myself with worry. In my mind that heap was vanishingly small, melting under the weight of my anxiety like fool's wealth. It would surely be stones by morning.

It came that I would sneak to the coal in the night, tiptoe through the house to look at it, a paranoid miser counting out chunks. I would comfort myself, filthy my fingers until I felt better, but before I had walked the length of the hall it was creeping to nothing again, ready to give me nightmares. More than anything I feared the cold; as world without fire was a world at an end. Oh, but I was afraid.

When the electricity went off, I had an awful shock, and it seemed to me an inexplicable thing, as though the sun had refused to rise. It was the bills of course; those envelopes that came through the door, but back then such things were beyond me. How was I to know of quarter-lies, of black and red printed letters? They were not mine anyhow, but addressed to my mother and marked PRIVATE.

When finally, blood-faced with shame, I picked one

open and uncreased the paper inside, I tried to comprehend the writing, honestly I had, but really, what hope had I? And if I understood, how might I have known how to pay? So we had to manage without lights.

My grandmother brought us candles sometimes, but somehow the fear of running out began to interfere with the fear of darkness, and I started to store them unlit, cached against some uncertain future. In the meantime I wandered, stub toed about the house at night like a thing half-blind. In the meantime the mice got into the candle store and gnawed them all to sinews of wick.

But somehow we all went along; we ate from cans and walked from room to room as living things do. In time the mice seemed to regain some of their quickness, the jump-candle brilliance of lives burnt through very fast. They bred like echoes and soon we were a whole plague, the mice and I.

After a time I allowed poor Thomas back into our lives, as the mice were so many and so swift; it seemed that he should have as much right to the fire as the rest of us. So I opened the kitchen door, and together they made the merry play of life and dying, although for the mice it seemed a dance without music; joyless leaping. I do not think that Thomas killed many. After all, I fed him well on Spam and Ideal Milk.

There came a night when I sat out in the old red chair, with no thought in me but fire, the jumping and bright witchery of it, when I thought for a moment that I could hear something, as if the glasscutter crying of knives was closer by a mite. I held my head and listened as best I could, and perhaps there was a dryish sound, a scraping, but against the crackle of the grate I might easily have made the sound up.

As soon as I turned my mind away from flames, I came to myself a little; remembered my discomfort. For days I had been hurting inside my clothes. It seemed that I had grown a great deal lately, as though some anchor had come away from my insides. All of a trice I became a gawk-kneed adolescent, my wrists hanging beyond the cuffs of my dress, my cardigan armpits pinching.

The light in the grate was quite beguiling, and away from it the house was unbearable. Still, the splitting taut-ness that against my body was more than I could stand. With a kind of ruthlessness I leapt to my feet and turned to the door. I needed a different frock before my ribs broke, and so I went out to the stairs.

It was dark. I closed my eyes and began to creep upwards, preferring the black behind my eyelids to that that was beyond them. The mice all scuffed before me though, and scrabbled at my feet, and I was fearful that I might break them underneath my socks. I stopped where I was, before the turn in the landing, and I opened my eyes against that blindness, breathing slow until the banisters shone bone-pale amid the drifting shades of grey.

Among the dark the eyes of mice shone like some opposite kind of light, beacon bright. When I could see, when I knew that I would not crush them, I inched through the shadows and turned the handle on my mother's bedroom door.

The air was stale inside, stirring in chilly spirals; and goodness me it was like winter after the warmth and light of the parlour. I began to shake and could have died for shivering as I darted forwards to hunt for a new dress to wear.

The window was star-littered, with a witless, gibbous moon that made a splash against my mother's bed, silver and delicate as a slug-trails. I could hardly believe my bravery to be in here at all, but yet a dress of hers must be a better prospect than nakedness, or growing inside my child's clothing until I suffocated?

So shuddering with cold, I struggled free of my green dress, feeling the rip and give of the seams as I hauled it off my shoulders. Then I stood for a moment in that moon's stupid light, white limbed and astonished at myself. I dressed more slowly, pulled my mother's frock over this unfamiliar body, softened and round at breast and belly, but heretic-thin elsewhere.

When I was done I remembered her, my mother's sweat and rosebud scent, that unplaceable note of her that smelled of crying, and I felt wild-headed and guilty standing there. The mice all whispered forward and I held my hands to them; they did not condemn me, only shivered their backs in sympathy. Now at least I could swing my arms, and so I stole back down the stairs, breaking into a canter at the door with the relief of regaining the parlour and its lovely fire.

Thomas sidled into the parlour soon after, smiling like a robber. The mice in the parlour all clambered high, up to the picture rail and the bookcase tops; the cat craned his neck to see them but did not fuss. There would be no killing with me in the room.

When he jumped onto my lap he gave a start, smelling my mother on me, but as I stroked his back he seemed to calm. I was not my mother. His pelt began to warm against the fire, and I ran my hands against it, mackerel streaked and lead-grey, and he purred from the core of him and eased my heart.

Thomas was not so agile now, and he walked with a strange gait, pulling slightly to one side. One eye seemed a little milky and he had a split in his eartip from some battle in the garden. He was heavy against my lap; a mouse whispered to another from the shadows and the grate glowed. In time, even the purring petered out as the cat fell asleep. The house muttered to itself like an old man shaking his head, so low that I could hear it with the marrow in my bones.

The fire burned down to a glowing, quiet so that I could make out my grandmother in her attic rooms, her thinking a turmoil of wings, beating and frantic.

Somehow the metal voices from the parlour became clear, like a fork against glass. And as I sat like a point of silence, I perceived that scraping again, a scratching between the skirting and the floor; I bit my lip and listened. In time the scratch grew hideous, and my eyes opened wide as a hole appeared. I could not move.

My grandmother came then, suddenly, as though she had already been on her way. She nodded at the wall, where that point was twisting slowly, corkscrew-wise. It stopped for a moment, tasting at the air, with its tip right through the hole.

She had a bottle from the kitchen and was already unscrewing the top. 'Always remember,' said she, 'that rust is the thing.' And so saying, she strode up to the wall and poured that knife-snout with vinegar.

I was amazed, for it shrieked and pulled back into the dining room, quick as that. Poor Thomas woke at the sound and fled with a yowl, tail streaming behind and leaving claw digs in my thigh. The mice were perfectly quiet; perfectly still.

I went to stand before my grandmother; she took a moment to pinch my mother's frock in her fingers with a *Hm*. Then she took me with her and showed me how to soak a rag with vinegar and patch up the hole.

58
Mice

THE CREATURES OF the earth are tramping into the Ark by sevens and by twos, even though the sun is slapped overhead like a spoonful of margarine; even though it does not looks like rain. Here they are, every one; the zebra goes nodding and shying up the gangplank, shaking his great striped head. His mate is on board already, stamping her hooves against the coffin walls of her cell.

Although the Ark is surely much too small, the tortured queue of beasts stretches a mile into the distance; elephant and okapi; hummingbird and untouchable pig. There are no mice. Perhaps the Lord need not have herded mice for the Ark; perhaps they infested it already.

The angel of the Lord is standing astride the sky as though it were some invisible horse. His hair is brilliant and his raiment Persil-white. He is holding a sword that is short and broad like a hanging metal tongue, and there are clouds in his eyes that belie his majestic wingspan. Perhaps there will be no room for the archangel in this boat. Perhaps this too is God's perfect plan.

And so he plants his feet on clouds and keeps the order as the colour plate is devoured by mice, crossed and crossed by piddle and blunt claws. The page is glossy and diffi-cult to shred, and it stinks of printer's ink besides; still there is a kind of tang to the *Young Christians' Bible*, a toxicity that seems a little holy.

The offspring of the patchwork mouse prefer their nests to taste a little deathish. They are Mouse; they are humble and low against the ground, and birth is such a lit-termate with death that their cradles seem like graves. So it is that the zebra and the mighty elk are bitten up for a nursery; and the white-yellow Bible soil is rendered soft at last. The stoneware blue sky turns into tissue, and the abandoned teacup at the back of a drift of clothes becomes a shelter for birthing in.

The mouse that builds this nursery is herself a piebald thing, a kind of patchwork mouse; the daughter or grand-daughter of that other patchwork mouse, she who brought repentance to mousehood and revival of the old ways. This mouse is pendulous with her young; they clamour to be born at this very moment, and every swing of haunch is bone-hard labour. She tears and shreds, fusses at her picture snippings, for it must all be right before she pushes them into the air.

The child of the patchwork mouse pauses in her efforts, rests and polishes her face and right behind her ears. When she yawns, her teeth are yellow and bodkin-curved and terrible sharp. Her belly is pushing from the mice inside her, but she seems to be a thing made delicately, her heav-iness balanced by the spike of teeth and the jewellery maker's flick of her tail. The eyes of the patchwork mouse's child are black, for they know love and death like the mice of old.

The rightful life for a mouse is equivocal, made from neither euphoria nor despair. A mouse is made, in essence, for doubting, for balancing along the washing line strung between birth-making and the leaping out for death. Now Mother Owl has made them know these things, and has made it known in a manner fit for mice, without flash of revelation or frenzied revolution.

The patchwork mouse simply told her children the things that she had learned; the mouse that had been witness to it told her children, and another had overheard it from a nearby running-place. Soon every nest was filled with the dark comfort of Mother Owl and her eyes of golden syrup amber.

Before a week had scampered past, every new pup in the colony knew well that he was Mouse and mouse alone, small and humble and low against the ground. And thus, with whisper and whisker-twitch, the evil cult of the fairy light god was crumbled away. There is no god that does not wish to kill them, of course there is not; for the gods of mice are gods of death. This is as it should be, for mice are fleeting only; flashing sparks against the grinning void of the night. They burn for a little time, and they make the darkness a place of beauty. They cling against their skins until their skins let them go.

And at Mother Owl's behest, the cat has been permitted among the mice, to make them know their place, to drag his claws along their slightest trace of arrogance. They fear him, but they grudge him not his tithe of lives, although they do escape him if they can.

As to the future, why that is equivocal too, for every mouse deserves a crumb of hope. Perhaps they will all burn alive; perhaps they will not. In humility dwells the essence of Mouse, in quiet hope and the gathering of fluff. My, these are humble times; for a whole forever, Mother Owl has trodden these carpets; now her footsteps are as silent-winged as the air around her is loud.

Mother owl. May they be forgiven, the mice have lived these centuries with Mother Owl herself, and even so they have given themselves to idolatry, to the making of new and false religions. They have bled out whole life spans, entire generations, on the making of hatreds, the hoarding of guilt like bitter nuts. It is not right for Mouse to have the sort of voice that other creatures hear.

Mother Owl has been a patient teacher, and slow to chide. Mother Owl is as kind as a trap that cuts deep and sudden and hard; she makes no bones about despair or worthiness. She showed herself to them suddenly, turned her eyes from blue to amber and unmasked the scent of sky from her flesh.

Now her time is come; now they see the god in her, the wind and storm and tumult in her, for they are ready to understand. With every moment they see more of her, the more and more raw her power, high as a month old dustbin and as strong as a million slamming doors. Mother Owl is outgrowing her body; she is calling all the power in the universe towards herself, towards her mirror-grey hair and her eyes. She is too strong for flesh; she will scatter, surely. It has been a month of flapping curtains and of whistling in the ears.

And the child of the patchwork mouse is turning these things over in her mind. Her nest is flashed all over with colour; the tawny brown of lion skin and the secretive leopard's spots. At last the Ark is reduced to bedding, with a mouse curled up in its centre like an ancient secret, a rebus from the time before there were words. The corner that she has chosen is skeined and strung with cobwebs, and every hard straight line is soft, and dust-filthy. The child of the patchwork mouse breathes against the musty air and begins to give birth.

The forks and knives and spoons are whining again, singing like saws do, from their prison in the dining room. It is a tiny sound, almost as quiet as thinking. There is no blocking it out; it is a crying so shrill that it is the first thing that the mouselings ever hear. The child of the patchwork mouse licks her children clean, bites away umbilicus and afterbirth, one for every pup like the twin of each, the headless fleshy anchor that roots every life to its mother's.

Suddenly Mother Owl is there, and the bedroom door is smacked out wide, without her even touching it. The mice all cower back against shadow and stain, overawed and in the most frightful danger. Mother Owl might tear the roof off with a careless laugh. She strides inside and stands in the centre of the room, in the eye of herself as the universe turns.

The mice all stare, perfectly transfixed at the sight of Mother Owl, at the weather in her face, the fear of tiny birds, at the sounds of river and thunder and falling trees. Mother Owl stares back through each tiny soul, and suddenly her power is at its zenith. Every poor little whisker trembles like palsy; every heart patters a music of terror.

The child of the patchwork mouse crouches, frozen in her nest, and Mother Owl gazes through obstacles and dirty clothing, and she sees her there, her anxiety and humility and her squirming mouselings, and she nods as if satisfied. Then she is gone, fluttering small objects and paper fragments behind her like the ice-trail of a comet. And in her writhing wake, the mice follow nose to tail, dancing and prancing against their will, cascading the staircase and the gaps between banisters, where the morning is small and hard and not yet ripe, whilst Mother Owl goes to wake Marie.

Very soon after, she leaves the house with Marie at her heels, but when it seems that they are all to be stripped from their home, she glances backwards to the mice, breaks the tendons that had dragged them so, and the mice all scatter backwards.

The house is staring, disbelieving, at this woman who might drag the stars into new orbit, and then the god breaks into parts, returns her fragments to the places from which they were poached. The mice stare from the open door, and they see it happen, feel the moment when the garden sucks her in, when the light between her atoms grows dazzling.

Then the earth has her back, absorbs the realness and power of the grandmother; Mother Owl is the last part of her to break away, and she looks back one last time with her treacle-gold eyes; she closes one lid and opens it again, as if this is some gesture for humans, with meaning of its own.

Then Mother Owl pours into the air, into the glower of the dark before the sun breaks past the horizon; she flutters out on silent, insubstantial wings. It begins to hammer with rain.

59
Marie

WHEN I FLOATED to my senses I was half drowned by wings, the manic, metal whirring of feathers against air. Before my eyes were even open, I knew that she was there; my grandmother with her voiceless mind, her raw and whirling energy.

My grandmother was a storm, strong enough to tear a tree's arm off. The spirals that made her were loosening, until she was no longer tornado but gale, growing flatter, losing her form like a slowing top. When she came to me now there was something frenetic in her, as though her power grew huger, even as she lost herself. I could see that she was dying, if dying was the correct word. I could see that she would not hold together indefinitely.

I hardly saw her now, and when I did she would stride the house like a god, throwing up loose paper and making my hair grow static; the mice all stiffened at her coming and stared like things obsessed.

That morning was hardly even made begun, and when I rubbed my face and gathered my wits I was freezing cold as my eiderdown flapped around me, and the fire in the grate was fanned to a kind of hopeless fury.

Dawn was paling the parlour and I felt insubstantial beside her, an imaginary thing next to the matter that she contained, that spilt and swirled about her streaming hair.

I sat up, gazed at her. I had never seen my grandmother with her hair untied; it would have reached beyond her waist, although in that wind it flickered about her like a cape. She reached out and I took her hand; it felt like grasping stone. 'Marie,' said my grandmother, 'Marie, come and see!' and her voice was hardly human.

I battled through the air after her, struggling to keep my footing, and came through the smacking back door to stand with my grandmother in the garden. The sky was nothingy-white, as if she sucked on every real thing in the world, just to keep together.

There were birds everywhere, in every space; even the trees and hedgerows seemed to be gawping. I let go of her hand and backed away, the dew wetting my toes, the slick lawn treacherous.

'Marie,' said my grandmother, 'goodbye!' And so saying, she shattered, there and then, every tiny piece a feather. It was as if she had turned out to be an image only, a graven thing made of feathers and power; eyeless, without face or organs or bone. Even the clothes that she had seemed to wear proved suddenly to be a cunning weave of quills, grey and white and goldfinch bright, spinning out one last empty swirl. Then they settled on the lawn; littered it.

At the same moment the sky was filled with realness, fat and drenched with it, suddenly bruised with purpling clouds and the smell of electricity. The branches of the cherry tree wrenched as if some giant was throttling it by the neck, and then it clamoured with rain. The sky was filled with birds, crows among sparrows, hawk and dove and mistle thrush dancing through the throngs of each other as though they had quite lost their reason.

'But grandmother,' said I, 'the coal is running out!' My voice was lost inside that riot. Everything around me was unbearably *there*, and I was not accustomed to such concentration. I put my hands over my ears and sat down in the wet as the rain pummelled my back.

It rained like the end of the world as the day broke; water filled my ears and eyes until I thought that I might drown. Eventually I flinched to my feet and crept back indoors to find the mice all staring at the door as if they had been drugged. I was so flustered that I filled the kettle with water and plugged it in, as though by some miracle I might make tea. After a time I gave up, and fetched a can of Ambrosia Creamed Rice from the pantry, to fit body and soul together. Then I went to shiver before the fire and eat it from the tin.

I could not get warm that day, and neither could I settle in the parlour. I felt as lonely as could be; hours went by and the rain smeared down, and after a time I decided to go outside again and be wet. If that rain was the last of my grandmother then I would at least stand in it until she was gone.

The garden had grown calmer, although water bled from the sky as though it might rain forever. The feathers were limp against the grass like sodden leaves; I walked over them to the back fence, to look at the spot where I had buried my mother.

That was where I found the child, curled up and naked in the fence's mean shelter, convulsing with cold. She regarded me with trouble in her face and bared her teeth very slightly. I hardly knew what to think.

I extended my hand to her, asked her name, but in reply she gently growled and shrank into the shadow of the fence. I felt as though I might faint; at the sight of her face, my brain sang with memory. I shuddered and plastered my hair from my face to look at the sky. I was not alone. I need not be alone after all.

If I left her be, this naked child would freeze to death out here. If I let her be she might never come to rescue my heart again. With a stare that I hoped seemed laden with authority, I reached towards her as she snarled, braced myself for a bitten hand.

She did not hurt me though, so I hauled her into my arms; I was as gentle as I could be, but I forced her to walk with me; in this way we two staggered towards the house. She made no sound at all. Once in the parlour, wrapped in a knitted blanket, she gazed at me solemnly as I made a huge fire with the last of the coal, and set a pan of water on the top to warm.

As the parlour grew hot, the rainwater steamed from our hair and the child's shivering subsided. She watched me very carefully as I found soap and shampoo, and laid out towels on the hearthstone. I wet a flannel and reached towards her very slowly, making no sudden movements.

Meeting no immediate resistance, I began to wash her, soaping great muddy streaks from her flanks and her back. In time, the child seemed to relax in my company, and I dared to come up very close to dab at her face and neck, the corners of her eyes. When I had washed her hands for her I could find no clippers, so in the end I bit off her nails with my teeth.

I soon gave up with any hope of conversation; apart from her growl out in the garden, she had uttered nothing. She held out her foot for me, passive as I tried to lather out the black that ingrained her, every inch.

Her hair was dark and long; at the thought of it I almost despaired, thinking that I might never brush it, but it was lush and oily and it hardly bore a single knot. As I combed, that child seemed fairly to purr. Her cheeks grew ruddy with the heat from the fire, and the scent of lily-of-the-valley soon replaced the wet-dog odour she had carried in from the garden.

Light from the grate weaved in her eyes; when she smiled at me, I saw that she had lost her two front baby teeth. I smiled too, and dressed her in an old frock of mine, with thick woollen tights; then I braided her hair into two thick vines.

All this while the mice had been gathering, one and two and then a thousand, all assembled but hanging back, quivering and staring at the child. She looked at them too, knitting her face as though raking through her memory for something. After a very long pause, and quite suddenly, she sat up and brushed her fingers down her cheeks. I could actually hear the gasp of the mice, all at once, like tiny draughts over candles.

I did not want to share that moment with the mice, for I knew, however dimly, that I had waited such a time for this, and so I replaced the blanket round her narrow shoulders; then I lifted that little thing right up onto my lap, blanket and all, and I rocked her in my arms until we fell asleep together in the firelight.

60

Knife

THE CUTLERY IS as plaintive as viruses are, as the cancer that crawls in a lung. There are patches of the wall that are really quite thin, and for every blunted knife that snubs its teeth against the wall, two or three knife-children will spring, little and scuttling and cute as cuticle trimmers.

61

Marie

I WOKE BEFORE it was light, and for a few moments I was alone again. My arms contained nothing at all and my back was crunched from sleeping in the chair. My grief was indescribable then, for in my dreams I had found my other half. I had invented for myself a childish playmate, as one conjures stories in one's head to fend off madness. There was a minute in which I fixed my eyes to the ceiling, not moving my head, loath to tip my vision to the parlour, to the waste land of my home.

Tears rivered my face and collected at the root of my throat, at the collar of a nightdress I had stolen from my mother. My nose ran too, for my crying was not a pretty thing; I did not care, and so I simply let it run.

I could hear the house complaining softly at the ache in the scullery window; I could hear the nickel snickering of the cutlery in the dining room. There was no sound of wings, for now even my grandmother was gone.

Then I heard a sniff, a human sniff; delicate as of one breathing in the scent of violets, and I snapped my body straight, so fast that I heard my neck click and felt a sudden wash of giddiness. The child from the garden was sitting on the hearthstone, in the fire's dying warmth.

She was surrounded by mice, perched upon from lap to head with them, every one very still, none of them looking up. She tensed at my movement, thickened the muscle of her jaw, but she did not flinch or cower. I pawed over my nose, my sodden cheeks, tried to staunch my silly tears.

We remained like so for a long time, moving only ribs and eyelids, blinking and breathing in the fire's ruddy dawn. Eventually the sun replaced the coal as the fire burned lower, turned our precious fuel to ashes.

I had nothing in my head to say to her; nor it seemed, had she any words for me. And whilst I watched this tiny stranger in my blue denim pinafore, I found I knew her with all my heart, with the tissues of my belly and the red in my bones. I knew her better than any creature alive. The child looked back at me likewise, her little face open and wise, but wild as a tangle of bindweed.

She was perhaps half my age, or maybe a little more. We had no photographs in our house, despite the box-Brownie on top of my mother's wardrobe. Still, looking at her was as good as a childhood snap of my own self, or a child's drawing, uncanny and accurate, snatched away by my mother and torn up between her hands.

Nevertheless, here was she, a kind of myself, fashioned with the left hand, shaded dark where I myself was light: brown eyed, black haired, ingrained with the soil of the garden. She was tiny. I saw her there, in my own little-girl dress, and I felt waves of compassion for her, such a small thing against the bigness of the world.

I think inside there was a kernel, some peach stone of sympathy for my own self also. It seemed a tragedy that any human creature should be that small, to have such slender brittle wrists or fingers so very thin. Her eyes were terribly liquid and her collarbones so exposed; she seemed as though she might tear at moment, break against the weight of air and early sunlight. Perhaps she understood, for she sat quite motionless and seemed to wait for me to assemble my thoughts.

The mice, all this while, just crouched where they were, gripping the child with their paws and their curly tails, as a bigger creature might fling its arms and bury its face in the beloved's shoulder, refusing to let go. Yet they did not seem jubilant, filled with ecstasy at this apparent reunion; rather they were quiet with a kind of sorrowful joy. The child seemed to comprehend this too, and she just let them be, although surely their toenails must have been jagging at her skin.

The light evolved as the sun moved and I realised that I was hungry. Then I was filled with shame, for what of this poor child? Who was to say when she last ate? I bowed my head at the thought, then inched to my feet, gently, lest I should scare her. When I left the room, her absence bit me.

We dined against the hearthstone, on tins of fish and pineapple rings, dipping our fingers into syrup and pilchard sauce. She ate like a little dog, bolting her food so ravenously that at first I felt forced to dole out food a little at a time, lest she should devour all of what was meant for us both.

The hunger in her great dark eyes strangled my appetite; I gave in and let her wolf the lot, and a can of artichoke hearts and pickled beetroot besides. It gladdened me to watch her eat, to stain her mouth dark red, to see such need satisfied so easily. When she was done, she snuffled at her fingers and then polished her face with her hands; I could have died for delight. She regarded me gravely, and I smiled, as fond as can be.

Then there was a barking of knuckles at the door, followed by a wrenching as the door was tried from the outside. At the same time, I heard the wet gribbet of a throat being cleared, and I realised with a dripping horror that it was rent day, and here was the rent man come for his dues. I scalded to my feet, tipping up the balance of the mice, kicking the empty tins behind the wash basket, out of sight.

I rushed to the hall and then up the stairs, sick at the knees, calling for my grandmother. But she was gone, turned to a rainstorm in the garden, and she could not have helped me one bit, not ever again. There would be no more gifts, no more of her queer demonstrations, no spiteful love or rattling feathers. I choked on my panic. How would I ever manage? What was I to do?

The banging on the door grew bad-tempered, and so I tiptoed back downstairs and opened the door, almost yanking the rent man right over, who had been cupping his hands at the sunburst window, peering through the red and yellow glass. He spread out his lips for me, showed me a row of teeth.

'Ah, Marie! There you are,' boomed the rent man with an overheated smile, gazing frankly at my chest. He had a breadcrumb adhering to the sweat on his upper lip, a shaving cut against his jowl. I lowered my eyes and smiled at the floor.

The rent man strode past me and let himself into the parlour. He shoved the door to and said that young Marie must have cash aplenty, to have been burning such a fire in the middle of the summer. I gazed around, frantic, but the child was nowhere to be seen.

The rent man parked himself in the red armchair, and asked me where was Mummy. And then he corrected himself with a favourite-uncle chuckle, saying that he'd just as soon deal with Marie herself, as she was here. Wasn't she such a grown up now (he lowered his voice), so much nicer to look at than Mummy anyhow. I had a dreadful urge to punch the rent man.

Then I was struck with a wonderful idea; I turned back

to the door, crying 'Grandmother? Oh, you are home!'
The rent man's face fell. And I ran to stand at the top of
the stairs and conduct a conversation with myself. Finally
I returned to inform the rent man that my grandmother
was dreadfully sorry, but the post office had been shut and
that there was no rent money for him today.

I stood before him, scarlet and shaking, and I told him
that we would most definitely have means to pay him
double next week. And with the most incredible bravery,
I met the rent man's ham-jelly eyes, and I held his stare,
fists bunched by my sides, tall as him.

The rent man said that we would just see about this,
young woman, we would just see, and his voice was huge
and deep and it made the house itself cower. Then he was
off, leaving the front door wide and crunching off to his
car, which whined at the twist of the key.

I limped back to the parlour, scanning the empty room,
hunting for the child but reluctant to call out. Anyhow, I
mused, what name would I call?

Presently I began to hear a new sound, low and soft
as breath over a bottle. The pitch modulated, a gentle
droning. Bobbing my head, I tried to follow it, finally following my ears to the recess beneath the sideboard. There
was a tiny fold of blue cloth visible from the shadows,
under the scrolling mahogany. The note paled and sank
again, lifting like the music of pigeons. A slow smile crept
over my face. The child was singing.

62

Mice

IN THE PLAYROOM, the musty, ancient broom cupboard, sits the childling with her face all creased in wonder. Things have barely stirred in here these last years; the dust is a little thicker and more grey, and the smell of damp has matured. To the childling and the mice it is a smell like brandy, rich and brown and filled with bright notes of mould and sombre tones of memory and sorrow.

The childling is holding her body very still, motionless as a cherry stone in the earth; as a mouseling listening in the night for the heartbeat of its missing dam. She blinks her huge eyes, as tiny a creature as ever a monster was. She could eat them all if she chose to do so. She does not belong to them; she is human after all. She like Marie, the same as the frizz-mother before she turned mouse. They are disappointed.

The mice all gaze at her, flummoxed at this big thing who had been hidden from them so long. But now it falls upon the mice to comprehend this childling, to unstitch truth from blasphemy, for she truly exists, and yet Mother Owl has reminded them of their own little place in the world. She is no possession of theirs.

Yes, it must be a further test, although this time not a test of any fairy light god. The mice sit in their concentric rings and they stare at their own sacred childling, the unwitting source of so much love and despair.

This time, this time more than any other in the endless history of mousehood, this time they must comprehend truly, must understand who or what this child is to them. And every mouse knows with a pain in his flank that he has killed for this moment, that he murdered the wretched suffering frizz-mother, all because of now, all because they supposed that she had put the childling forever beyond the embrace of mice.

They considered her their own, Mother Owl help them, they had so considered this creature their belonging, that they ripped out the mind of another animal, the frizz-mother who surely was as much worth their pity as any ruined soul of this house. There is no scent for the horror they feel, no picture in their heads nor squeak or gesture for the pain of this understanding.

The child seems to know nothing much of this, although she followed them to this prehistoric site readily enough, as if the time had simply come for her to explore, to repossess this strange old house and the universe of ceilings, after aeons of underground pit and the endless sky beyond the garden. She simply sits and sniffs the colours of the olden times whilst the mice watch. And it seems to them that in her expression, in the mute wisdom of her face, there is a hint of the owl.

Underneath the bobbled pile of her woollen tights, the childling can feel the dig and pullings of splinters. Slowly she shifts her legs, finds another way to sit. Them she spreads out her clever paws and runs them lightly against the sacking and the floorboards, brailing through the cobwebs as if she were fishing. Her fingers light on little things: a metal car, corroded with rust and rodent urine; and a cotton reel that is pale like a plastic vertebra. She finds a brownish clothes peg that is thready at the ends where baby teeth once chewed the wood to fibres, and she seems to start at it; the mice all sniff hard and sway a little as she fits it to her mouth. The childling, beloved of mice, lifts her face and gazes at the ceiling, the lumpy ceiling that cradles the staircase.

She discovers that she loves every fat bulge, every craze and stain of wet and age and soaked-in guilt. And then, for some reason, and the first time in forever, she dips her head again and her eyes begin to pour with salty water. Beyond the door, they can hear Marie, plodding along the hallway, then up above them, fitting a shoe into every stair tread.

The mice are concerned, and perplexed also; they crowd closer still and they catch the drops as they fall, try to drink them or absorb them in their fur, lest any of this moment be lost. Now she is here, come at last as if in some reply to their repentance; Mother Owl has at last released the childling to them, that they might prove themselves humble. In the failing light, it seems to the mice that they can hear Mother Owl outside the window even now, her silence, the absence that she is, and the darkness.

The childling sits on her haunches and cries as Mother Owl sweeps past the house, enfolds all of them in her queer comfort. The mice all close their eyes and empty their tiny lungs, for here at least is their blessing; Mother Owl has seen them there with her light bulb eyes; she has caused the face of the childling to rain and she has given mousehood its little grey doubt at last.

They have no huge redemption to make after all; no new fate to create, no false god to scribble across the empty spaces in the air. There is simply this massive and beautiful creature, and the sweet rot of this ancient play-room, and the fate that Mother Owl shall pick for them all. Perhaps they *will* burn, or sleep for a hundred years.

They shall shred up the fate that is given to them, and with it they will line their nests, whether it be so sharp as to ribbon their skin, or soft enough to bear a litter into. So they climb up over the childling, and they taste her raining and they try to make it stop. In time she seems to grow calm, and then she reaches out again and gathers up another toy with her fingertips.

This one is a little bear, the twin of a teddy that was owned by the other child, by Marie. This bear is blanket blue, or rather it was at one time; the childling can smell the blueness on it, the sweat and the love that has leached into the softness. This thing here is a half-forgotten picture book, with pork rind for its cover and poetry of smells inside. The childling takes this as well, gathers a little heap of toys onto her lap as the mice all splay their fragile paws, and hold her as best they can. Mother Owl sweeps past and past the house; they can feel her emptiness and her tender wings.

It is in this that at last the lesson is learnt, in this silent hour in the cupboard under the stairs; they are only mice. They are small, and humble and low against the ground. Mice are for dying, for doubting, for making a little beauty, a little love. The childling is returned to them only at the end of an age of strife, only when they finally understand that in her is embodied no great work of mice. She is just a sad thing, a poor thing as they are. She is come that they might love her, nothing more.

As the mice are thinking, the feet of the other human creature come back down the stairs and wander this way and that; there is a great commotion in the kitchen that makes them all freeze like dead things and listen, as Marie smashes up a dining chair. Then everything becomes quiet again and the child clambers to her feet.

For a few minutes the mice all watch as the childling gathers things, bobbins and cup-handle teethers and a rattle that is half a tin of sugar cubes. She frowns as her hands become too full, and squats to her knees again, as if trying to puzzle this out.

There is a sudden cough from the parlour then, a sort of sobbing, throaty noise, and the childling leaps at it, scattering toys and mice. They flee for their lives as she crashes through the door, teddy bear still in her fist, to find her sister.

63

Marie

SINCE MY GRANDMOTHER soaked back into the garden, everything was much too strong, over-coloured like neat orange squash. And I, who was so accustomed to a dilute world, was overcome with it, the too-sweet wind gusts; the slimy lawn and the clouds in the sky that coated the tongue and the back of the throat. I could hardly stand it, and was dogged by pains in the head and a ringing in my skull from the clashing air.

Even the house, with its uncertain corners and yellowish paintwork, seemed a little affected, forced a little realer by her melting. There was a licking of pink in the wallpaper, where before I had seen only mauve, and I discovered the scent of my own self, animal-like and woody. The curtains finicked in new draughts and the thinking nerves of the bricks themselves seemed throbbingly loud. Right then, I could feel its heavy mind drowsing, lifting and sinking, muttering silently; the house was falling asleep.

It seemed that my grandmother had been made out of us, wrenched out of everything like a kind of essence, the unknowable soul of our household. It was only after she had gone that I think I truly understood the puzzle that she was; for even as I had feared her, she had made me safe. I had not realised, either, just how much of the world that she contained; how grey things had become with every passing night.

I am not sure why she came apart as she did, nor why she should have grown so very strong. There was a kind of sense to her demise, though; it seemed fit that she should end her days with electrical spikes and rain and thunder. I missed her solidness, and the tread of her feet against the stairs.

The garden was like unwatered Kia Ora as I stood at the step and flinched at the afternoon. It was harsh enough to suffocate. I had wandered here again without quite considering why; as if I might somehow discover her in the garden, pinching the thorns off rosebushes, or stalking through the spraddled flowerbeds with blackish vials of blood.

My grandmother was nowhere to be found; she was everywhere. I could breathe her; I turned my head away from the sky, after-images colliding in my eyes. She left me seven days ago. I hoped it was seven; I would have made a note, counted out the time, except that the only biro I could find was dried out and useless, splitting the paper but making no mark.

It was probably seven days. When it came to eight days since she shattered, the rent man would come again and I was terrified. I would owe him double. He would be very angry. And however was I to protect myself now; protect this other child? I was the provider now, and my grandmother's rooms were locked, secure as a tomb. I crept up the stairs to look; the door might as well have been nailed.

Even as rent day loomed I dared not think of it; instead I busied my head with the worries of fuel. There was no coal left to burn, so with what might I make a fire? Already the cold was collecting in my fingers, and I had come to fear darkness like a cave dweller. So I pulled the door shut behind me and I pondered the notion of burning.

With what could I bear to part? What objects need I burn to keep my creatures alive? Like a clockwork thing I made my way upstairs and found myself in my old bedroom. I swept my gaze across my musty bed, and peeled off an armful of sheets that smelled of mushrooms.

The books were almost gone already, eaten to spines of gluey string by mice, dragged into skirting holes and crevices. I found the skeleton of my *Young Christians' Bible* and tucked what remained of it underneath my arm for the fire. Everywhere there were neat little droppings and scraps of this and that.

I dragged my feet towards the heap of my toys, and found myself a Ludo board and a broken plastic boat. A drift of dolls and stuffed animals stared from the floor like some stupid audience, politely admiring dust motes and cracks in the plaster.

I picked up a few, but then I had a glimpse of their future, smiling through the fire, splitting threadbare fur until they were only kapok and brand-hot glass eyes. My skin crawled; I threw their little bodies back towards the corner with my heart pounding. I had better not burn my old frocks either, for the child must have something to wear.

She crept from the parlour this morning, had laid her hot little hand against my cheek and walked away. I had been horrified, but the mice all got up to go with her and so I felt a little eased. They all trooped into the hall together and I eavesdropped with my fist in my mouth until I heard them all pattering up the stairs. I suppose I could not begrudge her the right to explore.

That first night and the day after, the child had stayed with me, hardly moving, sharing my air and holding my fingers in her hands. All that time the mice had held their peace, even as they clung against her skin. I had dominated her attention, kept her selfishly close, that I might stroke her like a cat, make her burrow her head into the gap between my collarbone and chin. And she let me; that little wild thing from the garden patiently bore me and my hysterical cuddles. She gazed into my face with her back very straight, and her face not quite smiling.

But now (I stood outside my old room and listened), she sat nearby, communing with mice. I could feel them; hear their whispered thinking. The house heaved within its dreaming, groaned with its rafters, making my teeth hurt. I shook my head at the state of us all and bore my strange kindling downstairs.

Evening dropped like a cloth and I began to panic, hunting in the gloaming light for something solid to burn. Plastic and paper was all very well, but we had to have wood, something to burn slow, keep us alive all night. I needed fire, needed light to push away the blackness, make safe my child, my mice, my own trembling self. There was not fuel enough in all the world for a darkness like ours.

I should have gone outside and gathered sticks. I should have thought of what to do before. I daren't now, I thought, daren't leave the back door's gloomy refuge, for the garden was mutating to a hugeness of black, new and solid since my grandmother had shed herself into it. I stood at the scullery window, gulping and counting out my fear, and then jumped as a massive pale owl drifted from the cherry tree like some unspeakable power.

Its eyes were puddles of nothing and it threw itself at the window, talons arched in front of it. I ducked my head and hid my face, as if it might break the glass with its claws, but at the last instant it wheeled away and was off through the night. The house must have felt my flinch, for it moaned again, this time in real distress. I put my fingers against the sweating plaster, but then my eyes lit on a dullish gleam underneath the stone sink.

It was the head of a little hatchet; it had lain there for so many years that I had never quite noticed it. When I crouched down to see, there was a whole tool box, ruined and rusty, swaddled with spider webs. I lifted things out one by one; I had never really examined such objects, much less seen them put to any use; their weight and tact-less edges made me think of the rent man.

Nonetheless, the hatchet was a thing that I knew, for the woodcutters of my storybooks had brandished these at tree and wolf, and so I took it with me into the kitchen. It was a sudden inspiration, or else a kind of sudden fury, that caused me to take that axe to a dining chair; it broke beneath my hammering and chopping, until of a sudden I had wood enough for a fire, for a few days even, if only I was careful to save it.

I staggered with all my bits to the parlour and dropped them on the floor with a clatter. I made a little blaze with one of the very last matches; then I sat and watched the baby flames as the house ground its old brown jaws and whimpered. I could feel its hurt with the pains in my head; it was doubled up around the dining room like an animal curled around a wound.

Its sadness felt like my own somehow, and I resolved to do my best to comfort the great miserable thing; a flea comforting an elephant, but a loving flea at least. I reached behind the red armchair for my eiderdown and then I lugged it like a corpse along the floor; at the chimney-breast I swathed myself inside it, leaving my back bare against the plaster.

I sat as still as anything, as a mother with four little mouse-children used my shoulder for a lookout post. Scrapings from the other side of the wall made them freeze, then scatter suddenly. The cutlery was nosing at the brickwork again, hunting for a way through, singing their thin serrated music and flipping their sinuous blades.

The house continued to thrash; infrasonic bellows coughed up from the cellars. I laid my face against the plaster, stroked that cold old wall like the flank of a carthorse. It was huddled thus, cheek against cheek, that I shared the house's dream.

I saw it as it saw itself: clear skinned, without the pits of weather and the lichen that now itched one whole side. A heavy-rumped parlour maid scurried from the attic to the lower floors, which rang with the bickering of children. Their motion was so rapid that it was shocking to see; it was only when the figures were still that I could hope to observe them.

The girl held a top to her chest, refusing to give it up; a boy in a sailor suit struck her with the whip, cutting at her bare shin. I gasped, heaved with the violence of it. Then there was a jumble, an awful tangle of years and lives and meanness, and I realised the liquid evil of creatures that are not made as houses are. These things of meat did nothing but hurt, jagger and wound each other and the house with their fists and boots and electric drills. I was aghast at it, but rooted by the feet. I might never escape them.

Then it seemed that some of the trillion moments that I dreamed of were familiar. I dreamed of fairy lights, and paper chains that noosed up the corners of ceiling and wall, of the hundred nasty nicks from drawing pins.

I saw a younger woman, and a man that I did not know. I was puzzling at this when the woman made a gesture, a hugging of herself that made me recognise her. It was my mother; it must have been, but then I lost her again amidst the clutter of images, the tiny killings and scrapings and sofas dragged along my floors.

My mother was in the kitchen, murdering trifle

sponges, fracturing them in her finger bones amidst a chaos of kitchen things: Paxo boxes, Birds mix; a great frozen turkey carcass. The man was wobbling atop a kitchen chair, jabbing and jabbing with a thumbtack at the wall, a string of tinsel impaled against it. However much he hurt the distemper it would not stay in, and presently the point squashed out sideways, quite flat.

They were talking together all the while, speaking and speaking, louder and louder still. She upset a jug full of boiling jelly, scalded the carpet with it. He trod awkwardly from the chair, fell sideways and blamed her. The kettle began to scream.

I did not understand what happened after that, only that hours rattled by and voices rose and fell, that a baby began to wail upstairs and nobody came. The voices of people are a rapid kind of trilling, like the singing of flesh-eating birds, and I tried to look away, to focus my mind elsewhere.

But all that I could really see were the violences, and so I watched the poor baby for a long while, the boiling rage of her crying, her little face red and hot and streaming tears like an overflow pipe. She cried a long time, until she seemed to grow exhausted and I saw her dark eyes glisten in the light from the hall.

But there was a sickness in me, a new and catastrophic sickness, and I hunted from room to room as one might search through pockets, although I already knew perfectly well where the malady was. I felt the copper taste of blood in my floors, and I shuddered so hard that my foundations broke. Sore as a scree slope, I turned to look at the slime trail of red between the kitchen and the dining room.

There was a scraping from the sideboard, a metal whine that sounded like the end of every living thing. I heard the music that follows Armageddon, when the knives shall wake and lick up all the gore; when the knives shall inherit the whole earth, with no creature left to witness but the stones and ruined houses. Nausea soaked inside me as the inmates of the knife drawer turned from one thing to another; from dormant to savage, from needless to starving. I was terrified; I was terrified.

I woke to find that I was sitting up, sobbing at the darkness with the child shaking my shoulders. She had a soggy blue teddy bear in her hand, bitten out of blanket by lots of little teeth. I saw the black in her eyes and then I knew utterly who she was. She was my sister, my twin; she had cried and then listened in the night as my mother killed a man. Forcefully, I perceived the welt around the dining room, the thickened air that held it removed like a canker from the rest of the building.

The child knelt down and placed herself in my arms; I held her close and tried to calm myself. For a long time, I could not.

64

Knife

THERE IS NOT much light to see by, and there is hardly any colour. As the rain spats the painted window, as the chimney wails, the tones of everything are shades of steel and tarnish. From an inch above the carpet floor, the world is wide and stark; a fish knife flips its back and rears right up against its ivory handle.

Perhaps that ivory remembers being an animal, once; perhaps its brittle flexion calls to itself a trace of the plains, of the ancient plodding wisdom of the elephant. But if there is some tiny relic left inside of the world of things with souls, there is no sign. The fish knife quivers, twists this way and then the other, watching through its edges, scanning the waste-grounds of carpet. It does not look up to see the ceilings.

Here and there are flecks of brightness, where the meagre light catches tine or spoon-edge; these patches are quite bleached and the fish knife can barely make them out. Cutlery is not made for daytime. Knives do not give a damn for the life-giving sun, and when it has burned itself to a throbbing crimson eye they will not mourn it for a second.

There is no colour in the universe but red. There are argent greys and the dullness of lead; there are a trillion notes of white and black, but red is the only colour. Red is the glory of bloody things; the poetry of flesh and warm skin tearing. Red is the only colour; red is delicious and hot and liquid; red is the sunset of the old order.

There is no red to be seen; no red to taste in this old rank air; there has been no red for long famished months. And it seems that the cutlery has found a taste for it, this ruinous life beyond dormancy; they might have bided their time for twenty thousand years, but now they know the lick of meat they will never rest again. The hunger of a carving fork is the agony of worlds; is long as a nuclear winter, and the cutlery seethes amongst itself like boiling.

The fish-knife has not smelt red for savage ages and it is hungry, screeking and aching and starving for redness. But there is no colour, not a trace but the sterile shine of metal, and they cannot eat each other. They cross and cross each other's paths like sharks in shallow waters, and the carpet pile is shaved to canvas string and fluff. The fish knife flats its blade again and tumbles to the floor; it has no thinking in its nerves but the high scream of starvation.

There is no jot of intelligence in it, any more than a cockroach is wise, yet a fork or spoon is all made out of nerves, nerves and little more, nerves that conduct in massive flattened sheets. Where a blooded thing has nerves in fragile threads, where a houseish thing has nerves in lumbering brick and lath, a fish-knife has nerves of nickel, layers and layers of them, razor sharp at the edges. They conduct at half the speed of sound, unimpeded by synapse or autonomy, knowing no sensation but feeding and hunger and the pain of corrosion.

They are not bright enough for fear; they hardly know themselves to be living, but the leap of impulse makes them fleet as flies. A bluebottle will twirl into the air an age, a century before the hand swiped at it, seeking to smatter it against a windowpane. Such creatures are made differently, swift and precise of movement, brainless and unkillable and very much faster than soft-fleshed things of meat.

The wall is wearing very thin, so thin that odd molecules of red are beginning to percolate through from the parlour. The fish-knife slithers towards the eaten parts and knows that there is red behind it. The other side of the wall is gorgeously warm; betrays itself with the sounds of living blood, with the scuffs and voices and lung-wet exhalations. The prisoners of the dining room will feed; if they had to, they would carve a channel in a mountain for a taste of red, but now the wall is nearly through.

Then there are shoes beyond the door and the dining room grows deadly silent. The wood is thinner than a wall by inches and might have been screwed through weeks ago, but a knife cannot easily wield itself. If they could jump, lift off the floor, then they might have murdered the household a long time since. If they could jump, they might have cleared the metal barricades underneath the door, might have twisted like corkscrews and broken out in a trice.

But they can only scrape or cut a thing by bracing on the ground, by forcing point or blade or digging edge against the leverage of handle and floor. When the cutlery makes war with flesh, comes out to possess the universe, the revolution will come at floor level with torn feet and splitting arteries; in time whole cities shall fall as low as the knives; the knives will finish them off when their throats are flat against carpet and tarmac.

The footsteps die away and the cutlery returns to munching at the wall; to the house it is like having a peptic ulcer, an endless chewing bellyache. But house meat is not red, and the fish knife does not care a toss about its pain.

65

Marie

THE NEXT MORNING the rent man jattered the letterbox before six; he came like a burst water pipe, or food poisoning. He was catastrophic; he filled our ears and made us crawl at the skin.

He tried very hard; he shoved his shoulder at the front door and seemed astounded that it was secured. The rent man called, 'I say! I say!' though the sunburst window as if he were trying to hail a cab, as if some fellow had stolen the cap from his head. Then he scraped his way past the blackberry bushes to the back door, trailing filthy language from his mouth as he went.

I had been expecting him, of course. Last night I had even managed to shut the back door fast, though it half finished me to heave on it so hard; by the time I managed to drag it past the stick in the frame, I was sweating and trembling like a person in a fever. It must have taken me twenty tries, every one an act of such hugeness I surprised my own self.

It was clear that that door would never open again, and I think that the house itself was pleased that I had shut it properly after all that time, as though a dislocated joint had been forced back in place at last. I could hear it that night, testing at the hinge and catch, humming and hahring to itself in absentminded approval. That made me smile, even in the midst of all that unease.

When the rent man had found his way to the concrete patio, he was probably very hot himself; there was a redness in his voice, a kind of flush that I could see with my mind, plain as a nosebleed. The rent man was scarlet in the face, and creased all the way from brow to brow; I expect there were little veins standing out against his head, and his scalp was probably uncomfortably damp. He rattled at the door handle, then beat at it with the heel of his hand.

'I know you are in there,' said the rent man, red and loud and we could hear it from the parlour. 'I know you are in there,' said he, and then he seemed to change his mind, or at least alter tack, for he suddenly brightened his tone and called out, 'Mrs Ashkin? Are you there?'

'Marie, dear,' called the rent man and I closed my eyes, 'Marie dear, is your mummy home? I have some lovely lollipops in my jacket you know!' Then he opened his palm and slapped the wood once, as one might a face. The poor house blinked, quite astonished.

By the time the rent man found his way to the front of the house again I was so giddy that I could not tell if I were still sitting upright. The child and I held each other's wrists and huddled against the wall, comforting ourselves, the windowsill above our heads offering some mean protection. The rent man smeared the glass with his fingers and the smear of his lip as he held his face and tried to see us through the parlour window.

I grit my teeth and quaked as the rent man spat the landlord's name through the pane, invoked him like some mediaeval Satan. The landlord would hear of this. We should all be evicted, thrown out on our filthy ears. The rent man told my long-gone mother that he would return with the master keys, and perhaps the police too, for it was all that she deserved. And then he turned and cursed and swaggered off to his car, which he scratched against the fencepost with a horrible screech.

The child stared at my face with dumb terror; when he had finally gone from earshot she undug her fingernails from my arm and left me with three half-moon welts where she had gripped so hard. I stroked her face, said, 'Shush, shush,' under my breath, for an explanation would have been entirely useless, and I hadn't the heart for one anyhow.

As the pounding of our nerves subsided, I began to hear something else, far nastier than any rent man. The scritch of metal could be heard again, digging and cutting at the adjoining wall, relentless, brainlessly persistent. There was a busy quality to it this time, a new kind of urgency, a disaster waiting for its birth.

The cutlery was starving. Of course it was; any fool could have guessed that; and now that I had seen them with the house's poor consciousness I could imagine them with the most awful clarity. I knew for sure about the mice, the man that my mother stabbed, the snippy fate of every poor corpse that was dumped in there. The cutlery was famished and it would eat the very brickwork. We should be dissected in our sleep.

I tossed my head and jumped to my feet, for I fancied then that I could see light through the wallpaper, as though the breakthrough would come at any moment. The child cowered at my haste, as I fled for the scullery, as I dug around for tin cans in the rubbish, and a handful of rusty clout-nails from the box beneath the sink. I even unearthed a few bits of zinc sheeting, and I sandwiched these between vinegary tea towels and nailed them along the skirting boards, blacking one thumbnail, grunting and whimpering to myself as though fending off a nightmare. Then I stood back to examine my handiwork, and wondered whether it would all prove useless.

At the end of it I was tired to the death, and I crawled to the red armchair with my head aching and a pulling at my belly where I had strained a muscle, and fell asleep without a single thought. I did not dream, only listened with sleeping ears to the echoes of my hammer and the curious nibbling of knives.

I woke later, hours or minutes later; for the clock said half past six and it was still dim, or else night was falling, and I could not tell which. I fed the fire with the *Motorists' Atlas of the British Isles* and handfuls of pot pourri, and then I went in search of the child. I found that the scullery window was wide open, and with a jolt of fear, I clambered through and into the garden, praying that I had not lost her.

She was on the back step; she turned to me, cautiously, and then raised her feral head to snuff at the air. Her hair hung black over her eyes. I smiled at her, rushed with relief that I was not abandoned, and it was almost with a chuckle that I hurried over the patio towards her.

She narrowed her eyes, seemed to warn me off. I stopped, half turned away, almost embarrassed. Perhaps I should busy myself elsewhere, pretend that I was not watching her like a spy. I decided to gather sticks. I walked out to the cherry tree and beyond it, to a sapling of scraggy plum, thumb-thick at the branches, wondering if I might be able to fell it with my blunt little hatchet. Meditatively, I rubbed at the new hardness that was developing along my forearm. Perhaps I could at that. I felt capable, then, like a grown-up would feel.

I turned my hand, palm uppermost. It was not the little pale thing that I remembered. Grained with dirt, callused from breaking wooden things, this hand may as well have belonged to someone else, I thought. A long splinter was visible, stuck in the skin of my index finger. I put my hand to my mouth to nibble through the top layer, to get it out.

The sensation of skin between my teeth was so repulsive, that although it did not hurt, I could not bear to continue. My grandmother used to take out splinters by picking and picking with the point of a leatherworking needle. I could never do that to the child, even if she had let me.

With a pang, I looked up to see if she was still here. There she was, on all fours on the vegetable patch in my tartan dress and holed tights. She wore no shoes, and would push them off with her toes if I tried to force them upon her.

I put up my hand to shield my eyes, for the sun seemed to be rising; I watched the child inch forward, sinuous as a snare. There was something foreboding in her manner, something so very wild, that I merely stood, almost afraid, watching. The child tilted her head, very slowly, so as to free a lock of hair from her staring eye.

Her little body hunkered down to earth, soil showing black between her outspread fingers. Then she moved forward again, slow as paralysis. Her hands curled until the fingers were dug right into the mud, and the child drew back her lip, uncovered her milk teeth. She seemed to be glaring at the cherry tree. I put my finger into my mouth and waited. She did not move.

And then, the child leaped like a flame. She surged up the horrified tree in an instant; the cherry tree exploded with wings and the cries of small birds. She had jumped so hard that she landed on the second branch, high as my head. Lightly she dropped to the ground again, the long body of a squirrel caught in her jaws. I stood, stiff and stranded as a scarecrow.

There was a long hush in the garden. The birds had settled on the guttering and trees again, and it took a time for the wind to remember to blow, for the sun to continue its stunted dawn. The birds began to sing again; my finger held the imprint of my bite.

The child sat at the foot of the cherry tree with a fresh bright scratch on her brow. She smeared at it with the flat of one wrist, and then she bit into her squirrel. I pushed my hands through my hair, and the movement made the child look up; for a moment her eyes were baleful and she uttered a long growl that showed the red in her teeth.

I shivered for an hour or two in the garden, pretending not to watch the child as she devoured every inch of that squirrel, snapping at the spine with the sides of her teeth like a dog at a marrowbone. After an age, the fury in her seemed to die back and she sniffed and licked at her fingers and arms, polished her face with them and looked over at me again. Then the child crept over to the open window and climbed back inside. I followed carefully.

66

Mice

THE NIGHT BELONGS to Mother Owl; the woollen-scarf darkness and the fear. The night belongs to Mother Owl because it is the time of birth-making, of shadows and secret things. When the night comes there is nothing but her, the nothingness of her, and the light from the grate is made only to see the blackness by.

The whimpers of newborns make a joy to see the silence by. The love of Mouse for its own, for the strange huge children that they adore, this love is to show them the quiet that comes after love is at an end, the empty pulse of a torpid heart, the enormity of everything that is larger than a mouse.

This is what makes them so very beautiful, the brilliance and dancingness of tiny lives. This is a thing that they know with their guts and whiskers. They are Mouse; small and humble and low against the ground, and any pretension to greatness is futile at best.

For its part the parlour is paradise at three o'clock in the morning. The fire is sinking into itself in the grate, casting the room with a colour like the inside of some colossal womb. And the odour is mystifying and glorious, making poetry of the universe of Home; here are burning cushion covers, dust turned into smoke. There are lavender bags in the fire, and the stink of their purple burning is a magic spell recited in air.

It is sumptuous and gorgeous and perfectly terrifying, for this is how the house shall smell when it is licked up in flames, when fire climbs out from his sooty ironwork cradle to claim his black and red inheritance. He will make the beauty of this house complete; this is the way of life and death. This is the will of Mother Owl.

Marie and the childling are huddled together like littermates; like sleeping continents, crouched side by side in the frizz-mother's ragged armchair. They do not even know that they are embracing so, for the childling had remained by herself for hours, waiting like a fox in the quiet of the scullery.

Even the mice had not dared sit with her, for she smelled dangerous to them today, bloody like a creature fed upon killed things. All afternoon she had seemed more like owl than mouse to them; some unknowable creature from the leaf-smelling space beyond the back door. This too is the will of Mother Owl; she reveals the nature of beings, reminds the mice that no thing alive is uncomplicated.

She is so familiar to them, yet she teaches a lesson of wildness, of safety and the danger of things taken for granted. So she sat by herself like a moonless sky, with blood in her teeth and a terrible sadness to her that could rupture the heart. She sat and held her knees against her chest, and slowly the smells of wind and death sank away from her; slowly the tension in her bones grew looser and she turned her head to see the mice, to snuff the fire smoke from the parlour. When finally she was the childling that they knew again, she released her smile and crept to the parlour.

By then Marie was asleep, cold despite the warmth. She was sleeping the way in which she had hunched all evening; as stiff and uncomfortable as a coat hanger, and she never even stirred when the childling crawled up under her arm and clambered onto her lap. But the mice all saw, and in their small grey way, they were happy.

Since then they have watched them both as the night time threw her great cold feathers against the flanks of the house. They have sighed like microscopic draughts as Marie found her twin in her sleep, as they folded their limbs together and slept amongst each other, and grew cosy.

Now it is the holy time, which belongs alone to the silences of mice. And somehow there collects in the air a sense of the sacred, a kind of frightened reverence, for the mice plan to make a sacrifice to Mother Owl. They have saved a gift of immense wealth. Behind the washing basket, fluff-studded and glistening gold, there is a whole slice of Prince's cling peach.

The mice all tip their noses, each to each, and the shadows on the wall leap and play like demons in a forest, and the parlour is as eldritch as can be. The breathing of the girls is a rise and falling in the atmosphere, which is fragrant with the killing magic of burning shoes, so they gather up their terror and their slice of peach and begin the journey to the attic.

It makes a luscious sticky trail along the carpet, as wonderful a moving thing as any holy procession. Instead of flower carts there are little globs of syrup, and the aromatic glory of it is purer than the rarest incense. A brownish mouse is shoving with his paws, with the push of his forehead, doing his best to move that slice along before him. Before the red chair is even passed he is soaked with it, the sweetness of his burden. Juice coats him, stings his eyes as he pushes, as his claws sink into that yellow flesh. It takes super-mouse effort to shove it beyond the gap beneath the door.

Thomas is waiting in the dank hallway, waiting with his muzzleful of teeth, with his eyes playful-bright and the end of his tail lashing. The peach slips through first, with the brownish mouse behind it, pushing and squishing. He is a sugar mouse now, syrup anointed, and when he unflattens his back, he finds himself gazing at the cat's hypnotic eyes, which are golden and a little like those of an owl.

The seconds that twirl past are enormous and quivering; the brownish mouse freezes like a drawing, his fingers folded against his chest and his chin lifted to his killer. Thomas pauses for a moment, lifts his forefeet, rears into the sky without making the slightest sound.

In that eternity the whole house becomes a new thing, black and fire-bright together: magic and beautiful as the instant of death or birthing. The brownish mouse comprehends this; the agony and mercy of Mother Owl, and he finds his life bitten away in a fierce kind of joy.

Thomas pounces. His paws, as they strike, are at the same time warm and blanket-soft, sharp as a smashed light bulb. Then the brownish mouse is all over with. The cat lifts his feet slowly and catches the little body up in his teeth, shaking his head, kittenish and pleased.

The other mice creep through the gap, shocked. They are noiseless, and very, very many, and they swarm the hallway in silent crowds. They are in no danger now, for the beast is sated. Thomas barely glances up as he carts his prize away, to skulk with it beneath the kitchen table; the mice all stare after him and then they turn back for the peach. Now there is a little blood amongst the slick of syrup; this is as it should be. They take an age to heave it up the stairs.

No mouse has ever set its toes in the grandmother's rooms, in the Queendom of Mother Owl. None has ever dared to; yet in his tiny head, every one of them has wondered what kind of place is past that lead-painted door.

Perhaps there is nothing at all. Perhaps the door opens into sky and void, or there again, perhaps the nest of Mother Owl is a little as those of mice are; perhaps she tears up clouds and furry creatures to make the place for her children soft. The grandmother is no more, but Mother Owl is watching them in every small move of their hearts. They shall go to her, then, with their sacrifice of food; they shall show Mother Owl their humility, make their homage. They are Mouse; they are small and humble and low against the ground. They will show her their fear, that she should know they have understood their lesson.

By the time they have reached the attic, the peach is in several pieces and quite filthy. The mice all look at one another sidelong, each one quaking. After a time, one brave soul pushes her shoulders through the door-gap, puts her face into the den of Mother Owl, and the others follow suit.

The skylight is open to the night and the walls are soft with wings of every kind. There are the petrol-spill wings of pigeons, the drab of sparrow and the crow's utter black. In the draught the feathers ripple and the attic sounds like flying; they overlap each other, leaving no gap of wall at all.

There is no bed like the things the humans slept in, only a huge oval mirror and a bank of shelves, bearing books all bound in delicious leather. Mother Owl is not there, not upon the knotted floorboards, not hiding in the absent light from the naked socket. They gaze about and they sniff, but she is not here. The mice are a little flummoxed, but they stow the peach in the space beneath the bookshelves, where she is bound to find it.

And now the mice should leave, for they have accomplished the thing that they set out to do, but the nature of mouse is impetuous, and curiosity is ever their downfall. There is a scarf hanging from one shelf, a scarf made of silk that almost touches the floor. Now a mouse is a tiny thing, and it barely weighs an ounce or two, so when a pale grey mouse finds herself overcome with madness, she shins right up with hardly a pull at all.

The others stare after her as she is lost from sight. She has discovered a row of glass vials, tiny and bright like a row of milk teeth; she has discovered a great long thing that humans use to make marks on paper. There is a bottle of Quink that stains her curious snout and makes her sneeze. When she polishes at her face, her paws and mouth turn blue.

The mice on the floor cannot bear it, this ignorance, for one of them is exploring and they themselves are not. Mice are made for discovering, and so it is that they forget to be humble and low against the ground, just for a second, and they begin to clamber up the scarf by ones and twos, then ten and twenty, and the tiny weight that a mouse is mounts up and the scarf is pulled right away, along with the ink stained mouse and half a dozen of the glass vials that had rested against it.

The vials hit the ground as the mice do, falling around like a strange kind of hail; as the mice bounce, the glasses burst and spatter shards everywhere. And as they break, small things are released: the high, over-strung songs of little birds, every one living and panicking and suddenly set free. Perhaps they are souls.

The attic is quite mad with them for a second or two, chaotic with the singing that flutters around the mice, the smashing, falling glass, and the scarf that tumbles slowly down like mercury. The mice all scramble for safety; they scat on cut paws, beneath the door, down the stairs. Mice seethe into the parlour with terror gulping at their backs as the birds' voices all find the window and soar out of it into the sky. And somewhere, way beyond, Mother Owl is laughing.

67

Rent Man

THE SUN WAS not quite above the hedge that clung to the side of the lane to the house. It was unpleasantly bright against the eyes of the rent man, which were rather bloodshot at the best of times. The rent man was a trifle hung-over, which was a little unfair, as he had not consumed all that much the afternoon before.

He rounded the corner to the driveway with unaccustomed ease, as today the rent man had parked his big red car at the bottom of the lane. Today, the rent man did not care to announce his presence; today he was on a secret mission. He smiled at his own fancy, pictured himself as Mr Steed. Inside the rent man's mind, his paunch turned muscular and his scanty hair Brylcreem-slick, and he turned his head to either side, furtive and wiry as a stoat.

The coast was clear and the house stood there as ever, cracked across its face, the gutters hairy with stalks of grass, the windows cataracts of filth. The rent man hooked his thumbs into his armpits, stood a while and studied everything like a work of art, pleased with the dereliction of it all.

Proper upkeep was a condition of the tenancy; he would have them all slung in the gutter. The rent man lingered over the image of that nasty old woman squatting on the tarmac of the high street, snotty tears coursing down her pinched granny's face.

Then, with a slight stiffening of his trousers, he imagined the mother gazing up at him, wordless pleading in her eyes. The rent man considered her, and young Marie too, with her little breasts and her delicate face, like an illustration in a book. Perhaps he would offer them clemency, should they prove sufficiently grateful. It might prove to be an interesting day.

The rent man stood back with that thought in his head and suddenly felt remarkably cheerful. Then he put his fingers to his pocket and discovered the master key there. The copper Yale would fit the lock of the front door; he would slide it into its hole very gently, would push at the door and creep in to see what he would see.

The rent man was beginning to sweat as he fished it from his pocket and held it to the sunlight. He undid the door with great tenderness and then began to ease his weight against it, when all of a sudden Thomas, who had been shut inside all night, made a break through the crack, head down low, streaming between the rent man's very shiny shoes. He hissed a curse and swiped a kick at the cat, felt the toecap connect with its haunch and felt much better. The cat fled.

Then the rent man stood like an Indian hunter, as if by effort of will he might unmake any noise that he had already caused, and slowly he let the moment absorb him again. Perhaps he might find one of them undressed! Finally, trembling with anticipation, he let himself in.

68

Marie

WE SAT IN the perfect light of dawn, the last two girls in the whole wide universe, in our shabby haven. It was not cold; the bath towels were piled in the grate, fizzing and hissing and making the air around us gentle; making the wallpaper glow.

I kept the fire alight always, for it seemed that our way of life was on the wane already, and so it mattered not a crumb if my oxblood sandals were eaten by the fire, or that the cookery books were gone. I might never remember how to make a drop-scone now, or mix up batter for pancakes, but there was no milk, nor any gas to light for the stove. And the last match was spent, so if I let the flames die out then I should never get them lit again.

So it was that we basked in our paradise like Eve and Adam, our hearts naked and perfectly pure, even as our earthly flesh was dirty. The child had been in my arms as I woke, nuzzled up against my side, with no trace about her of that squirrel but a dry streak of blood on her cheek.

Yesterday I had been frightened of her, disturbed by her sudden violence, this alien ability to murder a living thing. But of course, she was forced into her shape by the world, forced and distorted. If I never had tin cans to open, perhaps I might have grown into a different sort of creature. Perhaps life would have made me cruel, a killer, or a seer of elves and pixies.

I watched her sleep for a long time, until I understood at last that her hunting was no thing that I should resent; any more than I should hate Thomas for his catching birds, than my mother for her crying, than the mice for tormenting her so.

The nature of creatures came to me then; I think that at last I truly understood my life. It was no triumph after all, and not a bit of comfort. Her jaw muscles moved beneath the pale of her cheek, and her chin was a small sharp triangle, and she had nobody in all creation to keep her safe but me, and I had nobody at all.

Then her eyes flickered and lit against my own and I embraced my sister; after a moment she put out her slim hand and stroked it through my hair. Even though it was a kind of comfort, that touch made my eyes silver with tears.

Every corner was alive with mice, watching or resting, with their backs like greasy pearls in the sunrise. It seemed that we all felt the need to stay together, as if every sort of beast needed the others to assure herself that she was real, to hold to some fool's notion of strength in numbers. Perhaps we were all just afraid to be alone. The cutlery was a nest of wasps, nervy and buzzing like a light bulb before it blows.

The wall that stood between us and the dining room was thinning like laddering stockings, but without the consolation of the fire I could hardly bear the thought of living. I think I would sooner have had my throat cut than die in the kitchen, of loneliness and cold and the uncaring dark.

I laid the lambskin on the embers, gently, so as not to quash the flames, and then on a strange whim, I pulled my mother's dress over my head and poured it into the fire too. Behind the sofa I had found an old nightdress that was almost clean, with lacy cuffs and a high tight throat, and when I put it on I felt like an angel. I rummaged in the laundry basket and discovered a little one that had been mine, and the child did not object when I dressed her in it.

Then we sat facing the fire as I sang to her; I combed her hair and sang the only holy song I knew. I sang the lines

'*Amazing grace, how sweet the sound*
That saved a wretch like me!'

over and over, because I thought that was the whole song. I discovered that my voice was low and sweet and pure as a dove's voice, and was surprised, as if I had never sung before in all my life, as if this might be my first and only song. The hair of the child was like broken coal against her nightdress, and I knew that I should never braid it again, for it was meant to cascade exactly as it was. She was beautiful, and I cried and combed it through with my clawed fingers.

The door banged open, so hard it caught the wall and bit a dent in the plaster. The house jumped, cringing like a kicked dog, and I could feel it holding its breath as if braced for something. The mice all skeltered away in a trice. The rent man planted himself in the middle of the floor with his mouth curling, with his hands in his pockets. He said, 'Hello sweetie,' as if he had been rehearsing what to say before he came.

I jumped to my feet, and the child hid her body behind mine. With a leer, the rent man nodded his jowls at her and began to snigger. He called me a dirty little mare, and said that he had always known I would be an early developer, that certain things always ran in families, didn't they. Or maybe, said the rent man, this kid was one of his, as mummy and he had been rather good friends, did I know that? He asked me where my mother was but I only stared, and so he smiled, red in the face.

The rent man's face turned beatific then, almost paternal, and he tugged at the folds of his trousers just above the knees, and dropped into a crouch. With a brief rummage at his pocket, with the face of a Sunday school teacher, he twiddled his fingers at the child's face. She shied sideways, as he produced a glossy lollipop from behind her ear. The rent man told her to run along and play. She made no move whatever to take it from his hand. Her flinch seemed to offend him, for then he scowled and stood up, and I heard the crick of his knees.

The rent man jammed his fists into his pockets and began to drone about wear and tear, and a deplorable lack of upkeep. I gazed at his mouth as he moved his lips, dark pink and fleshy like some obscene plant, a flower made of meat. He spat as he talked, flecked his tie with small white dots, and I dredged my brain for words, those noises of mouth and throat that used to come with such ease. I shook my face and tried to understand.

I supposed he meant the house. I had no defence to plead; it was filthy and overrun with the mice, but here I was, doing my best. I tried to convey this to the rent man, but he scraped my excuses aside with a sweep of his square-nailed fingers and announced that a little tart like me deserved nothing better than destitution. He stepped his plastic shoes right up to my own bare toes, and he was shaking as he shoved his face at mine, and the sound of his mind was like a suffocating dog, straining at a choke collar, fit to die.

All this time, the child had crouched behind my back, but as the rent man began to enjoy the sound of his voice, I heard her begin to growl softly. I became aware too, of a scraping crescendo from the dining room. With a sidelong glance at the wall, I glimpsed a streak of silver and jumped. The child had seen it too, and her lips drew right back over her teeth, as she began to snarl, high-pitched and savage.

The rent man's threats trailed off as his eyes followed mine to the wall. With a nibbling like rats on a water pipe, a part of the plaster and brick went right through. I rushed to the corner for rags and vinegar, ignoring the spluttering of the rent man, who demanded to know the meaning of this, by god. I was forced to actually splash the blade of a carving knife before it zipped backwards with a shriek. My hands were shaking too much for me to put the lid back on the vinegar, and I fumbled with the bottle for ages as the rent man made a sort of gulping motion with his mouth.

I swear to you that I tried to stop him. That is, I would have done, but in the moment I was so horrified that I simply clamped my hand over my mouth and froze like a mouse. With a bullish shake of his head, the rent man had marched from the parlour, and wrenched open the door to the dining room, heaved through the barricade, grazed a semicircle in the carpet. The child slipped out quietly and stood at his back. I think it was she that closed the door behind him.

For several seconds, I heard the insistent clicking of the light switch as the rent man tried to make it work in the gloom. The child wandered back to my side as he uttered an irritable *tsk*, and seemed to be saying something, although whether I was supposed to hear it or not, I could not say. Then, we heard a short nasal sound, like a very loud sneeze or a shout that was cut off too quickly. I took the child by the hand and led her to the red chair by the fire.

As we gazed at the flames, there was a sort of heavy crumple, like a roll of carpet falling over, and a snipping, snipping, snipping that went on for hours. We heard it as we plugged the hole in the wall. We heard it as we feasted on tinned pineapple and corned beef. We heard it as we stoked the fire and fed its flames with cardigans. We heard it as we leaned together in the warm until we fell slowly asleep. We heard it in our dreams and in the horrified groans of the house.

69
Mice

IN THE VERY dead of night there is no sound but fire and the snipping, the scissor noises of the cutlery as it feeds. Beneath the bay window in the parlour, in a crack behind the skirting board, there is a little nest moused out of dish-cloths, all loops and tangles and knots. Amongst its fusty warmth is a brownish mouse like a left-out apple core, and her child, the only crawling thing amongst her six still-born brothers.

This pup is a female, seventh from a litter of seven, and her tiny heart is wise as an owl's. Every one of her litter-mates was dead, grew alongside her in the womb with their pulses flickering but their heads unformed and brain-less. She was made to be born alone; before she ever filled her lungs with air, she knew of loss. In the dark night of the uterus, the albino understood the ecstasy, the tragedy of mousehood; she knew herself to be a miracle.

They curl together in their nest like Madonna and Child, gazing into the secret of each other's eyes. The prophet's eyes are red as the glass on the sunburst window, red as dusk; the brownish mouse, her mother, is mes-merised and could watch her infant for the rest of her life.

Written in this mouse-child's eyes is the crumb of hope, the uncertainty of futures. The albino is more poetess than prophet after all, for she is not afraid; she sees the universe as it might be and does not shudder. She does not squeal of doom, not when her face encompasses the universe. The mouse that is brown like an apple core can see her own birth, the flick and twitch of her own small life, the hundred deaths that she might suffer.

Perhaps they shall burn, shall end their days in fire, die as the first poor prophet did when he saw the future. The thought of murder sickens the mouse mother's soul, for that guilt is a mutation, coiled inside her DNA. There again, perhaps they will be spared, for who can second-guess the will of Mother Owl? In death and hope there is glory, the mouse mother can see it now, and every act of chance is divine beauty.

In her, the mouse-mother can see the spectrum of doubt, every colour within it, from the dawning hues of afterbirth to despair's utter black. There is poetry in this, for the nature of Mouse is small and humble and low against the ground; there is no fate chosen for mice than the whim of bigger things, of gods.

So here is another prophet, dropped from the sky's talons: a second albino. This time there are no fairy lights to turn her fellows against her, no mouse-made religion to deny her truth. Even so, there is a thrill of fear clawing up the mother's backbone, for what will the others think? Will they snatch her away, call her a monster, throw her to the fire?

She cannot be a monster though, for she is so pretty. She is Arctic pure, white and soft as Andrex paper. Over hours her coat is showing through like soap-lather, as if all the weeks of her life are slipping by very quickly, as if she is growing as shrewd, as old and calm as an elderly year-ling.

If this snowy thing is a singing mouse, she makes no sign of it; neither does she murmur and squeak as a pup will. All that there is within this creature is silence and the reservoirs of love that keep a mouse's hope afloat. Perhaps the desert wanderings, the forty years in the dining room and hallways were not all useless after all, for the mice have altered their essence a little; these days they seem strung together from fear and love both. Perhaps they could never kill again; perhaps their altered nature would make such a thing impossible.

The cutlery eats and eats and eats, and the albino knows their fury and their hunger, their blind and thoughtless evil. Her mother looks and sees her terror reflected, the jittering fears of knives and fire and ruination. But it does not matter, for their fate lies upon a whim. In her pup's beacon eyes, in the landscape of her face, the albino's mother can read the million paths a creature might take, the hundred trillion damnations or savings of little lives.

The rent man is dead. The mice hardly knew he existed, hardly cared, but now his meat, the rawness of him has made a stink in the house that will only clean away in the flames. Such a portent has not been known for long centuries, yet every mouse knows well his theology, whispered in his seashell ears from the first night of his life.

This enormous human death, the awful joy of knives, tells of cosmic matters. Each mouse knows in his claws that the new albino is curled against the night; each can hear the throbbing silence of the song she is not singing.

So they come. The space behind the skirting is very narrow and they do not seek to force their way inside, instead the colony gathers just beyond, amongst the sighs of the childling and Marie, who are dreaming of cutlery. They come by the hundreds and they wait, until the albino and her mother are ready to let them see.

When she comes out to them she can barely crawl, for she is very young, and her paws are tiny and fine as fingers. She is perfect and strange; she is mouse and not-mouse;

she is white as the wings of the owl; she is babe and old sage all at once.

They see the sky in her; they see futures rise and fall in her little face; they see the very smallness of mouse. Suddenly the mice all comprehend themselves as the gods see them; they are silly things, exquisitely wrought. The albino clings to them as they lift her up, and they feel her frailty. They do not wish her harm; they bear this infant along with them and go to look at the night.

From the scullery window the dark is billowing huge and the moon is obscured by the rain and smearing clouds. The mice set down the albino on the sill and she turns back to gaze at them with eyes like the garden, wild and magic and full of mercy and danger. And when Mother Owl comes out of the watery sky she circles only once around the house, for it seems that they do not need her after all.

70
House

THE SUNRISE FLICKERS against the sky in shades of gore as the night is eaten away, scavenged clean by the cold and the circling rooks. The light is painful against window and roof-tile, for if there was any scrap of mercy in this old cold earth, the sun would not have risen again.

The house sits on its crumbling haunches and stares into the atmosphere, where day and night is written and unwritten again. This eternal scrambling, the liquidness of every moment of air, is awfully cruel for creatures without joy; forever the atoms of the sky are dragged through patterns of weather; never still. The sky churns like food chewed in a mouth; it is making the house feel sick.

And yet that hateful sun climbs, infests the garden, insists on itself, and the slates on the house are spiky like hackles, itching and bristling and letting in the dew. The house would snarl if it could, would howl at the sky and thrash in its prison of foundation pit.

Instead it rumbles and groans; it lets its stare become catatonic, fixed and dangerous. The morning is raw and gusty; wind picks at the branches of the cherry tree, lifts each leaf and lets it go, as if testing its nerve, testing its zeal for living. The tree hangs onto them, morosely, ill with sympathy for the house and its wound.

It has been a whole day since the rent man's life parted

with his skin; at this exact moment the knives are tussling for his tendons, hacking at the bones to joint them. His polyester trousers lie in playful ribbons like a kind of awful bunting, and his comb-over is ruined forever. There is even a lollipop, lying abandoned on the black-soaked carpet, the stalk of it bitten into little sections.

The rent man's teeth are growing loose, and he has mislaid his car keys in the recess beneath the sideboard; a cheeky family of nail scissors have snipped out a chunk of torso and dragged it under there to liquefy in privacy.

If they were to sneer their points, to look upwards, they would have a view of the knife drawer and its dug out belly, of the gouged-through path from drawer bottom to floor; they might even make out the green rags of baize that once swaddled them warm. They are much too busy to look up.

The rent man's soggy remains have slicked the floorboards, have collected amongst the trillion residues of sacrificed mice, of that other severed man from years ago. The rent man clogs the indentations where the nails are hammered in; he tastes of metal and grease. He is vile; he is utterly vile and the house has not any means for spitting.

The house has hardened now; its sadness is transforming. That pain, the colossal exhaustion has developed into a sort of rage, has become a solidness like gallstones, and it will never sleep now, not ever again.

Instead it grinds its joists to stumps and measures the aching in the scullery window, the decaying mortar between chimney bricks and the tickle of the wasps' nest down its throat. The cherry tree would make some gesture if it could, but it is rooted in the earth and has no language for things that are not cherry pips or wood.

The time flags around them both, boils in fast-motion; in the afternoon there appears an owl, out against its nature in the broad daylight. The house stares at it for a little while, for it somehow seems familiar, but its heart is beyond caring what it sees now.

All the house can comprehend is its own affliction, and the murderous creatures that infect its innards like worms. All life is hateful, it seems; bloodish animals, things of metal, live only to cause pain, to grieve each other. They have no regard for houses at all. And the lot of a house is the worst, for what is a house's purpose but to stand as witness, victim to every bloody whim? There is no use to being a house; it would be better to be reduced to rubble, to be the sand on a beach, shed into forgetful grains on the bottom of some peaceful sea.

71

Marie

I woke very late with gluey eyes and a throbbing in my chest; I woke feeling like I did the time that my mother gave me too much Benylin. I had been coughing for days, hacking until I was sick, hanging on to the backs of chairs and door handles. My mother had grown cross with it; perhaps she thought I was coughing on purpose, just to spite her.

She woke me in the middle of the night with a huge wooden spoon in her hand and a sort of aggressive kindness on her face. She had filled the spoon with half a bottle of syrup. I have a recollection as if from a dream, of a dark-pink lake, glossy and rolling-thick, oozing off the side of a gritty slab of wood. It would not fit into my mouth, not quite, but I tried my best anyway.

I woke up the next day, well past noon, my cheek stuck against the pillowcase, with Benylin sloshing slowly in my head, thicker than sardine oil. I daren't lift my face for fear that I might disturb that vile meniscus, reel myself to liquid or topple my head from my shoulders.

My grandmother came to look at me in the evening; the coldness of her palm against my face made me struggle and whine and fight for sleep. 'You'll live,' she had said, simply, as though this had been a question in some doubt.

The day after the rent man, I felt like that again, raw

and sweet and nauseous. My head was so full I daren't move my jaw, in case everything that had happened should tip out of me in a rush. I sat up carefully, straightened out my back, rubbed my eyes with the pads of my thumbs.

The house was moaning to itself, clearing its throat again and again, rocking and cracking and slowly dislocating its bones from the sockets, testing the pain of it, hurting itself as if it wanted to. There was a fixity to the gesture, as of pushing and pulling a loose tooth, worrying at the root until it would come away with a surge of broken nerves and blood.

The room was full of mice, each one busy, washing their faces or whispering in corners, tending to squeaking infants or gazing about. They looked expectant, as if they were up to something, some private business known to mice alone. They looked up when they saw me stir, and then glanced away quickly, considered each other's faces as if wondering.

The child was standing very still, her ear against the ruined wall, fingers spread against it and her teeth bared. There was daylight to be seen through the holes, and in places it seemed the plaster was not there at all, the illusion of a barrier being made only by the thickness of the wallpaper. Suddenly the sight of her little tender feet and holey tights terrified me, and I jumped to my feet with a gasp and pulled her away from the wall.

There was probably not the slightest risk to her standing there. There was nothing to be seen of the forks and knives, nothing but the sounds of them, seething beyond the wall like ants, slithering and scissoring the rent man, sawing against bones and trouser buttons.

She could probably have sat down in the dining room quite naked; they were busy with feeding and had no interest in catching prey. Even so, I did not want her there; the very thought of knives made me want to scream, to lift the whole world up in my arms and hold it out of danger's way.

So I grabbed her; she looked at me with incomprehension as I dragged her away. I found myself embarrassed, let her go again, stroked her hair out of her eyes. For a moment I thought that I might be about to vomit.

Then I raised my head and faced the parlour and a sudden urge rose out of me, to be safe, to make safe our queer little household. We were so many, so easily hurt, and here was I in my mother's clothes, the biggest one of all. I felt like a saint for a moment, a dead martyr that must comfort the souls of millions, pacing heaven with her fingers in her ears, frantic not to hear the prayers of the desperate living. Then the second passed like a giddy spell and I found myself laughing.

I spent a useless hour trying to clean the house; somehow it seemed the only thing that I could do. I pushed the carpet sweeper up and down in the parlour, but it jammed right up with little silky hairs. The child and the mice all looked on, amazed as I smeared at the windows with vinegar and screwings of newspaper from the scullery.

I pulled out the sofa and the red chair and swept beneath them; I rediscovered my mother's Crying Boy and found that I felt a little sorry for him after all. I picked up every last sock and underslip and I piled them atop the washing basket, and the dust that I kicked up everywhere made me wheeze. Everywhere were morsels of dust-fleece; little stranded, broken objects. The house began to hum to itself.

I even found a tiny model of a mouse, all made in bits and pieces; the mice all started at the sight of it, quite horrified. I knew what it was, I think, or at least I almost knew, but there was nothing to be done, not now. I went down to my knees and looked it over, saw all the little things it was woven from; I recognised my mother's dressing gown, her brown dyed hair and the silver chain from around her neck. I picked it up and turned to the mice, but not a single one would meet my eyes; so I fed it to the fire, very gently, and then began to weep.

The child came and sat with me as my shoulders shook, whilst the mice all loitered, shamefaced in the corners. When I was done with crying, the child smiled at me, pushed my own hair away from my eyes. Then we went along the mantelpiece, choosing things to burn: silk poppies, a Palm Sunday cross, and a tartan pincushion that had once belonged to me.

By the time the light was waning we were hungry, despite the horrible noises that rumbled the whole house, the eating and eating and eating of the knives. So I crept through the kitchen and came back with a lapful of cans, as many as I could carry, as many as did not roll from the hammock of my frock as I came. The mice all fled at the sight of me, lest a can of pineapple chunks should crush a little life to nothing.

When I was sitting they returned, sniffing and tutting at our ankles as I doled out Spam and pear quarters, laid little piles and puddles of food against the sooty hearth-stone. Then we devoured a week's worth of food, as if there was no tomorrow. We ate, and then we watched the fire as the house jittered; as the rent man spread his remains against the floor; as the draughts beyond the door grew cold.

It took a long time for me to register the fidgeting behind my elbow, the furtive gathering of bits and the respectful nodding of mice. When I finally turned from the flames to see, the mice had made a message for me, from a lolly stick and half a hair slide and a darning needle that must have been stuck in the carpet.

They had made an arrow that pointed at the fire, and

the sight of it made me feel betrayed by trusted friends, as if the mice were making jokes about my mother, as if all of this were not sadness enough. I hid my face in my hands and would not come out, like a sulking child, knowing all the time that I was being ridiculous. I hid my face in my hands until my arms lost all their nerves and I felt as though there was no moving blood left in me at all. After an age, I moved a little, and the cramp crawled through my muscles and I had to let my arms drop.

The mice all shuddered; perhaps they had been waiting for me. When they saw that I was looking, they all swept their eyes from me to the fire and back again. I saw that the arrow had been dismantled, and felt vertigo collecting inside my skull. Then I saw the child; she was sitting a little way off, leaning her flank against the chimney breast. She blinked at me, seemed to purse her lips before her gaze sank again to her lap.

She had a mouse perched on her knee. It was a tiny thing, the length of a thumb-joint, tail and all, like the work of some fiendish toymaker, made with copper wires and glue. It was pure white, and when I met its eyes I felt as though I were tumbling through air.

72
Mice

THE EYES OF the albino, which were watching before her birth, which have seen the inside of the womb, even as she was forming there in secret; the eyes of the albino are red and straining in the gloom.

She is a fragile thing, almost an idea only, clad in a coat of mouldy white. Her little tail is wrapped like string along the curve of her haunch, and she is not curled face-first against the flank of her mother, as mouse-children ought, but pointing the other way, staring into the parlour.

Her mother would rather have her hidden, safe from the cat, from the gods and prying muzzles, but the silence of her singing is far too loud. If she were snuggled with her infant in the hollow of her nest then the quiet would echo terribly, would thrum and throb and make the mother die of love.

It is a beautiful song, all the same, this strange not-music that cannot be heard, that vibrates against the backbone and the soul. It is perfect; it rings in the parlour like a saucepan lid struck at with a fork; bell clear; dangerous; pure.

And somehow the unmusic chimes with the cutlery's frenzy, with the zip and slide of metal over metal, makes it exquisite. There is glory in the end of life, no less than at its dawning, and the eyes of the albino are like light from the grate, are a prophecy of fire. The albino is a dream of death, beautiful and skeletal and just the same as a dream of hope.

She closes her eyes for a moment, and the parlour is the poorer for it; the mice all feel the loss of her gaze. They start and shudder and glance towards the mouse-mother and child, but then she looks again at them and they know they are not lost, even if all is destroyed after all, for the albino understands their glory.

The parlour smells like the end of the world, for so many house things are burning in the grate already, for the fury and misery of the house is a wheeze in the draughts. The rent man has become a colossal stink, and with every breath the albino draws in, scents of his blood and innards, of the sort of spite that could poison a whole watercourse overwhelm her. All of creation is quivering, ready for the apocalypse, lying carefully still. The childling just cocks her head and listens.

Yet Marie is sleeping like an infant atop a bomb; the albino is watching her, washing her in love and pity, for she is only a silly precious creature, as mice are. She wakens, jars the air with her fear and her darting movements, and every shudder disturbs the balance of the world. The end will happen very soon.

Hours tremble past. The albino and her mother watch the universe teeter, and the mouse-mother studies the curtains, the shuddering air beyond the windowpanes, and wonders what how it shall be for them. The albino turns to her dam to feed; her mother gives her the substance of her body, the milk that flows with her own blood.

Marie is busy with fidgeting, and suddenly she begins to clean, although to the mice it seems like the very opposite, for she disturbs the dust, drags out the armchair from its place, upends the washing basket and folds the filthy clothes. She shows up patches of the floor that have not seen the light for a decade, where the pattern of the carpet is shockingly pristine. The mice all watch in disbelief flee as she scatters them with the push of the sweeper, and their numbness is broken.

There is a mouse that is sixteen long months old, and his snout is grizzled with age; he has clambered up the bookcase, beyond the reach of poor Marie and her frenetic carpet sweeper. He is gazing down at all of creation, the sum and surfaces of Home, and he wonders about the land of the dead, where the soul might wander after Armageddon.

Perhaps death is like the garden, vast and open and impossible to fathom. Perhaps death is a great cold place, black and burned right out, with neither crevice nor grate-fire; perhaps death is a nest so vast that one might never find rags enough to soften it. He holds his paws together and watches a spider scale the wallpaper like a living hiero-glyph, and he wonders at it, the contents of its tiny scrib-bling mind.

And still Marie bustles down below his tail, even though the sweeper will not work, even though the air is choking-full of dust and old uncovered guilts. She is brushing with her hands at the red armchair, pulling off the cushions and dragging sweet papers and bits from down the sides. Then suddenly, the frizz-mother is in her hand, the frizz-mother in her sad little voodoo effigy.

The mouse upon the bookcase feels as though he is coming apart at the joints, as if he is floating in water, and he feels his own self twisted into finnicks of cotton and tags of dressing gown. He finds that his tail is a boneless flick of dishcloth thread, that he is made, is strung together by regret and cruelty and fear, that his heart is a tight little bundle of nail clippings.

And every mouse alive is staring at that wretched thing, feeling the hurting of those lolly-stick legs, knowing in his whiskers the pain of victimhood and the agony of the murderer who is left behind. That moment is long; the only thing that moves is a spider, shambling towards heaven. Marie cradles her mother and the mice stare, and it seems that the whole of the universe dangles. The albino turns to see.

Marie gazes at them all; they dare not meet her eyes, for suddenly she holds the fate of the world in her fingers. The air is jumping with gods and shadows, the ghost of the fairy lights, the prophet, the owl, the stoat, and the nameless leaping darkness.

The mice are holding their breath, and around them their belief is formless, waiting for the moment to take shape, to coalesce into this or that. Truth hangs like a spider, waits for the first hint of comprehension to make the next thing true. The religions of mice are born anew every moment; gods take shape or change their form and ripple through generations like wind through net curtains.

So the absent fairy lights, the spirit of Thomas, the childling cult and the fire itself all shiver in the atmosphere. But the moment passes and it is Mother Owl after all who has ordained this, for Marie is burning the witch's figurine, and here is Mother Owl's answer to the question of destruction.

She lays the frizz-mother in the fire like a mouseling and the flames lick her up, kindly, unhurt her stiffness and her guilt and her wounds; to the old mouse on the bookcase it is a part of him burning too. Now his cruelty is gone forever and he will always be perfect, purified and a little holy, but humble also and low against the ground.

Now Mother Owl is both killer and guide, for she is owl and fire together, and she strips away their impurities because they amuse her, but she loves them too. The next time that she circles past the window, her feathers are tinged with flame.

And then, because this is the dawn of a new age, Marie gets up from her knees and prepares a feast for them all; they nibble at corn and potato salad and orange spaghetti in voluptuous shining loops.

The fire is coming now; Mother Owl will take them to her wings before the sun rises again, and it seems that within their humility there might yet be a little room for rescue. Now the mice have learnt the error of meddling in the enormous affairs of humanity, but surely a tiny warning will not disturb the universe? So they take some little bits, and with hardly a speck of pretension in their souls they fashion one very small arrow and point it to the fire to prophecy the future for her.

Her reaction is queer, for she hides herself in her arms, as though she were burrowing the flank of some long-dead dam; the mice all sway with her pain, for she is motherless and has no teat to suckle on. Perhaps Mother Owl will make this one her own.

And the childling, who has remained all this time as watchful, as familiar and alien as a cat, sits in her place with Heinz Ravioli on the bib of her nightgown. Suddenly, as if at some divine calling, the albino breaks away from the warmth of her mother and tries to walk upon her baby paws although she is not a week old yet. The mice and the childling all fix their eyes upon her as she struggles on the carpet, and then the most astonishing thing happens.

The childling herself stretches out her arm, which is long as a branch, and she actually picks up the albino in her big blunt fingers. She is colossal and gentle as she carries that tiny thing through the air, lifts her to her face, and the mice all gasp, in case she means to eat her. She does not; she simply gazes into the eyes of the white mouse. The albino gazes back at her, and they discover that each knows the other very well indeed. Then she lays the baby mouse upon her lap and tips back her head and seems to spend a long time thinking.

73
Marie

The Bible clay was dry as delirium and I was trying to walk in big high-heeled shoes. I tripped right over as I ran and fell out flat, cut my knees and the palms of my hands; even though I called out for her to wait for me, my grandmother carried on stalking away.

I wanted to catch her up, knew that it was vital that I did so, but she did not care a bit whether I could follow her, so I cried like a little girl, 'Grandmother!' and my voice surprised me, for I was a little girl after all.

The very air was gnawing; my ears were full of sky and the sky was full of little teeth, biting and biting like the jaws of locusts. Although there was nothing to be seen, the sound was immense, as of a whale being nibbled to nothing by a thousand little fishes.

I shook and shook my head to rid me of the din, but it was no use at all, for the sky was full of nibbling teeth and that was an end to it. The noise was like a bent-back fingernail, and I cried for the death of the silence, the quiet that I remembered from the old days.

And somehow I spent so much time then, just crying, with gritty blood-grazed knees, that whole days and nights fell right there on the road to Emmaeus; plunging suns rose and collapsed beyond the hills before I remembered my grandmother. 'Grandmother!' I called, and I think that

I might have almost spotted her, half turned towards me, half smiling and not really there at all.

So I clambered to my feet amongst the sound of gnawing, and I stuck my feet into my shoes and tottered after her, and the desert track was lined with streetlamps. Then I remembered all the little things that I should have brought with me, and I panicked, hobbling down the desert tarmac and digging in my pockets as I went, for the little things were lost and I should have had them in my purse.

I clutched at my coat as I chased along the road, groped at the seams in case my little things had dropped inside through a tear, and nearly stumbled into an oncoming stream of cars, all lurching from a stop as the traffic lights turned green.

When I woke up the air was full of gnawing, for the mice were fixing their jaws on every surface of the parlour, as though they had entirely lost their wits. As I found my waking self, the child was pulling at my sleeve, wordless and sparkly with fear.

In the dim of the fire, the nervous flicker of tails and whiskers caused the darkness to seethe, as the mice chewed madly on anything there was to chew. Some were occupied meaninglessly on biting the mantelpiece, the sofa and the feet of the red armchair, but most of them seemed to be trying to escape the parlour. They swarmed the sash windows, gnawing the frames and wrecking their jaws against the putty that stuck glass to frame, frantic, beside themselves with busyness. I knew then that we were in danger.

The child stared into my face and then shied her head away, covering her ears with the flats of her hands. There was a sound in the room that rumbled lower than the staccato grinding of mouse against wood. One had to hold one's head at certain angle to make it out, but then it clattered like a slap against my ear. The chimneys were howling, swelling to cracking with the black night air.

I sprang to my feet and stumbled, struck my cheek against the skirting board and tried to stand up again, but the carpet was not still. The very floors were bucking as the house filled up its mighty lungs, braced itself for a long scream. I clung against the wall, found my way to my feet again and looked around for the child. She was squatting beside the window.

It gave way all of an instant. The glass fell inwards because of the wind beyond it, and many little souls were crushed beneath. At the same instant, the air was smashing with leaping bodies the colour of dust, all flinging towards the garden and its fragile skies.

Half a minute, and the child and I were alone in the parlour, watching the warmth from the fire grate fog the freezing air from outside. I wondered where Thomas was. Now that there was no competing noise of mice to mask it, the holler of air in the chimney made a sound like pouring taps. There was no whisper from the dining room; perhaps the knives were listening too. The fire roared in the grate.

The house gasped hard and bellowed. The chimney breast burst right out as the fire spilt like amber beads upon the hearthstone, upon the carpet and the old red chair. The child lurched towards me, pulled me away as the flames jumped over the fabric of it and licked at the wallpaper. The air began to fatten with smoke, piling in lovely folds towards the ceiling, obscuring the stains of damp and the cracking.

I stood still and watched, entranced by the beauty of it. In another minute, my mother's chair was a glowing staccato of bones and splinters, translucent and glorious like a message from a god, the flocking and the foam reduced to poison gas and flames. Then I realised that this was what it had always wanted, after all.

The inside wall was writhing in pain as the door to the hallway dropped in, with such a rush that the whole world exploded into flame. I found myself once more against my face, aware of the intricacy of the carpet's weaving, of the tiny hugeness of the universe an inch from the floor, of the lazy pressure of suffocation against my back.

With a scream of frustration, the child grabbed my hand, heaved at it, forced me to roll up to my knees again with something like disappointment. As I got to the empty window, she was already leaping through, the soles of her tights black and bloody and worn into holes.

The ceiling was collapsing in tatters as I followed suit. My knees snagged the glass in the frame, and I landed heavily against my shoulder. I found a milk bottle from centuries ago, rolled away from its old wire basket, a rain-ruined note still jammed down the neck. Soon afterwards, the red velour curtains caught.

The house coughed and coughed, thrashed in its stone bed, blazed as hard and as quickly as it possibly could, more beautiful than anything I had ever seen. With a splash, the windows in my mother's room shattered. Before long there were lights streaming between the tiles of the roof.

I thought of old clothes burning, of the toys from my childhood, of the dining room, of the rent man's lollipops turning liquid in the heat; the tears dried against my face as quickly as they came. My face grew raw; the child came to catch my arms again, to drag me away as far as the low wall, and we held each other as fire engines wailed against the wind with their strange, hollow voices.

We shivered together as the upper storey collapsed, as the house gave up its great slow ghost, as the night twirled flashing blue. The child put her little filthy hand in mine, and asked me a question with her eyes; I did not know the answer, so I let her lead me to the fields beyond the garden, to where the air was silent except for the barking of foxes.

74

Mice

THEN CAME THE great *Unhoming*. The *Unhoming* followed the time of *Echoing*. It marked the rupture of the old ways, the start of mousehood's long pull through the birth canal, to the terror and the wonder of the real world.

Until mousehood was *Unhomed*, he was as an unmade creature in the curl of the womb, floating and dreaming all of time away, with yet not a lungful of breath in his chest. Before the time of *Unhoming*, mousehood lived among wallpaper and banisters, which are a flat kind of flower, and a queer straight tree.

They were not wallpapers like these, whispers the mouse-mother to her children, for these walls do not grow plants within them, only tree roots and cracks, and there are no banisters here but the scrub beyond the gate. It is said that in the very olden times, the sun was not one great circle, but a good many small suns, one for the centre of every ceiling-sky, but this last might be a tale too far, for it was an ancient legend even in the days of *Unhoming*.

In the very olden times there were lots of little worlds; there was a great number of square rooms, connected together by doors, every one of them different. There was a kitchen world, where the shelves were huge as clouds; where food spilled from the cupboards in massive, clattering cans of metal that could only be opened with the teeth or the will of Mother Owl herself.

Yes, such was the magic of that ancient Home that the god herself had her nest there, higher than treetops, ringing and ringing with the flailing souls of little birds. Mother Owl had clad herself in human skin and cloth, or else in feathers and mighty rushing winds, or else the astounding moon of bed sheet white that smiles upon the face of mousehood even now.

There was a hell in the house, a real and certain hell, which was populated with demons far crueller than stoats. These were agents of the frizz-mother, but they outgrew her with their wit and keenness; in their way they were holy too, for they knew the evil in the hearts of all flesh.

The knives had a song like the sun against a broken bottle; they would streak out in the dark and slice the unclean to slivers, fearing no thing, even people. There were great big men before the *Unhoming* that existed only for harm and wrongdoing; any one of these was as big as the door of a barn, as violent and vile as a terrier. Imagine such a thing! But they had fallen at the snipping of the knives, for they had insulted Mother Owl in their hearts and done many secret sinful things besides, of which only Mother Owl may know.

The air beyond the nest is lean and cold and full of the stink of cows and diesel and the wicked trotting fox, to whom prayers are made at the ebbing of the daylight. The little mother, who is grey like a cobweb full of dust, pauses for a moment, feels the tremble of her heart and the magic of it.

She, her family, the whole race of Mouse, are just a mouthful on the edge of this glorious world. The black sky is richer than molasses, more exquisite than broken coal. Mice are the most beautiful thing upon it as they leap from shadow to shadow, or feed or fornicate or make their rituals to please Mother Owl in her trillion aspects.

The parlour was the cradle of fire, which was a gigantic orange thing that spat like cats, that was fierce and kind together like a summer all burned out at once. Before the *Unhoming*, mousehood had never perished with the cold, nor understood the perfect fear of the naked sky. They had never seen the stars or flinched at the prophetic singing of the bats at dusk, as they cry out their music and charm the felt-winged moths. They were poor things then.

Then the Owl called unto them, and the house began howl and to burn, and the dear Albino showed them the way that they must go. And the mice of the old times thought that their lives must all be spent, for that baby's wisdom sent them beyond the window, which was a sheet of ice encased in wood. The Albino's dam bore her in her teeth, as she was yet too small to scurry, and together they followed the path in the garden that the Owl marked out for them.

The way was terrible hard, for those were hardly mice at all, having never picked their way through blades of grass, having never felt the night against their fur. But the eyes of Mother Owl, the snowy pelt of the Albino, bore them on into the darkness, and they travelled a thousand inches or more with the blazing house at their tails. They toiled among the plants and tinfoil moonlight, and the Albino knew the way in which they must go, even as the garden bawled and crashed with disaster. It is said that the house itself cried for its pain, wailed to itself and shed its soul in a great blue light.

The Albino made no singing, and the sweetness of her silence made a trail through that chaos, and her mother carried her as she was bidden, and so it came that they were directed according to Mother Owl's whim, to the great muddy country beyond the concrete patio. And, though the way was a path of pure terror, they found their way at last to a great wooden doorway in the very soil.

The mice were filled with doubt, and they wondered among themselves what such a thing might be, but the Albino was not afraid and she struggled from the mouth of her dam until she was set down upon her tiny paws. Then all of mousehood gazed into her puddle-bright eyes and knew that all would yet be well. And she crawled before the others until she was atop that hollow space, and when she came upon a hole drilled into it, she pushed her body through.

Then every mouse alive was filled with courage and dropped in after her like furry drops of rain; Mother Owl had prepared that pit before the dawn of time itself, and so it was a perfect refuge for all that were afraid and close to abandoning their skins.

It was a fine hole, deep and almost dry, and padded like a featherbed with tangles of dishcloth string, with old clothing and handkerchiefs and plastic bags. The mice breathed in the scent of it and wondered, for it smelled so familiar to them and yet they could not quite determine where they had encountered such a thing before.

When they had picked themselves up and shaken their fur they turned to one another, seeking the Albino, but it seemed that after all she was not in the hole; for the only white thing among the mice was a single downy feather from the breast of an owl.

That was the first night.

Acknowledgements

Love and gratitude to Hilary Mellon and Caroline Forbes from the Bridges creative writing group. Thank you to George Szirtes for his unending encouragement and support, and the occasional slice of cake. To lovely Helen Ivory and Andrea Porter, to my big sister Na, and Kieron and Debbie from Rethink. To Simon Blue the 'puter doctor and Sue Dudley, who is an angel. In memory of Pinkie-Dinkie-Doo, the finest hamster that every trod a squeaky wheel.

Padrika Tarrant was born in 1974. Emerging blinking from an honours degree in sculpture, she found herself unhealthily fixated with scissors and the animator Jan Svankmajer. She won an Arts Council Escalator award in 2005 and has been working more seriously since then. *The Knife Drawer* is her second full-length book; *Broken Things* was published by Salt in 2007. Padrika quite likes sushi, although she tends to pick the fish out. She hates the smell of money.

Lightning Source UK Ltd.
Milton Keynes UK
UKOW06f2326180716

278701UK00017B/439/P